MR - - '16

DEATH WEARS A MASK

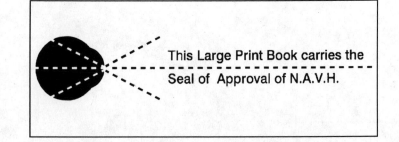

This Large Print Book carries the
Seal of Approval of N.A.V.H.

DEATH WEARS A MASK

ASHLEY WEAVER

THORNDIKE PRESS
A part of Gale, Cengage Learning

GALE
CENGAGE Learning·

Farmington Hills, Mich • San Francisco • New York • Waterville, Maine
Meriden, Conn • Mason, Ohio • Chicago

GALE
CENGAGE Learning·

Copyright © 2015 by Ashley Weaver.
Thorndike Press, a part of Gale, Cengage Learning.

ALL RIGHTS RESERVED
This is a work of fiction. All of the characters, organizations, and events portrayed in this novel are either products of the author's imagination or are used fictitiously.
Thorndike Press® Large Print Mystery.
The text of this Large Print edition is unabridged.
Other aspects of the book may vary from the original edition.
Set in 16 pt. Plantin.

LIBRARY OF CONGRESS CATALOGING-IN-PUBLICATION DATA
Names: Weaver, Ashley.
Title: Death wears a mask / by Ashley Weaver.
Description: Large print edition. | Waterville, Maine : Thorndike Press, 2016. | © 2015 | Series: Thorndike Press large print mystery
Identifiers: LCCN 2015041370 | ISBN 9781410484239 (hardcover) | ISBN 1410484238 (hardcover)
Subjects: LCSH: Women private investigators—England—London—Fiction. | Murder—Investigation—Fiction. | Large type books. | GSAFD: Mystery fiction.
Classification: LCC PS3623.E3828 D43 2016 | DDC 813/.6—dc23
LC record available at http://lccn.loc.gov/2015041370

Published in 2016 by arrangement with St. Martin's Press, LLC

Printed in Mexico
1 2 3 4 5 6 7 20 19 18 17 16

*For Amelia Lea and Dan Weaver,
the best little sister and brother
a girl could ask for.*

Love you, Mills and Danny!

ACKNOWLEDGMENTS

Once again, I owe a debt of gratitude to the many people who made this book possible. My heartfelt thanks goes out to all of them.

To my agent extraordinaire, Ann Collette; my fantastic editor, Toni Kirkpatrick; the amazing Jennifer Letwack; and the teams at Thomas Dunne and Minotaur Books. There aren't enough adjectives to describe how great this group is, and I can't thank them enough for all their efforts through every step of the process. I will never cease to be amazed at the magic they work in turning a document on my computer into a book. And a big thank-you to David Rotstein for his jacket designs and John Mattos for his jacket illustrations. I couldn't have imagined more perfect covers for my books!

To my writing buddies and manuscript readers for their friendship and feedback.

To the lovely ladies of Sleuths in Time for their camaraderie and support. I'm so happy to be part of a group of such talented writers.

To my gracious boss, Renee Grantham, who has helped my second career meld so seamlessly with my first. And to my coworkers at the Allen Parish Libraries for never being too alarmed at all my talk of murder.

And, finally, endless thanks to my family for their tireless love and encouragement, and to God for His many blessings.

1

LONDON, AUGUST 1932

It was amazing, really, what murder had done for my marriage.

Not that I wished to speak flippantly of such tragedy, of course, but I couldn't help but marvel at the way in which a brush with death had done wonders to improve things between my husband and me.

It had been two months since the events at the Brightwell Hotel, in which a holiday at the seaside had evolved into a double homicide and my nearly being killed. Murder was the last thing on my mind as I sat at my dressing table sipping a strong cup of tea in an attempt to fortify myself for the long evening ahead. Milo and I had been in town for less than a week, and I was still adjusting to the hours required by reemergence into society after an extended period of quiet country living.

A retreat to the country had been necessary after that dreadful holiday. Murder alone was enough to try anyone's nerves. But coupled with that awful event was the fact that my marriage had very nearly dissolved over the same period — not to mention that the entire thing had played out in lurid detail in every gossip rag in the country. Needless to say, it had proved to be a singularly unpleasant trip. It hadn't helped matters that I had very briefly and quite erroneously suspected that my husband might be a murderer.

We all make mistakes.

The mystery solved and misunderstandings resolved, we had departed for Thornecrest, our country home, and managed to smooth out the majority of our differences. However, such idylls couldn't last forever. Milo's occasional visits to town increasing in length and frequency, it had become apparent to me that he was growing restless. Though I suspected London society was not exactly the place to live down such events in quiet anonymity, I thought it better to accompany him back to our London flat than leave him to his own devices.

Things weren't yet perfect, perhaps, but I was happy. We were happier together than we had been in a very long time.

I glanced at Milo's reflection as I powdered my nose. He was seated behind me on an ebony velvet chair, resplendent in his evening clothes, flipping through a magazine while he waited for me to finish dressing.

"Have you seen this issue of *The Mirror*?" he asked.

"You know I don't like to read that tripe," I replied. "Why? Are you in it? I shouldn't think you've been in town long enough to garner any such attention."

"You are, in fact, wrong. But this time I am not alone. Allow me to read you this rather juicy bit of gossip." He cleared his throat for dramatic emphasis. "Mr. and Mrs. Milo Ames have been seen together in public again after the Brightwell Hotel Affair, quelling, at least temporarily, the speculation that a split is imminent."

"Does it really say that?" I asked, horrified. Despite my hopes that things would have died down by now, it appeared the gossipmongers were still atwitter.

"It certainly does," he answered, "complete with photographic evidence of our blissful reunion. It's a rather good picture of you, Amory." He folded the paper and held it up so I could see the photograph of the two of us emerging from a restaurant two nights before. I turned from the mirror for a closer inspection. I was certainly not the person to whom the eye was drawn. That honor, as usual, belonged to Milo. He looked superb in his evening clothes, his smooth, handsome features in three-quarter profile, light from the flashbulbs glinting off his black hair. It was absurd, really, how well he photographed.

"The prime minister went out just before us," I said. "I thought they were photographing him."

"Nonsense," Milo said dismissively. "Why should they want MacDonald when they could photograph you?"

"Or you for that matter," I replied, knowing from long experience that my husband was a favorite subject of the society columns. His cinema-star good looks and the endearing tendency to find himself in compromising situations had earned him that dubious distinction. I didn't add aloud what I was really thinking: that it was nice to be the woman in the photograph with him for once. Things had certainly improved.

I turned back to the mirror and picked up the necklace of sapphires that lay on the dressing table, raising it to my throat. "Help me with this clasp, will you? It always sticks."

"Certainly." He tossed the magazine aside and rose from the chair.

Coming up beside me, he fastened the necklace, his fingers warm against my skin. This was one of my favorite pieces. The sapphires complemented the backless blue gown and emphasized my dark hair and fair coloring.

Milo's bright blue eyes met my gray ones in the mirror. "You're very beautiful, Amory," he said.

Then, his hands on my arms, he leaned down to kiss my neck, sending a shiver clear through me. "Remind me again why we're going to the Barringtons' tonight," he murmured against my ear.

At the moment I was having a hard time remembering. "Mrs. Barrington is an old friend of my mother's," I said.

"All the more reason to avoid her."

I ignored this remark and went on, despite the fact that Milo was making it very difficult to concentrate. "When she found out we were in town, she was most anxious that we should come and dine with her, and I think it was very nice of her to ask us."

She had been rather insistent on it, in fact. I had been a bit puzzled by her eagerness to see me, considering we had not crossed paths in years, but I thought it could certainly do no harm to spend an evening in her company.

"It will be a lovely evening," I said in an unconvinced tone.

"It would be a much lovelier evening if we stayed at home."

I turned to look disapprovingly at him, and he seized the opportunity of access to my mouth, kissing me even as he pulled me up from my seat and into his arms, knocking over the dressing table stool in the process.

I dimly heard the telephone in the foyer ring and Winnelda, my maid, answering it. A moment later, she tapped hesitantly on the door.

"She'll go away," Milo whispered.

"You're quite incorrigible." I laughed, pushing myself back from him.

He released me, somewhat reluctantly, and I turned to right the stool and smooth my dress and hair before calling, "Yes, Winnelda? Come in."

She opened the door the barest of cracks, as though afraid to look in. "Your car is ready, madam."

"Thank you. We'll be right out."

She closed the door, and I turned to my husband. "We'd better go."

Milo sighed heavily; I couldn't have agreed with him more.

A half hour later, we pulled up in front of the Barringtons' home in one of the more fashionable districts of London and were welcomed into the marble-floored foyer, where my furs were whisked away by a silent maid as the butler led us toward the drawing room.

Before we could enter the room, however, Mrs. Barrington came sailing out of it, arms extended, the rings on her fingers flashing like flames in the light of the crystal chandelier.

"Mr. and Mrs. Ames, I'm delighted that you've come!" Mrs. Barrington was an attractive, buxom woman who looked remarkably hearty for her sixty-odd years. Her features were strong and distinct, keeping her from conventional beauty, but she was striking nonetheless. Her Christian name was Serena, but it was hearty robustness rather than serenity that radiated from her. As she came at me, I had the feeling that she might pull me into a tight embrace.

Instead, she squeezed my hand rather enthusiastically. "Amory, my dear, I'm so pleased to see you. I feel as though it's been ages."

"It has been rather a long time, Mrs. Barrington. Before my marriage, I think."

"I believe you're right. And speaking of your marriage, this charming gentleman must be your husband," she said, turning to Milo.

"Yes. Mrs. Barrington: my husband, Milo Ames."

She held out her hand and he took it. "How do you do, Mrs. Barrington," he said.

She gave him an appraising look, and her approval was plain on her features.

"I've heard a great deal about you, Mr. Ames." It seemed that she had decided to like him despite that fact, for she smiled brightly at him. "It is a pleasure to meet you at last."

"The pleasure is mine, Mrs. Barrington, I assure you. You have a lovely home."

"I'm sure it's nothing compared to your house in Berkeley Square. Are you staying there now?"

"No, the house is closed for the time being. We're at our flat. It's much more convenient."

"Yes, I'm sure it is. I'm sometimes of a mind to get a flat myself. So much less space to look after. Well, if you'll come this way, I'll introduce you to the others."

The drawing room was a large, lovely

16

room with dark paneled walls, high molded ceilings, and parquet floors covered with very good rugs. There were several pieces of quality furniture scattered about, many of them occupied by our dinner companions.

"Delighted to see you again, Mrs. Ames," said Mr. Lloyd Barrington, rising to greet us. He was a stout, mustachioed gentleman with graying dark hair, warm brown eyes, and a winning smile. There was something calm and steady about him that complemented his wife's exuberance.

Mrs. Barrington introduced other guests in turn. They were Mr. Douglas-Hughes and his American wife, whose names were familiar due to the sensation their marriage had caused the previous year; the tennis star, Mr. Nigel Foster; Mrs. Barrington's nephew, James Harker; pretty blond sisters, Marjorie and Felicity Echols; and a stunning, dark-eyed woman named Mrs. Vivian Garmond, whose name I had heard in some capacity I couldn't quite recall.

In my head I counted off the guests and realized that we were still short one gentleman. I was only vaguely curious who it might be, which made the answer all that more surprising.

"Mrs. Barrington, I must insist that you introduce me at once to this lovely stranger in our midst." These words were spoken in a low, pleasant tone by a gentleman who had just come in from the foyer.

"Oh, Lord Dunmore," said Mrs. Barrington, and something in the way she said it made me feel as though his sudden presence was not quite a pleasant surprise. "I didn't know you had arrived."

Lord Dunmore. The name was very familiar. The increasingly outlandish exploits of Alexander Warrington, the Viscount Dunmore, were currently an excessively popular topic of London gossip, proving a welcome distraction from my own little scandal. A recent string of lavish parties had resulted in some particularly sordid rumors. I didn't pay much heed to the details, so I was not certain of all the social improprieties of which he had been accused. I knew enough, however, to be slightly surprised at his presence.

"Only just, Mrs. Barrington, but I see I've come at the right time." He walked to where Milo and I stood with our hostess.

His gaze flickered over the gathering, encompassing the other guests, and I took a moment to appraise him. He was indeed handsome, though there was nothing in particular that made him so. It was just an overall attractiveness, a combination of well-formed features, a rather nice figure, and an unmistakable air of confidence. His dark brown hair was neatly parted and fashionably slicked. Eyes of a pale blue that might have tended toward coolness were warmed by a pleasant expression. I could see at once why he was successful with women.

"Lord Dunmore, allow me to introduce you to Mr. and Mrs. Ames."

"Mr. Ames and I know each other. How are you, Ames?" Lord Dunmore answered, glancing at Milo by way of greeting before coming back to me. "But Mrs. Ames and I" — he took my hand in his — "have not yet had the pleasure."

"How do you do, Lord Dunmore."

His eyes stayed on mine for a fraction longer than was customary, and his hand had not yet released mine when Mrs. Barrington spoke.

"I suppose now that everyone is here, we may as well go in to dinner."

"You have assembled the usual group, I see," Lord Dunmore observed, relinquishing his hold on me to cast his gaze around the room once more. He seemed to be looking at one person in particular, but when I turned to follow his gaze I could not determine on whom it had rested.

"Yes, I suppose I have," Mrs. Barrington

said absently. "Shall we?"

Everyone began rising from their chairs, preparing for the migration to the dining room. As a general hubbub ensued, Mrs. Barrington suddenly clutched my arm, pulling me slightly aside, and leaned to whisper in my ear. "Watch my guests, Mrs. Ames. I should like your opinion of them."

I looked at her, my surprise and confusion apparent on my face.

"It's a delicate matter. I'll explain later," she whispered as Lord Dunmore approached to escort her into the dining room.

I glanced at Milo to see if he had witnessed that rather strange interaction, but he was talking to one of the Miss Echols and didn't seem to have noticed.

I took Mr. Barrington's proffered arm somewhat distractedly. Very much perplexed by my hostess's mysterious appeal, I cast a look around at my fellow guests, feeling vaguely uneasy as we all went in to dinner.

2

Seated at the table and pondering Mrs. Barrington's strange request, I found myself, despite my reservations, trying to detect within the dinner guests any hints of illicit conduct. I really couldn't imagine what it was I was meant to observe, for the company was excellent.

Mr. Nigel Foster sat to my right. As befitted an athlete of his caliber, he was fit and trim. Wavy dark hair and bright blue eyes resulted in the boyish good looks that his legions of female fans adored, and the quickness of his movements gave the impression that he contained a great welling of energy just below the surface.

"I'm a bit starstruck to be sitting beside you," I told him. "I've seen you play many times and have always greatly admired your tennis game." That was an understatement. His skill on the court was exceptional, and, despite an unfortunate loss at Wimbledon the year before, his name was usually mentioned among the greats of the sport.

He offered me a ready smile as he waved away the compliment. "I play because I love the game," he said. "It has afforded me the opportunity to travel a great deal, another of my passions. I have been fortunate in that respect."

"You've been on a tour, I believe?"

"Yes. And afterward I had a rather long holiday in Greece and then Italy. I haven't set foot in England for nearly a year, so it's been nice to be home."

"It's been rather a long time since I've been to Greece," I told him.

"I've always longed to go there," Felicity Echols told me quietly.

"I'm sure you'd enjoy it," Mr. Foster said with a smile.

"Felicity and I both long to travel," Marjorie, her sister, added. "We've never been outside England, but one day soon we shall see the world."

Though they were similar in appearance, it had not taken me long to distinguish between the Echols sisters. Felicity was a sweet, somewhat vague young woman with wide green eyes and glossy golden hair. There was something bolder, sharper about Marjorie. She had clear blue eyes and a quick, lively manner that I expected could turn boisterous given the right occasion. Her words were spoken with a decisive air that was in marked contrast to her sister's soft, somewhat breathy voice.

"I wouldn't care to go to Greece just now," said Mr. Barrington, "what with the political situation there."

"Oh, Lloyd. Let's not talk politics." Mrs. Barrington sighed.

"Well, Mr. Douglas-Hughes will agree with me, I'm sure."

"The political situation has certainly been a bit unstable as of late," answered the gentleman in question cautiously. "What the elections will bring remains to be seen. If Venizélos is not reelected, it is difficult to say what the effect will be."

Connected to the Foreign Office, Mr. Sanderson Douglas-Hughes was quite well-informed on political matters, I was sure. However, it was not solely in that capacity that his name was familiar to me. I had been interested to meet him and his wife because we shared the unfortunate distinction of having our marriages publicly picked apart by society columnists. Mr. Douglas-Hughes came from a very old and wealthy family, and I well recalled the sensation it had caused when he had married an American dancer named Mamie Allen.

The gossips had played up her occupation as a dancer, lending it sordid undertones as if to imply she had spent her nights dancing the hoochie-coochie in some New York burlesque, but I had heard that she had, in fact, been a ballroom dancer on Broadway. She was tall and extremely thin, and there was a calm gracefulness about her that I was sure must have pleased even the stoutest defenders of the Douglas-Hughes legacy. She was a lovely woman, pale with a halo of striking red hair that could only have been a natural hue. There was something very warm and open about her, and I found myself liking her at once.

"There are so few places Sandy will take me for fear of sudden rebellions or uprisings," she teased. "I am really beginning to believe that ignorance is bliss."

It took me a moment to realize that she was referring to her husband. It amused me to learn that the elegant Mr. Sanderson Douglas-Hughes had been given the pet name "Sandy" by his wife.

"Bliss is being married to you, my love," he returned with a smile, "which is why I find it prudent to be cautious."

As his wife had done, Mr. Douglas-Hughes impressed me favorably. In addition to his obvious affection for her, there was an easy friendliness in his manner, a sense of calm that matched her quiet poise. I imagined a pleasant demeanor and a cool head were assets in the Foreign Office.

"Mr. Ames, I understand you're acquainted with Helene Renault. A friend of mine said he'd seen you together last weekend. She's a lovely woman. I've never met a film star. What's she like?"

This abrupt and rather startling speech came from Mr. James Harker, Mrs. Barrington's nephew. Like his aunt, Mr. Harker was also robust and lively of manner. He had a round, pleasant face that lit up when he smiled, which he seemed to do often. He had reminded me of a happy and amiable child upon introduction, and the impression was strengthened now as he waited with apparent guilelessness for the answer to his question.

It seemed to me that conversation faltered a bit as those around me tried to listen without appearing to do so. I had no knowledge of Milo's acquaintance with the French actress, so I was as curious as anyone to hear what his answer would be.

Schooling my features into polite disinterest had become habit when discussing Milo's behavior with strangers, so I fancy there was no expression on my face as my eyes rose slowly from my plate to look at my husband across the table. His gaze was awaiting mine, and I could read no sign of discomfort in it.

"I don't know her at all well," Milo answered with a perfect ease. "We've met once or twice at social events."

"I was certain someone told me that the two of you were quite good friends."

An awkward silence descended like a veil over the table, and I felt suddenly cold. A sad sort of sinking feeling that I had not experienced as of late seemed to hit me squarely in my chest.

It seemed Mr. Harker was the only one at this dinner unaware of the fact that this entire conversation was extremely uncomfortable for everyone, excepting perhaps Milo, who remained completely unruffled in the face of Mr. Harker's clumsy interrogation.

"I'm afraid you were misinformed," he replied smoothly.

"Yes, but . . ."

"This crème anglaise is quite delicious," Mrs. Vivian Garmond said suddenly. It was almost the first word I had heard her speak at the dinner table. So calm and natural was her delivery, however, that her deflection seemed the normal course of conversation.

"Yes, it's wonderful," Mrs. Douglas-Hughes put in. "The entire meal has been lovely."

Conversation ensued again as the guests sent their compliments to Mrs. Barrington's chef, and I breathed an inward sigh of relief. I had no wish to air out the difficulties of my marriage before a room full of strangers.

Everyone went on as though nothing had happened, though I saw Lord Dunmore looking in my direction, a vague expression of amusement on his features.

Mrs. Garmond was sitting directly across from me, and when she looked at me I thought I detected something like understanding in her expression.

I was curious about Mrs. Garmond, for she did not seem to be on particularly friendly terms with any of our fellow guests, let alone our hostess. If anything, it seemed that Mrs. Barrington had avoided her throughout the evening. I had noticed, however, the way her dark eyes followed Lord Dunmore when he wasn't looking. I could not help but wonder if there was some sort of connection between the two, although I had also noticed that the viscount had not glanced at her more than once or twice throughout the course of the meal.

What Milo thought about the incident with Mr. Harker I didn't know, for I studiously avoided his gaze. Though he was not technically responsible for my current embarrassment, it was not the first time his conduct had subjected me to a dreadfully uncomfortable moment, and I felt no inclination to be gracious in the face of Mr. Harker's implications. I was all too aware of the plausibility of the story.

As to the question of the true nature of his acquaintance with Mademoiselle Renault, that was something I didn't care to ponder at the moment. There would be time enough for that particular discussion in the privacy of our home.

I forced the issue from my mind, determined to think instead of Mrs. Barrington's puzzling request that I observe her guests. As I wondered what could be so mysteriously noteworthy about someone seated at the dinner table, I had no way of knowing that Milo would soon be the least of my worries.

The last course finished, we stood to move back to the drawing room for coffee. Mrs. Barrington came to me as we entered the room, distress evident on her features, and spoke in a low voice. "You must forgive James his faux pas, Mrs. Ames. He's always saying the wrong things."

"It's quite all right, Mrs. Barrington. You needn't apologize." The less said about it the better, in fact.

She shook her head. "He doesn't think before he speaks. It's always been an unfortunate habit of his. He doesn't mean anything by it. He's a sweet boy, but so gauche at times. I'm sure he didn't mean to imply that . . . I'm sure your husband isn't . . . well, most of the time, James doesn't even realize that he's said anything offensive."

"Milo knows rather a lot of interesting people," I replied vaguely. "I was not at all offended. Truly."

"It's good of you to say so, dear." She was frowning, looking not at me but at her nephew, who was talking animatedly to his uncle. "And yet . . . I worry sometimes that his tongue will get him into trouble." Still looking preoccupied, she moved away to see to the coffee.

People naturally fell into little groups for conversation, and I took a seat on a burgundy-upholstered divan near the fire with my cup and saucer in hand. I would do my societal duty and mingle in a moment, but I needed a bit of fortification first.

The incident at dinner had thrown me a bit more than I liked to admit. I had been certain my marriage was improving these past two months, but perhaps I had been mistaken. I had been wrong before.

I hazarded a glance in Milo's direction. He was engaged in conversation with Mrs. Barrington, who was no doubt repeating her apologies. He laughed at something she said, touching her arm in a reassuring manner, and she smiled, clearly relieved. There was no sign of discomfiture in his demeanor, and I found his imperturbability to be highly irritating.

"Are you by nature a solitary soul, Mrs. Ames?" I looked up, surprised to see Lord Dunmore standing before me, drink in hand. I hadn't noticed him approaching.

I could hardly deny it, as he had caught me in an isolated reverie. "I do find myself enjoying solitude upon occasion, my lord."

"Perhaps that explains why I've never had the pleasure of your company before this. I'm surprised we haven't had more mutual engagements. But perhaps you are often abroad with your husband." He indicated the divan. "May I?"

"Of course."

He took a seat beside me. It was not a very large piece of furniture, and I felt his nearness at once. There was nothing at all improper in his manner, but there was a certain sort of pull about him, a confidence that I suspected stemmed from his rumored popularity with women.

"I was delighted to meet you this evening, Mrs. Ames. Had I known that you and your husband were friends of the Barringtons, I should have urged them to invite you long before now."

"Oh, are you an old friend of the Barringtons?"

"Yes. My father and Mr. Barrington were at school together. They'd meet up for drinks or to go the races, and my father would sometimes bring me along. Mrs. Barrington sends along the odd invitation when she's in need of another gentleman."

"I should hardly call you merely 'another gentleman,' Lord Dunmore. I imagine your attendance at dinner is something of a social coup."

He smiled. "You flatter me, Mrs. Ames. I am not intriguing as all that. Besides, I rather like Mr. and Mrs. Barrington. Dinner with old friends is often so much less tiresome than dinner with a group of strangers. Although, I will say that the Barrington dinner parties usually include many of the same people, so I was delighted to see fresh faces this evening . . . your fresh face, in particular. I suspected the wife of Milo Ames was likely to be a beauty, but you surpassed even my high expectations."

It seemed the viscount's reputation for excessive charm had not been exaggerated.

"Now it is you who are flattering me, Lord Dunmore," I said.

"Not at all." His eyes flickered over my face, and he smiled. "One cannot flatter with the truth, after all."

"Mrs. Barrington was kind to invite us this evening," I went on, trying to divert the conversation back along a more suitable course. "She and my mother are quite old friends. I am not much familiar with any of the others, however. Are you very well acquainted with them?"

"I know them all in one way or another." His gaze traveled around the room as he detailed his connections to our fellow guests. "Like your husband, Mr. Douglas-Hughes belongs to my club. We cross paths occasionally. He's a very proper gentleman." I suspected that, coming from the viscount, this remark was meant to be disparaging.

"James Harker and I were at school together," he continued. "The man's a thorough dolt, though I suppose you've realized as much. Even at school, he was a snoop and a talebearer. Mrs. Barrington adores him, of course, but he's always in one awkward scrape or another."

I digested this bit of information without comment.

"And Mr. Foster?"

He hesitated ever so slightly. "Mr. Foster I don't know well, though I've long been an admirer of his tennis game. We're often thrown into society events together. I believe he and Mr. Barrington have bonded over a love of sport."

I noticed that the viscount made no mention of the ladies present. Given his reputation, I wondered if he knew any of them better than he let on. It was a wicked thing for me to think, but it did cross my mind.

I looked to where Felicity and Marjorie Echols seemed to be inquiring of Mrs. Garmond about her dressmaker. They were examining her gown and motioning to it occasionally, in deep conversation. Mr. Harker sat a short distance off, watching the conversation with apparent interest. I wondered if perhaps one of the ladies had caught his eye.

Mr. Foster appeared to be surveying the scene with amusement before he moved to Mrs. Garmond and struck up a conversation.

"Are the two of you conspiring?" asked Mrs. Barrington as she approached us.

"I certainly was," said Lord Dunmore, rising until Serena Barrington had seated herself in a nearby chair. "I was just about to ask Mrs. Ames to come to my masked ball and was trying to think of sufficient inducement for her to accept."

Mrs. Barrington smiled. "Oh, yes. The masked ball! You should certainly come, Mrs. Ames. It's going to be quite an event. We've been talking of it constantly."

I was surprised at the urging from Mrs. Barrington. From what I had heard, Lord Dunmore's parties were not the type of thing I would expect her to attend, let alone enjoy. Then again, I was well aware of how gossip and gross exaggeration went hand in hand. Perhaps there was nothing so very wrong in his parties after all.

"You see, Mrs. Ames?" he asked, turning to me, his eyes alight with amusement. "Mrs. Barrington insists. Do you enjoy masked balls?"

"It's been ages since I've been to one," I replied, "but I very much enjoyed them in my youth."

"Come now, Mrs. Ames. You still seem very much in the full bloom of youth to me," he replied, in a voice that was just low enough not to be heard distinctly by Mrs. Barrington. It was not so much the compliment that was inappropriate but the intimacy he ascribed to it.

"You seem rather young and carefree yourself," I answered tonelessly.

He smiled. "Perhaps too much so. I expect you've heard rumors about me."

It seemed there was a vague challenge behind the words, as though he knew that I was thinking of what I had heard about his parties. "I don't listen to gossip, Lord Dunmore. I find there are so many more worthy things to occupy my time."

He lifted his glass. "Well said, Mrs. Ames . . ."

Mrs. Barrington had watched our exchange with apparent interest, and some other emotion I could not name.

"I can see we shall get on splendidly. You'll come to my ball, won't you?"

"When is it?" I asked, not entirely certain I cared to encourage him.

"Tomorrow night, in fact. But you needn't wear fancy dress. Many of us wear evening clothes with our masks. I can recommend my costumier at Friedrich's. Bertelli is his name. Many of us use him. He can make you a mask in no time."

"I'll speak to my husband about it."

"I expect he'll agree if you want to go."

"Perhaps." I wasn't certain, however, that I did want to go.

"It's short notice, I suppose. If you can't make it, I plan to have another party in two weeks. If you're like me, however, short notice is much better. I hate waiting for things." He smiled as his eyes came to mine. "I find that lengthy anticipation is highly overrated."

Before I could formulate any sort of response, he had risen to his feet. "If you charming ladies will excuse me now, I'll just go have a word with Mr. Barrington."

Her eyes on his retreating form, Mrs. Barrington leaned toward me. "Have you encountered him before tonight?" I thought it an odd choice of words, but I supposed "encounter" was an apt enough description.

"No. Tonight was the first time I have met him."

"He's handsome, don't you think?"

I was not at all sure what this was leading up to, so I ventured a hesitant agreement. "Yes, I suppose he is."

"Of course, you'd do well to have little to do with him." Under other circumstances such words might have caused offense, but I had the feeling Mrs. Barrington was merely trying to offer a friendly warning.

From what I had seen of Lord Dunmore, it was probably warranted.

"We haven't crossed paths before now, so I doubt we shall see much of one another in the future," I replied.

Her gaze came back to me. "You think not? I'm afraid you don't know how persistent he can be. I've seen him look that way before," she said vaguely.

"You spoke earlier tonight of my watching your guests, Mrs. Barrington. What was it I was to watch for?" It was something of a non sequitur, perhaps, but I was very curious and our secluded seat by the fire presented the perfect opportunity for quiet conversation.

This captured her attention. She leaned closer. "I will speak plainly to you, Mrs. Ames: someone has been stealing from me."

I was at a loss as to how to reply to this bit of information, and I could not immediately perceive why it was that she should choose to share it with me. I didn't have to wait long to find out.

"I knew at once, of course, that you were just the person to help me." Her gaze met mine expectantly. "I want you to find out who it is."

3

I did my best to hide my considerable surprise.

"Mrs. Barrington," I said carefully, "I don't know how I could possibly . . ."

"You investigated that murder business on the coast; theft should be quite a simple matter."

So there it was. I was taken aback that she should choose to connect the two crimes, if indeed this was a case of theft.

"That was a very different situation. One I undertook out of necessity. If someone has stolen something from you, you should contact the police."

"I don't want the police here," she said quickly. "I . . . I rather think this needs to be kept quiet."

"I really don't think . . ." I tried again.

"Let me tell you the facts before you say no. If you cannot or will not help me, I will accept it."

"Very well." I had to admit that I was faintly curious. It could do no harm to listen to what she had to say, after all.

She looked around, as though making sure we wouldn't be overheard, and then began speaking in a low, unhurried voice. "My husband has always been fond of giving me extravagant gifts, though he knows perfectly well that it isn't necessary. He does spoil me so, the dear. As a result, I have rather a good collection of jewelry. It's only the last few months that I've begun to notice that things are missing."

"Missing?"

"Yes. It started first with the loss of a ruby earring. It disappeared from my jewelry box, and I turned my dressing room upside down looking for it. A week later, I found it in the drawer of my bureau, though I'm certain I had searched there."

"Perhaps you overlooked it."

"I thought so too, at first. But now I don't know. The next thing to disappear was an emerald ring. It happened a month or so after the incident with the earring. It was a bit large for my fingers, but I wore it to dinner one night, here at home. When I discovered it was missing, I assumed it must have fallen off and one of the servants would discover it, but it has never turned up. Then,

39

not two weeks later, a diamond bracelet that I wore disappeared."

"Were you dining at home that night as well?" I asked.

"Yes. As with the bracelet, I thought I might have misplaced it. I was certain that it would come to light eventually."

"Perhaps it still will," I said. I was harboring the hope that Mrs. Barrington might merely have misplaced these things. It would be the simplest and most satisfactory explanation.

"I hoped so, but I'm rather certain now that that is not the case."

"As everything was lost here at your home, do you think, perhaps, one of the servants . . ." I hinted delicately. I did not like to insinuate such a thing. One had to be careful when suggesting wrongdoing on the part of the domestic staff. Even the whisper of suspicion could ruin a domestic career. It was unfair to assume that they would resort to stealing merely because they were in a position to do so, but one had to concede that such things had been known to happen.

"Yes," she agreed. "At first, I thought that the most likely thing. I'd instructed Fenton, my butler, to keep a watch, and I fully expected that the culprit would eventually be caught. Until last week, that is."

She paused dramatically, raising her eyebrows for added significance.

"What happened?" I prompted, sensing this was what was expected of me.

"While I love everything that Lloyd has given me, the prize of my collection is a diamond brooch he gave me when we became engaged. It was a replica of the Eiffel Tower in gold, encrusted with diamonds and tiny pearls. We met in Paris, you see, and it was a little reminder of how we came to be together. He had it designed especially for me with our engagement date engraved on the back; it's one of a kind."

"It sounds lovely." I too had diamonds I associated with Paris, a necklace Milo bought me when we honeymooned there.

Almost without thinking, I glanced in Milo's direction. He and Mr. Douglas-Hughes were speaking, but he happened to look my way at almost the same moment I looked his. His eyes caught mine, and I looked away.

"I had a dinner party a fortnight past," Mrs. Barrington was saying, "and, as it was our wedding anniversary, I wore it. But it seemed the clasp was loose, so I removed the pin and placed it in that little ivory trinket box on the mantel." She nodded toward the fireplace. "I meant to collect it later and have it sent to be repaired. However, after I had bid all my guests good evening, I went to retrieve it and found that it was gone."

As much as I had harbored hopes to the contrary, the circumstances certainly were suspicious. This business was becoming more intriguing than I had initially believed.

"Of course, I was frantic," she went on. "The thing is very valuable, of course, but it has far more sentimental worth to me than anything else. I searched the room, then the house, hoping I had misplaced it somehow, but I knew perfectly well that I hadn't. I put it in the ivory trinket box, and at the end of the evening it simply wasn't there."

"But the servants . . ."

"There had been no servants in the room all evening, save for Fenton, whom I trust implicitly. And even if I thought him capable of such a thing, I'm quite sure he was nowhere near the mantel all evening."

"Then who . . ."

"Don't you see?" she asked with a conspiratorial whisper, her eyes making a quick sweep of the room. "It must have been one of my guests. My dear, who else could it be?"

My impulse was to dismiss the entire thing

at once as some kind of misunderstanding, but my instincts told me differently. I thought for a moment, digesting all of what she had just told me. She was quite right, of course; it didn't seem it could be anything but deliberate theft. Nevertheless, it seemed absurd that anyone wealthy enough to be included in the Barringtons' circle should be forced to stoop to pilfering from their host. Certainly none of the guests here tonight seemed capable of such a thing. I seemed to recall that Lord Dunmore, for example, was in possession of the Dunmore Diamond, a jewel of some renown. I thought it unlikely he would have use for Mrs. Barrington's Eiffel Tower brooch.

"Did you ask any of them about it?"

"Certainly not," she said, obviously horrified at the suggestion. "I didn't like to make a scene. You know how poorly people react if they think they are being accused of anything."

I did indeed. If she thought accusing someone of theft was bad, she had never been forced to confront a murderer. That had proved to be an extremely disagreeable experience.

"Who was there that evening?" I asked.

"The same group that is here tonight."

And then I understood. The sudden invitation, the insistence that I accept, had all been a part of the ploy. The truth of it was that I had been invited to dinner under false pretenses. It was perfectly obvious that Mrs. Barrington had lured me here under the guise of a simple dinner party in order for me to ferret out a thief in our midst. I didn't think it was at all a nice thing to do, yet I couldn't keep myself from asking a pertinent question. "Was that the same group that was there each of the three times that something went missing?"

"Yes, I believe so. I've been over it in my mind, and I think it was the very same group each time. Well, all except Mr. Barrington. He was called away on some business the night my brooch disappeared. He was so upset, poor dear, when I told him my lovely anniversary gift was missing."

"I find it difficult to believe that any of your guests would do such a thing," I said carefully.

"But it seems one of them must have, doesn't it?" she asked pointedly. "I don't like to accuse anyone, naturally, but facts are facts."

"Perhaps." I didn't quite know what to think. It was all so fantastic.

"Well?" She looked at me expectantly.

"Well, what, Mrs. Barrington?"

"Are you going to help me?"

"As intriguing as this is, I'm still not sure how I can be of help to you."

She looked disappointed, as though her expectations had not been met. "You haven't any ideas as to how we may catch the culprit?"

"I'm afraid not." I hesitated to venture my misgivings as to the guilt of one of the present company. I thought it much more likely that one of the servants had escaped her notice that evening, though, admittedly, Mrs. Barrington did not seem to miss much.

"Well, we shall think on it," she said. "I will come up with something. But you will help me, won't you? I don't expect you to catch the thief red-handed and wrestle him to the ground or any such thing."

Well, thank heavens for that.

"Another dinner party would do, I suppose, though it may be a while before everyone is free again. There are so many parties and such that are . . . Oh, I have it!" she cried so suddenly that I nearly flinched. "Lord Dunmore's masquerade ball tomorrow night! He's invited you to it. Mr. Barrington and I are attending as well. Everyone here tonight will be there. It's the perfect opportunity to lay a trap."

"Mrs. Barrington . . ." I felt I should try

to dissuade her, though I had the impression that feat might be comparable to stopping a runaway train at this point.

"I'm going to wear some jewels to the ball, put them in the path of the suspects, and see if someone will steal them."

"I don't think . . ."

"It's the perfect plan," she interrupted. "Where I'll need your help is keeping an eye on each of the suspects, helping me direct them, so to speak. And of course you'll serve as a witness when we catch the thief."

"What exactly do you intend to do if you succeed in your plan?" I asked, hoping to draw her back to the more realistic side of things. I wondered if perhaps she had not quite thought the thing through, but I should have known better.

"It's perfectly simple," she said, with a wave of her hand. "When confronted, the guilty party will quite naturally be so embarrassed and eager to keep it all a secret that he will return all of my things. That's all I want: the return of my beloved brooch. Will you help me?"

I hesitated. This entire thing was madness, and I knew perfectly well I should distance myself from any involvement in her schemes. And yet . . . What could it hurt, really? If there was nothing to it, no one would be the wiser. If she was right, perhaps I could lessen the damage if something socially catastrophic were to occur.

"I suppose I will, Mrs. Barrington," I conceded.

"Splendid! I just knew you would! Let me tell you what I have in mind." She outlined a plan in which she would leave a bracelet in a spot where each of the "suspects" would be sure to know about it. Then it was only a matter of waiting for the culprit to take it. My part in the scheme would be to draw attention to her bracelet at some point in the evening so that the thief would know where to find it, and then I could take part in what Mrs. Barrington called "the negotiations." That is, convincing the villain to return her purloined baubles.

The plan was simple enough, but I was not at all convinced it was going to succeed. For one thing, I still had my doubts that any of the guests tonight were involved in the disappearance of Mrs. Barrington's jewelry. For another, the entire strategy reminded me of a very poorly written mystery play I had once attended in the West End.

"I feel so relieved that you've agreed to help me, Mrs. Ames," she said, grasping my hand warmly in hers. "I'm sure we shall straighten this business out in no time, and you'll be glad you agreed to assist me."

I highly doubted it. Against my better judgment, I had agreed to help Serena Barrington catch a thief, and I could only imagine what sort of trouble would come of it.

Lost in various disconcerting thoughts, I was silent as we walked from the Barringtons' home. Milo's hand rested lightly on the small of my back as he escorted me to our waiting automobile, and I wondered if he could detect the tension in me.

As Markham, our driver, pulled away from the curb, Milo sank back against the seat and began pulling loose his necktie. "Well, that was just as dull as I imagined it would be."

"Really?" I replied, looking out the window at the darkened streets. "I thought it was a rather interesting evening." It had certainly been more than I had bargained for. My mind was still spinning.

"What did you make of the viscount?" he asked. "Were you dazzled?"

"He's invited us to his masquerade tomorrow night."

"Ah, so it's you who've dazzled him. I

might have known. He certainly seemed to be enjoying your company."

I said nothing, and after a moment the silence seemed to grow heavy.

I could feel him looking at me in the darkness.

"What are you thinking about?" he asked at last.

"Nothing in particular."

"Yes, you are. You're thinking of what that idiot James Harker said."

I glanced at him. "It was of no consequence." My tone said otherwise, and Milo knew it.

"As I said at dinner, I barely know Helene Renault."

"I'd rather not discuss it now, Milo." I glanced pointedly up at Markham, who could hear every word we said.

Milo took the hint, but rather than letting the subject drop as I had wished, he slid closer to me on the seat, his arm slipping around me, and leaned to whisper in my ear. "It's simply another of those nasty rumors."

I didn't trust myself to reply.

"Look at me, darling."

I turned to look at him, not taking into account how close he sat. My mouth nearly brushed his as I looked into his eyes, so very blue even in the darkness of the car.

"There's nothing to it. Truly."

I knew that I wanted very much to believe him. Perhaps I could. I had doubted him before, and it had very nearly been disastrous.

I sighed. "Very well."

He smiled and lowered his mouth to mine.

"Milo," I whispered, pulling back after a moment. "Not now."

Milo shot an impatient glance at our driver before turning his attention back to me. "I am sure Markham is aware there are occasions when a man would like to kiss his wife."

If he wasn't, I'm afraid he was well aware of it by the time we reached home.

4

I had not found the time by morning to tell Milo of my strange conversation with Mrs. Barrington. Very likely he would have brushed it aside as the far-fetched imaginings of a bored society doyenne. And perhaps I was the least bit afraid he would attempt to dissuade me from getting involved in an affair that was, admittedly, none of my concern. That did not prevent me from deciding to attend the ball, however. Milo, though not especially enthusiastic, had agreed to accompany me.

The day was a whirl as I made preparations. Though I was the first to admit I had a very serviceable wardrobe, I could find nothing that I thought suitable to wear to a masquerade thrown by the Viscount Dunmore. Though my modiste had promised to try to find something appropriate, I had not yet heard from her by the time I began to ready myself for the ball, and I had determined that I would have to choose a gown from among my own things.

Winnelda, my maid, stood behind me, watching my preparations in the mirror, her head tilted slightly to one side. She was a petite, pretty young woman, and her reflection reminded me of a woodland pixie standing over my shoulder.

"Your hair looks lovely." She leaned to examine it. "Just like a cinema star."

"Thank you." I had had it freshly waved that morning, though I somehow doubted the effect was as glamorous as she seemed to think.

"I've always longed for dark hair like yours," she continued wistfully. "But both of my parents were pale as winter whey, so I suppose it wasn't to be. And I don't suppose I'd look quite right if I dyed it . . . not that I'd do such a thing."

"Your hair is quite pretty as it is, Winnelda." It was true. Her natural shade was a startling shade of platinum that would have made Jean Harlow envious.

"Thank you, madam."

I reached for my perfume bottle, and she rushed to hand it to me, fairly pushing my hand away in the process. "Here you are."

"Thank you."

"And which gown have you chosen? Will

you wear the blue silk?"

"The black satin, I think." I nodded toward the dress draped across my bed. Though not extravagant, it was a striking dress and would not be out of place at Lord Dunmore's ball.

Winnelda didn't care for black, it seemed. I was certain I saw her grimace in the mirror, but I ignored it. It was best, I had learned, to pay no attention to her frequent opinionated responses.

She was not, strictly speaking, a lady's maid. In fact, she had been hired by Milo, in my absence, to look after the flat. Before her arrival, we had made a point not to have domestic staff at the flat. A woman had come in to cook and clean, and we had enjoyed the absence of domestics observing our every move.

Since our return to London from the country, however, Winnelda had inserted herself into my daily routine in a manner that was all-encompassing, if not completely effectual. I had found that her enthusiasm was undiminished by any of my tactful attempts at discouraging her, and she had assumed the roles of parlor maid, cook, and housekeeper with undisguised zeal. I hadn't had the heart to advertise for another lady's maid, mine having left my service two months before to be married, and so here Winnelda was, making a likable and well-meaning nuisance of herself in every imaginable capacity.

I picked up the dress and moved behind the black lacquer changing screen. Milo entered just then, and Winnelda slipped from the room. She was, it had become plain, somewhat overawed by Milo and made rather obvious attempts to stay out of his way.

"Darling?" There was something in the way he said it that roused instant suspicion. He had been on the telephone in the hallway, and I knew instantly that no good had come of it.

"Behind the screen," I answered.

My instincts were confirmed as he continued. "I'm afraid something's come up. I've got to dash off. Make my excuses for me, will you?"

"It's a bit late to cry off now, isn't it?" I asked the question mildly, for I knew perfectly well that there was little chance Milo would be convinced to change his mind. He had never been very reliable, except for when it came to doing just as he pleased.

"Yes, I know. But it's rather urgent. Rumor has it that Frederick Garmond is in rather dire straits financially. He may be

ready to sell off his Arabian. I've been trying to buy the beast from him for a year,
and Kelvin's just rung up to say Garmond's
arrived at my club. I need to speak to him
before someone else does."

"Can't it wait?" My dress fastened, I came
from around the screen.

"I'm afraid not. I can't have someone else
buying that horse."

I bit back an angry retort, turning instead
to the mirror and powdering my already-
powdered nose, determined to give every
indication of indifference. "Very well."

"I may be able to drop by Dunmore's ball
later this evening, if all goes well."

"Don't inconvenience yourself on my account," I answered, almost managing to
keep the edge from my tone.

He came up behind me as I smoothed my
hair, but I refused to look at him in the mirror.

"Don't be cross with me, darling," he said.

"I'm not cross."

"Yes, you are. You've done up your buttons wrong."

I started to reach behind me, but his
hands were already there, unfastening my
dress so he could redo them properly. I was
irritated that my frustration should have
presented itself in my wardrobe, but it

would have been childish to brush his hands away. His fingers moved assuredly but without any great haste, and I wished there were fewer buttons on the gown.

"There," he said after a moment, his hands dropping to my waist. "You're quite presentable now."

"Thank you."

His eyes met mine in the mirror, waiting, I supposed, for protests I did not intend to give. I certainly wouldn't beg him to accompany me. If the horse was so important, let him go to it.

"I'll probably be quite late," he said. "Garmond will no doubt require a bit of liquoring up before he'll sell."

"I may be late myself," I answered.

"Indeed? Well, try to behave yourself with Dunmore," he said dryly. He dropped a kiss on my neck, then turned and left the room.

I fought back my annoyance and the sudden desire to remain at home because of my spoiled mood. But Mrs. Barrington was expecting me. Besides, I was not going to let Milo ruin my evening. I was perfectly capable of enjoying myself without his company.

I was nearly ready when I heard the bell.

A moment later, Winnelda came into the room carrying a large box. "This has just come for you, madam."

"Thank you." I took the box and set it on the bed, then picked up the attached card. "From my dressmaker," I told Winnelda, cutting the string and pulling back the lid.

As the box opened, my eyes widened, and Winnelda gasped loudly as I pulled out the gown and held it up.

"Begging your pardon, madam," she said, "but that's ever so much more beautiful than the black satin."

I felt a bit conspicuous arriving at Lord Dunmore's home in a gown of scarlet satin. It was far more extravagant than anything I would normally wear, but a masquerade called for a bit of added glamour. At least, that was what my modiste had assured me in her note. Looking at the ostentatious ensemble now, I hoped I wasn't going to call unnecessary attention to myself.

The gown had an intricately beaded bodice with very short sleeves that gave way to a low-cut neckline that might have been overly revealing on a more buxom woman, and the back plunged quite low as well. The gown was fitted from bodice to hip, giving way to a flowing skirt, with chiffon inlays that fluttered when I walked, the effect of which was rather like floating on a red mist.

A red beaded mask and red satin gloves completed the costume.

I was swept through the doors of Dunmore House and into the cavernous entrance hall with a group of other people. As we were all masked, it was a bit difficult to tell who was who, but there were several individuals I recognized, including an illustrious author, two members of Parliament, and an earl. It seemed that, whatever rumors abounded about the viscount's parties, they nevertheless held appeal for the crème de la crème of society.

I had heard of the opulence of Dunmore House, and I found the reports were not exaggerated. The entrance hall was a gleaming expanse of marble floors that ran from the doorway to a grand red-carpeted staircase. There was a door to the right that I assumed was some sort of sitting room, and beyond that was the entrance to a corridor that led to the other rooms on that side of the house. The tall gilt doors to the ballroom were on the left. I moved with the wave of people into the massive ballroom and was embraced by the swell of music coming from the orchestra in the corner. It was a beautiful room with gleaming parquet floors and ivory walls with gold-leaf molding. Crystal chandeliers glittered overhead, and golden sconces on the wall held candles that gave off a warm glow that electric lighting couldn't match.

The room was lavishly but tastefully decorated with an abundance of floral arrangements, and I detected the scents of rose, jasmine, and gardenia, along with subtler scents, hanging pleasantly in the air. I noticed many of the blooms that had been selected were out of season. It was apparent that the viscount had spared no expense on this ball, down to the last detail, and I wondered briefly what sort of impact such excessive parties made on his bank account.

"And who might this stunning creature be?" said a voice behind me. I turned to the approaching gentleman. He wore a half mask that obscured his features. Nevertheless, I recognized the posture and tone of voice. It was Lord Dunmore himself, arrayed in flawless evening dress and a mask of silver and black diamonds. Even masked, I supposed it would be difficult to mistake him for anyone else.

"It's a lovely party, my lord," I said, as he took my hand in his.

"I see you have found me out." He smiled. "I suppose, then, that I must confess I recognized you the moment you walked through the door. Some things cannot be hidden with a mask." His eyes ran over me in an appraising way. "You're a vision. Red suits you perfectly."

"Thank you. Your home is magnificent."

"You're too kind. I'm so glad you've come. But where is your husband?" He glanced around as though Milo might be lurking somewhere behind me.

"I'm afraid he was called away on urgent business."

"Oh? Well, his loss is my gain." He held out his hand. "Might I have the honor of this dance?"

"Of course, my lord."

He escorted me to the dance floor and pulled me to him in the manner of a man who is quite accustomed to feeling a woman in his arms. He danced beautifully, and I saw several women watching him as we moved about the floor, his warm hand against the bare skin of my back.

"I was afraid you wouldn't come, given the short notice," he said. "Imagine my delight to see you walk in, outshining every woman here, no less. I'm surprised your husband lets you out alone, looking as you do."

"Mr. Ames suffers no alarm on my account."

"Indeed? Well, he's a very fortunate man."

"And what about you, Lord Dunmore?" I asked, trying to deflect his flattery. "I wonder that some charming lady has not yet stolen your heart."

"Alas, Mrs. Ames, it seems the best of them are already taken."

I smiled, and we finished the rest of the dance in a comfortable silence. The song concluded, and he escorted me back to the edge of the room, where great piles of food sat on long white-clothed tables. A group of three women stood conversing near one of them. I might not have recognized them, but for the lovely red hair of the woman in a copper-colored gown. It was Mrs. Douglas-Hughes and, I realized, Felicity and Marjorie Echols.

"Hello, Mrs. Ames," Mrs. Douglas-Hughes said, as I approached.

"Hello, Mrs. Douglas-Hughes. And it's Felicity and Marjorie Echols, isn't it? You all look lovely."

"Now, what is the point of a masquerade if everyone acknowledges that they know everyone else?" Lord Dunmore complained good-naturedly.

"I think knowing people is ever so much nicer than conversing with strangers," said Felicity Echols, her wide green eyes accentuated by the glittering turquoise mask she wore. "One knows where one stands with everyone."

Her sister, attired in blue satin and a mask composed of flower petals, disagreed. "I think a masquerade is mysterious and romantic, myself. Not knowing is half the fun."

"I must agree with Marjorie," Lord Dunmore said. "There is something alluring about anonymity, isn't there? One might be anyone . . . do anything."

"An alarming suggestion." Mrs. Douglas-Hughes laughed.

"Where is your husband?" Lord Dunmore asked Mrs. Douglas-Hughes. "I'm going to pull him aside for drinks and billiards. Foster, too, if I can find him in this infernal crush. I believe he's wearing a tiger's mask."

"But the ball's only just begun," said Marjorie Echols, something like disappointment in her tone.

"Exactly. I should have begun drinking hours ago."

"Aren't you worried your guests will miss you?" I asked.

He smiled. "That's why I enjoy a masquerade; no one will know whether I'm here or not. And I'll expect all of you ladies to dance with me later." He took my hand in his. "Will you dance the midnight waltz with me, after the unmasking?"

"If you wish."

"Good. Ah, there he is," he said, spotting a gentleman I supposed was Mr. Douglas-Hughes. "If you ladies will excuse me . . ."

We watched him walk away. "I hope Sandy doesn't drink too much." Mrs. Douglas-Hughes sighed. "He never feels well when he does."

"What do the gentlemen do at balls in America, with alcohol being illegal?" Marjorie asked.

"They sneak away to drink just as they do here," Mamie said with a laugh. "Men, it seems, are much the same the world over."

"I've never known a man quite like Lord Dunmore," Marjorie Echols said, her eyes following his form across the room. "He's so handsome, isn't he? It's a pity about him, really."

"Surely he's not as bad as all that." I questioned lightly.

"Nothing unforgivable, I suppose. But there have been a string of showgirls and actresses. And then there's Vivian Garmond, of course. But you know about that."

"I . . . I'm afraid I don't," I confessed.

"Really? I'm surprised you haven't heard."

"Marjorie, perhaps you shouldn't . . ." began Felicity.

63

Her sister ignored her. "They're quite close. I've heard he pays for her house. They also say her young son looks very like the viscount, and he doesn't bother to deny it."

I raised my brows. While a mistress was sometimes considered de rigueur among the titled class, having it known so openly seemed to me a rather defiant step. Rumors and supposition were one thing; openly supporting a woman and practical admittance of an illegitimate child were quite another.

"Oh, she claims to have a husband that died, and people make a show of believing it, but everyone knows the child is his. I suppose he feels he needn't marry her when he can likely get a younger, well-connected woman to wed him, sordid reputation or not."

I digested this information silently. It made sense now, her inclusion at a dinner party where no one much wanted anything to do with her, the way her eyes followed the viscount when he wasn't looking. If it was true, it certainly did nothing to improve my opinion of Lord Dunmore. Then again, I had learned to take rumor with a grain of salt.

I glanced around the room, wondering if Mrs. Garmond was in attendance tonight. I had the feeling that she might be somewhere about the room, watching with her sad, dark eyes while the man she loved flirted with other women. If I came across her, I was determined I should make an effort to be friendly. I certainly knew something of what it was like to live under the shadow of scandal.

"Of course, she may not want to marry him," Marjorie continued. "With all the other rumors about him . . ."

"Marjorie, don't." It seemed that there was something almost desperate in Felicity Echols's whispered reprimand, though her sister merely shrugged.

"This is one of my favorite waltzes," Mrs. Douglas-Hughes interposed as the band struck up Lanner's "Die Romantiker." It seemed that she was very adept at seamless conversational detours.

"Yes, come, Felicity," Marjorie instructed. "Let's find someone to dance with us."

She led her sister away even as a gentleman approached Mrs. Douglas-Hughes and escorted her to the dance floor.

I stood for a moment, watching the festivities. Everyone seemed to be enjoying themselves immensely, but I saw nothing of the debauchery I had been led to expect. I will not say I was disappointed, but I was a bit perplexed that, forewarned as I had been of great wickedness, I had yet to see anything remotely scandalous.

Of course, the evening was still young.

5

Despite my initial reluctance to attend, I found myself genuinely enjoying the ball as the night progressed. I danced with several gentlemen, conversed with several notable figures, and sampled some of the very good food Lord Dunmore had provided. All told, I almost managed to forget that I had been commissioned to catch a thief. Almost, but not quite.

I had been keeping an eye out for Mrs. Barrington. I assumed our plan was still in force, but I had yet to spot her in the crush of the ballroom. I didn't even know what she was wearing or what type of mask she had chosen. It occurred to me that our plot was very haphazard indeed. If we had intended to accomplish anything, it would have behooved us to be a bit more organized. Nevertheless, I thought I should at least make an effort to find her.

From the corner of my eye, I saw a woman

I thought might be she stepping into the foyer, so I made my way through the crowds to follow her. It turned out, however, that the woman wasn't Mrs. Barrington, but a woman of similar build exiting the party.

I stood still for a moment, reluctant to return at once to the heat of the ballroom. The foyer was mostly deserted, and the air was much cooler there.

It was then I spotted a gentleman in the orange and black striped mask of a tiger coming down the stairs. Lord Dunmore mentioned Mr. Foster had worn such a mask, and I assumed the gentlemen had finished their game of billiards.

"Venturing back into the fray, Mr. Foster?" I asked with a smile.

He turned to me, and I realized at once that I had made a mistake. The mask was the same, the striped face of a tiger, but the build was not quite right, and the aura of confident athleticism was entirely absent.

"I . . . I'm not Foster," he said a bit haltingly. "I'm James Harker."

"I beg your pardon, Mr. Harker," I said. "It is I, Mrs. Ames."

"Mrs. Ames." There was something like relief in his voice as he pulled off his mask, revealing his red, perspiring face. "I'm awfully glad to meet someone I know. I find I don't care for all these masked faces at all."

"I thought you must be Mr. Foster. I believe he's wearing a similar mask to yours."

He frowned. "I haven't seen him," he said, dabbing at his face with a handkerchief. "I've been in the library upstairs. I've mostly been trying to stay out of the way. I only came down because I've an appointment with someone. I'm not much of one for parties, but Aunt Serena said it would be rude of me not to come."

"Do you happen to know where your aunt is?" I asked. "She's actually the one I've been looking for."

"I'm not certain where she is now," he said, "but it would be hard to miss her. She's dressed in a peacock sort of thing."

I didn't recall seeing her, but the description was clear enough.

"She's wearing some new jewels as well, sapphires, I think. My uncle must have bought them for her. He's always buying her things, you know. He dotes on her. Even his mask is blue to match her."

"Yes, she mentioned that he's very generous. Thank you, Mr. Harker. I'll just keep looking. If you happen across her, will you tell her I'm searching for her?"

"Certainly, though I don't expect our

paths shall cross anytime soon. I expect to go back upstairs. It's much more private there."

"I see."

"And when my appointment's over, I think I shall leave, despite what Aunt Serena says. Dunmore won't notice anyway. He isn't interested in my being here. It's the ladies that he's interested in. If you'll excuse me, Mrs. Ames."

"Certainly." I watched him go back into the ballroom, a bit bemused by his artlessness. He was an unusual gentleman, to be sure.

Well, if Mr. Harker planned on keeping his appointment, I supposed I should keep mine as well. I would have to wade back into the throng and locate Mrs. Barrington.

I reentered the ballroom and edged along the wall, politely declining two offers to dance as I went, attempting to spot Mrs. Barrington in the crowd. As the hour had grown later, the atmosphere of the party had begun to shift. The music, it seemed to me, had become faster, and there was a slightly more reckless air to the revelers than there had been at the start of the evening. I daresay that, not being even midnight, things were only beginning to warm up.

In the end, it was Mrs. Barrington who

found me.

"Mrs. Ames," she hissed. "Mrs. Ames! Over here!"

I turned and saw her standing near the French doors that led out onto the terrace. She had cracked one of them open to the cool night breeze and was fanning herself with a peacock-plume fan.

I made my way to her, admiring her gown of emerald and sapphire silk. There were elaborate inlays in the skirt that fluttered in the air. Somehow the flamboyant peacock attire suited her.

"Good evening, Mrs. Barrington. Your dress is lovely."

"Thank you, Mrs. Ames," she said without further pleasantries, clutching my arm and leaning in conspiratorially. "I've been wondering where you were. Our plan has been set into action."

I had been half hoping she had forgotten, but it was very apparent that she had not. "Yes, I've been looking for you, but it's so very crowded."

"Look at this." A brilliant sapphire bracelet appeared suddenly in her outstretched hand, like some sort of conjuror's trick.

"It's lovely."

"It's paste!" she cried delightedly. "Mr. Barrington had it made for me. Isn't it

71

clever? It's almost prettier than the real ones! I'm not sure I could tell the difference. I'm quite certain the thief shall be tempted to take it. I've been flashing it about all evening. I'm sure each of the suspects has seen it by now. And I've made a show of telling the others I plan to rest in the upstairs library for a while and that my bracelets are too tight and I must take them off. I saw those silly Echols girls not twenty minutes ago, and I could see perfectly well that they were ogling my jewelry. I also mentioned it to Mrs. Douglas-Hughes and Mrs. Garmond, in passing."

I wondered if her suspects had found this all to be as obvious as I did.

"Accompany me to the library, dear, and we shall lay the trap. Lloyd and the other gentlemen have gone upstairs to play cards or some such nonsense, so it shall be easy enough to find them and apprise them of my location."

I sighed inwardly, thinking of the futility of it all. "All right, Mrs. Barrington."

We made our way across the crowded ballroom and back into the foyer, where it appeared that more guests were arriving. We nodded politely at the latest arrivals and moved past them toward the stairs. A set of wide gold and crimson carpeted steps led upward, facing the front door from across the expanse of marble flooring, and then split off into two curving staircases that wound upward, parallel to the first set, before meeting on the first-floor landing. There was a railed gallery that overlooked the stairs and foyer, breaking up a long hallway that ran from one side of the house to the other.

We took the stairs together, skirting a group of two men and two women who were sitting at the landing, engaged in some sort of earnest conversation.

On the landing, we took the set of stairs to the right. It seemed Mrs. Barrington was familiar with the layout of the house, for she led me down a hallway straight ahead to the first door on the left, which was the library. It was a lovely room with very good furniture and shelf upon shelf of leather-bound books. A fire had been lit in the fireplace and crackled warmly. It reminded me a bit of the library at Thornecrest and was the sort of room in which I could have spent many comfortable hours.

She sank into a chair away from the fire and let out a great sigh. "It's so warm downstairs," she said, "all those bodies packed so closely together. I'm not as young as I once was." She laughed boisterously as she flipped open her fan of peacock feathers and began to wave it rapidly in front of her face. "Oh, bother," she cried suddenly. "This bracelet is forever getting caught on my dress." She pried loose the fabric that was caught at her wrist and took off the bracelet, setting it on the table beside her. "I think I shall leave it just here for the thief to find. In a few moments, I'll move to sit behind that screen," she said, indicating an impressive piece of Oriental design. "I'll be ready to pounce upon the bandit when he comes. Or perhaps I'll just sit here and pretend to sleep, then spring upon the culprit as he reaches out to take it."

"What if nothing happens?" I asked, secretly hoping that neither of her alarming suggestions would prove necessary. "It may be a while before anyone will screw up the courage to try."

"I'll wait," she said. "It feels lovely to get off my feet. These shoes are much too tight. Just come back in a while. Perhaps the culprit will have showed himself by then. If you'll just try to find the gentlemen and casually mention my jewels . . ."

"I think Lord Dunmore said something about a game of billiards."

"The billiards room is downstairs, my dear, but they aren't there. You recall I said they've come upstairs to play cards. I found the billiards room earlier, and they'd all gone. I'm sure you shall find them in no time, however."

She laid her head back in the chair and closed her eyes, and I realized that I had been dismissed to carry out my errand.

I left her reclining in the chair and went again into the long, wood-paneled hallway.

I stopped for a moment and glanced around. The hallway on this side of the stairwell extended far into the shadows, with several doors along either side. I had no intention of barging into rooms until I located the one in which the gentlemen were playing cards. No doubt if I returned downstairs and asked, someone would be able to direct me to the correct room.

A grandfather clock stood against the wall near the door to the library, and I noted the time. It was nearly half past eleven. I would fulfill my duty and then perhaps wait an hour more. After that, I would go home. I highly doubted anything eventful would occur tonight. In retrospect, the entire plan seemed rather ridiculous.

The group still sat on the landing when I reached the stairwell, and I heard their excited voices as I approached.

"Isn't that Helene Renault that's just

come in, the film star? Isn't she beautiful? I've seen all her pictures!"

"Look at her jewels! They're magnificent."

Curiosity got the best of me, and I walked toward the railing, hoping to catch a glance of the fabled actress.

"Who is the gentleman with her?" the other girl asked in a low voice. "Even with the mask, he's ever so handsome."

I had reached the railing by then and had a good view of the foyer below.

The girl was right. The thin black mask did little to hide his good looks . . . or his identity.

It was Milo.

6

I felt myself flush cold and then hot as I stepped back from the railing to avoid being seen, my head reeling. Milo had accompanied Helene Renault to Lord Dunmore's masquerade. So this was what had become of the horse he was desperate to buy.

I walked back up the short flight of stairs to the shadowed hallway. Standing in the semidarkness, I closed my eyes and drew in a deep breath, willing myself to remain calm. It would do me no good to fly into a fury; it never had.

I could hear the increased murmur of voices below, and I knew the cinema star's entrance had caused a stir. No doubt she was basking in the glow of the sensation her late arrival had caused, even as she clung to my husband's arm. They made a stunning pair, I would grant them that. Milo, tall and dark, was the perfect complement to Helene Renault's sleek blond beauty.

I suddenly felt very tired.

Too many emotions hit me all at once, and I knew only that I wanted to go home. I decided to change my strategy. Mrs. Barrington had said the gentlemen were playing cards somewhere on this floor, and I intended to locate them without going downstairs for directions. I would find Lord Dunmore, wish him a good evening, and be on my way. There were so many people in the ballroom, I could leave without ever encountering Milo.

I walked down the long hall, my skirts rustling around me in the relative silence. A door suddenly opened, and Felicity Echols emerged from it, closing it quickly behind her. She turned and nearly collided with me, barely stifling a gasp.

"Oh, Mrs. Ames!" she said, a bright flush creeping up her cheeks. "I . . . I was just lying down for a moment. It was awfully hot in that ballroom."

"Yes, just what Mrs. Barrington was saying earlier," I replied. "So many people."

She nodded, almost too vigorously, and I felt she seemed more nervous than the situation warranted. "Indeed. I felt I must lie down for a moment," she said again.

"Mrs. Barrington is resting in the library," I noted, feeling, in addition to the need to move the conversation along, that I might as well play my part as well as I could before exiting the party. "I was looking for Lord Dunmore. Have you seen him?"

If possible, her flush brightened. "No, I don't . . . that is, not since earlier this evening. I . . . I think he may have gone downstairs."

I nodded. "Thank you."

"Oh," she said suddenly, putting a hand to her face. "I've forgotten my mask. If you'll excuse me, Mrs. Ames . . ." She reentered the room, shutting the door behind her.

I didn't believe that Lord Dunmore was downstairs. In fact, I suspected there was a good possibility that he recently had been keeping Miss Echols company in the room from which she had just emerged. However, it really was none of my business. It seemed that I had enough illicit liaisons to worry about in my own household.

I walked farther along the long hallway, listening as I went. At last, I seemed to hear voices behind a door. I knocked and was rewarded by a call to enter.

I opened the door and found Lord Dunmore, Mr. Douglas-Hughes, Mr. Foster, and Mr. Barrington sitting around a table, cards in hand, their masks discarded. The empty-eyed masks looked up at me from black and silver, glittering peacock-blue, gold, and tiger-striped faces.

The gentlemen had turned to look at me as I opened the door and then began to rise from their seats as I came into the room.

"Please, gentlemen, don't get up," I said. "I didn't mean to intrude."

"Not at all," Lord Dunmore said, coming to usher me into the room. "We're delighted. We could use a respite from the game. Foster is entirely too good at everything he sets his hand to. Doesn't seem fair he should be a champion at tennis and a perfect billiards prodigy, but now he's trouncing us at cards as well. It's uncanny." He smiled as he said it, but it didn't seem quite sincere. I thought Lord Dunmore seemed a man who wouldn't much like to lose.

"Mere luck," Mr. Foster said dismissively.

"Well, I am sorry for the interruption." I turned to Lord Dunmore. His hand, which had lingered on my back, fell away. "I've only come to wish you good evening. I'm afraid it's time for me to leave."

"Nonsense," he said, glancing at the clock on the wall. "It's not even midnight, and you promised me the dance after the unmasking."

80

I hesitated. I didn't want to appear rude, but neither did I want to stay any longer than was absolutely necessary.

"We're nearly finished with this hand. Wait at least until midnight." There was something in his coaxing command that I could not refuse.

"Very well," I assented. After all, why should I be forced to flee the party just because my husband had decided to arrive with another woman? Two could play that game. "I shall save my last dance of the evening for you, Lord Dunmore."

"Excellent." He reached out and squeezed my arm. "I knew you wouldn't want to disappoint me, Mrs. Ames."

I was unsure how to respond to this, so I said nothing.

As the gentlemen resumed their game, I remembered suddenly that I had told Mrs. Barrington I would mention her location to the possible thief in our midst. "I've just come from speaking with your wife, Mr. Barrington. She's resting in the library because she found it crowded and hot downstairs. I believe she may even have fallen asleep."

"Serena's always getting overheated," he murmured, his eyes on his cards.

"She showed me her lovely sapphire

81

bracelet, but she said it was hurting her wrists and needed to take it off. Such a lovely piece."

"Hmm," her husband replied, laying down a card. Though he knew about Mrs. Barrington's ploy, he seemed singularly disinterested in taking part. I couldn't say I blamed him.

"I'll just go back and check on her," I said, by way of excusing myself, having done all I could to try to induce the men to thievery. They all seemed much too engrossed in their game to think of Mrs. Barrington's jewelry.

"I'll meet you downstairs in a few moments for the unmasking?" Lord Dunmore asked.

"Very well."

I exited the room and made my way down the hallway, half wishing I had insisted upon leaving. I really was rather tired, and I wanted to be home and out of this heavy dress. I supposed it wouldn't hurt me to dance one dance with Lord Dunmore, however. I was just as capable of making a spectacle of myself as Milo was, and I thought I just might enjoy it. In preparation, I located a powder room and spent a few moments refreshing my makeup before again venturing into the hall.

"Hello, Mrs. Ames." I started and looked up. I had been so lost in thought that I had not heard Mrs. Douglas-Hughes approaching.

"Hello, Mrs. Douglas-Hughes," I replied, as cheerily as I could manage.

"Call me Mamie, won't you? Douglas-Hughes is such a mouthful."

I smiled. "Certainly, if you will call me Amory."

"I'd like that. I'm just looking for Sandy. It's nearly midnight, and he shall dance with me if I have to drag him down the stairs. I tried the billiards room, but someone told me they'd come upstairs for cards. The house is massive, isn't it?" She looked at the hallway ahead and then over her shoulder at where the hallway extended beyond the gallery toward the other side of the house. I don't have any idea where to look."

"It's the room at the end of the hall." I directed her to the doorway from which I had recently emerged. "I understand Mr. Foster is trouncing them soundly."

She paused, and her expression was hesitant, as though there was more she wanted to say. I thought I might know what it was.

"I've seen my husband has arrived," I said, to relieve her of the burden. I was glad my voice betrayed nothing of my true feelings.

83

"Yes," she answered carefully. "He came in a few moments ago."

"He has the charming habit of popping up places unannounced at the most inconvenient times."

"You weren't expecting him, then." Or her. Those last two words were implied.

"No. I wasn't."

"I suppose that's very . . . awkward."

"I've grown somewhat accustomed to it," I replied tonelessly.

"I'm not trying to pry," she said. "I just thought that maybe you would like someone to talk to." She laughed self-consciously. "I suppose it's very American of me, but I just wanted to be sure you were . . . all right."

I smiled again, more naturally this time, charmed by her thoughtfulness. "Thank you, Mamie. I appreciate that. I'm quite all right."

She nodded, sensing that I had no wish to continue along this topic at present.

"I'll just go get Sandy then. I'll see you later, Amory?"

"Yes."

She continued on down the hall, and I headed toward the library. With any luck, Mrs. Barrington would still be there resting comfortably. I hoped she was not put out with me for abandoning her little scheme to go home, but I had felt all along that it was somewhat preposterous, and I was in no mood to play along at present.

I pushed open the door to the library, prepared to offer my excuses, and found Mrs. Barrington collapsed against the back of her chair, sound asleep and snoring softly. I hesitated, wondering if I should perhaps awaken her, but I decided against it. There was no reason to disturb her, especially not now, as I intended to leave at the first convenient moment.

A glance at the table showed that the sapphire bracelet was no longer in sight. It seemed improbable that the thief might actually have struck in my absence, so I supposed Mrs. Barrington had tucked it away before she drifted off. Well, our little charade would have to wait for another time.

I left the room, closing the door softly behind me.

The hallway was deserted, the quiet broken by the muted sounds of the ball drifting up from below: swelling music, the murmur of voices, and the occasional clink of china and crystal as the guests sampled the delicacies of the lavish buffet.

I glanced again at the grandfather clock and saw that it was a quarter to midnight. Nearly time for the unmasking.

Lord Dunmore said he would meet me downstairs, so I supposed it was time to make my way back to the ballroom. I dreaded bumping into Milo, but the place was so crowded that it was unlikely. In any event, there was no need for me to go on behaving as though I were the guilty party.

I reached the railing and looked over at the stairs leading down into the foyer. The group still sat there at the top of the lower staircase, conversing as eagerly as ever. There was no sign of Milo.

I started down the staircase and was halfway to the landing where the group sat when my foot slid out from under me. I grasped at the railing, but it was too late. I could not regain my footing. My ankle twisted painfully as I tried unsuccessfully to catch myself, and I fell down the last four steps, ending in an ungraceful heap at the landing, my dress tangled around me like a great sea of red foam.

The four young people who had been seated on the stairs below me stood at once, and both of the gentlemen started up toward me. "Are you hurt?" one asked.

"Mrs. Ames!" Lord Dunmore had appeared at the top of the stairs, from where I had just come, his face once again obscured by his black and silver mask. He was down the steps and at my side in the space of an instant, leaning down to help me up. "Are you all right?"

"Yes. Just clumsy, I'm afraid." I wrestled my skirt, which seemed to multiply in volume the more I moved. I was quite sure my face must be as crimson as my gown by this point, especially with so attentive an audience. At least the top half of my face was hidden behind a mask.

Somehow Lord Dunmore managed to extricate me from the folds of my dress and help me to my feet. I winced as I tried to stand on my right ankle, and I gripped the banister, knowing my ankle could not support my weight.

I smiled at the two gentlemen who still stood watching, though I rather expect it came across as more of a grimace. "Thank you for your concern. Please don't let me disturb you."

Rather reluctantly, they made their way back down to their ladies, and I was relieved when the four of them sat again and resumed their conversation.

Lord Dunmore was watching me carefully, his arm still around me, his hand at my waist. "You've hurt yourself, haven't you?" he asked. "You've gone quite white."

"It's only my ankle. I'll be just fine in a

moment," I told him, though the pain seemed to be getting worse the longer I stood.

"Let me help you."

"Yes, perhaps I had better go back up and sit down for a moment."

I tried to take the first step and lurched as the pain shot through my foot. I clenched my teeth. I was prepared to sit on the bottom step, when, without another word, Lord Dunmore swept me up into his arms.

"Really, my lord," I said in a breathless mixture of surprise and embarrassment. "This isn't necessary."

"Of course it is. You need to see a doctor."

I sighed. "I'm sure it's quite all right. If you'll just have my car sent round, I'll go home. I'm sure my ankle will be right as rain in the morning."

He ignored me and continued to carry me up the stairs, and I could see the interested group on the lower staircase looking up at us until he moved beyond the railings and down the hall.

He moved past the library and then the room where I had seen Miss Echols, and I briefly wondered what had become of her. She certainly hadn't passed us on the stairs. He stopped before a door midway down the corridor. Still holding me in his arms, he reached out and turned the knob before pushing the door open with his foot and carrying me inside. It was a beautiful bedroom, done in dark wood, emerald silks, and flocked wallpaper.

He deposited me gently on the bed, and I pulled my mask off, glad to be rid of it.

"Perhaps I had better look at it," he said, removing his mask as well.

I studied him for a moment but could discern no ulterior motives in his expression. In any event, Lord Dunmore had certainly witnessed more scandalous things than a twisted ankle.

I pushed my skirts aside, and he sat on the edge of the bed, taking my foot gently in his hands. "It's begun to swell," he said. "Let's get rid of this shoe."

He slipped my shoe off and dropped it on the floor. I had to admit, it did feel a bit better already.

"And now your stocking," he said.

"Lord Dunmore . . ."

He smiled. "I assure you, Mrs. Ames, I act with pure intentions."

I raised a brow, but offered no further objection. It would be extremely difficult to remove it myself, and I was certain the doctor would want it removed in any event.

His hands slid up my leg, and he deftly and expertly unfastened the stocking from my garter and began to slip it off.

It was at that moment that the door opened and Milo made one of his extremely inopportune entrances.

7

Lord Dunmore reacted as though he was caught removing another man's wife's stocking every evening. Then again, perhaps he was.

"Hello, Ames." For the space of a moment, he glanced over his shoulder at Milo, who no longer wore his mask, and then turned his attention back to me. With perfect equanimity, he finished sliding the stocking down my leg and peeled it off, careful not to jar my ankle. I shifted a bit uncomfortably and found I could not quite meet Milo's gaze as the viscount's warm hand brushed against my bare foot.

"Hello, Dunmore," Milo replied. "This is quite the party you're having."

Lord Dunmore smoothed out the stocking and handed it to me. "Good silk," he said with a smile before turning his gaze back to Milo. "Yes. I hope you're enjoying your evening as much as I've been enjoying mine."

"Never a dull moment," my husband answered. His tone was friendly enough, but I could never be quite certain what he was thinking. After all, this scene did look rather bad, and Lord Dunmore seemed disinclined to offer excuses. In fact, I was not altogether sure he wasn't enjoying himself.

"Your wife's taken quite a tumble," he said.

"Indeed?" Milo replied dryly.

"I fell down a few stairs," I interjected. "Rather clumsy of me. It's nothing."

"I shall send for the doctor, nonetheless," Lord Dunmore said, rising unhurriedly and depositing my foot carefully back on the bed. "I'll ring him from my bedroom. Keep an eye on her, will you, Ames?"

"Certainly," Milo replied, stepping out of the doorway so Lord Dunmore could pass.

The viscount departed and closed the door behind him, leaving us alone. We looked at one another. I supposed the situation warranted explanation, but I was loath to explain things to Milo when he was always so very cavalier in justifying his own highly questionable behavior. In fact, I couldn't seem to summon up any feelings of shame, especially after the embarrassment that he had inflicted on me this evening.

He walked to the bed, and his gaze fell upon Lord Dunmore's mask where it lay discarded atop the blanket. "At least only masks and stockings have been removed thus far," he said. As usual, it was nearly impossible for me to gauge his reaction. I had to contend with a vague look of amused speculation that gave no indication of his true feelings.

I said nothing. I felt I was doing a fairly good job of hiding my own feelings, considering I was furious with him.

Instead of attempting to fill the silence, I straightened my skirts around me, careful not to shift my ankle, which continued to throb steadily. It was quite swollen and beginning to turn an unflattering shade of purple.

"I'll have the car brought round and send for Dr. Easton. He can see you at the flat."

"Thank you, but if Lord Dunmore has rung his doctor already, I may as well see him here." I would have, in fact, preferred to see my family doctor in my own home, but at the moment I felt stubbornly disinclined to give in to Milo's suggestion.

"Very well." His eyes shifted to my ankle, and I wondered if he had doubted my story up to now. "How did you manage to fall down the stairs?"

"I'm not certain how it happened. I was coming down the stairs, and my foot just slipped out from under me."

"Very unfortunate."

"Yes. What are you doing here, Milo?"

"I happened to step into the foyer and saw Dunmore sweep my wife off her feet and carry her up the stairs. I thought it prudent to follow."

I ignored this remark and its inherent insinuation. "I meant why did you come to the masquerade?"

"My business with Garmond was conducted much more quickly than I expected, and I decided to come to the masquerade after all, to surprise you."

"Well, you certainly did that," I retorted irritably.

"Yes, so I noticed." His eyes ran over me. "You look absolutely stunning in the gown, darling. It's not the one you were wearing when I left."

"No, it's not." The more he spoke, the more averse I felt to offering any explanations. Let him make whatever assumptions he liked.

"I'm sure there was not a man here who could take his eyes from you. Though, I'll admit, I would have preferred that you end up in my bed at the end of the evening rather than Dunmore's."

"Indeed?" My brows rose. "I thought perhaps you had made other arrangements for tonight."

"Ah." The corner of his mouth tipped up. "You saw me come in with Helene."

"Yes. The illustrious Mademoiselle Renault, whom you barely know."

"There is a perfectly simple explanation."

"There always is, Milo," I said tiredly.

"You don't see me causing a stir just because I happened to find Dunmore peeling off your clothes in his bed."

"This isn't his bed."

"A technicality."

"I don't want to talk about it now," I said. "I'm in rather a lot of pain and . . ."

My words were cut off by the loud sound of something very like a gunshot coming from somewhere down the hall.

I started. "What on earth . . ."

"It sounded rather like a gunshot to me." Milo turned toward the door with his usual unhurried elegance as I made an almost unconscious move to get up from the bed and gasped in pain as I jarred my ankle.

"Stay here, Amory," he commanded me. "I'll be back in a moment."

"Milo, perhaps you'd better not . . ."

But he had already reached the door and smiled back at me. "Don't fret, darling. I'm sure it's nothing. Then again, we can't be sure. Perhaps Dunmore has been caught stripping the clothes from some less understanding gentleman's wife."

I might have thrown something at him had anything useful been in reach. But he had already closed the door behind him.

With a sigh, I adjusted my skirts again and carefully slid my legs off the bed until my feet rested on the floor. My twisted ankle was quite swollen at this point, and I knew it would be impossible to stand on it. I attempted it, nonetheless, and just managed to catch myself before I took another tumble to the floor.

Grasping the bedpost for support, I hopped quite ungracefully to the foot of the bed and then toward the door. I'm sure I made quite a sight, bounding across the room like a rabbit in a billowing red ball gown. I reached the door and, leaning against the wall for support, cracked it open and looked out into the hallway.

I could hear the music and the din of voices coming up unworriedly from below, and I could only assume the partygoers had not heard the noise of the shot. Perhaps the music had muffled it.

It had been difficult to tell from which direction the shot had come, but I could hear voices coming from down the corridor. I pulled the door open a bit further and leaned out. Nigel Foster and Mr. Douglas-Hughes stood outside the door of one of the rooms. Though my knowledge of Lord Dunmore's floor plan had grown considerably over the evening, it was not one of the rooms I recognized. It seemed to be a few doors down from the room in which the gentlemen had been playing cards.

"Good Lord," I heard someone say from inside, and it sounded like Mr. Barrington. A moment later, my guess was confirmed as he came out of the room, followed by Milo and Lord Dunmore. They closed the door behind them, speaking in low voices. Maddeningly, I couldn't make out anything that was being said. Lord Dunmore left the group and disappeared into another of the rooms. Mr. Barrington stared straight ahead for a moment, his face slack and gray. Then he visibly drew in a breath and squared his shoulders. He went off in the direction of the library, an air of resolution about him.

Milo came back down the hall a moment later, and I pulled the door open further to greet him before he reached it. "What's happened?" I demanded.

He sighed. Without a word, he swept me up and carried me back to the bed, depositing me none too gently in an untidy heap upon the satin bedspread. "You shouldn't be walking on that ankle."

"I hopped," I told him, with an impatient wave of my hand. "What was that noise about?"

"It's the Barringtons' nephew."

"James Harker?"

"Yes."

"What's happened?"

He hesitated for only a moment. "I'm afraid he's killed himself."

I had hoped, after the events at the Brightwell Hotel, never to put myself in the path of sudden and unnatural death again. Of course, I suppose I really had very little say in the matter. If one is determined to kill oneself in a public place, there is not much the bystanders can do about it.

Milo didn't offer any details, and I didn't want to know, not really. He had been in that room, and I could only assume it must have been dreadful.

"Will you be all right here for a few moments, Amory?" Milo asked, drawing me out of my reverie. "I have something I must attend to."

Our eyes met, both of us knowing perfectly well what, or rather who, it was.

"By all means," I replied, too tired to think of anything more cutting to add.

"I'll be back in a moment."

But he wasn't. Apparently, Mademoiselle Renault was in need of greater consolation than I, for Milo had not returned by the time Lord Dunmore came back to the room.

Though the viscount carried himself with his usual confidence, his face was grave.

"You've heard, Mrs. Ames?"

"Yes. It's so terrible."

"Are you all right?"

"Yes, of course. How is Mrs. Barrington? Has she been told?"

"Mr. Barrington is with her now. She's terribly upset, naturally, but quite composed."

I felt sorry for the woman. In the short time that I had observed them together, it had become apparent to me that she was very fond of her nephew. I'm sure his unexpected death would be hard on her.

"The police should be here soon," he said. "I don't think the guests downstairs know what has happened. I suppose they'll find out soon enough, however. If you'll excuse me for a few moments, I should probably wait for the police to arrive."

"Of course. Thank you for looking in on me."

He left me alone and I knew he must be right about the other guests not knowing, for the music carried on below as though nothing had happened. People were dancing, eating, and laughing, blissfully unaware of what had occurred upstairs. I envied them.

A few moments later, the doctor Lord Dunmore had contacted appeared and examined my ankle. He was a stout, white-haired gentleman who went about his business with brisk efficiency.

"Nothing broken," he said when he had finished his examination. "Just a nasty sprain. You should probably stay off of it for a few days and let it heal."

It was a better diagnosis than I had expected, but the thought of being bedridden was not an appealing one.

He seemed to sense my feelings, for he added, "If you'll give me your address, I can have a cane sent around to you in the morning. That should help you get about when necessary."

"Thank you, doctor."

He left without saying anything of the other business, though I was certain he must have spoken to Lord Dunmore. It was frustrating in the extreme to be stuck in this bedroom. I wanted to be able to help in some way, and I couldn't even walk.

A moment later, Lord Dunmore knocked and came in again, this time followed by a man who could only have been a policeman. Dressed in a brown suit and a serviceable wool coat, he had a stern, humorless face. My initial impression was confirmed as Lord Dunmore made the introduction.

"Mrs. Ames, this is Inspector Harris. He's going to use the library to interview the others that were upstairs at the time, but I told him you were injured."

"Good evening, madam," the inspector said, casting his dark eyes over me in a vaguely disapproving way, as though it was rude of me to lie there while being interviewed.

"Good evening."

"I'd like to ask you a few questions. You were, I understand, in this room at the time of the incident?"

"Yes."

"What time was it that you heard the shot?"

"Sometime near midnight, I think."

"And had you seen Mr. Harker earlier in the evening?"

"I saw him once."

"Here on the first floor?"

"No, on the stairwell, but it was quite some time ago."

"Did he strike you as behaving oddly?"

"Not particularly, no. I didn't know him at all well, of course."

Harris nodded, as though he had suspected as much. "Very good. I think that will be all. If there's anything else, I will let you know. Good evening."

He turned and left the room without further ado.

"Charming fellow, isn't he?" Dunmore said with a wan smile. "Forgive me for leaving you alone again, Mrs. Ames, but I suppose I had better follow him to the library. The others are all quite shaken up."

"Yes, of course," I said.

He went again from the room, and I was left alone with my thoughts.

I couldn't understand why Mr. Harker had killed himself. I cast my mind back to our encounter. He had seemed a bit harried, perhaps uncomfortable in his surroundings, but I had had no inkling that he was about to do anything drastic. In fact, he had expressed plans for the rest of the evening that seemed at definite odds with the contemplation of suicide. I supposed one never really knows what is going on in the minds of other people, but there was something about it that didn't seem right.

A few moments later, his business with Mademoiselle Renault apparently concluded, Milo came to collect me.

"I've had the car brought round," he said. "Are you ready?"

"Have you spoken to that police inspector?"

"Yes. I had nothing of interest to tell him. I'll carry you to the car."

"Very well." There really was no point in resisting. I knew perfectly well that I couldn't walk. "Get my shoe, will you?"

He picked it up and put it in his pocket, ignoring the discarded stocking. Then he scooped me up and carried me from the room. Lord Dunmore met us in the hallway. "Going so soon?" he asked with a smile. He kept up a façade of casual affability, but his eyes looked tired.

"Thank you for your hospitality, Lord Dunmore," I said. "I'm terribly sorry about everything."

"It is I who am sorry about all this," he said, taking my hand. "I can't imagine why . . ." His voice trailed off, and he went on with grim cheerfulness. "I'll drop round in a day or so to be certain your ankle is mending."

"You needn't inconvenience yourself, my lord."

"On the contrary, Mrs. Ames. I shall look forward to it immensely." His gaze moved then to Milo, as though he had forgotten I had been resting in my husband's arms for the duration of our conversation. "Good night, Ames," he said, patting him on the shoulder. "Thank you for coming."

"Good night, Dunmore."

Milo moved down the hall. As we passed the room where James Harker had shot himself, I couldn't resist looking through the open door. The body had been covered, and it felt immensely unreal that the shapeless lump on the floor had been an affable young man conversing with me in the foyer only an hour or so before.

There was a policeman on his hands and knees on the rug beside the body, closely examining the floor. It struck me as vaguely odd, though I couldn't quite make out why.

I couldn't help but think there was something peculiar in all of this. For one thing, it was very strange indeed that all of the guests at Mrs. Barrington's dinner should have been in such close proximity to this tragedy. In the next few days, I would pay my respects to Mrs. Barrington and perhaps see if she still harbored suspicions about the theft of her jewelry. It had crossed my mind that the recent thefts and the unfortunate death of Mr. Harker might be in some way related.

A thought came to me suddenly.

"Milo?" I asked as he carried me down the stairs. "Who else was on the first floor with us when it happened?"

He paused a moment to think it over. "When I went into the hall, Dunmore, Barrington, Foster, and Douglas-Hughes were already there. That inspector also had both the Echols sisters and Mrs. Douglas-Hughes in the library."

An odd, uneasy feeling settled over me.

It was Mrs. Barrington's group of suspects, almost to the person.

8

The ball was still in full swing as Milo carried me across the foyer and out into the night. The revelry had increased to the degree that our departure generated very little notice. I suspected I was not the last woman that would be carried out before the night was over. That is, if the party was allowed to continue. Apparently, the arrival of the police had been handled with extreme discretion thus far, but something like this could only be kept quiet for so long.

Milo deposited me on the backseat, and it was only then, with my body no longer pressed against his, that I realized how cold the night had become. Lord Dunmore's butler had brought out my fur, and Milo handed it to me. I draped it over myself, trying to cover my bare arms as Milo went around to the other side of the car and got in. He sat close, but not quite touching, and neither of us spoke.

In addition to feeling distraught over the tragedy that had just occurred, I couldn't help but be furious about Milo's arrival with the French actress. I also suspected that Milo, beneath his calm exterior, was in something of a temper over finding Lord Dunmore removing my stockings.

I could only imagine what Markham thought of our cool behavior toward one another. What a difference one night could make.

We pulled up in front of the flat after riding the rest of the way in a silence heavy with mutual disapproval. Milo got out before Markham could open the door and came around to assist me from the car.

"Perhaps if I just leaned on you," I said, hoping in vain that I might be able to walk on my own.

"Nonsense," he interrupted, sweeping me up into his arms.

The doorman and the lift operator both took in the scene with perfect equanimity, but I was relieved once we had reached the privacy of our flat. Winnelda, I hoped, was asleep, and Parks, Milo's valet, had been given the night off. Milo frequently dispensed with Parks's services; I had always suspected it was because Milo didn't like witnesses to his misdeeds.

He carried me into the dark bedroom and deposited me on the bed before he switched on the lamp. The room was decorated in black and gold, and the lamplight seemed to do little to push back the shadows; perhaps it was just that everything seemed darker this evening.

"Shall I send for Dr. Easton?" he asked.

"I saw the doctor while you were . . ." My words trailed off. "He says it's only a sprain."

I sat up, easing myself to the edge of the bed, and reached to unfasten my dress as the chiffon of the skirt caught beneath me and welled up around me. What had started out as a dream of a gown had turned into an incredible nuisance. I couldn't wait to be free of the wretched thing. Unfortunately, the side closures were difficult for me to undo myself.

"If you'd wake Winnelda for me," I said, not wanting to disturb her, but wanting even less to ask him for assistance.

He ignored my request as he sat beside me on the bed, the mattress shifting under his weight, and began to unfasten the innumerable little hook closures that held the dress closed.

I looked down at the top of his dark head as he leaned to unhook me. I wanted to say something, but I didn't know where to begin. Things had been so much better between us as of late, but I could feel the old uncertainty beginning to creep back in.

Almost before I knew it, he had gathered up the gown and slipped it over my head, tossing it in a heap on the floor. I was left sitting in my slip. And one stocking.

"Does it hurt?" he asked, glancing down at my bare and swollen ankle.

"It throbs a bit," I admitted.

Milo rose and poured a glass of water from the pitcher on the bedside table. Then he took two aspirin from the bottle in the drawer and handed them to me.

"Here you are."

"Thank you."

I gingerly shifted my foot back onto the bed and sat back against the pillows, swallowing the aspirin.

Milo didn't look at me as he took off his necktie and dinner jacket, tossing them across the back of a chair. He broke the silence as he removed his cuff links. "You know I dread above all things the conventional role of a jealous husband, but I feel I should warn you about Dunmore."

Had I not been exhausted and in pain, I might have found the irony of his admonishment to be laughable. As it was, I managed a very civil reply.

"There's no need. I have no interest in Lord Dunmore."

"He has an interest in you," he said mildly, "and he is generally known as a man who will stop at nothing to get what he wants."

"I'm more interested in what you want, Milo."

"Meaning what?"

"Are you having an affair with Helene Renault?" The words were out almost before I realized I was going to say them. I had not intended to be so blunt, but there it was.

His eyes met mine. "No, I'm not."

I must have expressed silent skepticism, for he sat down on the edge of the mattress and continued. "I met Garmond at my club, but then we decided to go out for dinner and drinks. When I was leaving, I happened to run into Helene. She asked where I was going and insisted upon accompanying me. She has heard about Dunmore, you see, and was anxious to meet him."

"Isn't that a bit of a coincidence?"

"Perhaps, but it's the truth."

I leaned my head against the black-velvet tufted headboard and looked up at him. I had long ago recognized the flaw in my reasoning when it came to Milo. It was that I always wanted to believe him, no matter how dubious the story. This time was no different. I could feel myself relenting, despite the implausibility of his explanation.

"As I told you before," he went on, as though he knew that I was on the verge of accepting this far-fetched account, "I barely know the woman."

"That's not what the papers will be saying tomorrow." Just when things had begun to settle down, I would once again see the cracks in my marriage flashed across the gossip columns.

"I'm afraid the cause célèbre of the hour is much more likely to be the unfortunate Mr. Harker," Milo replied.

"Why would he do it, do you think?" I asked, my thoughts diverted for the moment.

"I expect theories abound in plenty, and I assume they will be made available to the press. You shall probably read all about his secret gambling debts and other assorted sins in tomorrow's paper."

"He seemed a nice young man," I said, ignoring Milo's cynicism.

He rose to finish undressing. "Those are frequently the kind that get themselves into trouble and can see no alternative but to end it all. Shame and embarrassment are sometimes unbearable for respectable peo-

111

ple. That's why it doesn't pay to worry about one's reputation."

Milo certainly followed his own credo there; he had never been embarrassed in his life.

"Perhaps. But it was rather a drastic thing to do at a ball." I frowned as I thought about it. It wasn't at all the sort of thing I would think Mr. Harker would do. Despite our initial and publicly embarrassing meeting, the impression I had formed of him at the ball had been one of a retiring, private man. If he was inclined to end his life, I would have expected it to be done at his own residence, not in the house of a man he barely knew — and during the middle of a masquerade ball at that.

"Milo, do you think it odd . . ."

"No," he said, cutting me off, as he handed me a nightgown he had retrieved from my bureau. "And you shouldn't either. I know perfectly well what kind of schemes that brain of yours is concocting, and no good can come of them."

I frowned at him, but he ignored me.

"I'm going to sleep in the guest bedroom so I don't bump your ankle in the night," he said, as he tied the belt of the black dressing gown he had put on over his nightclothes. "Do you need anything else?"

There were so many things I wanted to say, but instead I shook my head. "I'm fine, thank you."

"Very well. Good night, darling."

He dropped a kiss on my lips and departed the room, leaving me feeling dissatisfied and unsettled about the entire evening.

The feeling of dissatisfaction had not waned as the gray light of early morning began to filter through my curtains. Despite the hour at which I had gone to bed, I found I could not go back to sleep. I lay abed for what seemed like hours, willing myself to rest, but at last I gave it up and rose, pulling on a negligee over my nightgown.

I hobbled from my bed to the black velvet chaise lounge and propped up my foot. It was quite sore this morning, but the swelling seemed to have gone down somewhat. I hoped to be up and walking again by the next day at the latest, doctor's orders or no.

I was surprised when the door opened and Milo came in carrying a tray. He was almost never awake at this hour. I wondered if this was a sign of an attempted truce on his part.

"I've intercepted Winnelda and brought your breakfast," he said.

"Bless you for that. I'll tell her all about

the ball later," I said. "After I've had some coffee."

"How's your ankle this morning?"

"A bit better, thank you," I answered.

"Glad to hear it." He set the tray on the table. "She's made you toast and jam, which, though not especially substantial, might be for the best. I'm still not sure I'd trust the girl to do more than boil water. And I thought you might be interested in this." He handed me a copy of *The Times*.

I had been hoping to avoid the papers, but I knew I would have to face them eventually. The events of last night were only more fodder for the gossip machines. Like it or not, I had become part of another scandal.

I took the paper from Milo and unfolded it. The headline was there in bold letters, and it was worse than I had expected: SUICIDE AT LORD DUNMORE'S BALL: DEAD MAN BELIEVED TO BE JEWEL THIEF.

"Jewel thief!" I exclaimed. "What on earth . . ."

"Read on," Milo said, reaching to pour coffee from the pot into my cup.

I read aloud. "Last evening, the ball held at the home of the Viscount Dunmore was the scene of an unexpected tragedy when Mr. James Harker, nephew of Mr. and Mrs.

Lloyd Barrington, shot himself in one of Lord Dunmore's upstairs rooms. A later examination of the body revealed the presence of several sapphires, believed to be from a bracelet belonging to the deceased's aunt, Mrs. Barrington."

I gasped and looked up at Milo as he complacently stirred sugar into my coffee.

"Mrs. Barrington's bracelet?"

"It appears so. I told you the young man's sins would come to light."

My eyes scanned the article. "Mrs. Barrington revealed that bracelet appeared to be the one she had been wearing earlier in the evening. She also divulged that other items of jewelry were missing from her home, including a priceless brooch and a diamond bracelet. The combined value of the items is estimated to be in excess of ten thousand pounds."

"Not exactly a queen's ransom," Milo observed.

I looked up. "But those sapphires were paste."

One of Milo's dark brows lifted as he paused, my cup raised halfway to his lips. "Indeed? You seem privy to information that *The Times* was not able to extract from the rather voluble Mrs. Barrington."

I flushed, realizing I had revealed more

than I intended. I fancy I was able to smooth out my features rather quickly, but not quickly enough to escape Milo's notice. He was, as always, irritatingly perceptive. "Amory, have you been involving yourself in things you shouldn't again?"

"I don't know what you mean," I replied.

"Don't you?" He challenged me with a knowing look.

I was spared the effort of summoning up an indignant response by the ringing of the telephone.

"I wonder who that could be at this hour," I said.

"I'm sure we shall soon see."

A moment later, Winnelda tapped hesitantly at the door.

"Come in," I called.

She cracked the door and stuck her head inside the room as she always did, her eyes averted as though afraid of finding us in the throes of passion.

"Yes, Winnelda? Who's calling?" I asked.

"It's Mrs. Barrington, madam," she answered, her gaze still trained on the floor.

My eyes met Milo's, something very like interest flickering in his.

"Thank you, Winnelda." I made a move to rise, but Milo was up before I could get to my feet.

"I'll speak to her, darling," he said. "You shouldn't be walking with your ankle as it is."

"Milo, I would like to speak to her . . ."

But he was already to the door, Winnelda scurrying to get out of his way.

He reached the telephone a moment later, and I could hear the low, pleasant murmur of his voice as he spoke. The conversation lasted for some minutes, and I supposed Mrs. Barrington was being treated to the full array of his considerable charms. I hadn't the slightest doubt she would be captivated by the time he rang off. Much to my chagrin, I could not make out what he was saying, and I supposed they would be done speaking before I could hop to the door to eavesdrop. I gritted my teeth at the utter inconvenience of it all.

When he came back into the room, I could barely contain my curiosity.

"Well?" I asked. "What did she say?"

"She wanted to see you, today if at all possible. She hadn't heard, of course, that you have been injured."

"It's only a sprain. Did she say what about?"

"You really must be careful of your ankle," he said, taking his seat and picking up my coffee cup, which he seemed to have commandeered. He infuriated me by taking a leisurely sip before continuing. "In any event, I've invited her to have tea with us this afternoon."

I was slightly mollified. At least I wouldn't have long to wait before I discovered what it was she wanted.

Milo drained the last of the coffee from the cup and rose from his chair. "I have some other matters to attend to, but I shall be back in time for tea." He leaned to brush a kiss across my cheek. Then he was gone, and I leaned back against the divan, more exhausted, if possible, than I had been a few moments before.

I managed to pull myself together quite nicely by teatime. A somewhat fitful nap, a hot bath, and a smart new dress of indigo silk did much to improve both my appearance and my disposition.

Using the wretched cane the doctor had sent, I was able to get around well enough to oversee Winnelda's preparation of the tea things. We had just finished setting the table when the buzzer sounded.

"She has arrived punctually," Milo said, coming into the room. He had come home moments before, looking characteristically well turned out in a charcoal-gray suit.

A moment later, Winnelda showed Mrs. Barrington into the room and left us alone. I think the girl was afraid she would spill tea on someone if she tried to serve, and I rather expected she was right. She really was a sweet little thing, but I was not at all certain she was cut out for service.

Mrs. Barrington was dressed in a subtle navy ensemble and her features were somber, but the air of resilience hadn't left her. I thought I detected a sense of determination about her, and I wondered what it was that she had come to say.

"Mrs. Barrington," I said, extending my hand to her. "I'm so sorry about your nephew."

"Thank you. It's been rather a shock." She said it in an automatic way, as though there were other things on her mind. While her tone was a bit more subdued than normal, I still detected the now-familiar underlying strength. Whatever her reason for coming, she had not come here to weep over James Harker, that much was certain.

Milo had stood when she entered and moved to greet her. "Hello, Mrs. Barrington. Allow me to offer my condolences."

"Thank you."

"How do you take your tea, Mrs. Barrington?" I asked, as Milo pulled out her chair and she sat.

We settled for a moment into the comfortable routine of teatime. There was something very soothing about the familiar ritual, and the soft clinking of china and silver filled in the empty spaces in the conversation.

"I suppose you're wondering why I've come," she said after emptying her cup. She set the cup and saucer on the table before her and squared her shoulders as though preparing for some taxing activity.

"Well," I said carefully, "I . . . was a bit curious when Milo told me you wanted to come today."

"So soon after James's death." Her perceptive gaze trained on me. "But I expect you know that's why I'm here."

I was still as puzzled as ever on that score. I really had no idea why she had come. I glanced at Milo, but his features were pleasantly impassive, as though we were discussing the weather.

"I supposed it had something to do with the missing jewelry about which you had spoken to me," I said at last.

"No, it isn't that," she said. "Not exactly, though goodness knows I wish I had never bothered about the jewels. If I had never bothered about it, James might still be alive.

Of course, there is no way of knowing that for sure, and one mustn't dwell on the 'if only's,' must one?"

"I . . . no, I suppose not," I answered vaguely. I wasn't quite sure what she was getting at. I wondered if she suspected her nephew had killed himself over guilt for stealing her things. It was what the papers had implied, but that did not mean it was true. Mrs. Barrington was a kind woman. If Mr. Harker had confessed, I had no doubt she would have forgiven him in an instant. No, I was certain there was more to James Harker's suicide than the theft of a few of Mrs. Barrington's jewels.

"What is it about your nephew's death that brought you here?" Milo asked. It was a rather straightforward question, but Mrs. Barrington didn't appear to mind. In fact, she seemed to relax ever so slightly.

"Have you seen the papers?" she asked.

"I've been reading *The Times,*" I said, before adding hesitantly, "They said that you recognized the jewels found in your nephew's pocket."

"Yes, I told the press that the jewels were mine and that the other things were missing," she said. "They would have found out in any event. It saved time, and it served my purpose to do so."

My eyes flickered to Milo's. We were both wondering, I think, where this bizarre conversation was leading.

"Perhaps he had a good reason for taking them," I ventured, when she didn't continue.

"James didn't steal my things, Mrs. Ames."

I hesitated, choosing my words carefully. "I know it's a horrible thought, especially given the circumstances, but . . ."

"You don't understand," she said abruptly, and I could almost picture her impatiently swatting my erroneous assumptions aside. "He knew that the sapphires were paste. I confided my plan in him before the ball."

I was silent a moment while I considered what this information meant.

"Then he would have had no reason to steal them," Milo said. He made no attempt to hide the interest in his voice.

"Exactly. And there is more. The jewels were not all there. You remember the bracelet, Mrs. Ames?"

I nodded. It had been a very distinctive piece.

"It contained twenty-two stones in total. Only four were found in James's pocket. And there were a few more scattered about the floor."

"Did the police recover the rest?" Milo asked.

"No. They searched the room but didn't find them.

"Then that means . . ." I said, the implication of her words startlingly clear.

"Yes. Now you see why I've come," she said. "Poor James didn't kill himself. He was murdered."

9

"Murdered?" I repeated, though somehow I was not really surprised. It had been in the back of my mind since last night that something was amiss in all of this, and it seemed that now my suspicions were confirmed.

I hazarded another glance at Milo. His countenance was completely unruffled, but there was a watchful look in his eyes that went beyond his customary indifference.

"Yes," Mrs. Barrington said. "The theft of my jewels and James's death are obviously connected. I just haven't determined why or how."

I poured myself another cup of tea as I allowed the implications of what she was saying to settle around me. As far-fetched as it might seem, the events appeared too closely connected to be mere coincidence.

"The police are aware of your concerns, of course?" Milo asked, as though it was perfectly natural to announce at tea that one's relative had been recently murdered.

"Yes, I spoke with them again today. They said they are content to let the rumor of suicide stand for the time being. I suppose it will give them more time to muster forces or whatever it is that they do. Poor James. I'm sure he would be mortified to have everyone think he would do such a thing, though anyone who knew him is bound to disbelieve it. And, of course, if it will help to catch his killer, I suppose the end justifies the means."

She looked at me, as if expecting me to concur.

"But why come to us?" I asked, finding my words at last.

"Don't you understand, Mrs. Ames? I need you now more than ever." She turned to look at Milo. "And you too, of course, Mr. Ames. Your help will be invaluable."

"But surely the police . . ." I began.

She shook her head. "The police will do what they can, of course, but they cannot go where you go, Mrs. Ames. They haven't the influence in our sphere that you do. You know that people of our set won't be open with policemen . . . but they will be open with you. You were able to do it before, on the south coast. I'm asking you to do it again now."

"I . . . I don't think . . ."

Milo was watching me, and I wished that he would say something.

"Please," Mrs. Barrington said before I could refuse. "If you think there's anything you can do to help, I should be deeply indebted to you."

How could I refuse her?

"All right, Mrs. Barrington," I conceded, albeit with grave reservations. "I'll do what I can."

"Bless you," she said, rising from her seat. I rose with her, and this time she did embrace me, pressing me tightly against her ample bosom. She released me and turned to Milo, whom I suspected she would have enjoyed embracing as well, and settled for squeezing his hands warmly.

"I shall be busy with arrangements. The police say we may be unable to bury James until next Monday, a week from today. Will you come and have tea with me next Wednesday?"

"Yes, that should be all right."

"Excellent. A week should be ample time for you to gather evidence. I shall see you then." And with that she swept out of the room and was gone before I could have Winnelda show her out.

After the front door had closed, I turned to look at Milo, who had resumed his seat and was placidly eating a watercress sandwich.

"What do you make of that?" I asked him.

"Very interesting," he said, though one certainly couldn't have determined his interest from his tone.

"I don't know what to think," I said, still looking at the door through which Mrs. Barrington had departed. "I'm not certain how I feel about being involved in another murder investigation."

"You like it," Milo said.

"I beg your pardon?"

"You like the idea of plunging headfirst into this tangle. In fact, I'd hazard a guess that you're thrilled at the prospect."

I was incensed at this assumption, whether or not it was true. "Whatever gave you such an absurd idea?"

"When you poured your tea after she told you about the murder, your hands were perfectly steady. It didn't upset you in the slightest."

"That's nonsense."

He sat back in his chair and scrutinized me. "And now your eyes are unnaturally bright, like liquid silver."

"Oh, don't be ridiculous," I huffed.

127

"Come now, darling, you may as well admit it."

The buzzer rang again, sparing me the necessity of having to answer his ludicrous accusations. "Mrs. Barrington must have thought of something else," I said.

However, it was not Mrs. Barrington who entered the room behind Winnelda, but an enormous basket of red roses, from under which the delivery boy was attempting to refrain from knocking into anything of value.

"Just set them there," I told him, surprised. Winnelda steered him to a corner. The bouquet was nearly as tall as the boy himself. Milo tipped him, and Winnelda ushered him out before hurrying back into the room.

"Aren't they lovely, madam," she said with delight. "The most beautiful thing I've ever seen!"

"Yes, they're very lovely," I said, as I made my way carefully to the flowers and plucked out the card. *My humblest apologies and sincerest wishes for your speedy recovery*, it read. *The night was an utter failure, but I promise to make it up to you. — Dunmore*

"From the viscount," I said.

"Oh! How very thoughtful of him!" Winnelda cried. "He's such a gentleman, isn't he, madam?"

" 'Gentleman' is not the word I would use," Milo remarked over his teacup.

"He wishes me a speedy recovery."

"Yes, I'm sure he does."

Ignoring his tone, I turned to Winnelda. "Will you get some water for them?"

"Yes, madam."

She went to the kitchen, and I turned back to Milo. Of course he would sneer at the flowers. Not only did he have general objections to Lord Dunmore, but extravagant floral arrangements weren't much in Milo's style. I, on the other hand, thought it was quite a sweet gesture. I didn't share Milo's concerns. Lord Dunmore was something of a flirt, perhaps, but there was nothing serious in his attentions. He certainly had no cause to believe that I would be receptive to them.

"Well?" I prompted Milo. He had said surprisingly little about Mrs. Barrington's revelations, and I was curious to know what was going on behind that impassive face of his.

He looked up at me. "Well, what? Shall I applaud Lord Dunmore's taste in roses?"

"I don't give a fig about the roses," I told him crossly. "What do you think we should do about Mrs. Barrington?"

He rose, tossing his napkin onto the table. "I think you're going to do just as you please, no matter what I say. There is, at least, one positive thing about the situation."

"And what's that?"

"I was in the room with you when the murder occurred this time. You can't possibly accuse me."

He was smiling, but I sometimes wondered if that rift had been completely mended. Things had been tense and uncertain at the Brightwell, but the plain fact remained that, for a few mad moments, I had believed him capable of murder.

"Aren't you curious about James Harker's death?" I asked.

"Vaguely," he admitted. "That doesn't mean I think we should go wading into matters that do not concern us."

He was steadily moving toward the dining room door as we spoke.

"Where are you going?"

"I have to meet up with Garmond again to finish settling matters about my horse. And then I've a dinner engagement with a few friends. You don't mind, do you?"

"Not at all," I said, refusing to acknowledge the disappointment washing over me. "Have a nice evening."

■ ■ ■ ■

Milo left, and I did not allow myself to think about where he might really be going. I was not so naive as to accept his carefully reported plans for the evening at face value.

I felt again the sensation that things were beginning to fall apart at the seams, that the happiness we had constructed so carefully over the past two months was beginning to crumble.

I hobbled mournfully into the sitting room but found I was not to have the luxury of solitude in which to pity myself. Winnelda followed me and began dusting things in a very conspicuous way. She had been waiting all day with thinly veiled impatience for me to relate the events of Lord Dunmore's ball. I was sure that bits and snatches had come her way throughout the day, and she wanted a full report, which I had been thus far too harried to give.

Now, as I sat in one of a pair of ivory-colored leather chairs before the fireplace, she was making her presence known by cleaning everything near me as energetically as possible. When she nearly knocked over the Lalique vase on the mantel, I thought it time to put an end to her domestic charade.

"Would you like to hear about the ball, Winnelda?"

"Oh, yes!" she said, dropping the duster and perching on the chair opposite me with startling speed. "I've been ever so curious, though I didn't like to say so."

"Yes," I replied. "I thought you might be."

I gave her a condensed version of events, with just enough of the grim details to satisfy her appetite for the macabre. Though she tried to hide it, I knew that her tastes tended toward the sensational, for I often found her scandal sheets hidden about the premises.

"That's ever so strange," she said when I had concluded. She had settled back in the chair by this point and was frowning as she contemplated my tale. "It doesn't seem quite like a gentleman would do away with himself at another gentleman's ball, does it, madam?"

This was, in essence, the same thing I had thought myself.

"It was quite a shock," I said vaguely.

"And just think, you were just down the corridor from the scene of a tragic death," she went on, something disturbingly like envy in her tone.

"If I had been able to walk, I might have been able to be of more use," I said, refusing to acknowledge, even to myself, that my aid might have been more akin to snooping.

"I'm ever so sorry you fell down the stairs," she said. "It must have been frightfully embarrassing."

"Thank you, Winnelda. Yes, it was very unpleasant all around, though mercifully there weren't many people to witness it."

I thought suddenly of the four young people who had been seated on the stairs. I wondered if any of them had heard the shot that had killed James Harker. If so, one of them might have seen something of use. I wonder if that inspector had spoken to them. I thought back to the humorless expression of Inspector Harris and surmised that he was not an overly imaginative sort of person. Perhaps, if I were to . . .

"That reminds me, madam," Winnelda said, drawing me from my traitorous thoughts. "One of your shoes seems to be missing. I was putting your things away before tea and forgot to mention it."

"I believe Mr. Ames put it in the pocket of his dinner jacket."

"I'll just fetch it so that I can put them together in the closet. Things will be tidier that way, and then you can finish telling me all about it."

She disappeared out of the room before I

could say that I had told her all there was to tell. She was back a moment later with the offending shoe in her hand. "I found it in Mr. Ames's pocket, just as you said. How was it that you fell, madam?"

"I don't know what happened. My foot just slipped out from under me."

"I suppose he'd had the floors waxed for the ball." She flipped the shoe over, examining it. "Was something broken, madam?"

"No, just a sprain."

"Begging your pardon, I meant something glass?"

"I don't think so. Why do you ask?"

"There seems to be a piece of colored glass lodged on the bottom of your shoe. Perhaps that was what made you slip."

She picked at something lodged between the sole and the heel.

I frowned. "A piece of . . . may I see it?"

She dropped it in my hand. I opened my palm and looked down at what appeared to be a sapphire glinting softly in the warm, flickering light of the fireplace.

10

I knew the prudent thing would be to telephone the police at once. This was undoubtedly a valuable piece of evidence and should be brought to their attention. However, I needed time to think. I wasn't ready to surrender my tiny piece of the puzzle just yet.

I held the sapphire up, letting the light play through the facets. I was no gemologist, but this looked very like the paste sapphires from Mrs. Barrington's missing bracelet. I had slipped on it while on the stairs. How exactly had it come to be there? It had been there before the murder, which meant that the jewels had been removed from the bracelet before James Harker had been killed. Had he removed the stones for some reason? Or had someone else done it? I could think of no reason why anyone would have wanted to remove the stones from the setting in the first place. It was all exceedingly bizarre.

The buzzer rang, and my thoughts were drawn to the present when, a moment later, Winnelda came into the room. "There's a Mr. Jones here to see you, madam," she announced formally.

"Mr. Jones?" I repeated searchingly, dropping the sapphire into my pocket. "I don't . . ."

The gentleman in question stepped into the doorway beside her.

"Detective Inspector Jones," I said, rising from my chair, my surprise evident in my voice.

"Good afternoon, Mrs. Ames."

For a moment, I was quite unsure what to make of this most unexpected guest. The inspector had been in charge of investigating the murder I had become so unfortunately entangled in at the Brightwell Hotel. When I had left the seaside, I had rather thought I would not be renewing our acquaintance anytime soon. Then again, perhaps he had come to London on business and had dropped by to wish me a friendly hello.

Somehow, in the light of all that had happened, that seemed unlikely.

I suddenly remembered my manners. "Come in, won't you?"

He came into the room, pulling off his hat, his dark eyes moving about in his customary observant fashion. He was what one might call nondescript in appearance, with dark hair tinged with gray and pleasant features, but there was something arresting about him that made one take notice. I motioned to the chair across from me, but he didn't sit until I did.

"Would you care for some tea?" I asked.

"That won't be necessary, Mrs. Ames." His replies, while perfectly polite, did not hide the fact that there was something formal in his manner. It brought to mind unpleasant memories of when I had known him in his official capacity. Truth be told, though we had eventually cultivated a somewhat cordial working relationship, he had been rather stern with me on more than one occasion about interfering in official police business.

It occurred to me that the timing of his arrival, one night after I had been at the scene of another unexpected death, might not be entirely coincidental.

"What brings you to London, Inspector?" I asked.

"I understand you were at the scene of another murder last night."

One could never accuse Detective Inspector Jones of being anything less than direct.

It was one word in particular, however, that caught my attention. "A murder," I repeated, feigning surprise. "They said it was suicide."

He looked at me as though he knew perfectly well that I was being disingenuous. "That is what we've told the press."

I frowned as he included himself in the actions of the police. " 'We'? Are you . . . I'm sorry, but I thought you belonged to the East Sussex police."

"I've transferred to Scotland Yard," he said. "As of last month."

"I see." He offered no further explanation, and I was not entirely sure whether I should be pleased or alarmed at this news. Inspector Jones and I had parted on friendly terms, but I rather suspected he would begin his customary frowning at my having been found at the scene of another murder — not that I could help it. It certainly wasn't my fault people went about getting themselves killed wherever I happened to be.

"I was given to understand . . ." I began. "That is, Inspector Harris . . ."

"Was good enough to turn the case over to me," he interrupted smoothly. "He is not with the Criminal Investigation Department, you see. When it became known that it was a murder, it was transferred to the CID."

"I see," I said again, though I was not entirely sure I did see. Inspector Jones was an extremely competent policeman and would, I was sure, prove an asset to the Metropolitan Police. None of this, however, explained his visit. Why exactly had he come to me?

"When I heard that you were at hand when the murder happened, I was particularly interested."

"It is rather an unfortunate coincidence," I admitted warily.

"Or a fortunate one, depending on how you look at it."

I waited. If there was one thing I knew about Inspector Jones, it was that he was not going to reveal anything until he was ready to do so. It was a particularly maddening trait of his.

"When I saw your name among the list of guests, I asked specifically to be assigned to this case. You may be surprised to hear it, Mrs. Ames, but I've actually come to ask for your help."

My brows rose. "Indeed? You're right, Inspector. I'm quite surprised."

"We have not released the fact that it was

a murder to the general public as of yet, but it is only a matter of time before the truth becomes known. The inquest will be in a few days. Once the verdict is decided, there will be no keeping it quiet. In fact, rumors are already beginning to spread. Inspector Harris, in a moment of investigative zealousness after he realized the jewels were part of a missing bracelet, decided to have everyone on the floor at the time of the murder searched for the presence of the rest of the jewels."

"That must have been after we left," I said. I thought of the jewel in my shoe, but decided to wait to reveal it until I knew more of why he had come.

"It raised no small alarm, I'm sure I need not tell you. Nearly everyone there at the time now suspects foul play, and I haven't the slightest doubt that news will spread like wildfire."

"And what is it that you would like me to do?" I asked. I was still a bit wary, as though I was treading on thin ice above unknown waters.

He looked at me steadily. "To begin with, I would like to know what you know."

"What makes you think I know anything?"

A hint of a smile flickered across his mouth. "You're much too modest, Mrs.

Ames. My sources tell me that you were wading into a mystery before the murder took place."

So that was it. He might have said so to begin with.

"You've spoken with Mr. Harker's aunt, Mrs. Barrington, I assume?"

"Yes, I spoke to her shortly before I came to see you. Mrs. Barrington had a good deal to say on the subject. From the first, she has insisted that it was murder. She also tells me that she had enlisted your aid to catch a jewel thief, and she thinks that the two incidents are connected."

"Perhaps I should start at the beginning," I said.

"That is usually best."

I told him of Mrs. Barrington's request at her dinner party and the subsequent events at the ball, including Mrs. Barrington's plan to catch the thief.

"She wanted to lay a trap at Lord Dunmore's ball," he mused. He hesitated a moment and then asked, "Was that your idea, Mrs. Ames?"

"Certainly not!" I replied, incensed. "I thought the entire thing very ill advised."

He looked at me with what might be described as skepticism.

"She fell asleep in the library," I told him.

"There wasn't much time between my leaving her and the murder, so someone had a short window of opportunity to take the bracelet."

"And, presumably, to murder Mr. Harker."

Unless Mr. Harker had taken the bracelet and then, for some reason, decided to end his life a short time later.

"You are certain, I suppose, that it couldn't have been suicide?" I asked.

"I'm afraid there's no question of that. Mr. Harker was killed with a single bullet wound to the head at very close range. From the . . . state of things, it was not immediately apparent, but upon further examination, the medical examiner is quite sure." I winced a bit at his careful avoidance of the unpleasant details, but he continued in his usual professional manner. "The angle at which the bullet entered his head is not consistent with a self-inflicted wound. In fact, it seems as though he may have been surprised and shot from behind before he could turn completely around to face his assailant."

Someone had killed him while his back was turned. "Then it was a very deliberate murder," I said.

"Yes. I'm afraid there can be no doubt."

My mind spun at these implications. "And how is it that I can help?"

He leaned forward a bit in his seat, his steady eyes resting on mine. "I know I have had issue with your, shall we say, *methods* in the past. I think, however, that in this situation, your social expertise will prove ideal. I don't want you to do anything foolish, of course. But if you should happen to be in touch with any of these people and should learn anything of interest, you will contact me?"

I paused a moment to let this sink in. I could scarcely credit that Inspector Jones was willingly asking for my involvement in the matter. Well, if he thought I could be of use, that was good enough for me. I had intended to involve myself, in any event.

"I'll be happy to do whatever I can, Inspector Jones."

He smiled. "I thought you might say that, Mrs. Ames."

"What happened to the gun?" I asked suddenly. "It was still in the room, I suppose, if it was originally thought to be a suicide."

"Yes. I'm not certain the killer intended it look like suicide, but the gun was left at the scene."

"If the killer wanted to make Mr. Harker's death look like suicide, it would ac-

143

count for the gemstones in his pocket. Perhaps they were put there to reinforce the idea of Mr. Harker's guilt."

"I'm not convinced. If the killer intended to make it look like suicide, he did a rather careless job of it. In any event, we're still attempting to determine to whom the gun belonged."

"Perhaps it belonged to Lord Dunmore," I suggested.

"He says no."

I wondered if Lord Dunmore would have admitted it, if the gun was indeed his. I had known my share of titled gentlemen, and it seemed that all of them had a great deal of assorted weaponry lying about their homes. That was certainly something to be considered.

"I understand there were jewels discovered in Mr. Harker's pocket." I charged ahead. I wanted to glean as much information as possible while the inspector was inclined to share.

"Yes. Four small gemstones. Three more were found on the floor near the body. Mrs. Barrington believes they came from her bracelet, but we have yet to find the setting or the rest of the stones."

"If he took it from his aunt, he must have done it shortly before he was killed," I said.

"It's strange that he should have taken them since he was aware that the sapphires were paste."

"Yes, Mrs. Barrington tells me that Mr. Harker was aware of her plan to catch the thief. If that is the case, I am at a loss as to why the gems should have been found in his pocket."

While we were talking about gemstones, I supposed I had better reveal my own little clue.

"There is something I should like to show you," I said. Inspector

Jones looked at me in a way that might have been interpreted as suspicious. "Indeed?"

"Look at this." I reached into my pocket and pulled out the sapphire, handing it to him.

I could tell he knew at once what it was.

"Already in the thick of things, I see," he said, though I was certain that his dry tone held traces of amusement. He rolled the sapphire around the palm of his hand with his thumb, examining it. "Just how did you happen to come by this, Mrs. Ames?"

"My maid found it lodged in my shoe only a short while ago. It caused me to slip on the staircase and turn my ankle. And there's something else, a rather telling fact. I was in one of the bedrooms with Milo waiting for the doctor when we heard the shot. I couldn't get up to see who was moving about. However, Milo noted who was there, and I realized that everyone who had attended Mrs. Barrington's dinner party was on the first floor at the time of the murder, all except Mrs. Garmond."

"Mrs. Vivian Garmond was, in fact, among those upstairs when the murder took place," he said.

This was a surprise. "I never saw her."

"She was in one of the bedrooms." While his tone was perfectly neutral, I gathered my own inferences from this bit of information.

I couldn't resist raising my eyebrows. Between Mrs. Garmond, Felicity Echols, and myself, Lord Dunmore had been keeping quite a lot of women in bedrooms.

"Rather tidy, all of the suspected jewel thieves being together on the same floor," I said.

"Yes, isn't it?"

"There were two men and two women seated on the stairs," I said, remembering the group. "They may have observed something."

"Yes, I've spoken with them. They've confirmed that after you fell, no one except for your husband came up or down the stairs. So that narrows the field of suspects considerably."

I thought it very clever of him to have already discovered the witnesses. He really was a terribly efficient policeman.

"Someone could have taken the servant's stairs," I suggested. "It's an enormous house. Anyone from the ball may have slipped past."

"Possible, but not likely. I've spoken to the staff. There were extra servants engaged for the ball, and they all did a great deal of moving about. It would have been difficult for anyone to have gone upstairs without detection."

"Then it does seem it must be one of Mrs. Barrington's original suspects. But surely it can be narrowed further. All the gentlemen were together when I saw them last. Can they confirm each other's whereabouts?"

He smiled ruefully. "As luck would have it, Mrs. Ames, the game had broken up shortly before the murder, and the gentlemen had dispersed."

"Nothing can ever be simple, can it?" I observed.

"Very seldom when murder is concerned."

I tried to recall the layout of the house. "Where was everyone when it happened?"

He pulled the familiar notebook from his pocket and consulted it. "Lord Dunmore said he had gone to ring the doctor for you."

I nodded. "Yes, he went out shortly before the shot sounded."

Inspector Jones looked at me intently. "Long enough for him to have fired it?"

I considered. "I suppose so."

He said nothing, turning back to the notebook. "Mr. Douglas-Hughes and his wife remained together in the card room. Mr. Nigel Foster had gone out to smoke on the balcony."

"Then the Douglas-Hugheses would have seen him if he had come back into the room and left."

"Not necessarily. The balcony stretches the length of three rooms and overlooks the little courtyard below. There are doors to two of the other rooms on that side of the house, one of which was the room where the murder took place. However, both doors appear to have been bolted from the inside."

"What about Mr. Barrington?"

"He had wandered off in search of his wife, but hadn't reached the library by the time the shot sounded."

"Mrs. Barrington was in the library, and you said Mrs. Garmond was in one of the bedrooms. What about the Echols sisters?"

He consulted his notes. "Miss Felicity Echols was lying down with a headache. Marjorie Echols was powdering her nose in the bathroom."

"So it seems everyone was alone at the time of the murder, save Mr. and Mrs. Douglas-Hughes."

"Provided they really were together, yes."

"So anyone might have done it," I said with a sigh.

"Precisely. And, as far as I can tell, no one had much of a motive. That's where you come in, Mrs. Ames. People may be inclined to talk to you. Perhaps you can discover some connections that it would be more difficult for me to find."

I nodded. "People do tend to talk. I'll see what I can find out."

"Did you notice anything suspicious at the ball?"

I cast my mind back. "I have been trying to think, but there was nothing that really stood out to me. Unless . . ." I suddenly remembered something that had somehow escaped me until now. "I saw Mr. Harker only once, on the staircase. He . . ." I stopped. Why hadn't I thought of it before? "He was wearing the same mask as Mr. Foster. A tiger's mask."

This seemed to interest the inspector.

"Mr. Foster was not wearing a mask when I spoke with him."

"No. I believe he discarded it when he was playing cards. All the gentlemen had. Do you think someone might have killed James Harker by mistake?"

"It's certainly something to take into consideration. I shall look into it."

"There's one more thing," I told him. "Mr. Harker told me he had an appointment with someone that night. He didn't say with whom, but it might be worth finding out."

"Yes, I'd say so. You've been most helpful already, Mrs. Ames," he said, rising from his seat. "I think that will be all for now. Don't trouble yourself getting up. I can show myself out. I'll check in with you in the next few days. As I said, if you can glean a bit of society gossip, it may prove useful. Don't do anything foolish."

"Of course not," I replied.

He stopped at the doorway and turned back. "By the way, how is Mr. Ames these days?"

I hesitated. "He's much the same as usual," I replied.

He seemed to consider that. "I see," he said, and then he was gone.

I felt sure that he had indeed seen just

what I meant.

When he was gone, I sat for a moment, lost in thought. This latest turn of events was quite unexpected. I would never have imagined that he would come to me for help, but I was very glad that he had.

Perhaps, as Milo had pointed out, the murder was really none of my business. Nevertheless, there was something about the ability to prove useful, to make a difference, that I found terribly appealing. I hadn't known James Harker well at all, but he hadn't deserved to die in that terrible way. If nothing else, I felt it my duty to do whatever I could to see that a murderer did not go free.

11

"I'm ever so glad he's gone," said Winnelda, coming back into the room and interrupting my reverie. "I'm all on edge whenever there's a policeman about. Not that I've ever done anything really wrong. But they do have a way of making one feel as though one *might* be guilty of something, don't they?"

"I have felt that way on occasion." I agreed with a smile. "But Inspector Jones is quite nearly a friend of mine."

"Oh," said Winnelda, clearly impressed. "I didn't mean to say anything improper."

"I assure you, he has made me feel on edge myself on more than one occasion. However, this time he actually came to ask for my assistance."

"Yes, I heard . . ." She stopped, flushing bright red. "That is, when I was passing the doorway . . . It seemed that I might have happened to overhear . . ."

I waved away her explanations. I knew perfectly well that it was very difficult for Winnelda not to listen to interesting things that happened to be said in her vicinity. I couldn't exactly blame her. A great deal of very interesting things seemed to be happening in the Ames residence as of late.

"Was it really murder?" she asked.

"It seems so. Of course, you mustn't say anything to anyone."

"Oh, no, madam! I won't breathe a word. But I've been thinking. It's very queer about that stone being in your shoe. It does seem that whoever dropped it must have been very careless. That is, if I had a sapphire, I would be very careful not to just drop it any old place, wouldn't you, madam? That is, you *do* have sapphires, and I've never seen you fling them about with no thought as to where they might end up."

"No, Winnelda. You're quite right."

The same thought had occurred to me, though perhaps a bit less verbosely. It was odd that a jewel, the procurement of which had somehow led to a man's death, should be so easily misplaced. Then again, it was perfectly possible that either Mr. Harker or his killer had dropped the stone in haste.

It seemed that all of this related back to the jewels. I felt that if we could make some sense of the theft, we would be on our way to solving the murder.

Mr. Harker had been found with four stones in his pocket, and a few stones were scattered nearby. It seemed, then, that he must have had possession of the bracelet at some point in the evening. If so, how had the stones come loose?

Another idea came to me. Perhaps Mr. Harker had taken his aunt's bracelet intending to try to catch the thief on his own. The encounter might have gone badly. Perhaps there had been a struggle and the thief had murdered Mr. Harker. It was a bit melodramatic, perhaps, but certainly not outside the realm of possibility.

It was also possible that someone knew he had the bracelet and, not knowing it was paste, had killed him to get it. How horrifying that he might have been murdered for paste jewels.

The problem was that there were so many unknowns. This was going to be quite a task.

I sighed. Sometimes it was very trying to be a detective.

I spent a quiet evening at home and was still sitting before the fire with a cup of tea when Milo arrived home. It was a quarter to one, and I was just beginning to wonder if he might not make it back when I heard a key in the lock. The front door opened, and I waited. He must have seen the light, for a moment later he was in the doorway, leaning against the frame.

Apparently, he had changed at his club, for he had gone out in a day suit and come home in evening clothes.

"Hello, darling," he said. "You're up late."

"I've been thinking."

"Oh, dear," he said dryly. "I hesitate to ask. Of what have you been thinking?"

"Things," I said vaguely. I was not feeling especially charitable toward him, and my response was not intended to encourage conversation.

I half expected him to continue on to the bedroom, but he came into the room and took a seat on the sofa. "It was a dull evening without you."

"Oh?" I took a sip of tea, my gaze on the fire.

"I wish you had been along, for you're much better company than Frederick Garmond. He's an utter bore. You might have made the evening bearable."

I recognized the subtle flexing of his charm, the maddening way he had of winning me over when I was cross with him. Even more irritating than this familiar tactic was the fact that I could feel it working. I fought against the inclination to be pleased with his comment.

"Did everything come off all right with the horse?" I asked with as little interest in my tone as I could manage.

"Yes, I'm going to Bedfordshire in the morning to collect it and bring it to Thornecrest."

In the morning. It crossed my mind that he could very well have sent someone else to do it. Geoffrey, the groom at Thornecrest, might have gone to Bedfordshire, but Milo was always very particular about his horses.

"Do you expect to be gone long?" I asked, wiping at a tea stain on my white china saucer.

"Not very. A few days or perhaps a week. I want to see him settled."

"Yes, of course."

It struck me that our conversation was suddenly oddly formal, and I felt somehow powerless to rectify it. Since the ball, we had not quite regained our equilibrium. Being married to Milo sometimes felt very like walking a tightrope. I always had the impression that one small step in the wrong direction could prove disastrous

Milo took a cigarette from the box on the table. He lit it and settled back in his seat, his eyes on my face. "Why don't you tell me what's on your mind, my lovely?"

I glanced at him, half surprised at his interest. For some absurd reason, I suddenly wanted to go and sit beside him and lean my head on his shoulder, as though everything was easy between us. Instead, I sighed, my mind a jumble of problems, personal and otherwise. "I wouldn't know where to begin."

"That sounds ominous."

"Detective Inspector Jones came to see me tonight," I said suddenly, deciding to ignore, at least for the time being, my growing concerns about our relationship and focus on the more pressing matter at hand.

Only the barest flicker of interest showed in Milo's expression. "Touring the big city, is he? It was nice of him to drop by."

I wondered if Milo suspected, as I had, that there was more to the inspector's visit than that.

"He's transferred to Scotland Yard, in fact, and has been assigned to the Harker case."

Milo's brows rose slightly. "How very cozy all of this is becoming."

"Yes, that's what I've thought. And there's more . . . He's asked for my help."

"Has he indeed? I suppose I needn't ask what your answer was."

"I told him I would do whatever I could, of course."

The corner of Milo's mouth tipped up. "Of course."

He was amused, but not much interested. So far, he had paid very little notice to Mr. Harker's murder. Somehow I had the impression that there was something else on his mind, that our conversation did not have his complete attention. I wished, as I had countless times before, that I could read his thoughts. He was so very closed sometimes.

I tried to draw him out. "Don't you think it strange that the list of people on the first floor when the murder occurred were the same people at Mrs. Barrington's dinner party, one of whom she suspects of being a jewel thief?"

"Perhaps it's just a coincidence. People naturally tend to flock in familiar groups. We'd all been together at the Barringtons'. It isn't so very strange that we should find ourselves grouped together again. Garmond and I dined tonight with Ivers and Billings from our club because we'd had drinks together yesterday. It's not so uncommon."

I shook my head. "There's more to it than that. There's something I can't put my finger on . . ." The thought came to me suddenly. "Is Mr. Garmond related in any way to Vivian Garmond?" I asked, making the connection between the two names that I should have made long ago.

"Dunmore's mistress? Distantly, perhaps. I've never asked him."

"You knew she was his mistress?" I asked, surprised.

"My dear, everyone knows it."

"You didn't mention it to me."

He shrugged. "I didn't think it noteworthy. Besides, what has she to do with any of this?"

"Perhaps nothing," I admitted.

"What else did you and the good inspector discuss?"

"I remembered tonight that Mr. Harker and Mr. Foster were wearing nearly the same mask. What if it was Mr. Foster that someone meant to kill?"

Milo seemed to consider this.

"Perhaps the killer murdered the wrong man by mistake," I suggested.

"Killing the wrong man would be rather a colossal mistake," he said.

"Just think of it," I said, warming to the tale. "The killer might have had a vendetta against Mr. Foster, snuck up behind him, and killed him."

"I suppose it's possible," he conceded without enthusiasm. "Nevertheless, I think it far more likely that James Harker was the intended victim. After all, one can't go around haphazardly killing people. Were I going to kill someone, I would make sure that I was killing the right person. It would be quite a nuisance to have all that planning count for naught."

Leave it to Milo to think of a mistaken murder in terms of the inconvenience it would cause rather than the moral implications.

I was not entirely convinced that my theory about killing the wrong man should be discarded, but I let it pass for the moment. Milo did have a point. It seemed quite unlikely. Besides, if the killer had murdered the wrong man by mistake, it didn't account for the gemstones found in Mr. Harker's pocket.

"What we have yet to determine," I said to Milo, "is why anyone would want the jewels so desperately in the first place. Granted, someone might steal something if it was lying about at Mrs. Barrington's house; it might have proved too tempting to resist. But who would want them or need them badly enough to kill for them? It just seems so senseless. After all, none of us are exactly in need of money."

"That we know of," he corrected.

It was a valid observation. What did I really know about the financial situations of anyone involved? Lord Dunmore, the Douglas-Hugheses, and Nigel Foster certainly didn't appear to need the money. That left only the Echols sisters and Mrs. Garmond as more obvious candidates. I would have to find out more about them.

I sighed. "It's all so complicated. I will have to see what I can discover."

He ground out his cigarette and stood. "You make an adorable bloodhound, my sweet, but I don't know that snooping about is a good idea."

I must say I found his reticence surprising. Though he would never admit it, I was certain that he had enjoyed the thrill of the chase as much as I had when we were looking into the affair at the Brightwell. Why should things be any different this time?

"Why ever not?" I asked.

"Because, if you'll recall, you nearly got yourself killed the last time. I should hate for you to get yourself into trouble while I'm away."

I bit back the urge to reply that he had never been much concerned about me during his absences before. Instead, I smiled with what I hoped was deceptive sweetness.

"Don't worry your pretty little head over me. I shall be just fine."

12

Whatever grand schemes I might have been concocting, the following days turned out to be frustratingly dull. I had forgotten the severe limitations placed upon me by my inability to walk properly. Despite my impatience, I knew I needed to give my sore ankle time to heal if I was going to devote my full energies to catching a killer.

Milo had set out for Bedfordshire the morning after Inspector Jones's visit, and I was left to limp about the house with only Winnelda for company. I spent a good deal of time sifting through her stash of scandal sheets, looking for any clues that might have been dredged up by the unwitting press. It would be helpful, I reasoned, to learn what I could about the suspects. By the time the week had passed, I knew more than I ever wished to, but none of it seemed at all important.

As might have been suspected, there was

very little to read about James Harker. He had appeared occasionally in the society columns, as the guest of some notable person or the other at various social events. He was often in the company of the Echols sisters, and I had seen photographs of him with Marjorie and Felicity appearing alternately on his arm. On the whole, his behavior seemed particularly unobjectionable, and I felt another stab of sadness that his life should have been ended so unexpectedly and so violently.

The tales of Lord Dunmore's misdeeds, of course, abounded in plenty. My purposeful avoidance of gossip had kept me in ignorance of most of them, and I was a bit surprised at the stunning variety of his rumored transgressions. Granted, they were interspersed with enough notices of various charitable contributions to prevent his reputation from slipping from tarnished to completely irredeemable.

I was surprised there was very little mention of Mrs. Garmond, at least in the recently published articles that Winnelda had on hand. Perhaps they had parted ways. It was quite possible that he had tired of her or that she had grown tired of his behavior. It was certainly trying to see the man you love appearing again and again in connection with other women.

"Oh, here's one on Mr. Nigel Foster, madam," Winnelda said, rousing me from my unpleasant reveries. She handed the paper over to me. She had been gleefully scouring page after page, pouncing upon tidbits of news that related to anyone involved in the case.

It wasn't much of a notice. "Tennis star Nigel Foster, who has been out of the country for several months on tour, missing Wimbledon after his failure to win last year, left his racket at home yesterday to attend a yachting race in the company of the Barringtons."

"Well, Winnelda," I said with a sigh, tossing the issue away. "I'm afraid we've reached the end of our stack."

"Would you like me to go out and buy some more?" she asked hopefully.

I stood, stretching my stiff neck. I had been sitting in one position for entirely too long. "I think we've had enough for now. My head is swimming."

"Oh! I think perhaps there's an issue in my room that I haven't read yet!" she said. "I'll fetch it."

The telephone rang, and Winnelda made a move in that direction, but I waved her away. "I'll get it," I said, already moving toward the foyer. At least I was finally able to walk without the assistance of my cane. I hoped I never had to see the wretched thing again.

"Hello?" I said, wondering who might be calling. I would not allow myself to hope that it might be Milo, for he rarely ever phoned when he was away.

"Hello, Amory?"

"Yes?"

"It's Mamie Douglas-Hughes."

"Oh, hello," I said, glad somehow to hear the friendly American voice on the other end of the line. "How are you?"

"I'm very well, thank you. I'm calling to see how your ankle's mending."

"It's much better, thank you. I'm getting around without my cane now."

"I'm so glad. Then on to my second reason for calling. I know it's short notice, but I was hoping you'd be able to join me for tea this afternoon."

"I'd love to," I replied immediately. I was sorely in need of a change of scenery, and this also presented a perfect opportunity to interact with another guest who had been at the "death party," as the papers were wont to call it, with typical lack of imagination.

The papers had initially reported that Mr. Harker had killed himself, and the speculation as to why had been varied and absurd, with hints that there had been some sort of torrid romance gone awry. After the inquest found that Mr. Harker had been murdered, however, the suggestions had become even more preposterous. My favorite of the theories put forth by the press was that there was a madman jewel thief loose in London whose true objective had been the theft of the illustrious Dunmore Diamond and who had killed Mr. Harker by mistake.

I had heard no more from either Mrs. Barrington or Inspector Jones. Mrs. Barrington had, I was sure, been attending to the details of her nephew's funeral, and I could only suppose that Inspector Jones was waiting for me to discover something useful.

Thus far I had been unable to determine the best course of action for gaining information directly from the sources, and so Mamie's invitation had come at just the right moment. I had had enough of research. I craved action.

"Wonderful!" she said. "Four o'clock?"

"I'll look forward to it."

We rang off, and I returned to the sitting room, where Winnelda was leaning over what I assumed was the magazine she had retrieved from her room.

She closed it guiltily as I came in and

stood quickly, trying very hard to look casual, despite the fact that she seemed to have gone pale. She was a sweet girl, but there was not a subtle bone in her body. There was something she was trying to keep from me, and I could only suppose it was about Milo. No doubt she had come across some lurid account of his having appeared at the ball with Helene Renault.

The buzzer rang before I had time to question her. "I'll get it, Winnelda," I called, walking once again toward the foyer.

I had no idea who might be calling. I pulled open the door to be faced with perhaps the last person I had expected.

"Lord Dunmore," I said, concealing my surprise. I had sent a note thanking him for the flowers and had not heard from him since.

"Hello, Mrs. Ames," he said, removing his hat.

I issued the invitation automatically. "Come in, won't you?"

I stepped back, and he came into the foyer, casting a brief glance at the black-and-white marble floors and gray-striped papered walls before turning his attention back to me. "I hope I'm not intruding."

"Not at all."

"How's your ankle? On the mend?"

"Yes, it's much better, thank you."

I wondered why he was really here, but I did not have long to wait.

"I was passing by and thought perhaps you'd like to go for a drive with me."

Passing by, was he?

"It's a lovely day," he continued. "I heard that your husband has gone away, and I thought perhaps you could use some company."

News certainly traveled quickly. I wondered who had told him that Milo had gone to Bedfordshire.

"We could drive out to the country," he went on. "I know several very nice scenic spots. Then perhaps lunch and . . ." He shrugged as his voice trailed off, leaving his meaning to hang in the air between us. Lunch and whatever happened to come afterward.

I found myself surprised at his directness. I had been warned that the viscount moved swiftly and without hesitation, but I had not expected anything of this sort. "Thank you, Lord Dunmore, but I don't think that will be possible."

"Have you another engagement?"

"Yes," I answered. "As a matter of fact, I have."

"What about tomorrow?"

I hesitated, not wanting to be rude but wishing my disinterest to be clear. "While I appreciate the offer, I don't think that would be a good idea."

"Surely you don't object to my company?" He smiled as if the question was absurd, and there was something strangely appealing about his utter lack of self-consciousness.

"I am certain that you are excellent company, my lord, but I am sure you are aware how it would look if we were seen driving about together."

"I thought you didn't read the gossip columns."

"That doesn't mean I wish to be maligned in them."

"Maligned?" His brows rose. "For taking a simple drive with me?"

We were both very aware that he was offering more than a drive, yet we both went on politely ignoring the fact.

"I am married, after all," I said at last, making note of what should have been the most obvious point.

"But not happily, I hear."

I stiffened slightly at the inference. "Even if that was true, it wouldn't make any difference."

His mouth tipped up at the corner. "It

does to most women."

"I am not most women, my lord," I answered coolly.

He smiled suddenly, quite a warm smile that seemed to evaporate whatever tension had been rising. "No. No, I can see you are not. I apologize if I've caused offense."

"Not at all," I said, as though I received such propositions every day. "I appreciate your invitation, but I'm afraid I must still decline it."

He nodded his acceptance good-naturedly. "I hope to see you again, at any rate. You'll come to my ball this weekend, won't you?"

"You don't mean your next ball will go on as planned?" Perhaps it was rude of me to ask, but I was surprised he intended to go ahead with his ball when a murder had been committed at the last one.

He seemed amused by my question. "I suppose the proper thing might have been to call it off, but considerable planning has gone into it and canceling things is tedious. Don't you think so?"

"I suppose so," I conceded. Not that tedium was an acceptable excuse for tactlessness.

"Then you'll come?"

I hesitated.

"I promise to behave myself." His eyes

twinkled as he spoke, and I understood perfectly well that Lord Dunmore was never any more well-behaved than was strictly necessary.

"I . . . I shall try to be there." All things considered, I certainly didn't intend to miss it, but I didn't want to appear too enthusiastic.

"Good, good."

He walked toward the door then, and I followed him. He put on his hat and turned to me, extending his hand. I took it, and he squeezed mine gently. "You're really quite a remarkable woman, Mrs. Ames," he said. "That husband of yours doesn't deserve you."

"Thank you," I said, for lack of something better to say.

"I look forward to our next meeting. Good day." He turned then and left.

I closed the door behind him, still not entirely sure what had just happened.

13

The Douglas-Hughes residence was located in Grosvenor Square, a large yet charming house of pale stone with dozens of gleaming windows.

I rang the bell and was a bit surprised when Mamie herself opened the door. "Hello, Amory," she said with a smile. "Please come in."

I entered the foyer and saw a frowning butler standing slightly behind her. "It's all right, Henson," she said, closing the door behind me. "I was just passing through and thought I might as well get the door."

"Very good, madam," he said stiffly, his disapproval fairly wafting at us as he walked away.

"He gets very angry with me," she said, leading me into a comfortable parlor decorated in a sleek, modern style, "though he's much too proper to say anything. I'm not used to butlers. Sandy tells me that I will grow accustomed to it, but so far I have been nothing but a nuisance to poor Henson and the rest of the staff. I'm forever doing things for myself that they don't think I should be doing. I imagine they're all fed up with me."

"Oh, I sincerely doubt it," I said with a smile. I imagined the staff was enchanted with Mrs. Douglas-Hughes. She had that rare combination of elegance and genuine warmth, which, combined with her American informality, made her a charming conversationalist.

"I have adapted very readily to teatime, though," she said, pouring the steaming liquid into a cup emblazoned with the Douglas-Hughes monogram.

I took my cup and saucer from her. "How long have you lived in England?"

"Two years now. It really is a wonderful place. Different from New York, of course, but also the same in many ways. Have you been to America?"

"Yes, although it's been quite some time. My cousin Laurel is on a steamship bound for there now. She's going to visit a family friend who lives in Manhattan."

"How very nice. It's always more pleasant to visit places where one has acquaintances." She paused for a moment before going on.

"If I'm honest, I will say that it has not been as easy for me to make friends here as I had hoped. Of course, there are social acquaintances, but it's not the same. As soon as we met, I felt immediately as though we were going to be friends."

I smiled, only a bit caught off guard by her frankness. "Well, thank you. I should like that."

She smiled brightly, and I found it hard to believe that people would not wish to befriend her. It was true that many women of our social circle might look down upon Mamie's social origins, her nationality, or possibly both. However, I had felt the same instinctual regard that she had felt for me, and I hoped that we would indeed become friends. My only truly close friend was Laurel, and I felt her absence all the more now that I had no one with whom to discuss all of my most recent contretemps.

"You were a dancer in America, I believe?" I asked. I had heard the various accounts of her past, but I was curious as to what the real story was.

"Yes, I danced in several revues on Broadway. Not a chorus girl, you understand. My partner and I would do dance routines: waltzes, the foxtrot, the Charleston, a bit of tap dance, that sort of thing. I'm also a great admirer of ballet, but it hasn't much taken hold in the States yet. Dancing was my greatest love . . . until I met Sandy."

I smiled. "How did you come to meet him?"

"He was in New York for some sort of political thing, and the gentlemen came to one of the revues. He sent a note to my dressing room afterward. I didn't often go out with men from the audience, but something about his sweet, formal little note caught my attention. He took me to dinner, and the rest is history." She smiled fondly, and I could detect no trace of sadness in the relinquishment of her profession.

"You seem very happy," I commented.

"Oh, we are. Of course, Sandy is away with his work more often than I like. And he's so secretive about it sometimes. Government conspiracies and all that, I suppose. But on the whole we have been extremely happy."

"Do you still dance?" I asked.

"Oh, no," she said. "I don't have much of an opportunity for that now. Of course, at balls and things I enjoy it. But as for dancing professionally, I find I don't miss it much. There are so many other things to occupy my time. With Sandy's role in the Foreign Office, we're forever attending different functions. He says he gleans public perception of current events when he attends social occasions. I think that was why he insisted we attend Lord Dunmore's ball. It's not really the sort of thing he would have enjoyed otherwise. He finds the idea of masks and disguises and such to be silly, and I was a bit surprised he wanted to go."

"It was terrible about Mr. Harker's death, wasn't it?" I said, pouncing upon the opening she had given me.

"Yes," she answered. "It was just awful! I could scarcely believe it when they told me what happened. And now to hear that it was murder. It's almost too much to believe."

"I was in one of the bedrooms waiting for the doctor when the shot sounded," I told her. "Were you still upstairs?" According to Inspector Jones, she had been in a room with her husband, but I wanted to hear her account firsthand.

She nodded. "Sandy and I were in the room where the men had been playing cards before they all wandered off. We were discussing a bit of political gossip when the shot sounded. It flashed across my mind that there may have been an assassination, and now it seems I was not far wrong. Perhaps that is why there continues to be something about that night that bothers me."

"It was so dreadfully unexpected," I said, to prod her along.

"Yes, but it wasn't just that," she continued, a thoughtful expression on her face. "There's something else, something that someone said that night that made me think . . ." She smiled suddenly, looking a bit embarrassed. "It's quite possible that my mind is playing tricks on me after everything that happened."

"What do you mean?" I pressed her. I didn't want to appear too inquisitive. Then again, a mysterious death was bound to be a subject of interest, and there was no reason why I should not appear intrigued.

"I don't know exactly." Her brow furrowed as she thought. "It was just when I heard that they found those jewels in his pocket, it made me feel that I had seen or heard something earlier in the evening that made me wonder . . ." She laughed. "I'm probably imagining things. Sandy tells me I have a typically American imagination. The Hollywood influence, he calls it."

I longed to question her further, but I didn't want to tip my hand, as the Americans said. Though I felt instinctively that I could trust Mamie Douglas-Hughes, I knew that my involvement in the mystery of James Harker's death was probably best kept quiet for the present. If an opportunity came to confide in Mamie at a later time, I would certainly do so. For now, I thought it best to tread carefully.

"I suppose it was quite a shock to everyone who had recently dined at the Barringtons' home," I said. "To know we had just dined with Mr. Harker, and now he is dead."

"Yes, I'm so sorry for poor Mrs. Barrington. We're often in company with the Barringtons because Sandy and Mr. Barrington are very chummy. They like talking politics for hours on end. I didn't know Mr. Harker well, only from the dinner parties. He always seemed very nice, even if he was a bit awkward. I feel sorry for Felicity, too."

This stopped me. "Felicity Echols?"

"Yes. I never heard anything, of course, but I think she was a bit sweet on Mr. Harker."

"I didn't know," I said.

"It was just an impression I got. Of course, I doubt there was anything really going on between them. Felicity's so quiet. She's a sweet thing, but Marjorie's a bit frightening, isn't she? I don't mean that in a negative way. I just mean that she's very brash. She reminds me of some of the girls I knew from the revue, flashy and confident. She runs with a rowdy crowd, I believe. And she drags poor Felicity along with her. I think Mr. Harker would accompany them out sometimes as well. That's why I had the impression that he and Felicity might have been an item."

This was an interesting bit of news. I wanted to ask her more, but Mr. Douglas-Hughes suddenly appeared in the doorway.

"Ah, here you are, darling," he said. "And Mrs. Ames. I'm delighted to see you."

"Good afternoon, Mr. Douglas-Hughes."

"Amory and I are having a delightful time," Mamie said. "We're going to be great friends."

He smiled affectionately at his wife. "I'm delighted to hear it. You must watch out for her, Mrs. Ames," he said, turning to me. "She has the charming habit of completely winning people over when she sets her mind to it."

"Oh, Sandy's always teasing me," she said laughingly. "He claims he fell in love with me against his will."

"I had the firmest intentions of remaining a bachelor, wholly dedicated to my work," Mr. Douglas-Hughes told me. "However, one evening in Mamie's company, and I was hopelessly smitten. She quickly brought me to heel."

I tried to imagine the words "smitten" or "brought to heel" ever being even remotely applicable to Milo and failed utterly.

She laughed and reached up to touch his hand on her shoulder. "You shouldn't say such things in front of people!"

I felt a little pang at the way they looked at one another. It was obvious that they were very much in love.

"You must excuse us, Mrs. Ames," he said. "I'm afraid Mamie's scandalous American behavior is rubbing off on me."

I smiled, admiring the ease of their exchanges and their affection for one another. Had Milo and I ever been that way? It suddenly seemed very difficult to remember.

"Will you drink tea with us?" she asked him.

"I'm afraid I haven't much time. I've an appointment with Sir John."

Mamie wrinkled her nose at the mention of the foreign secretary. "You'd have a better time with us, although we're being a bit morbid. We were talking about poor Mr. Harker's death."

"Indeed? That was quite a tragedy." He said this almost tonelessly, and I couldn't help but feel that there was suddenly a slight change in his manner, as though it was a topic he wished to avoid. Naturally, this made me want to pursue it.

"I didn't know Mr. Harker well," I said, "but he seemed a pleasant gentleman. His murder was so shocking a thing to happen in such a public place."

"Yes, I think we were all a great deal surprised, though I'm sure the culprit will be apprehended shortly," he answered blandly, thwarting my attempts to draw him into the conversation. "I'm afraid I've got to be off. Don't wait dinner for me, my dear. Mrs. Ames, it was lovely to see you again."

"It was nice to see you as well, Mr. Douglas-Hughes."

He excused himself, and I found I was a bit disappointed. I suspected that careful neutral replies were no doubt the stock-in-trade of Mr. Douglas-Hughes's profession, so his reserve was not necessarily unusual. Nevertheless, it seemed that he was especially disinclined to discuss Mr. Harker's death. Perhaps he knew more than he was willing to say.

Mamie changed the subject then, and there was little I could do to change it back without appearing either suspicious or morbidly curious. We talked about pleasanter things, and I thought that we would indeed be good friends.

At last, I rose to leave and Mamie walked me to the door. "Sandy and I are having dinner with some friends Thursday night at Restaurant Boulestin," she said. "It's become one of my favorite places. If you feel like coming, we'd be delighted to have you."

I wondered if any of the other guests might be on the list of suspects. There would be potential for me to learn more about what had happened on the night of the ball. However, there was really no way that I could ask who else would be attending.

"Thank you. I shall try to be there."

"Wonderful! You don't need to call me or anything. It's nothing formal. Just come if you feel like it. We'll make room at our table."

I left the Douglas-Hughes home a while later, lost in thought. What had I learned today? It hadn't been much. However, it was interesting to know that Felicity Echols might have been involved with James Harker. The papers had suggested a lovers' quarrel. It seemed far-fetched, but I couldn't rule it out. I would need to find out more about the relationship between Miss Echols and Mr. Harker.

I also wondered what it was that Mrs. Douglas-Hughes felt she had observed. I would have to bring it up again casually the next time we met.

The flat was quiet when I returned home that evening after some shopping and a light dinner. It was Winnelda's night off, and I realized suddenly that I had become unaccustomed to silence. She was growing on me.

I changed into a blue silk nightdress with a sheer ivory negligee thrown over it then went into the kitchen to make myself a cup of tea. I intended to pass a quiet evening reading before the fire. I needed a distraction from my marriage and the murder, if only for an hour or two.

I set out a cup and saucer on the countertop and took the tea tin down from the shelf. As I opened the tin, the lid slipped from my grasp, fell to the floor, and rolled across the room and behind the dustbin. I leaned to retrieve it, and something caught my eye.

There was a gossip magazine shoved in the dustbin, its cover half obscured by some crumpled parchment paper. I frowned. It was unlike Winnelda to throw her scandal sheets away. After all, it was her accumulated collection that had proved so useful to us this afternoon. Why might she have wanted to dispose of it? I could only suppose it was the article about Milo and that Renault woman. It was sweet of her to want to shield me.

I picked up the magazine and thumbed through it, curious. I suspected a picture had been taken of the two of them when they arrived together at Lord Dunmore's ball, and I wanted to get a better look at her than the one I had had from the top of the stairs. I couldn't help but be a bit curious about my husband's rumored inamorata, after all.

I turned the page and stopped cold. I could literally feel the blood draining from my face before it rushed through it again in a fierce wave of heat.

The photograph had not been taken at Lord Dunmore's house. The magazine was new, dated the day Milo had left for Frederick Garmond's estate.

It was indeed a picture of Milo and Helene Renault, but I was quite unable to get a good look at her face as I had intended, for it was obscured by his.

Her arms were thrown around his neck, and they were kissing.

I'm not entirely sure how long I stood there staring at it. The photograph had been captured while they were in the backseat of an automobile. It was difficult to make anything out, really, except for the fact that they were clearly enjoying one another's company. Her fur-draped arms were around his shoulders, and she was leaning into his embrace, her mouth pressed against his.

After a moment, I had to concede that Winnelda had had the right idea. I crumpled it up and put it back in the dustbin. I noticed as I did so that my hands were shaking, whether from shock or the intense fury I was attempting to contain, I didn't know.

I drew in a deep breath and forced myself to remain calm. It was by no means the first time this had happened. There had been other women in other photographs, but I could not escape the fact that none had been as blatant as this. There was no way to explain a kiss away.

I fought down an immense wave of sadness. There would be time enough to deal with this when Milo returned home. Until then, I would push it away to some far corner of my mind and not think about it. It was a skill I had mastered over the years.

With supreme effort, I calmly finished making my tea and took it to the parlor.

My eyes fell on the photograph on the mantel of Milo and I on our wedding day. I looked so very young, so radiantly happy. Milo looked as elegant as always, but he looked happy, too. Looking at the photograph, I would have sworn that we were very much in love.

I sighed. Our wedding day seemed so very long ago. I had truly believed then that we would be happy together for all the days of our lives. Did I still believe it? I just wasn't sure anymore. I fought the urge to pick up our wedding photograph and hurl it across the room. Instead, I sat and drank my tea.

14

I slept very poorly, but I was determined to put on a good show for Winnelda. It didn't seem to have worked, however, for she took one look at me and cheerfully suggested a bit of rouge to "improve my color."

My makeup duly applied and a cheerful dress of rose-colored crepe selected, I set out to determine my first order of business for the day. I certainly didn't intend to sit at home moping as though my world had come to an end. I was hurt and deeply angry, but giving rein to either of those emotions was not going to be useful at present. There was still a mystery to be solved, and I needed to see what other information I could glean.

I had spoken with Mrs. Douglas-Hughes and, though quite unsatisfactorily, with her husband. It would be more difficult for me to arrange a meeting with the other suspects. Typically, crossing paths with the women would be easier to accomplish, though in this case I could think of no good means of doing so. The Echols sisters I didn't know at all well. I had not been acquainted with them before Mrs. Barrington's dinner party, and I could think of no excuse for contacting them now. I could think of even less of a reason to contact Mrs. Garmond.

As for the gentlemen, I had very little means of putting myself in their paths in an inconspicuous way. This served as yet another reason for me to be angry with Milo. Were he not traipsing about the country making a spectacle of himself with his mistress, he might have proved himself useful.

What I needed was another source. Someone who was disconnected from the murder itself but might still have information that would be useful.

I thought suddenly of Yvonne Roland. I dismissed the idea at once, but I couldn't seem to shake it completely. An extremely wealthy widow, she charged through polite society with terrible speed, gathering up information like a squirrel gathering nuts. Though I had never ascertained the particulars, she had some type of connection with the gossip columns, and I wondered if there might possibly be anything that she could tell me. I hadn't the slightest doubt that she had been following the story in the papers.

I pondered the hazards of contacting her. With my own situation being what it was, I suspected it would be difficult to keep her from prying into my personal affairs. Then again, she would probably know things about the guests of Lord Dunmore's ball that would be nearly impossible for me to find out myself.

I decided to take the risk. After all, I knew her game and would go in prepared to beat her at it.

At four o'clock, I was ushered into Mrs. Roland's parlor. She had been delighted to hear from me and had insisted I come to tea that very afternoon. She lived in a large but comfortable house she had bought for herself after the death of her most recent husband. She went through husbands at a somewhat alarming rate, but it had never been known to dampen her considerable zeal for society life.

A harried-looking maid had shown me to the parlor and disappeared as soon as she had announced me. I had expected shelves of bric-a-brac, an abundance of aspidistra, and at least three cats. I was correct in two of three surmises. The parlor was decorated very much in the Victorian style, with dark flowered wallpaper, heavy golden drapes, lush plants in porcelain pots, and a great deal of ornate furniture crowding the room.

There were no cats, however. Instead, I found the lady holding court for the two Pomeranians and a fat Pekingese lying before her on silk cushions on the rug. The trio of animals began yipping at me in harmony as I entered.

"Hush," she said, and the dogs were immediately silenced. I was rather impressed with their obedience. Then again, I did not find it surprising that the forceful Mrs. Roland should have the same effect on animals as she did on people.

"Mrs. Ames," she said, rising to meet me, extending a hand that fairly glittered with assorted rings of all descriptions. "I'm delighted that you've come to see me. It's been much too long! After the events at the Brightwell, you know, I have been thinking how we simply must have tea. In fact, I had just thought this very morning that I should phone you. I've been wanting to see you, my dear. I feel that we have so much to discuss!"

I felt a vague sensation of unease, as though I had been drawn into the spider's web unawares.

"And then you rang me up, and now here you are! It must be fate! I'm delighted."

"Thank you for having me, Mrs. Roland," I said, as I took the seat she indicated, an impressive piece with a heavy wooden frame and garish embroidered upholstery.

Mrs. Roland herself was no less impressive. She was as much known in society for her ostentatious ensembles as she was for being a notorious quidnunc, and today was no exception. Her henna-red hair was swept into an intricate coiffure that served to highlight a gold-beaded headpiece Cleopatra might have envied. If ancient Egypt had inspired her headdress, she must have taken her wardrobe cues from the Greeks, for she was dressed in a long, elaborately draped gown of puce, the folds of which brushed one of the dogs as she swept past and set it to barking again.

"Ferdinand, be quiet," she commanded as she settled herself back into her chair. "You must excuse my little ones, Mrs. Ames. They're very excitable. Have you any dogs?"

"We've some hounds at Thornecrest. Hunters, not house dogs."

"Sugar or milk?" she asked, leaning over the silver tea service on the table.

"Two sugars, please."

192

The beads of her many bracelets clanked against the pot as she poured.

"Are you fond of dogs?" she asked, handing me my cup.

"Yes, I suppose I am. We had a mastiff when I was a child. He was called Archibald, and we were the greatest of friends."

"You should get a sweet little dog, Mrs. Ames. I find them to be a great comfort." She said this with a significant look, and I knew that we had already come to the topic I had been hoping to avoid. I felt again the sensation that she had invited me here to question me and not the other way around. "I'm sure, with your husband away as often as he is, you find yourself quite lonely sometimes."

It was not a very subtle hint, but I felt disinclined to elaborate on the situation. It was not that I wanted to shield Milo, but neither did I want our personal difficulties to be any more on display than they already were. "Perhaps a puppy would be nice one day."

"Of course, dear. But you needn't put on a brave face with me. We're old friends, aren't we? After all, I'm no stranger to philandering husbands. My first husband was a handsome devil, just like Mr. Ames, though perhaps not *quite* as handsome. He broke my heart more times than I can remember, and many's the time I thought I couldn't take it another moment, but love's not a thing you can turn on and off with a switch, is it? I loved him until that unfortunate accident carried him off."

I was beginning to think that I had overestimated my abilities and that coming here was a very bad idea indeed.

"I know young people don't like to talk about their problems," she said sweetly, misinterpreting my bewildered silence for embarrassment, "but if you need a sympathetic ear, you have only to ask. And I'm the soul of discretion, my dear."

"Thank you," I said politely in the face of this tremendous untruth. "I know there have been quite a lot of things printed about my husband lately, but you know how the papers exaggerate things."

"Helene Renault is a beautiful woman, naturally, but she's lacking something. She hasn't got your elegance, for one thing. Of course, men don't take much note of such things. It seems that all it takes is the whiff of French perfume and a few garbled syllables to draw them like bees to honey." She shook her head. "It's a pity. But I shouldn't worry much, Mrs. Ames. In the end, I should be very much surprised if she holds his interest for long. After all, your husband is quite mad about you. That much was quite plain to me at the Brightwell. And your other young man, Gil Trent. What has become of him since that wretched hotel business?"

She was referring to my former fiancé, who had also been involved in the events at the Brightwell Hotel. "I had a letter from him a few weeks back," I told her. "He's quite well."

"Splendid! You wouldn't have suited in the long run, I don't suppose, but one must hope he will find happiness with someone else."

"Do you know Mrs. Vivian Garmond?" I asked abruptly, as it had become apparent there was no possible means of politely shifting the conversation in sight.

"Poor Mrs. Garmond," Mrs. Roland tut-tutted, diverted from her monologue on my marriage. "Now, that Lord Dunmore is a different matter. He is a scoundrel. He's handsome enough, I suppose, but I don't see why it is that women go weak at the knees over him. Vivian Garmond should have known better. She's a clever girl from a good family, but I suppose even clever girls can lose their heads."

"You know her then?"

195

"I knew the family. Overton is their name. She went abroad a few years ago . . . Turkey or Greece or some such place . . . and came back a widow with an infant son." She placed definite skeptical emphasis on the word "widow."

"Coincidentally," she continued, "Lord Dunmore had been abroad at about the same time and came back shortly after she did. They immediately took up with one another, so it's commonly assumed he got her in trouble and refused to marry her. Everyone realizes what's going on, of course, but she maintains the pretense that her husband was killed and people go on pretending to believe it. However, I, of my own knowledge, have never been able to ascertain exactly when and where her husband seems to have died. After all, that's the sort of thing one remembers. I remember all my poor husbands' deaths."

I blinked and managed a sympathetic smile. "Yes, Mrs. Roland, I'm sure you do. Surely there must be some record of a Mr. Garmond dying?"

She shrugged. "I suppose one could find out, if one really cared to. I'm not much acquainted with the Garmonds myself. After all, if they've welcomed her into the family, who am I to discourage them? Of course, I don't know why they care to claim her, the way she runs after Dunmore, despite the parade of women going through his bed."

She stopped for breath, and I wondered if I could insert another question into the conversation. She beat me to it, however. "But here I am, running on about Lord Dunmore, and you've become acquainted with him yourself. You were at his ball when that murder happened, weren't you?" There was a sudden sharp look in her gaze, as though she was a predator closing in.

"Yes," I answered casually, "but I had injured my ankle and wasn't there when it occurred. I'm afraid I could be of no help at all."

"Poor dear," she said, and I didn't know whether she meant my injury or the fact that I had been excluded from the excitement.

"I suppose it was someone after the jewels?" she asked, trying to draw me out.

"I'm afraid I really don't know," I said honestly, and she frowned as though I had disappointed her.

"Poor Serena must be very upset. I haven't called on her yet, as I imagine she's busy with preparations."

"I wasn't aware you knew Mrs. Barrington." I imagined the two of them together and determined they would be a force to be reckoned with indeed.

"Serena was distantly related to my second husband. We have stayed in contact since his death, though we don't see each other much."

"I believe Mr. Harker's death has been very hard on her," I said. "And on Mr. Barrington."

"Perhaps. I don't know him well, but I believe he was never terribly fond of the nephew."

"Well, it was very sad, all around," I said, trying to steer the conversation back on course. "I was discussing it with Mrs. Douglas-Hughes only yesterday." As I had hoped, this set her off again.

"Mrs. Douglas-Hughes is a fine woman," she said. "One expects Americans to be a certain way, doesn't one? But she's not. She's quite a refined, lovely girl. I don't know, if I'd been doing the matching, that I'd have aligned her with Sanderson Douglas-Hughes. He's a gentleman, of course, but I don't know how much time he can devote to her when he is so very devoted to his work. Must be difficult for a man to concern himself with domestic life when he's always got his nose in foreign affairs."

"Mr. and Mrs. Douglas-Hughes seem quite happy together," I put in.

"Yes? Well, I hope so. One wonders if such a creative sort of person can be happy with a solemn gentleman, but opposites have attracted before this, haven't they?"

She didn't seem to need my confirmation, for she charged ahead, picking up steam. "This isn't his first brush with a mysterious death, I believe. I seem to recall that there was some foreign fellow a while back that was supposed to be working with Mr. Douglas-Hughes in some capacity but died rather unexpectedly. I suppose those things happen when one involves oneself in government. Those Echols girls were there, too, weren't they? I'm not surprised, for it seems that wherever there's trouble, Marjorie Echols isn't far behind. I've heard she was after James Harker, though goodness knows why she should want such a dolt . . . may he rest in peace."

"I was given to understand that it was Felicity who cared for Mr. Harker," I managed to interject.

"That may very well be. I should think that would only encourage Marjorie."

I supposed I might as well go through the list of suspects while she was in full-disclosure mode, so I jumped to the next of them. "I was pleased to have met Mr. Nigel Foster, as I have long been an admirer of his."

She hesitated as if searching her rumor reservoir, and I wondered if the gossip mill had actually ceased to grind. She recovered quickly, however. "I don't know much about Mr. Foster," she admitted. "Sporting events have never much been my forte. He's a handsome young man. I believe there was a girl a while back, something about an engagement, I think, but she was in an accident, and then they broke it off. The girl moved to California or some such absurd place."

"I see." I didn't recall reading any such thing, but Winnelda's gossip magazines had only extended back a few months.

"So many interesting people in attendance at the ball. If only I had been there," she lamented. She picked up a cookie and bit into it contemplatively. "I wasn't invited, of course, but half the people that attend his parties have not received invitations, so I shouldn't have let that stop me. Perhaps I'll attend the next one. I understand he throws them in rapid succession. The family's always been given to excess. His father was a libertine as well. I suppose he's still going to have the one this weekend."

"Yes, I believe he plans for it to go on as scheduled."

"I thought so. Lord Dunmore is not one to let tragedy put a stop to his fun. Well, perhaps I shall make an appearance. Have you seen the diamond?" she asked suddenly.

"The Dunmore Diamond? No, I haven't."

"It's a necklace that belonged to his great-grandmother, a monstrous diamond from India, I think. What good it's doing locked away, I don't know. I saw it once on Lord Dunmore's mother. Poor dear, she was much too plain to do it justice. Oh," she said, bringing her cup to her lips and taking it away again, "somehow my tea's managed to go cold. I can't imagine how I let that happen!"

I left Mrs. Roland's house a bit exhausted, and not until she had secured a promise from me that I would consider taking a puppy from the next litter of Wilhelmina, the fat Pekingese.

My own reputation had escaped relatively unscathed, and I had gained some very useful background information. For one thing, it seemed that the cloud that hung over Mrs. Garmond's past was darker than I had suspected.

I thought back to what Mrs. Barrington

said about James Harker's always saying things he shouldn't. Was it possible he might have known something about the elusive Mr. Garmond? Then again, everyone commonly assumed the child was Dunmore's. Would evidence to the contrary be worth killing for? Perhaps. People clung very hard to the masks they wore.

The masks . . . I wondered again. Had it been a coincidence that Mr. Harker and Mr. Foster had worn the same mask? I was sure that Inspector Jones would have investigated that avenue by now. I felt vaguely irritated that he had not yet been in touch. I would have to telephone him tomorrow and find out what he had learned.

I reached home and promptly gave Winnelda another night off. I had a lot of thinking to do, and I thought it would best be done in silence. She was willing enough, as two of her friends had invited her to the cinema, but when it was time for her to leave she hesitated.

"You're certain you'll be all right, madam?" she asked a bit worriedly. "I won't leave if you'd rather I didn't."

"Yes, thank you, Winnelda. I'm going to rest for a while. I'm quite tired."

My nights of poor sleep were catching up with me. I lay down when she had gone, intending to close my eyes for just a little while. I was surprised when I woke up in a darkened bedroom. I had slept later than I intended.

I rose and went to make myself a cup of tea. Winnelda had left dinner for me, but I found I wasn't very hungry. Instead, I made myself some toast and took it with my tea into the parlor.

As I nibbled on my toast, I mulled over what I knew, which didn't appear to be much. No one seemed to have a very clear motive for murder. It all seemed to come back to the theft of the jewels, but I still had a hard time believing that any of the suspects would have been desperate enough to commit murder for a bracelet. It had to be more than that. There was something that was missing, some part of the mystery that had not yet come to light. But what? I didn't know where to look next.

I was pulled from my musings as I heard the front door open.

"Is that you, Winnelda?" I called. She was back earlier than I had expected.

"Not even close," said Milo, coming into the room. I felt myself tense at his unexpected appearance. I hadn't prepared myself for his arrival, and felt strangely at a loss. I set my teacup down, and, to my annoyance, it rattled slightly in the saucer.

If he noticed anything amiss, or if he was feeling any guilt, he gave absolutely no indication of it.

"I got the brute settled faster than I had imagined. He's a magnificent animal, but I think he'll rival Xerxes in terms of surly temperament. I left him in Geoffrey's capable hands. We'll have to go back to Thornecrest for a weekend soon."

He came to where I sat and leaned to kiss me, but my voice stopped him.

"I can smell her perfume on your coat, Milo."

His eyes met mine, and I could see then that he knew that I knew. The cloying scent of rose hung in the air, as palpable as my anger.

I stood, unable to bear the pretense of civility any longer. "I'm going to bed. Good night."

"Amory . . ."

"Good night."

I left the room without looking back, and Milo didn't come after me.

15

Once again, I couldn't sleep, and I felt much worse in the morning than when I had gone to bed. The mirror clearly reflected the effects of my miserable night. I looked pale and drawn, and I suspected that no amount of makeup was going to help.

Nevertheless, I bathed and dressed in a becoming black Bruyère suit. Then I walked resolutely from my room, ready to meet Milo, should it even prove necessary.

I didn't want to face him, but there was a very good possibility he was still in bed, or perhaps even gone from the flat. I assumed he had slept in the guest room, but for all I knew he had gone back to Mademoiselle Renault. In any event, I didn't intend to hide from him.

I sat down at the table and poured myself a cup of coffee, gratified to see that my hands were perfectly steady. I had absolutely no appetite, but I didn't want Winnelda to know that I was upset. I was fairly certain she could sense something was amiss, however, for she went about on tenterhooks and refrained from her normal morning chatter.

Milo came into the room a few minutes after I did and sat across from me. Neither of us spoke, and the tension was heavy in the air. Despite his habitual nonchalance, I could tell that he was treading carefully, trying to gauge my mood.

"Amory . . ." he began at last.

I shook my head slowly, not looking up from my coffee. I didn't want to talk to him, not here and not now. It wasn't only the possibility that Winnelda might overhear. I simply didn't feel ready.

He didn't press me, and for that I was grateful. I picked at my food, pretending to eat it while my mind raced in a thousand directions. What could I say to him? What was there to say? It was perfectly clear where we stood; the only thing to be determined was where things would go from here.

"Will you go for a walk with me?" he asked at last. I supposed he had seen through my pretense of eating breakfast, for all I had really done was move my food about the plate.

I looked up at him for the first time since

he had come into the room. His gaze was steady, calm. I wished desperately that he didn't always look so very sure of himself.

I hesitated as I considered his request. A few moments of staring at my breakfast plate had still not prepared me for the conversation ahead, but I supposed it was better to get it over with. At least a walk would give us privacy. I wondered if he thought I would be less inclined to make a scene in public. He needn't have worried; I didn't intend to make things difficult.

"I'll get my coat," I said.

I put on a cloche and fetched a light coat and gloves from the bedroom and cast one last glance at myself in the mirror. I looked much more composed than I felt, and I was glad of it.

Milo was waiting for me in the foyer. He helped me into my coat, and we went out into the hallway, down the lift, and out of the building in silence.

We stepped out into the cool morning air. It was a lovely day, complete with a light breeze and chirping birds. The kind of day that was perfect for lovers out walking. I suddenly wished the weather was not quite so nice. I suspected that gray skies would be more suited to the scene we were about to play.

There was a little park not far from the flat, and we started in that direction without conferring. It occurred to me how strange it was that we should be so in harmony in some things and so completely discordant in others.

Milo seemed to be waiting for me to speak, giving me time to decide what I wanted to say. This thoughtful courtesy, coming at a time like this, was somehow almost painful.

"I don't know why I'm surprised," I said at last, breaking the silence. My voice sounded stronger than I had expected, and I was relieved. "I shouldn't be. Perhaps I should have expected it. But the plain fact remains that I was shocked to see that photograph."

"Yes, I was afraid of that. I had hoped to warn you before you saw it."

"That would have been kind of you," I said icily. "But, then again, I suppose it's usual for the wife to be the last to know."

"It's not what it looks like, if that's any consolation."

I let out an incredulous laugh, my hands clenching in the pockets of my coat. "Come now, Milo. Is that the best you can do?"

"It's perfectly clear that now is not the time for explanations. You wouldn't believe me if I gave them to you."

I gave him a brittle smile. "Yes, you're right. I see no conceivable way this could be explained away, though I'm sure you've had time to formulate a lovely story."

"It isn't what you think."

"Everyone knows perfectly well what it is," I answered calmly. "Half of London is talking about it. There's no need for you to deny it to me."

"I am not having an affair with Helene Renault." There was something very like patience in his tone that set me on edge. It was as though he thought I was the one who was behaving irrationally.

I stopped and turned to face him. This walk had been a bad idea. I wasn't ready to maintain my composure in the face of his lies.

"I don't want to talk about this now, Milo. I need some time to think."

"What does that mean, exactly?" he asked.

I looked up at him. "It means I'd rather you stay at your club, or at the Ritz, or go back to Thornecrest. I don't care where . . ." He could stay with Helene Renault if he was so inclined. Anywhere but with me at the flat.

"Amory . . ." He sighed.

"Please, Milo." The words came out as a

209

whisper, and I drew in a breath before continuing in a steadier voice. "Let's not make things any more difficult than they already are."

His eyes moved across my face, and I forced myself to meet the searching blue gaze unflinchingly. I needed him to see that I meant it. This wasn't going to be brushed off as easily as all of his past escapades. It was time he realized that I was not going to turn a blind eye forever. There was always a final straw.

"Very well," he said at last. "I'll go now and send Parks later for my things."

"I think that would be best."

And still we stood there looking at one another. There was a wall between us, and I wondered if perhaps it was insurmountable. It all seemed so very hopeless at the moment.

"Shall I telephone you in a day or two?" he asked. His tone was polite, and I could read nothing in it. As usual, he revealed only what he wanted me to know and nothing more.

"Yes," I said. "That should be fine."

He reached out and took my hand in his. He held it for just a moment before squeezing it. Then he let it go and turned and walked away unhurriedly without looking back.

I watched him for a moment, and then continued walking toward the park. I tried and failed to sort through the whirlwind of emotions I was experiencing. I didn't know whether anger or sadness was foremost among them. I only knew that, in our conversation, there had been no remorse, only excuses. Time and time again I had accepted his explanations, believed him because I wanted what he said to be true. Well, I wasn't going to do it this time. I couldn't.

I reached the border of the park and sat down heavily on a bench. I felt like I should cry, but in truth I was too weary for that. Things had been building to this moment for a long time, and now that it was finally here, I felt only a numb sort of acceptance. It was as though I had known that our happiness the last two months had been too good to last.

It was all such a wretched, infuriating mess.

And perhaps the most maddening thing of all was that, despite everything, I was still terribly in love with him.

When I felt sufficiently composed, I walked back toward the flat. There would be plenty of time for thinking things over when I had fully collected myself. Sitting alone in the park, airing out my emotions for all to see, would not solve anything.

I had nearly reached the flat's entrance when I spotted a familiar figure emerging from it. Detective Inspector Jones.

Given my somewhat flustered emotional state, I will admit that the thought of turning and dodging around the building to avoid him occurred to me. However, by the time it had, I had been spotted. I had wanted to speak to him, at any rate. I supposed now was as good a time as any. Sulking about my rapidly deteriorating marriage certainly wasn't going to solve James Harker's murder.

I waved and walked toward him, hoping the effects of my tumultuous morning weren't apparent on my face, though I rather suspected that was hoping for too much.

"Hello, Mrs. Ames. I've just come from your flat. Your maid told me that you were out."

"I've been for a walk in the park. How are you, Inspector?"

"I'm quite well, Mrs. Ames," he replied pleasantly, his eyes resting on my face in that unnervingly perceptive way of his.

"How are you?"

There was, I thought, more than common courtesy in the question, but I brushed it aside.

"I'm fine, thank you, Inspector. As a matter of fact, I was just thinking over a couple of matters and wanted to discuss them with you. Won't you come back upstairs?"

Though I was not exactly feeling up to company in my present state, perhaps it would help me to get my mind off things.

We rode up in the lift together, and, once in my flat, Winnelda took his hat and coat with an impressively becoming decorum, considering her views on policemen. The fact that the inspector allowed himself to be divested of his outside garments seemed to indicate a shift in our relationship. Some of his officious formality had eased ever so slightly. Furthermore, he accepted a cup of black tea from the pot Winnelda brought into the parlor. I could not help but feel that we were now practically old friends.

"Mr. Ames has gone out?" he asked, when we had settled into our seats. There was something searching in his gaze that made me suspect he knew more than he let on. I wondered if it was possible he had encountered Milo on his way back from our walk.

I decided to be direct. One could only

hide things from a detective for so long, after all. "Have you seen the photograph that has been circulating?"

He did me the justice of not feigning ignorance. "I have."

"Yes, I thought you might have." Not much escaped Inspector Jones. "I've asked him to stay elsewhere for the time being. I have a good deal to think over."

"I see."

I didn't elaborate, and he mercifully let the subject drop.

"What was it that you wanted to talk to me about, Mrs. Ames?"

I was glad for the change in topic and charged readily ahead. "For one thing, I wanted to ask if you had looked into the possibility that Mr. Harker might have been killed by mistake. After all, it's not outside the realm of possibility that someone might have wanted to kill Mr. Foster. Did you investigate the similarities of their masks?"

"I spoke with Mr. Foster. He seemed unaware that Mr. Harker was wearing the same mask on the night of the incident."

It was not entirely surprising. The house had been crowded with guests; Mr. Foster might not even have crossed paths with Mr. Harker.

"That doesn't, of course, preclude the fact

that someone might have mistaken one man for the other," I persisted.

"That seems unlikely. You see, we have positively identified the gun as belonging to Mr. Harker. His valet informed us that Mr. Harker had removed it from the drawer where it was normally kept and put it in his pocket before leaving for the ball."

This was another development I had not foreseen. "Mr. Harker was shot with his own gun," I said slowly.

"Yes."

"But why would Mr. Harker bring a gun to Lord Dunmore's ball?"

"I can only assume he thought he might have occasion to use it."

"Then he was expecting trouble. But what was Mr. Harker doing in that bedroom with jewels from the bracelet?" I asked, more of myself than of Inspector Jones. And then an idea occurred to me.

"Were you able to determine who he was meeting that night?"

"I'm afraid not. I questioned all the guests, including his aunt and uncle, and they all told me they had no knowledge of Mr. Harker's whereabouts in the hour preceding the murder."

"Nevertheless, he told me specifically that he was looking for someone. It seems now that that meeting had turned out to be deadly. Perhaps he knew who had been stealing Mrs. Barrington's jewels, decided to confront the thief, and arranged a meeting in one of the upstairs bedrooms. Perhaps things went wrong and the thief killed him."

It didn't quite explain how the killer might have shot Mr. Harker from behind with Mr. Harker's own gun, but I felt that I was at least getting somewhere.

Inspector Jones seemed less impressed with my theory than I had been. "It's possible, but it still leaves several unanswered questions."

I resisted the urge to note that it answered more questions than had thus far been addressed by the police.

"As we have ascertained, James Harker was shot from behind," Inspector Jones said, astutely finding the weak point in my theory. "That seems to indicate he was surprised."

"He could have set his gun aside and turned his back for a moment. The killer might have taken advantage of the opportunity and killed him with it."

"Perhaps," he conceded.

I had the sudden feeling that there was something he wasn't saying.

"There's more, isn't there? There's something you aren't telling me."

He smiled. "Surely you are aware by now, Mrs. Ames, that I cannot tell you everything I know. After all, you're not working in an official capacity."

As his irksome officiousness once again raised its ugly head, I noticed that he had not yet so much as sipped his tea. No doubt he had taken a cup simply to appease my desire to be hospitable, but it did not mean that this was a social call.

"It was you who came to me, Inspector," I reminded him coolly.

His smile broadened at my sudden hauteur, and I wondered if it was possible that he was teasing me. "Indeed, I did come to you, Mrs. Ames. You're a very perceptive woman, and I find our conversations most enlightening."

I wish I found things enlightening. It was all such a jumble. People had been everywhere, running about in masks. Really, it seemed a setting tailor-made for murder.

"It all comes back to the jewels," I said, as a theory began to take shape in my mind. "Mrs. Barrington's paste sapphire bracelet went missing while she slept in the library. Suppose the meeting had nothing to do with the murder. Well then, perhaps James Harker saw the thief come out of the library and confronted him. A struggle might have ensued in which the bracelet broke, scattering the jewels across the hallway floor. The thief and Mr. Harker might have gathered them up hastily, missing the one that I later slipped on when going down the stairs."

I was warming to my imagined account now, and Inspector Jones let me continue uninterrupted, his expression betraying nothing. "That would also account for the jewels found in Mr. Harker's pocket. Perhaps Mr. Harker then suggested that they step into one of the bedrooms to discuss the matter. Perhaps he even put aside the gun he had brought along as a sign of a truce, not knowing the thief would decide to use it against him." I stopped, quite pleased with my speculations.

"An admirable theory, Mrs. Ames," Inspector Jones replied. "However, there is one flaw in it."

"Oh? And what is that?"

"You theorize that they struggled over Mrs. Barrington's paste bracelet and that resulted in the loose stone on the steps. Well, I came today to let you in on a little secret. The jewel you found in your shoe was not paste. It was a genuine sapphire."

16

"But that can't be!" I exclaimed.

"I'm afraid it is," he replied calmly.

"I don't understand. Mrs. Barrington specifically told me that they were paste."

"It seems they were. Mr. Barrington has confirmed that he brought the bracelet to a jeweler and had a paste replica made. Perhaps the bracelet was taken as you theorized. However, at some point during the evening, someone dropped a genuine sapphire in the hallway or on the stairs."

"But no one else has reported anything missing?"

"No."

"This is maddening!" I exclaimed. "What of the stones in Mr. Harker's pocket?"

"They were paste." As was typical of Inspector Jones, he related one astounding piece of information after another without batting an eye. I wondered briefly if he ever found himself flummoxed, but I highly doubted it.

"Were the paste gems from the bracelet?" I asked.

"I've questioned Mrs. Barrington about it, but she can't be sure. It seems likely, but, if so, neither the setting nor the other paste jewels have been discovered."

I let out an exasperated sigh. It seemed that every time I began to make sense of things, something occurred to turn my theories topsy-turvy.

"You've certainly given me a lot to think about, Inspector," I mused. Much more than I needed at present.

"Yes, and I've taken up enough of your time, Mrs. Ames. Thank you for the tea." He took a perfunctory sip and then set the cup on the table before rising from his seat.

Winnelda appeared from around the corner, where she had apparently been lurking, and gave the inspector his hat and coat.

"I'll be in touch."

"Good afternoon, Inspector."

He left, and I sipped my cold tea as I pondered these newest revelations.

Inspector Jones had confidently ruled out a case of mistaken identity, and I was inclined to agree with him. Though I hated to admit it, Milo had made a point when he noted that killing the wrong man based on the mask he wore would be a very careless thing to do. Mr. Foster and James Harker had a similar build, perhaps, but that was where the similarities ended. I found it hard to believe that anyone, given a moment to observe Mr. Harker, might have mistaken him for the tennis star. Besides, the killer had used Mr. Harker's gun, so he — or she — must have known on whom they were using it.

There was, of course, another option: that Mr. Harker had been killed because of something that he knew. He might have been privy to information someone was afraid he would share. It was, perhaps, unlikely, given the growing mystery surrounding Mrs. Barrington's jewels. Nevertheless, it was something to take into account.

I sighed again, deeply. It all seemed very like trying to untangle a spider's web.

Winnelda reminded me that I had an engagement with Mrs. Barrington that afternoon.

"I'd forgotten all about that," I admitted, rubbing a hand tiredly across my eyes. So much had happened since I had agreed to have tea with her.

"Shall I telephone and tell her you're ill,

madam?" she asked, watching me anxiously. She really was a very sweet girl, and a perceptive one. Despite my best attempts at maintaining a carefree front, I knew that she was aware that everything was not all right.

"No," I said at last. "Thank you, Winnelda, but perhaps it will be good for me to get out for a while."

In truth, I was also glad to avoid being alone. Once things had settled down and I was left alone in the quietness of the flat, I knew I would be forced to make some sort of decision about my marriage. It was much easier to keep pushing it to the back of mind, like some unpleasant chore to be dealt with later.

I arrived at the Barringtons' home and was shown to one of the smaller sitting rooms, where Mrs. Barrington awaited me.

Despite the fact that she had asked me to come, she seemed distracted and a bit surprised to see me. "Oh, good afternoon, Mrs. Ames."

"How are you, Mrs. Barrington?"

"As well as can be expected. Can I offer you tea or perhaps some coffee?"

"Thank you, no. I don't wish to impose. I know that things are difficult for you right now."

"Yes," she said, sorrow flashing across her features. "I never thought to have lived to see James laid to rest beside his poor parents."

"I'm sorry." I knew that, beneath her strong exterior, she was mourning her nephew deeply.

She waved a hand, visibly drawing in a breath and squaring her shoulders. "We needn't talk about that now. Have you learned anything new?"

Inspector Jones had not told me to keep the information about the gemstones to myself, but I was naturally inclined to be cautious when sharing information. I thought it would be prudent not to reveal the truth about the sapphire that had been discovered on the stairs. I was certain Inspector Jones would question her again about her bracelet when the time was right.

"Nothing that seems to mean anything at the moment," I answered. "It seems, however, that everything comes back to the jewels. You told me it was an emerald ring, diamond bracelet, and the Eiffel Tower pin that went missing, correct?"

"Yes. And, of course, the sapphire bracelet at the ball, though that was paste."

"Mrs. Barrington, have you any idea how your nephew got hold of the paste sapphires in his pocket?"

She shook her head. "I've pondered that for hours, Mrs. Ames. James was aware of my plan to try to flush out the thief, so my only theory is that he might have taken the bracelet from the table in the library while I slept with the intention of luring the thief somehow. Why the stones should have been loose in his pocket and where the setting might have gone, I haven't the faintest idea." She had drawn much the same conclusions as I had.

"Can you describe the other pieces for me?" I asked. It seemed as though a description of the missing items might prove useful.

"Certainly," she said. "The emerald ring was a square cut in a gold setting. The bracelet was made of square stones, set in silver. I think I've a photograph . . ."

She stood, walking to a nearby table, where several photographs were displayed in frames. "Yes, here it is."

She brought over a photograph of her and her husband. A diamond bracelet was clearly visible on her wrist, and I made a mental impression of its design.

"I've described the Eiffel Tower pin to you already, I believe," she said, returning the photograph to its place.

"Yes," I said. "Thank you, Mrs. Barrington. I'm hoping that somehow we will be able to recover that piece at least, since it has sentimental value."

"I don't have much hope that it will ever turn up," she said sadly. "Mr. Barrington said he will buy me another, but that wouldn't be the same."

"Let's not give up just yet."

"You're quite right, dear," she said with a smile. "I have a great deal of faith in your abilities."

I only hoped her faith would prove to be justified.

"Serena, I'm going out for a while . . ." Mr. Barrington had come into the room and stopped when he saw me. "Oh, hello, Mrs. Ames." His face looked drawn and tired, but he smiled warmly.

"Good afternoon, Mr. Barrington."

"Going out, Lloyd?" Mrs. Barrington asked.

"Yes, I'm meeting Nigel Foster for a drink at our club. He rang up to offer his condolences and suggested a drink. You don't mind, do you?"

"No, not at all. It will be good for you to get out of the house for a bit. Mrs. Ames and I are discussing the murder and how the jewels might have come to be in James's pocket."

He hesitated and didn't, I thought, look much pleased with this bit of news. I wondered how comfortable he was with my involvement in the matter. After all, a murder in the family was a private affair. It was likely he didn't care to have the details paraded about for outsiders to see. Now might not be the best time for questions, but I didn't know when I would have another opportunity to ask.

"I know it's difficult," I said quickly, "but I think there must be something that we're missing that will help us discover who might have done it. It's only a matter of going through what we know and putting all the pieces together."

He passed a hand across his face. "Yes, of course. I'm sure you're right. It's just been so dreadful." He took a seat in a chair across from me.

"Have you any theory as to what might have happened or who might have done it?"

"I don't know, Mrs. Ames," he said tiredly. "I've turned it over in my mind, but it just doesn't seem to make sense. It seems that it must have been he who was stealing my wife's jewels. Perhaps he didn't remember they were paste. He was forgetful at times."

"Oh, Lloyd. You know James would never

do such a thing."

"I wouldn't think so," he conceded. "Then again, he must have taken the bracelet that night. There's no other way the jewels could have ended up in his pocket."

"If he took it, then why wasn't the setting found on his body?" she challenged.

He sighed. "I don't know. I don't know anything anymore, Serena."

I felt very much out of place in the midst of this private conversation, but neither of them seemed to mind that I was there. In fact, it was almost as though they had forgotten me for the moment.

"James must have discovered the thief," Mrs. Barrington told him firmly. "He took my paste jewels in order to carry out the trap and was killed for it. That's the only thing that makes any sense."

I had the distinct feeling that Mr. Barrington was skeptical of his wife's theories. I wondered if he secretly had suspicions of his own about what Mr. Harker might have been doing with the bracelet.

"I passed Mr. Harker on the stairs that evening," I told them. "He said he had an appointment with someone. Have you any idea who it might have been?"

Mrs. Barrington shook her head. "I haven't the faintest idea. James didn't much care for balls and things, but he said he was going to come along anyway. Perhaps that's why he decided to attend."

"What about his mask?" I asked suddenly. "Do you know why he chose a tiger?"

She frowned. "Now that you mention it, I was a bit surprised by his choice. But James often had little whims."

"Mr. Foster also wore a tiger mask." I mentioned this casually, but I saw that both of them looked a bit surprised at the connection.

"Do you suppose it might have been Mr. Foster that someone meant to kill?" Mrs. Barrington asked.

"Let's not get carried away, Serena," her husband cautioned her.

"It was Lord Dunmore's ball. Perhaps he had something to do with it."

She was desperate, searching for answers, but I knew that answers must be supported by facts. I thought of Lord Dunmore's calm, confident manner and found it hard to believe that he would ever condescend to something as vulgar as common theft. "It does seem unlikely that he should steal anything," I said carefully.

"Yes, you're right," she replied, suddenly deflating. "After all, what should he want with my things when he has the Dunmore

Diamond? It's just so maddening. Which of them could it have been? What we need is a chance to observe everyone. If there was only some way . . . In fact, I think I may have an idea."

"Oh?" I questioned cautiously. Mrs. Barrington seemed inclined to rope me into harebrained schemes I tended to regret later.

"Lord Dunmore is going on with his ball this weekend, isn't he? If I know him at all, he won't let James's death interfere. He loves nothing more than a good scandal. With a mysterious death at his last ball, everyone in London will want to be invited. It would be just the sort of thing he enjoys. Well, if we can get all of the suspects back into the same place, in similar circumstances, we're bound to discover something. Perhaps we can even lay another trap. In fact, perhaps we can get Lord Dunmore to help us!"

"Serena . . ." Mr. Barrington sighed.

She waved away his protest. "Let me think a moment. I have it!" She clapped her hands together in triumph, causing me to blink. "I have it! The Dunmore Diamond!"

This was not going to be a good idea. I could tell that at once.

"Good Lord, Serena," Mr. Barrington

said. "Have you gone mad?"

She ignored him. "What if he made a show of it at the ball? The thief wouldn't be able to resist."

"But Mrs. Barrington," I reasoned, "I don't think this is a professional jewel thief we're dealing with. The thief took things when it was convenient, not things of this magnitude."

"Well, even if that's so, what if he brought it out and mentioned to all of the suspects that he was going to leave it in a certain place? The thief wouldn't be able to resist trying to steal it."

I thought this unwise in the extreme, but somehow I could not completely dismiss the idea out of hand.

"What if Dunmore is the killer?" Mr. Barrington asked, more, I thought, to discourage her than because he thought it probable.

She was undaunted, however. "Well? Even if it happens that Lord Dunmore is the killer, we've already established that he wouldn't have needed to kill James for the jewels. If he murdered for something else, perhaps in the carrying out of our plot he will tip his hand."

She had a point, but I could not quite agree wholeheartedly with her plan just yet.

"With everything that's happened, do you think Lord Dunmore would be inclined to do such a thing?" I asked.

"Certainly. He's reckless, and he enjoys doing scandalous things. He just needs a bit of prodding, someone to put the idea into his mind."

There was no doubt in *my* mind just who she had *in* mind.

Mrs. Barrington was growing more enthusiastic by the moment. "Perhaps if you were to talk with him, Mrs. Ames. He fancies you. If you . . ."

"Serena," Mr. Barrington interrupted. "You can't ask Mrs. Ames to . . ."

"Oh, I didn't mean anything improper, Lloyd. But perhaps it would work."

The idea, though somewhat unorthodox, had its merits. I had no doubt that she was right about the viscount. I thought he would love the opportunity to once again be the talk of London, but there was still the question of how such a thing could be used to our advantage. "Even if he could be convinced to do such a thing, how will that help us?"

"We can trace his steps, Mrs. Ames. We can trace the steps of the killer. We'll be looking more closely this time, watching the people who are there. If someone thought it was worth killing James for my bracelet, then he or she may be desperate enough to strike again. We will just need a bigger prize, and the Dunmore Diamond ought to do very nicely."

17

And so it was that, against my better judgment, I found myself standing at Lord Dunmore's front door the following afternoon.

I had debated the idea all night and throughout the morning as I went about various errands. One errand, of a particularly sensitive nature, had been rather unpleasant, and I was glad for the distraction the mystery provided. There would be time enough to consider the implications of that particular errand at a later time.

In the end, I decided that it couldn't hurt to pay a call on Lord Dunmore and try to gauge his receptiveness to the idea. Though I thought that perhaps it was a foolhardy thing to do, I couldn't argue with the efficiency of it. If there was a way to get all the suspects back into the same place and to present them with an opportunity they couldn't resist, we might be able to catch the thief, and thus reveal the identity of the killer.

I arrived unannounced as Lord Dunmore had done when he dropped by the flat. I was not even certain he would be home, but I thought perhaps it would be best to make my visit appear impromptu.

The butler showed me to a magnificently decorated sitting room that was across the foyer from the ballroom, and I had not had time to seat myself in an exquisite Louis XIV chair when the viscount made his entrance. He was impeccably dressed and groomed as always, and there was an energy that came into the room with him. I thought again how easily women might find themselves captivated by his charms.

"Mrs. Ames! I'm delighted to see you." He came forward and caught my hands in his, squeezing them warmly before indicating that I should be seated. "To what do I owe the pleasure?" he asked, taking the seat across from me.

I had been caught up in Mrs. Barrington's rather contagious schemes, but now, sitting before Lord Dunmore, the entire thing seemed preposterous. It was beyond me how on earth I might convince him to parade his family's heirloom jewelry about when someone had been murdered for something much less valuable at the last ball.

"You'll think me quite mad if I tell you," I said at last.

He smiled, and it was a very charming smile. "I find madness to be much more interesting than sanity, Mrs. Ames. You have captured my attention."

"Perhaps I should start at the beginning. I visited Mrs. Barrington yesterday, and we were talking about poor Mr. Harker's death."

Was it my imagination, or did something in his expression change ever so slightly? Whatever emotion had been at the surface, he had managed to disguise it before it could make itself completely known. "And how is Mrs. Barrington faring?"

"Fairly well," I said. "She was quite fond of her nephew, so all this has been very hard on her. I think perhaps that is why she has come up with a rather strange idea."

He was wary now. I could sense it. Though his features maintained a perfectly pleasant expression, something in his posture had changed ever so slightly. Whatever else he might be, Lord Dunmore was not a stupid man. I was going to have to be careful.

"What kind of idea?" he asked, a watchful expression on his face.

Though I didn't know him well, I had rather suspected that he was the sort of man who could best be guided by subtle suggestion rather than direct requests, but I had decided to be straightforward. I wasn't sure it had paid off. I thought it unlikely I would succeed in convincing him, but I supposed I might as well go ahead with our slipshod plan while I was here.

"Mrs. Barrington thinks we may be able to convince the thief to strike again if you put the Dunmore Diamond on display."

It seemed that whatever he had been expecting me to say, this was not it. My answer appeared to actually relieve his mind in some way. "Does she, indeed? I think that sounds a bit far-fetched."

"I thought the same," I told him. "But she's a bit eccentric, isn't she? She seems to think that the thief might be willing to try again. Of course, if she happens to be right, I would hate to put either you or the Dunmore Diamond in danger."

The word "danger" seemed to have the opposite effect than I had intended.

"It is an interesting idea," he said. "I'll think it over. After all, there may be nothing to it, and there would be no harm to satisfy her whim."

I was a bit surprised. "Thank you. I'll tell

her you're considering it."

"And is that the only reason you've come, Mrs. Ames?" he asked. He had relaxed into his chair, but there was an intensity in his gaze that I might have found unnerving were I not hoping to play on his apparent interest in me as a means to an end. If I could form a friendship with him, I might be able to learn something.

I hesitated, allowing uncertainty to pass across my face. "Not the only reason, I suppose."

He waited, a vaguely expectant look on his handsome features.

"I felt perhaps that I was a bit rude to you when you called at my flat," I admitted at last. In truth, I thought I had spoken to him just as he deserved, but he was more likely to prove helpful if I was a bit more polite.

"I'm afraid I expressed myself badly," he said. "It wasn't my intention to offend you. It's just that I somehow find it difficult to mind my manners when in your company, Mrs. Ames."

He really was very good. Somehow he had wrapped an apology for his forward behavior in another advance. If I hadn't lived with Milo for nearly six years, I might have been taken in by his false repentance. As it was, I was well versed on the use of charm in lieu of sincerity.

"Well, now that we have cleared that up, perhaps we can be friends." I hoped I wasn't giving him the wrong impression, but I felt it was important to keep him on my side if I was to catch a killer.

"If we're to be friends, I wish you'd call me Alexander," he said. "It rolls off the tongue a bit more easily than Lord Dunmore."

I supposed there was no harm in it, so I nodded my assent. "If you'll call me Amory."

"I should love to."

"Well," I said, rising to my feet. "I suppose I've taken up enough of your time."

"Nonsense. I would gladly spend a good deal more time with you."

I was sure he was perfectly aware of how outrageously flirtatious he was being, but I chose to behave as though he were only being polite. "You're too kind."

He accompanied me out of the sitting room and back into the marble-floored foyer. Our footsteps echoed in the empty house. It seemed so much different, colder, without the people flowing in and out and the murmur of voices. I was very aware of Lord Dunmore's presence beside me. Something about the way he walked close by my side, yet just far enough away to avoid crowding me, bespoke more than friendly interest.

It seemed, however, that the house was not quite empty after all, for just as we reached the middle of the foyer, I saw someone come around the corner of the landing on the staircase. I was surprised to see that it was Mr. Douglas-Hughes.

I thought that he hesitated for a fraction of a second, and then, when he realized he had been seen, made his way down the rest of the stairs.

"Hello, Mrs. Ames." He greeted me warmly enough, though I had the impression he was not especially happy to see me. Or, more accurately, that I had seen him. I did wonder what he was doing here.

"Good afternoon, Mr. Douglas-Hughes." I realized suddenly that my own presence here might be construed as questionable, so I added, "I just dropped by for a few moments to speak with Lord Dunmore."

My excuse for being here did not induce him to offer his own. It was possible he was merely paying a social call on Lord Dunmore, though somehow I doubted it.

"Mamie tells me you'll be dining with us tonight," he said.

"Yes, I plan to be there."

"Good, good. I'll look forward to seeing you then." He glanced at Lord Dunmore. "No luck upstairs. Is it all right if I check the ballroom once more?"

"Certainly. I'll join you there in a moment."

Mr. Douglas-Hughes turned to me and smiled. "Until this evening, Mrs. Ames."

I watched him go and turned back to Lord Dunmore a bit expectantly.

"It seems his wife dropped an earring at the ball. He told her that he'd come and look for it. She was afraid the servants wouldn't find it."

This explanation gave me pause, and I tried to determine why.

We reached the door, and I turned and extended my hand. "Thank you for seeing me, Lord Dunmore."

He took my hand and held it.

"Alexander," he corrected. "And it was my pleasure, I assure you. I'll certainly consider Mrs. Barrington's suggestion . . . In fact, I have a proposition for you."

"Oh?" I asked warily.

"Have dinner with me tomorrow night, and I'll give you my answer."

I hesitated. On one hand, it would be an excellent opportunity to find out more about his whereabouts on the night of the murder. On the other, I suspected that too much time in his company could only lead to trouble. Though I thought I had made my disinterest in anything more than friendship quite clear, I was fairly certain that my scruples would not deter him much.

"I don't know if that would be a good idea," I said at last, sliding my hand from his grasp.

"Why not?"

"For one thing, there's bound to be talk if we're seen together."

"What if there is? After all, sometimes it's best to fight fire with fire."

I knew that he was referring to Milo and Helene Renault, but I didn't wish to discuss that, not now and not with him. Besides, just because Milo had been behaving badly didn't mean I felt any inclination to do the same.

"One fire is quite enough at present," I replied.

"Well, we needn't go out in public, if you'd rather not. I have an excellent cook. We could have a quiet dinner here."

Everything he said was perfectly proper and polite, but there was an undertone to his words, something in his body language, that let me know the invitation was for more than dinner.

"I don't think that would be a good idea either," I replied. There was something thoroughly unwholesome about Lord Dunmore, and I thought it would be best not to give him any undue encouragement.

He smiled again, a knowing smile. "Perhaps a compromise then? I know a nice, quiet place where we're not likely to be seen."

Some part of me was signaling that I needed to tread carefully, but I felt that I could scarcely refuse if I wanted him to agree to the scheme Mrs. Barrington and I had concocted.

"That might be all right," I said at last.

"Excellent. Shall I pick you up?"

I hesitated for only a fraction of a second before I nodded. "That would be lovely."

"Until tomorrow then," he said with a smile. "I shall look forward to it immensely."

I left the house and walked toward where Markham was waiting with the car. A frown furrowed my brow as I considered all that had just happened. There was something troubling me, and it wasn't only that I had just made a dinner engagement with a notorious rogue.

What really bothered me was that Mr. Douglas-Hughes had claimed that Mamie had lost an earring and that he had come to search for it. I had cast my mind back to the ball, and I was certain.

Mamie Douglas-Hughes hadn't been wearing earrings.

I was hoping for a few quiet moments when I got home to try to settle my thoughts. Alas, it was not to be.

"Mr. Ames is here, madam," said Winnelda, rushing at me with a somewhat wide-eyed, panicked expression on her face as I came in the door. The poor girl obviously thought I was going to fly into hysterics at the presence of my husband.

"Is he?" I replied calmly, removing my coat, hat, and gloves. I had not expected him, and I was not certain I was ready to see him. Nevertheless, there was nothing to be done about that now.

"Yes, madam. He's been waiting in the parlor for thirty minutes."

"Then I suppose I better not keep him."

I turned resolutely toward the parlor, irritated that he had arrived without warning. I was only glad that I had been out and he had been forced to wait. Milo hated waiting.

He was thumbing through a book, but he put it aside and stood as I came into the room. He was dressed in a light gray suit

243

and, for some absurd reason, looked even more handsome than usual. Perhaps it was a side effect of his newfound amour. I felt vaguely ill as the image of Helene Renault in his embrace flashed through my mind.

"Hello, darling," he said, completely at ease.

"Hello."

"How are you?"

"I'm fine. You needn't stand on ceremony, Milo. Sit down."

He sat, his eyes on my face, as I chose a chair on the opposite side of the room. As usual, I could determine nothing of what he was thinking from his posture or expression.

It seemed the same could not be said of me. "You're looking a bit peaked, Amory."

"Thank you," I replied wryly. "You always say the loveliest things."

"Are you feeling well?"

"I'm feeling fine, thank you." I did not bother to hide my annoyance. "Have you come to inquire after my health, or is there some other reason you're here?"

"I've come to ask you to have dinner with me," he answered, unfazed by my terseness.

I studied him, a bit surprised by this request. "Why?"

"For the pleasure of your company."

"I should have thought you had more pleasant company with which to occupy your time."

"Helene's gone back to Paris, if that's what you're wondering."

"I wasn't wondering," I snapped. His saying her name in that casual way upset me more than I liked to admit.

"She went back the night that photograph was taken. I haven't seen her since, nor do I care if I ever set eyes on her again."

It was too little too late. The damage had been done; one couldn't undo an affair by breaking it off.

"I don't want to talk about her, Milo. Her whereabouts are of no interest to me."

"They're of no interest to me either," he replied, a hint of impatience in his voice. "You'll agree, however, that we need to talk."

"Yes, but I told you I would let you know when I was ready. You said you would telephone me."

There was something in his expression that made me wary, and I soon found out that my instinct had been correct. The conversation had not gone well thus far, and so he decided to change tactics. "I've found out something rather interesting that may have a connection to James Harker's

245

murder."

He had my attention immediately, and I hated him for it. "What is it?" I asked, with barely a hint of curiosity in my tone.

His mouth tipped up at the corner, and I knew I had been had. "Come now, darling. You aren't going to feign disinterest? Not with me."

"Well, what did you learn?" I demanded, irritated that he had seen through my ruse of indifference.

"I'll tell you," he said, rising from his seat. "At dinner."

"Milo . . ."

"I'll pick you up at eight?" One dark brow was raised in what felt distinctly like a challenge.

I wavered. I was sorely tempted to tell Milo and his information to go to the devil. Then again, I was terribly curious. There was no telling what he might have learned or how important it might be to the investigation.

"Very well. If you insist," I agreed ungraciously.

He smiled, and my irritation deepened at the flutter it caused in my stomach. "Your enthusiasm flatters me," he said dryly. "I'll see you tonight."

And he left without further ado.

18

I was feeling restless, but I took a cup of tea in the parlor and tried to settle my nerves.

It was very like Milo to try to catch me off guard, and I was determined that it would not happen this time. Whatever he had to say at dinner, I was not going to allow myself to be wooed by pretty speeches . . . or even by excellent clues.

I was determined to remain unimpressed by whatever it was that he was going to tell me. After all, what could he possibly have learned? I tried to think of whom he might have encountered who would know something that might relate to Mr. Harker's murder.

The thought came to me suddenly. Frederick Garmond. Milo had recently purchased his horse, so it would be easy enough to contact him and lead the conversation along to the shocking murder of James Harker at Lord Dunmore's ball. If Mr. Garmond was distantly related to Vivian Garmond's deceased husband, perhaps Milo had learned something about her past.

Well, if he was going to tell me something about Mrs. Garmond, perhaps I could beat him to the punch. Perhaps I should try to speak to Mrs. Garmond on my own. I was vaguely aware that this newfound competitive streak might not be an exceptionally flattering trait, but I didn't much care at the moment. I was determined to trump him if I could.

But how to speak with Mrs. Garmond? I wished there was some way I could contact her without calling attention to the fact that I suspected she might be involved with murder. Then again, I could really think of no good reason why she might have murdered James Harker. Perhaps the direct approach would be best.

"Winnelda," I said. "Will you ring the operator and see if you can telephone Mrs. Vivian Garmond? I'd like to speak to her."

"Oh, she won't be at home, madam," Winnelda said. "She's gone hat shopping this afternoon."

I stared at her. "How on earth do you know that?"

"A friend of mine is the cousin of a girl who is rooming with a girl who works for

Mrs. Garmond. We're all maids, you see, so it's the sort of thing that interests us. I saw my friend at the market today, and she mentioned in a roundabout way that Mrs. Garmond always has the loveliest hats, and she was going shopping for a new one this afternoon."

"Good heavens," I breathed. "Winnelda, do you mean to tell me that information on Mrs. Garmond's whereabouts has traveled the distance of four maids in the space of one morning?"

"Oh, word gets around, madam," she said impressively.

It was certainly something worth noting. I could only imagine the sort of things that had "gotten around" about Milo and me.

She seemed to interpret my thoughts, for she added quickly, "Not that I'm much of one to gossip, Mrs. Ames. Mostly I just listen to what the others have to say."

I was suddenly struck with how useful a source of information Winnelda's connections might prove to be.

"What else have you heard about Mrs. Garmond?"

"Well," Winnelda said, "I don't like to spread tales about, but they do say that she is not receiving company from a certain gentleman as often as she has been in the past."

"Lord Dunmore, you mean?"

Winnelda nodded. Apparently, my knowledge of the situation was enough to open her informational floodgates. "Lilly — that's my friend — says that Jenny, her roommate, says that Gladys — that's Mrs. Garmond's maid — is concerned about Mrs. Garmond as of late. Gladys says she seems more than usually sad, and she's been cutting back on the household expenses, though Gladys said that she's been trying not to make it obvious."

"And yet she has the money to go hat shopping," I observed.

"Oh, well, as to that, a new hat does wonders for cheering a woman up," she told me sagely.

"You're quite right, Winnelda," I said contemplatively. "In fact, I think I may be in need of a new hat myself."

I had never visited Madame LeFleur's hat shop before. In fact, I suspected my milliner would be affronted in the extreme to know I had even set foot in a competing establishment. Nevertheless, Madame LeFleur's was familiar to me, and I could tell at once that it catered to a selective clientele. The interior was elegantly decorated with thick carpet, rose-colored silk-papered walls, and rows of beveled mirrors that reflected the light of the glittering crystal chandeliers.

At a glance, it seemed that the merchandise, displayed on assorted stands, shelves, and haughty mannequin heads, was also very high quality. The materials were expensive, the embellishments artfully arranged, and the styles the height of fashion. I was impressed.

There were only a few women in the shop at present, and none of them took notice of me as I entered. Winnelda's sources had been correct, for I saw that Mrs. Garmond was with one of the salesgirls along the wall, sitting on a stool of ivory satin. I tried to appear as though I didn't notice her as one of the other women came my way.

"How may I help you, madam?" she asked.

"I'm just looking for a nice new hat."

"Certainly. Are you looking to have something designed for you, or would you like to purchase something premade?"

I glanced around at the rather extensive inventory. "I'm certain I can find something ready-made. You seem to have a very nice selection."

"Thank you, madam. I'm sure we'll have

something that will suit you very well," she said. "Anything in particular?"

"Something modern, I think," I said. I had no real need for a hat, but Winnelda was right about the therapeutic effects of buying one. "I have nothing particular in mind, though I have a lovely red wool suit for autumn that could benefit from a new hat."

She stepped back and studied my face for a long moment, her head tilted to the side. "You have very lovely features," she pronounced at last. "You'll need something set back from the face, to frame it. I think I have just the thing. Excuse me for a moment. I'll be back directly."

"Thank you."

She walked away and began looking over the hats that rested on a shelf on the other side of the room. Her absence gave me the opportunity to try to work my way over to Mrs. Garmond.

I walked slowly along, looking at some of the creations on display. The designs were very modern, and, despite my ulterior motives for coming, I found myself looking forward to seeing what the salesgirl would bring me.

I stopped not far from Mrs. Garmond, picking up a hat in a startling shade of canary yellow. I suspected it would look ghastly with my skin tone, but I picked it up and put it on, walking toward the mirror next to the one where Mrs. Garmond sat.

She glanced my way as I approached.

"Oh," I said, feigning surprise. "Hello, Mrs. Garmond."

"Hello, Mrs. Ames." Though I wouldn't have said, exactly, that she was happy to see me, it didn't seem as though she was uncomfortable with my sudden arrival.

"That's a lovely hat," I said, indicating the one she was wearing, which was of deep garnet felt with braid detailing along the brim. She turned back to the mirror and studied it. "I do like it," she said.

It was an elegant hat, and I suspected it was likely to be expensive. If she was no longer relying on Lord Dunmore for financial support, she must have been able to keep herself in style in some other way.

The saleslady came back to me and held up a black felt hat with a narrow brim and netting and feathers that sat at a jaunty angle. I was not at all certain it would suit me, but I removed the yellow hat and took it from her. I set it on my head and surveyed myself in the mirror. I had to admit, it was a flattering style.

"Stunning," she said, with what sounded like finality. "It's perfect for you."

It seemed as though I was going to have very little say in the matter.

I turned my head to study it from another angle. It was rather a lovely little hat, and I thought it would complement my suit very well. Just because I had come to glean information did not mean I couldn't take advantage of the locale. "I'll take it," I said.

"Excellent. I'll wrap it for you. Is there anything else?"

"I think I'll look around a bit, if I may."

"Certainly. You've only to call if you need me."

"Thank you."

She took my hat away, and I glanced around at the others on display. The more I looked, the more I began to like.

I picked up a navy blue close-fitting hat with a netted veil.

"How have you been faring since the ball?" I asked Mrs. Garmond, as I put on the hat. She had made no attempt at conversation since I had greeted her, and I knew drawing her out would likely be difficult.

She turned with what could only be described as a guarded expression. "I've been fine. Why do you ask?"

"I was rather shaken up by Mr. Harker's death," I said casually, arranging the netting on my hat, my eyes on the mirror. "I can't seem to stop thinking about it."

"Oh, yes," she said, as though she had forgotten about it. "That was dreadful. So shocking."

I wondered what else had occurred at the ball to make murder of secondary interest.

"Who do you think might have done it?" I asked bluntly.

There was the faintest pause before her cool eyes met mine. "I'm sure I have no idea."

It seemed she was not going to be a font of theories.

"I was actually upstairs when it happened," I went on. "I had twisted my ankle, you see, and was resting in one of the bedrooms."

She turned and looked at me then, her gaze suddenly shrewd. It occurred to me to wonder for the first time if she might have been annoyed by the attention Lord Dunmore had paid me at the ball. I hadn't noticed her anywhere there, but that didn't mean she hadn't noticed me.

"I hope your ankle is feeling better," she said, though it seemed a response made more from politeness than sincerity. I was not making any headway in this conversation. It seemed that the more we spoke, the more aloof she became.

"Oh, it's much better, thank you. It was a lovely ball before that." I picked up another hat, one made of forest-green felt with leaf detailing.

"Alexander always throws lovely parties." There was something in her pointed use of Lord Dunmore's Christian name and the acknowledgment of their history that suddenly made me suspect that her coolness might be grounded in uncertainty over my interest in him. Her next statement confirmed it.

"You've been seeing rather a lot of him lately, so I hear."

So that was the way it was. She suspected that I was encroaching on her territory. I wondered just where she had heard that bit of inaccurate information. "Not really, no," I said. "I barely know him, in fact."

Her eyes seemed to study my face in the mirror, as though she was trying to gauge my truthfulness in it.

I thought about the dinner at Mrs. Barrington's and the night of the ball. I had seen very little interaction between the two of them. I wondered if they were simply keeping their relationship as discreet as possible. Somehow, given what I knew of Lord Dunmore, I thought that unlikely. It seemed to me that the two of them must have had a

256

falling out. Perhaps she worried that he would move on rather than return to her. Well, she needn't concern herself on my account. Even if Lord Dunmore had set his sights on me, I had no interest in a flirtation.

I wondered if there was any way I could get her to talk about what had caused them to drift apart, but, given her frigid demeanor, it seemed unlikely in the extreme. I would have to ask Winnelda to ask Lilly to ask Jenny to ask Gladys what might have transpired.

"Someone mentioned they had seen him at your flat," she said. Her tone was too casual, and I knew she was wondering what I would say.

"He dropped by in passing, to see how my ankle was mending."

I didn't know if she believed me, but she seemed to have thawed ever so slightly when she spoke again. "To tell the truth, I think he was more affected by the events of the ball than he likes to admit."

"I can imagine," I replied, wondering what she meant by this. I had detected very little sign of it in his manner yesterday. Then again, Mrs. Garmond knew him much better than I. He wouldn't have been likely to share such things with me.

"I saw him this morning," she continued, "and he mentioned how troubled he was by everything that has happened."

She'd seen him this morning, had she? Perhaps things were not as strained between them as I had believed. I wondered if he had mentioned that I had called and that we had a dinner engagement for the following evening. It might have accounted for her coolness toward me.

"I still find it hard to believe that such a thing happened under all of our noses. Did you hear the shot?" I asked.

It seemed to me that she hesitated ever so slightly before she answered. "No. I was in the ballroom at the time, and the music was too loud."

That was curious. Inspector Jones had told me that she was in one of the bedrooms when the murder had happened. For some reason, she had chosen to tell me a deliberate lie. Perhaps it was because the truth might have proved embarrassing for some reason, but there was always the chance that her lie was meant to cover something more sinister.

I picked up another hat, this one a strangely shaped brim that would be sure to draw attention, and perhaps not the positive kind. I put it on. "I had only just met Mr.

Harker at the Barringtons' dinner party. Did you know him well?"

Again, it seemed as though she hesitated. "Not very well, no. We came into contact not infrequently at social occasions, but we were not what I would call friends."

There was something in her manner that gave me the impression she was keeping something back. I had not as yet made any connection between the two of them, but I wondered if there was something she was hiding.

It was apparent I was not going to learn much more from the reticent Mrs. Garmond. I searched my mind for some other point of common interest. "I have been pleased to make the acquaintance of Mr. Foster. I have long enjoyed watching him play."

She dropped the hat pin she was holding and bent to pick it up, answering me as she did so. "I'm not very fond of tennis."

I barely heard her reply, however, for I had noticed that the collar of her blouse slipped down, and I could make out dark marks along her collarbone. Bruises.

I looked away as she sat back up, so she would not see that I had noticed. I studied a crimson beret with much more attention than it merited.

"I think that would suit you," she said, rising and gathering up her handbag and gloves. "You do look lovely in red. Good afternoon, Mrs. Ames."

"Good afternoon."

I finalized my purchases with the salesgirl and gave her the address of the flat for them to be delivered.

I left the shop not quite sure what I had accomplished. I had learned very little from Mrs. Garmond, though it was interesting that she had lied to me about her whereabouts at the time of the murder. I wondered if her lie had anything to do with the bruises. It was possible she had injured herself in some way, but the bruises had looked very much like marks left by fingers. Perhaps she and Lord Dunmore were not on friendly terms, after all.

If there was anything more she knew, I didn't think I would be able to get it out of her. I supposed I would just have to wait and see what sort of information Milo had been able to gather.

I was forced to admit that it had not been an entirely successful trip from an investigative standpoint. On a positive note, however, I had acquired five new hats.

19

A few hours later, I stood before the mirror, surveying myself with dissatisfaction. I was hard-pressed to determine what to wear to dinner with my husband. On the one hand, I felt that I should try to look as well as possible in order to keep up appearances. On the other hand, I didn't want him to think I had gone to any particular trouble on his account. I purposefully avoided wearing blue, as Milo had always preferred me in it.

The gown I had settled on was of forest-green silk that looked well with my fair skin and gave a hint of color to my gray eyes. It fit me very nicely, but it was not particularly enticing, and I decided it would do well enough. I wanted to give Milo no encouragement, for I did not have high hopes that our evening would end well.

In fact, I knew perfectly well how things would go. He would try to explain away his behavior, and I would long to believe it, despite the evidence. I knew, however, that if I gave in, we would be back where we started, with no true resolution of our problems. This made me more determined than ever that I would not give in to his charms.

He came into the house without ringing the buzzer, but I noticed that he didn't seek me out in the bedroom. Instead, I found him smoking in the parlor, listening indifferently to the radio.

He stood as I entered the room, leaning to ground out his cigarette. "Good evening, darling."

"Hello, Milo."

He came to me and brushed a kiss across my cheek. "You look stunning, as always."

Naturally, the same could be said of him. I didn't return the compliment, however. He knew perfectly well how good-looking he was and didn't need me to say so.

"Where would you like to dine tonight? Criterion?"

"As a matter of fact," I said casually, "I was hoping we could go to Restaurant Boulestin, for a change of pace."

I had not forgotten Mamie's invitation, and I did not intend to tell Milo about it until we arrived. I knew he wouldn't have agreed to dinner with company when he wanted me alone to work his wiles.

He had coerced me into dinner with the promise of information, so I felt not the slightest qualm about bringing him unknowingly to dinner with the Douglas-Hugheses.

If he suspected anything behind my unusual choice of restaurant, he gave no sign of it. It was not a restaurant we often frequented. Nevertheless, we did sometimes choose restaurants outside of our normal haunts, so the suggestion was not enough to elicit suspicion.

He helped me into my coat, and we went to our car.

We talked very little on the drive to Southampton Street. Milo knew how much I disliked talking in front of Markham, and the things we had to say to each other were of a more private nature than usual.

I had eaten at Restaurant Boulestin once or twice before. The food was excellent, and the wine-colored carpet, vibrant murals, and hanging balloon lights created a festive atmosphere.

As we walked into the restaurant, I looked about for Mrs. Douglas-Hughes. She was normally easy to spot with her flaming red hair, but I didn't see her at a quick glance. The crowded interior and bright décor proved a bit inhibitive to locating her. Luckily, a voice caught my attention.

"Good evening, Mrs. Ames."

I turned to see Nigel Foster approaching. I was happy to see him, for I had wanted the chance to converse with another of the suspects and had hoped at least one of them would be present at dinner.

"Good evening, Mr. Foster," I said warmly, as he took my hand. Though I had encountered my fair share of celebrities, I was still a bit in awe of Mr. Foster. It was not often, after all, that one came into contact with one of the greatest athletes in the country — the world, for that matter.

"Mrs. Douglas-Hughes said that we should perhaps expect you," he told me with a smile. "I was glad to hear it, for I'd been hoping for the opportunity to see you again."

His gaze turned to Milo, whom he had apparently just noticed behind me. While he was too polite to show surprise, I could see the interest in his expression. Mamie had not known Milo would be attending, and I supposed that Mr. Foster, like the rest of London, had heard about Milo's latest scandal. It seemed very unlikely that we should be dining together, but perhaps it would do something to quiet the rumors a bit.

"Good evening, Mr. Ames."

"Good evening," Milo said, and I detected the slightest trace of wariness in his tone. He was beginning to suspect something was afoot.

"You're joining us, aren't you?" Mr. Foster invited. "Our table is just over here."

Milo spoke up before I had the chance. "I'm afraid we won't be able to . . ."

I elbowed him in the side, none too gently.

". . . refuse such an invitation," he finished smoothly.

"Excellent! We'll be delighted to have you both."

He turned and began making his way through the crowded room toward a table in the corner. Milo took my arm as we followed him and leaned down to speak in my ear. "For the record, I took your rather aggressive cue unwillingly. I didn't intend to share you this evening with other gentlemen, celebrated athletes or no."

"It's not a matter of sharing."

"Indeed? You must have missed the way Mr. Foster looked at you before he noticed me standing there."

"Oh, posh," I said. "This dinner may be an opportunity to learn something important, Milo. We can talk about your peccadillos another time."

"Amory . . ."

I ignored him and reached the table before he could ply me with excuses.

The gentlemen rose as Mr. Foster pulled out my chair and we all exchanged pleasantries. The party consisted of Mr. and Mrs. Douglas-Hughes, Mr. Foster, a member of Parliament and his wife, and, to my surprise, Marjorie Echols. She was seated beside Mr. Foster, and I couldn't help but wonder if they had come together. Miss Echols did not display any sign of particular affection toward him. In fact, if I read her body language correctly, she seemed a bit uncomfortable beside him. Or perhaps it was only nerves or the excitement of being out with so famous a gentleman.

"I'm so glad you could join us, Amory," Mamie said warmly, her eyes moving from Milo to me and back again, "and you too, Mr. Ames."

"We're delighted," Milo said, with the appearance of perfect sincerity.

He was, of course, the picture of politeness; charm was a natural reflex for him. Nevertheless, I could sense his unwillingness to be a part of the group. I felt a bit bad about tricking him into a dinner party, but he might as well prove useful while he was here.

I leaned close to him. "Talk to Miss Echols about the murder," I instructed in a low voice. I had seen her bold eyes sweeping appreciatively over him since we had arrived at the table, and I was certain she would be more than happy to reveal to him whatever it was that she might know. If it was true that her sister and Mr. Harker had been involved with one another, Milo would be able to find out.

He let out an impatient breath, but a moment later he turned to her and began a conversation. He was apparently making headway, for her throaty laugh could be heard every so often, though I couldn't make out in the din of the room what they were saying to one another.

We all made pleasant, superficial conversation, but as the main course came I became impatient to try to learn something.

"I spoke with Mrs. Barrington yesterday," I said aloud, by way of easing the conversation around to murder. "She seems to be doing fairly well."

"The poor thing," Mamie said. "I feel so sorry for her. It must have been simply awful to lose someone like that."

"I didn't know Mr. Harker very well," I

267

said to Mr. Foster. "What was he like?"

"I'm afraid I didn't know him very well either," Mr. Foster admitted. "Mr. Barrington and I are friends, but I never spent much time in Mr. Harker's company. He seemed a pleasant fellow."

"We'd been to dinner at the Barringtons' several times when he was there, so we got to know him in a casual way," Mamie said. "He was so quiet, I'd often forget he was there . . . until he made some sort of outlandish remark that caught everyone off guard."

"Mamie," Mr. Douglas-Hughes said in an affectionately warning tone. "There's no need bringing that up."

"I didn't really mean to, Sandy," she replied. "But now that you've said it, I'll have to or everyone will simply die of curiosity."

"Oh, yes," I said lightly. "You must tell us now."

"Certainly," Mr. Foster joined in. "You can't dangle something like that in front of us and then refuse to tell us. We're all quite curious."

I saw Mr. Douglas-Hughes give his wife a subtle shrug, as though he knew she was going to go on with the story, so he might as well not oppose it. There was an affectionate resignation in his gaze, and I marveled at how easily I could read the fondness between the two of them.

"It was at dinner a few weeks ago," she said. "You were there at the time, Mr. Foster, though perhaps you weren't sitting near enough to hear what was said. We were all admiring Mrs. Barrington's jewelry when Mr. Harker commented quite loudly that she didn't really need such a collection, and it would be better off given to someone who could really use it."

I stilled, my fork halfway to my mouth as I took in this information. I glanced at Milo. His eyes were focused disinterestedly on the glass in his hand, but I knew him well enough to suspect that he was listening very carefully to what was being said.

"I supposed Mr. Harker felt strongly about some social cause he wanted to support," Mamie said, "but it made things a little awkward for all of us, the way he said it. Of course, it was sweet of him to care for the needy, and it just shows what sort of person that he was."

I glanced at Marjorie Echols. There was an odd expression on her face, but it was gone almost instantly, and I half wondered if I had imagined it.

"Poor Jim was always saying the strangest

things," she said, and her voice sounded strained beneath its artificial cheerfulness. "He was rather a dear, though. I'm sorry he's gone."

I wondered again if it was possible that she had been in love with him. It didn't seem likely. Her personality seemed ill-suited to someone like Mr. Harker. Stranger things had been known to happen, however.

"He always seemed a pleasant fellow to me," Mr. Foster put in. I saw him glance at Marjorie as he said it, and I suspected he was trying to soothe her feelings. I thought it kind of him to do so, though she didn't acknowledge his comment.

I had picked up my water glass when Mamie caught my eye. She raised her brows slightly and made a subtle nod toward the doorway. "I think I need to visit the powder room," she said to the table. "If you'll excuse me."

"I'll come with you," I said, taking her cue. "My makeup could use a bit of freshening up."

The gentlemen rose as we did, and I followed Mamie from the room. We entered the powder rooms. A row of red satin chairs sat before a long vanity that stretched along one wall. There was a woman there reapplying her lipstick, so I followed Mamie's lead and removed my compact from my handbag as we took two of the seats. We powdered our noses until the other woman had finished and left the room.

When the door had closed behind her, Mamie turned to me excitedly.

"I didn't want to say anything more at the table, but I thought of something else, the thing that was bothering me that I couldn't remember. It was at that same dinner. Before he said the charity line, he blurted out" — she affected an excellent British accent — " 'It's more the sort of thing a man would use to woo his mistress than give to his wife. Certainly you've no need for such adornments, Aunt Serena.' "

My brows rose. That was an interesting comment indeed.

"He then went on to say that he thought it would be better to donate things to the needy. I think it made her a bit uncomfortable."

"What sort of jewelry was it?" I questioned casually.

"I don't remember. It might have been a necklace. I really just remember how Mrs. Barrington looked so funny when he said it. It was as though he had struck some sort of nerve. I assume she was embarrassed at the crassness of the mistress remark, or perhaps at his insinuation that charity might be a better use for money. It wasn't really the thing to say at dinner."

"That is quite interesting," I said slowly, turning it over in my mind.

It was strange that Mr. Harker should have equated the jewelry to something one would give a mistress and that Mrs. Barrington had appeared deeply affected by the comment. Of course, it might have just been one of his awkward outbursts that had mortified her, but perhaps there was more to it than that.

Mrs. Barrington had made no mention of this incident, and I wondered if the piece of jewelry in question was one of the pieces that had gone missing. I would have to question her about it later.

"I wanted to tell you, but I didn't like to say it at the table. I thought it might make things unpleasant with talk of mistresses . . ." She stopped suddenly, a blush creeping over her face. "Well, now I suppose I've put my foot in my mouth."

"You've seen the photograph," I said.

"Yes. I don't like those awful gossip magazines, but I heard about it. And now I've blurted it out after speaking ill of poor Mr. Harker for doing just such a thing. I hope I haven't offended you."

"Not at all." It certainly wasn't her fault that Milo was incapable of behaving himself.

"It's really none of my business," she said. "Only, I know what it's like to be scrutinized by the press. If you'd like to talk about it, I'm willing to listen."

I hesitated. I was unaccustomed to discussing my private affairs with others, but there was something about Mamie's warm personality that made me feel I could confide in her.

I closed my compact, slipping it back into my handbag. "It has caused no small amount of strife, as I'm sure you can imagine."

"Did . . . did he admit to it, then?" she asked, concern apparent on her features.

"No," I answered wearily. "He says it's not what it appears to be."

"Well, maybe it's not." There was something so hopeful in her expression, I almost felt as though I should feel sorry for her and not the other way around.

"That would be easier to believe if it had never happened before," I said, looking at my expressionless reflection in the mirror. "But this is not the first time. Not nearly the first time."

"Oh. I see."

I managed a smile. Somehow the telling

of it was a relief. "There have always been explanations, of course. He's very good at making excuses. And thus far I've been very good at believing them. But it's easier to explain away a strange woman clinging to his arm than it is one kissing him on the mouth."

"He's terribly handsome," she said absently. "I suppose women are bound to flock to him." She blushed suddenly. "I suppose that was an impertinent thing to say. I'm sorry. Sometimes things come out before I have a chance to think them through."

I laughed. "You needn't worry about that. I find it refreshing when people say what they're really thinking."

"I only meant that I suppose women throw themselves at him without much encouragement."

"Yes, well, he isn't required to do such an efficient job of catching them."

She smiled a bit sadly at my response. "You're right, of course. But you're here together tonight. So are things on the mend? You're not . . . considering a divorce?"

"Divorce is not an easy thing in England," I said carefully.

She nodded. "I understand it's much more complicated here. It only takes six weeks in America, if you fly to Reno. It's almost too easy."

Six weeks. I wondered fleetingly if Milo and I would still be married now, were things so simple in this country.

"One can't simply obtain a divorce in England," I told her. "There must be proof of infidelity. I've known of couples who wanted a divorce and couldn't obtain one because neither of them was actually unfaithful. The husband has arranged to be 'caught' with a woman in a hotel."

"How very scandalous," she whispered.

"I believe it is usual for the husband to take the blame. However, in my case, there's no need for that pretense."

"I'm sorry," she said, and I was touched by the sincerity in her expression. Absurdly, I almost felt the need to comfort her.

"Nothing's been decided," I said. "I suppose I'll cross that bridge if it comes to it."

She held out her hand and gripped mine warmly. "I hope things work out for you, Amory. I truly do."

"Thank you, Mamie."

One could always hope.

I took my lipstick from the handbag, and a thought came to me suddenly. "I meant to ask you, did you find your earring?" I asked in a casual way as I applied a fresh coat to my lips.

"Earring?" she repeated absently, tucking a strand of her bright red hair behind her ear.

"I saw Mr. Douglas-Hughes at Lord Dunmore's house, and he said he was there looking for an earring you had misplaced at the ball."

It seemed to me she hesitated ever so slightly before she rose to her feet. "Oh, yes," she said. "I found it in our car. I suppose we'd better go back to the table before they miss us."

20

I felt, somehow, disappointed by Mamie's lie. Try as I might to reason it away, I could think of no reason why both she and her husband should claim she had lost an earring when she had not been wearing any at the ball. It was depressingly suspicious.

It was still on my mind as we said good night to the party and made our way out of the restaurant.

"I must say that was very well played, my dear," Milo said, as we stepped out into the night air.

"What do you mean?" I asked innocently, though I knew perfectly well to what he was referring.

"This business of allowing me to believe we were going to dinner to talk and instead dragging me into your little schemes."

"We're talking now, aren't we?" I asked, moving toward the car.

He caught my arm before we reached it.

"Wait a moment. I want to talk to you, Amory."

"We can talk on the way to the flat."

"In front of Markham?" he asked, brows raised inquiringly. He had me there, for he knew perfectly well where I stood on that score.

I sighed. "Very well. Then you may come up for a while."

"You know perfectly well that we cannot have a decent conversation with Winnelda creeping about the house."

"She's probably gone to bed by now."

"I want to be alone with you," he said in a low voice, and I ignored the little thrill the words evoked. I absolutely refused to fall prey to his charms this evening.

"Why?" I challenged.

"Because I have things I need to say."

I considered this, and he seemed to take my silence for assent.

"I'm staying at the Ritz. We can talk there."

"I don't think so, Milo."

"Why not?"

Our eyes met, and I could read the challenge in his. It wasn't that I didn't trust him. It was that I didn't trust myself. I was honest enough to acknowledge that I was entirely too vulnerable where Milo was concerned. Still, I wavered. Some ridiculous and hopelessly romantic part of me still hoped there was a chance to mend things.

"Please," he asked softly. "Just for a little while."

I sighed, unwilling to argue with him or myself any longer. "Very well. But only for a little while."

After a short drive, we pulled up in front of the hotel, the imposing façade aglow, and Milo assisted me from the car. The evening had grown cool, and I was very aware of the warmth of him beside me.

"I'll be down in an hour, Markham," I said.

"Very good, madam."

Milo took my arm, and we walked into the hotel and across the bright, gleaming lobby to the lift.

We arrived on his floor; walked down the long, carpeted hallway; and entered his suite of rooms. He switched on the lights, and I glanced around. The sitting room was lovely, with high ceilings, ivory walls and carpeting, and expensive furniture arranged around a marble fireplace. I could see through open French doors the adjoining bedroom and bath.

Milo helped me with my coat, and I took

a seat on the blue and yellow patterned sofa as he ordered coffee for me and then moved to pour himself a drink. It felt strange to be a guest visiting my husband's accommodations, and I felt somehow that I didn't want to discuss our marriage, not just yet.

"What is it that you've learned about the murder?" I asked him. "You told me you'd tell me at dinner."

"I have half a mind to keep it to myself after your little charade this evening," he replied, putting the glass stopper back in the decanter. "That was not how I had planned to spend my evening."

"I already had the engagement with the Douglas-Hugheses when you asked me to dinner; I thought I could kill two birds with one stone."

"Yes, well, stoning might have been preferable to an evening spent sitting next to that Echols woman."

"She seemed to find you charming."

He shot me a look as he took a seat beside me, drink in hand, and loosened his necktie. "She's certainly a talkative little thing."

"Did you learn anything interesting? Did she say anything about her sister and Mr. Harker?"

"She mentioned that they all spent a good deal of time together. There was a nightclub they enjoyed frequenting, the Sparrow, or some such ridiculous name."

I tucked that bit of information away for possible use in the future.

"Don't get any ideas, Amory," he said warningly, reading my thoughts with frustrating accuracy.

I ignored him. "Do you think she was in love with Mr. Harker?"

"Hardly. I imagine she and her sister found Mr. Harker something of an easy target."

"Using him for his money, you mean?"

"That would be my guess."

I wondered about Mr. Harker's financial situation. I hadn't even considered that possibility before now. "Was he well off, do you suppose?"

"Comfortably, I assume. His father was Mrs. Barrington's brother. The family is well off, I should say, though not exactly rolling in money."

I considered that for a moment. James Harker seemed the sort of sweet, vague young man who might be easily taken advantage of by a woman of the world. Might his money have had something to do with his death?

"What else did you learn?" I asked.

"Nothing much else tonight, but I telephoned Frederick Garmond and asked him about Vivian Garmond. Her deceased husband was only a distant cousin, but Garmond said the cousin went abroad a few years ago and died. Shortly after, Mrs. Garmond came home with a baby and the somewhat dubious account of their marriage. The family's accepted it, but it's commonly assumed that Dunmore got her pregnant and refused to marry her."

Milo's information was as I had suspected, then. That was much the same thing that Mrs. Roland had told me. I felt somewhat smug that Milo had not learned anything new.

"It's possible that James Harker knew something she wanted kept quiet," I said. "That seems unlikely, but I suppose we can't discount it. Winnelda also has it through her own little jungle telegraph that Mrs. Garmond has been having financial difficulties. It may be that she was desperate enough to steal the jewelry and Mr. Harker's death was an unfortunate by-product."

"That could be. However, her questionable widowhood was not the extent of his information. Garmond had something rather interesting to say about the Barringtons as well."

I looked at him, surprised. "What did he say?"

"To begin with, things aren't going as well as their lifestyle seems to indicate. Mr. Barrington had several investments that went awry."

"You mean they're not as wealthy as they seem to be?"

"That is exactly what I mean. Until very recently, Mr. Barrington had been losing money hand over fist. I understand things have been improving, but it will be difficult for him to recoup his losses, and things remain somewhat precarious."

I thought back to the night of the dinner party. Mrs. Barrington had mentioned taking a flat for convenience. Perhaps she had said it so that it wouldn't come as a surprise if they were forced to sell their house.

I considered the possible implications of this news. "Do you think she might have been selling her jewels and only claiming that they had gone missing?"

"It's possible, I suppose. What better way to acquire some much-needed funds than by selling off the jewelry? It could have been done inconspicuously."

"It would have been strange for her to ask for my help in locating them if she had taken them herself. Unless . . ."

"She was planning a murder," Milo and I said at the same time.

I smiled at him. In moments like this, when there was harmony between us, it was so very easy to talk to him. I wished it could always be that way. He must have noticed the wistful look on my face, for his expression grew more serious. "What is it?"

I shook my head, unwilling to unburden myself just now. "Nothing. Was there anything else you learned?"

He was still watching me, and I knew that he could tell that there was something more on my mind. He decided against pressing me, however, and let the subject drop for the time being.

"Yes, in fact. Not only are the Barringtons not as financially secure as they once were, I gather there was no love lost between Mr. Barrington and James Harker."

Mrs. Roland had mentioned as much, but I still found it surprising. "I thought the Barringtons were very fond of him."

"His aunt is, perhaps, but I was given to believe that Mr. Barrington was less than pleased with his nephew's contribution to the family financial situation. And, as you have heard, James Harker had the charming habit of putting his foot in his mouth."

"That seems to be the general consensus.

Were there any particular instances of note?"

"I gather Mr. Harker let slip at a dinner party that the family coffers were dwindling. Mr. Barrington was attempting to arrange some sort of business transaction with a gentleman who was present, but the deal later fell through. No doubt Mr. Barrington attributed this to Mr. Harker's careless talk."

"Mr. Garmond told you all of this?"

"Not all of it. I had an interesting conversation or two at my club. Mr. Barrington is an amiable and well-liked gentleman, but that doesn't mean people aren't willing to share bad tidings. People enjoy spreading word of misfortune much more than they do good news."

I was strangely glad that he had taken the trouble to glean what information he could from the members of his club. He had done it because he knew that it would please me.

"Who do you suppose inherits Mr. Harker's money?" I asked.

A glint showed in Milo's eyes. "That would be interesting to know, wouldn't it?"

Interesting indeed. Mr. Harker had been unmarried. It was entirely possible that his money would go to his nearest relations. I wondered cynically if Mr. and Mrs. Barrington might fall under this category.

Milo seemed to be considering this as well. "If Mrs. Barrington was planning a murder, it would have been strange of her to call attention to it. Unless she was attempting to throw us off the scent. That seems unlikely, however. She doesn't seem as though she would be inclined to create an elaborate setting for a crime she planned to commit."

"Mr. Barrington may have done it," I suggested. "If he didn't care for his nephew and knew about the earlier thefts, perhaps he used the opportunity to revenge himself. Or perhaps he was still angry with Harker about his past indiscretions. Then again, Mr. Harker has likely been making a nuisance of himself all of his life. Why should Mr. Barrington be more likely to kill him now than at any other time? I suppose it could have been a matter opportunity?"

Milo looked unconvinced. "At Lord Dunmore's ball? He could have easily killed him somewhere else much more conveniently and with much less risk of being caught."

I had to admit he had a point. "It was risky, wasn't it?" A thought came to me suddenly. "How did the killer know that he or she would be able to get away with it? There were people everywhere on the first floor. It seems that the killer must have used the opportunity to kill him rather than having planned it ahead of time."

"That makes sense," Milo agreed. "I think we may safely say that the murder was not premeditated."

"Nigel Foster seems a very unlikely candidate," I said, moving on to the other suspects. "Though he and Mr. Harker had some contacts, I don't see any reason why he might have killed him. Besides, I doubt he would risk his storied career over a few jewels."

"Not to mention murder is very unsportsmanlike," Milo added dryly.

"There is something else strange." I told of the story Mr. and Mrs. Douglas-Hughes had given about the missing earring. "If she didn't really lose her jewelry, what could Mr. Douglas-Hughes have been searching for?"

"Perhaps he hid the bracelet and went back for it."

"No," I said. "I refuse to believe Mr. and Mrs. Douglas-Hughes might have had anything to do with the murder."

Milo smiled indulgently. "So Sandy and his lovely wife have been singled out for your special brand of amnesty this time around. I've told you before, darling. You can't choose the people you like best and excuse them from your suspect list."

"I have an instinct," I responded archly.

"Ah."

"Mr. Douglas-Hughes is a very respectable gentleman. I can't imagine him participating in something as sordid as this. And Mamie . . . well, she's so very sweet and elegant. No," I said firmly. "I've made up my mind. Neither of them could possibly be the killer."

"I'll admit, Mrs. Douglas-Hughes is rather charming for an American. Her past is shaded in mystery, however. A musical revue seems a hotbed of sordid secrets. As for Douglas-Hughes, I imagine he has a great many secrets of his own. And James Harker was known for ferreting things out."

"They've already been picked apart by the press. What would one more secret matter?"

"People have been known to kill for less."

"You are so frightfully pragmatic this evening, Milo."

He smiled. "That, my dear, is the first time in my life I have ever been accused of that."

The coffee came then, and we settled into comfortable silence until the waiter had gone.

"This is a very lovely room," I said, looking about as I sipped my coffee.

When my eyes fell on Milo, I saw that he was looking at me intently, and I had to fight down the flutter in my stomach.

"No hotel can compare to one's home. I long to return to the comforts of a soft bed and a warm wife . . . or perhaps the other way around. How long is my banishment going to last?"

When he looked at me that way, it was so very difficult to forget how much I loved him.

"I don't know," I replied, summoning up my resolve. "I need time to think about everything, but, truthfully, I don't like to think about it. I'm sure you can understand that it's rather unpleasant for me."

"Will you let me tell you what happened?"

I looked into his eyes, trying to gauge his sincerity. "Will you be honest with me?"

"Yes."

"I'd rather the ugly truth than your pretty lies, Milo."

"I'll tell you the truth." He set his drink on the table and turned to face me. "It was one kiss. Nothing before, nothing after."

"Why did you kiss her?" I asked softly.

"I didn't kiss her. She kissed me. I didn't know she was going to do it."

"And poor, helpless thing that you are, you couldn't stop her," I said sardonically.

"Will you let me finish?"

I waved a hand for him to continue. I could already tell that I was going to find his story ridiculous, but I would give him the benefit of the doubt.

"They must have snapped the photograph at exactly the right time, for as soon as she did it, I disentangled myself from her. I dropped her off at her hotel immediately, and that was the last I've seen of her. There was never anything more to it than that. Everything before that was just rumor, and she apparently began to believe it."

"What were you doing with her to begin with? You told me you were going to Bedfordshire."

"I did go to Bedfordshire. I met her at the train station, and she asked me to have a drink with her. I didn't see any harm in it."

I sighed. "You don't expect me to believe that you didn't know her intentions when she's displayed such obvious interest in your company."

"I wasn't interested in her. I thought that was the material thing."

"No, Milo," I said. "The material thing is that you see nothing wrong with your behavior. Even if your highly questionable account of events happens to be true, even if that was the only time you've ever kissed her, it doesn't matter. If this is all some grand misunderstanding, as you claim, it still doesn't account for the fact that you care nothing about how things look."

"Why should I?" he replied. "Why should I care what people think?"

"Because I do," I replied, trying to keep my voice steady. "I'm tired of being made to look the fool. I know what people say: 'Poor Mrs. Ames suffers in silence as her husband parades his mistresses through the society columns.' Well, I'm not going to suffer in silence, Milo. Not anymore."

"I've told you. There was nothing in it."

"There's no use in going round and round about it," I said tiredly. "If I can't make you understand why I dislike your spending time dining and kissing and heaven knows what else with other women, then there's nothing else to be said."

I set my coffee on the table and stood, and he stood with me.

"Amory, this is quite ridiculous."

"I went to see Mr. Ludlow this morning," I said suddenly. I hadn't expected to share the fact that my unpleasant errand earlier in the day had been a visit to our solicitor, but now it seemed the moment to make it known. "I think you should know that I consulted him on the various . . . options that are open to me."

This news, I think, caught him off guard, for I saw the barest hint of surprise cross his features before it was smoothed away. "You don't mean to tell me that you're really serious about all of this?"

"Of course I'm serious," I replied, meeting his gaze levelly. "I've never been more in earnest in my life."

"You're thinking of divorcing me?" He asked the question in an expressionless voice, but his eyes on my face held an unusual intensity.

I shrugged helplessly. "Perhaps there's nothing else to be done. Perhaps we don't belong together . . ."

"Don't be absurd."

"There's no need for us to keep up the pretense of being happy if we're not. We wouldn't be the first couple of our acquaintance who . . . who couldn't make a go of it."

"I believe we said 'for as long as we both shall live.' "

If the moment had not been what it was, I might have laughed at the irony of his quoting our wedding vows.

"We said a lot of things, Milo. You don't get to pick and choose which apply."

"You know perfectly well you don't want

a divorce. For one thing, it will cause . . ."

"What?" I challenged. "Scandal? Embarrassment? Well, better to put up with it for a few months than for the rest of my life."

We looked at one another, and I could no longer read anything in his bright blue eyes.

"You've made up your mind, then?" His voice had gone cool, and I recognized that there would be no impassioned entreaties. I hadn't wanted any, but somehow I found myself disheartened that he should capitulate so easily.

"No," I replied, straining to keep my voice even. "I haven't said that. I only know I can't go on with the way things have been."

He didn't reply, and I picked up my coat. "We'll talk again later, Milo. Good night."

I went down to the lobby alone and waited for Markham to return and take me home.

21

I judged the evening to have been a catastrophic failure as far as my marriage was
concerned, and I was utterly exhausted by
the time I reached home. The day had been
much too eventful, and my head was fairly
swimming.

I hadn't meant for things to unravel so
rapidly with Milo, but I supposed it was
time for things to come to a head. He knew
now where I stood, and it was up to him to
determine what he meant to do about it. I
tried to fight back the nagging worry that
he might follow the path of least resistance
and allow me to divorce him.

Despite my unease and agitation over all
that had occurred, I had scarcely slid
beneath the sheets before I was sleeping
soundly.

I slept much later than usual, and before I
could rise, Winnelda came bustling into the
room with a tray of toast and coffee. "I

thought perhaps you'd enjoy breakfast in bed this morning, madam," she said cheerily.

"That's very kind of you, Winnelda."

As a matter of fact, I was still feeling rather drained from the events of last evening, and the prospect of lounging abed for another hour was distinctly appealing.

She set the tray down, arranging things on it for a few moments before stepping back and allowing me to pick up my coffee cup.

"Thank you."

She stood waiting, and I looked up at her expectantly. I had come to recognize that expression of barely concealed eagerness. "Is there something you want to talk about?"

"You're ever so perceptive, madam," she said with a smile. "You always seem to know just what I'm thinking. As a matter of fact, there is something I wanted to tell you. I've heard something rather strange from Lilly this morning, and I thought you might want to know about it."

"Have you?" I replied with interest. "What was it?"

"It's rather scandalous," she warned.

"I'm certain my nerves will bear up," I reassured her, stirring sugar and milk into my coffee.

"Well, Mrs. Garmond came home from her hat shopping yesterday, and Gladys said she was acting rather strange."

"Indeed?"

"Gladys says she's normally so very calm, but it seemed as though something had upset her."

I brought my coffee cup to my lips, contemplating this bit of news. She had encountered me at the hat shop. I wondered if I had somehow brought about this unexpected reaction.

"She had ordered dinner, but then she went out again without eating" — Winnelda paused for dramatic effect before adding, with significance — "and did not return home until this morning."

My brows rose. "I see."

There were, certainly, plausible explanations for her overnight absence, but I also thought it quite possible that she had gone to see Lord Dunmore, and that he had induced her to stay the night with him. If that was the case, however, what was it that had upset her, and why had she sought him out when they were rumored not to be on the best of terms?

"Weren't the servants worried when she didn't arrive home?" I asked.

Winnelda lifted her eyebrows. "I'm afraid

it's not the first time it's happened, madam. In fact, Gladys says that it used to be a fairly regular turn of events, up until recently."

"Thank you for telling me, Winnelda," I said, taking another sip of my coffee as I turned this bit of information around in my mind. "That is very interesting indeed."

I found I could not remain in bed after breakfast, for I felt a nervous energy and the desire to do something useful.

I decided that the next best course of action would be for me to speak again to Mrs. Barrington. Given what I had learned the last few days, I had several questions for her. I also needed to let her know that Lord Dunmore had agreed to consider dangling the Dunmore Diamond before the thief.

I rang her up, and she said that she would come to see me. In typical fashion, she wasted no time. She had arrived at the flat in less than an hour. I had barely had time to bathe and dress before Winnelda was showing her into the sitting room.

She settled herself in a chair, waving away my offer of coffee or tea. "Have you spoken with Lord Dunmore?"

"Yes, he says he will consider it."

"That's better than a flat no, I suppose," she mused. "Was there some other reason you wished to see me, Mrs. Ames?"

I decided it would be best to come directly to the point. She was not the type of woman who needed — or wanted — to be treated with delicacy. "Mrs. Barrington, someone mentioned last night that at a dinner party a few weeks ago, Mr. Harker had made a comment about a piece of your jewelry, and how it reminded him of a piece that someone would give to his mistress."

Mrs. Barrington's eyes widened. "Who told you that?"

"Mrs. Douglas-Hughes mentioned it," I said, seeing no point in concealing it. "I was trying to get information that might prove useful, and she recalled the incident."

Mrs. Barrington frowned. "James didn't mean anything by that. He was simply jesting with me. He was always saying strange things. It was just a way he had. He didn't know when he was being inappropriate."

"Did Mr. Harker have a mistress?" I asked.

"No," she said quickly. "James was a timid boy. He enjoyed spending time with the Echols girls because they're so lively, but it was never anything serious. If you think he would have wanted to give my jewels to one of them, it isn't so. James lacked cleverness, at times, but he wasn't stupid. The Echols girls could never have worn my pieces in public; I would have noticed. In any event, as I've said before, he knew the bracelet at the ball was paste. He would have had no reason to try to steal it."

"Which piece was it he referred to at dinner, do you recall?"

It seemed as though she wavered indecisively before saying, "It was the diamond bracelet, the second piece to go missing, but I can assure you it had nothing to do with the murder."

I had the sudden sensation that she was denying it too strenuously. I wondered if pressing her was the best course of action under the circumstances, but I had the distinct feeling that there was something she was holding back.

"Mrs. Barrington, is there anything you know? Anything you're not saying?"

"Of course not, Mrs. Ames!" she cried, a bit too spiritedly. "If I knew anything that could help to catch James's killer, I would certainly reveal it to you."

"Very good. We shall just have to hope that something else comes to light." For the time being, there was nothing more to be said.

Mrs. Barrington left, and Winnelda brought me coffee in the sitting room. I sipped it contemplatively. It seemed to me that Mrs. Barrington's story was not quite holding together. There had been something secretive in her manner today, as though there was something she wanted to keep from me.

I wondered if I was being unjustly suspicious. It was possible I was being influenced by what Milo had told me about the Barringtons' financial difficulties. Just because things were a bit tight for them, however, didn't mean that they would have had anything to do with the death of their nephew. Indeed, it seemed almost out of the question. Almost.

Without my meaning to think of him, my thoughts drifted to Milo. I wondered what he was doing at this moment. I wouldn't have been half surprised to find out he had decided to dash off to Nice or some such place without informing me. He tended to bolt at the most inopportune times.

Nevertheless, I could not help but hope that he had taken some of what I told him last night to heart. It had been difficult for me to speak so directly to him. I was accustomed to sidestepping our marital difficulties at every turn. However, I had come to the point where I could no longer remain silent on the subject. Five years had been too long. I was perfectly aware that my ultimatum might have been the nail in the coffin for our marriage. It was not something I took lightly. In addition to the heartbreak it would cause me, I was perfectly aware of the scandal that would ensue, of the social repercussions that would result if my marriage came to an end. But if that was the way it had to be, so be it. I had meant what I had said, and I would live with the consequences.

I stood up. I was feeling too restless to simply sit here. I was tired of thinking about things. I wanted to do something. But what?

My thoughts turned again to the apparent motive for murder. The missing jewelry seemed to be at the center of all of this, but where had it gone? Not only the paste bracelet from the ball but also Mrs. Barrington's other pieces. They had to be somewhere. Furthermore, where had the genuine sapphire come from? It seemed to have materialized out of thin air to vex me.

A thought came to me suddenly. If the thief had stolen Mrs. Barrington's jewelry out of desperation, it was just as possible that he or she would have tried to sell them already. I wonder if the police had investigated that possibility. I also wondered how one went about selling such things.

Winnelda seemed to have knowledge

301

about a wide range of things from her maid friends. I wondered if she could prove useful in this case.

"Winnelda," I asked casually as she came back into the room, "if one was interested in selling stolen jewelry, how do you suppose one would go about it?"

"I'm sure I wouldn't know, madam!" she exclaimed, properly scandalized by my question. "If you're missing jewelry, I can only tell you that I know nothing about it, and that I would never in a million years . . ."

"No, no," I assured her quickly. "I'm not missing anything. I am just wondering where such a transaction might take place."

She looked close to tears, and I felt bad for having frightened her.

"I only meant that, since you know so many people, you might have heard tales of where people would go to do such a thing."

"I don't keep company with *those* types of maids, madam," she said with great dignity.

"Certainly not, Winnelda," I soothed. "But it would be most useful to me if you could think of anyplace where one might dispose of jewelry secondhand."

"Well," she said, seemingly pacified by my appeal to her knowledge. "Lilly had a ring from her aunt that she was forced to sell when she lost her place once. She said she went to a shop on Whitechapel High Street. There are ever so many shops that way where one might sell things, jewelry and the like. I remember once, too, that Gladys told me she thought that Mrs. Garmond might have sold some of her jewelry from Lord Dunmore."

She had piqued my interest now. "Indeed?"

"Yes, Gladys heard her mention Whitechapel, and it was not the type of place that Mrs. Garmond would normally frequent, Mrs. Garmond being a fine lady. Gladys got to thinking about what Lilly had said about selling things and how Mrs. Garmond has been cutting back on expenses and thought she must have gone to sell some jewelry."

"Whitechapel High Street, you say," I mused. An idea was beginning to take shape in my mind.

"It's not a very nice place, though, madam. In fact, I think it's dangerous. One's always hearing about women being killed in Whitechapel, cut to ribbons and other sordid things."

I thought perhaps Winnelda was a bit out of date in her reading on that score.

"Besides," she added, as something of an

anticlimax, "they didn't give Lilly half of what her ring was worth."

"I don't think we need worry much about that, Winnelda."

She looked quite unconvinced. "Begging your pardon, madam, you're not thinking of selling anything?"

"Oh, no, certainly not." I thought it best to refute the idea quickly, before Lilly, Gladys, and company received news that I had begun to rid myself of all the jewelry Milo had given me. "In fact, I'm looking to buy something."

"Not from one of those places, surely? You're much too fine a lady to go to someplace like that," Winnelda protested. "With your lovely clothes and your elegant manner, they're bound to recognize you as quality and try to get too much money out of you."

"Perhaps you're right. I'd much rather shop in Mayfair."

"Oh, yes. It's ever so much nicer." Satisfied, for the moment, that she had done her part to discourage my strange whims, she went off to put the coffee things away.

I sat for a moment, the possibilities running through my head. If I could find Mrs. Barrington's jewels, it was very likely I would be able to determine who had stolen them.

I found it very interesting that Mrs. Garmond was known to have visited Whitechapel. Could it be that she had been selling the jewelry she had stolen from Mrs. Barrington?

There was only one way to find out.

While I knew that I had very little hope of stumbling across Mrs. Barrington's jewels in the first shop I visited, it was my thought that some subtle inquiries might lead me in the right direction.

Winnelda was right about one thing, however. I couldn't just waltz into a place like that asking questions. They would be bound to be suspicious. No, I would have to go with the pretext of trying to sell something. That meant there was only one option.

I would have to go in disguise.

22

My plan, once formulated, was put into action at once.

I located a dress in the back of my closet that had somehow escaped the charity pile. It was several years old, of a slightly dated color and cut. I had lost a bit of weight as of late, and it was ill-fitting, which I thought heightened the effect.

I took off my engagement and wedding rings and found a small ruby ring in the back of my jewelry box. I slipped it into my pocket.

I hadn't much experience going incognito, but I was of the impression that it would be best to hide my identity as thoroughly as possible. To that end, I put on too much makeup and mussed my hair a bit in hopes of appearing somewhat tawdry. I stepped back from the mirror and studied the effect.

Winnelda had watched my preparations in growing alarm. "Oh, I wish you wouldn't, madam," she had said, more than once.

"I assure you, everything will be fine, Winnelda."

"At least you'll have Markham with you," she said, as though to reassure herself. "He's a sturdy fellow and should be able to protect you if something goes amiss."

"I'll take a cab," I said. "If I have Markham drive me, it will call too much attention."

"I don't know, madam," Winnelda said, wringing her hands. "Begging your pardon, but I think it's an awfully risky thing to do."

"Don't fret. I'm not going to do anything dangerous."

"Perhaps I should come with you," she suggested. One look at her face was enough to make it plain that she hoped I would refuse. She needn't have worried, for I thought that her nervousness would only make me more conspicuous.

"I don't think that will be necessary," I told her. "I'm only going to make a few inquiries. Nothing is going to go wrong."

This did not seem to comfort her. "I do hope you're right, madam," she said mournfully.

I was undeterred by her lack of confidence and left the flat determined to learn something.

I took a cab to Whitechapel, and the drive gave me time to contemplate how poorly devised my plan really was. How on earth did I expect to locate Mrs. Barrington's missing jewelry in a sea of London pawnbrokers? I would have equated it to searching for a needle in a haystack, but I thought it unfair to haystacks. I felt suddenly that I had set out on a Herculean task. I supposed it wouldn't hurt to attempt it, however. After all, Hercules had succeeded.

Whitechapel High Street was bustling with traffic, and the car slowed, the driver glancing at me in the mirror. "Any particular pawnbroker?" he asked.

As I thought it might elicit suspicion to request the most disreputable of them, I asked him to stop at the first one we encountered.

He pulled up to the curb, and I instructed him to wait. Stepping out onto the street, I realized there were an alarming number of unsavory-looking shops. I fought down the rising feeling that I might have embarked on too great an undertaking and walked toward the shop nearest me, the three golden balls signifying a pawnbroker's shop beneath the faded sign that read ACKERMAN AND HEATH PURVEYORS OF FINE GOODS.

A bell, imprisoned by cobwebs, did its best to jangle as I entered. The place was just as I had imagined it would be, dark and musty with a generally unwholesome atmosphere. There were long, dusty glass counters filled with jewelry and trinkets of every imaginable description. I wondered how much of it might have been acquired by unscrupulous means.

The man behind the counter looked up at me as I entered, his shrewd eyes taking my measure in one practiced glance.

"Good afternoon," I said. I allowed a bit of uncertainty to come into my voice. I had determined that it would be best for me to act as though I was new to this sort of thing. No matter how much I hoped I might be able to turn in an excellent performance, Sarah Bernhardt I was not. There was no way I could convincingly portray a hardened criminal, so it would be easiest for me to act as a decent woman sliding down the slippery slope to thievery and ruin.

"What can I do for you?" he asked, still eyeing me in an unnerving way.

"Well, Mr. Ackerman . . . Or is it Heath?"

"Neither."

"Oh," I said. "I see. Well, I . . . do you buy jewelry here?"

"Depends."

"On what?"

"On the type of jewelry, where you got it, how much you want for it. Things like that."

"I have a ring I'd like to sell," I told him. "A ruby ring."

"Where did you come by it?" he asked.

I feigned nervousness, which was not difficult. "Someone gave it to me."

"Did they indeed?"

I heard the door to the shop open, but I didn't turn around. I was just beginning to warm up to my part. I hoped that I was making my story sound a bit dubious. "Yes. It was a gift from my employer."

"What do you do for a living?" he asked.

"I'm a maid."

I was not, by nature, a good liar. In fact, I was very much against it in practice. However, I consoled myself by the fact that this was a role I was playing. I only hoped I could maintain it.

"Well, why don't you let me see this ring of yours?"

I pulled off my glove and reached into my pocket to pull out the ring. He held out a rough, hairy hand, and I dropped it into his palm. He held it up, surveying it carefully, before his eyes came back to me.

"So I've found you out."

I turned at the familiar voice from the

doorway, unwilling, at first, to believe my ears.

It was Milo.

How in the world he had found me here, I didn't know, but I forced myself to keep from revealing my extreme annoyance at his unwelcomed presence.

"I was afraid you might do something like this, Mary," he said, disappointment in his voice.

Mary. So he was continuing the ploy then. I didn't know what he was up to, but I was sorely displeased that he had chosen to interfere in my affairs.

"As you can see, I followed you." Milo turned to the man. "She's taken the ring from my wife's jewelry case."

"Then that's a matter for the police," the man said, unalarmed. "You'd best deal with her elsewhere."

"No need for the police," Milo replied indulgently. "After all, I'm rather fond of Mary."

My eyes narrowed, but I held my tongue.

"Granted, she's not a very good maid," Milo continued. "More ornamental than useful, if you understand my meaning."

I clenched my fists to keep from snatching up some heavy object from a nearby shelf and hitting him with it, as he so richly deserved.

"We don't buy stolen jewelry," the proprietor said.

"No, no, of course not," Milo said pleasantly. "I'm only glad I caught her before she could go to someone who does. I'd hate for her to do something foolish. I'll make sure she doesn't try anything like this again. We're sorry to have troubled you. Come along, Mary."

He took my arm and fairly dragged me from the shop.

"What are you doing?" I hissed at him when we were out on the street, jerking my arm from his grasp.

He handed money to my cab driver, dismissing him without consulting me, and then took my arm again and led me to where his own cab was waiting. I thought about refusing to get into it, but I didn't want to make a scene.

"I was coming to see you when I saw you emerge from our flat questionably dressed and behaving in a highly suspicious way. I followed you, naturally," he said, as he slid in beside me.

"I don't like to be followed," I informed him irritably. "I've no need for you to monitor my movements. I'm perfectly capable of taking care of myself."

"It's a good thing I came along when I did. In another minute, he would have found you out, and I dare say he would not have been amused."

"He would not have found me out," I said. "I was doing just fine before you arrived."

"The ruse wouldn't have lasted much longer."

"Oh, really?" I retorted. "And what makes you such an expert on such things?"

"For one thing, you had taken off your gloves." He picked up my hand from my lap. "How many maids do you know with perfectly manicured fingernails?"

I pulled my hand from his grasp.

"For another, I'm afraid you've rather overdone it. Your face looks ghastly. I think you've confused the part of a maid with that of a tart."

I pulled a mirror from my handbag. Though I hated to admit it, he was right. In the light of day, my countenance was vaguely clownish. I took a handkerchief from my bag and began dabbing at the paint.

"I assume you're looking for Mrs. Barrington's stolen things. Well, I'll help you."

"I haven't asked for your help," I retorted. He ignored me as the car rolled along slowly and then stopped in front of another shop.

"Why are we stopping here?" I asked.

"Because the proprietor of this particular shop has been known to deal in questionably acquired goods."

"How did you learn that?" I demanded, irritated that he should have already begun inquiries along the same lines as mine.

"I have my sources."

He opened the door and got out. I followed him, protesting.

"Milo, I don't think . . ."

"Don't argue with me, Mary." He took my arm, and we walked into the shop.

Apparently, surly, unkempt gentlemen were standard in these types of establishments, for the proprietor here was nearly an exact duplicate of the one I had just encountered.

"What can I do for you?" he asked, his eyes moving from Milo to me and back to Milo.

"I'm looking for some fine jewelry," Milo told him in a bored tone, his eyes glancing disinterestedly around the shop.

The man ran his eyes over Milo's Savile Row suit in an appraising way. "I expect you'd find more of what you're looking for in some Mayfair jeweler's."

Milo smiled easily. "Yes, but I'm afraid any of those shops might provide an additional hazard. You see, I shouldn't like my wife to find out."

The man glanced at me, comprehension dawning on his features.

"I can appreciate that, sir," he said, his tone a bit more friendly than it had been before. I was incensed that Milo's insinuation should have been a point in his favor.

"I'd like something a bit different than the usual, something a wife probably won't appreciate."

"Must you always talk about your wife?" I asked pettishly. If I was going to play this role, I figured I may as well make a go of it.

"I'm sorry, darling, but it's not as though we can pretend she doesn't exist."

"You forget it easily enough at times," I shot back. Then I walked to the other end of the counter, pretending to examine the trinkets beneath the glass countertop. I thought perhaps the two men might commiserate in their mutual immorality.

"A bit skittish, is she, sir?" the man said, lowering his voice, though not low enough for his words to elude me.

"The high-spirited ones always are," Milo replied.

If he continued to talk about me as though

I were one of his horses, he was going to see just how high-spirited I could be.

"Women are strange creatures."

"They are indeed," Milo agreed gravely.

"I'd give that one what she wants," the man said. "She's one I'd hate to lose, if you'll pardon my saying so."

Out of the corner of my eye, I saw Milo turn to look at me. "That she is."

"What are you looking for?" the man asked him. "I've got some fine pieces that I don't keep on display. Anything particular you have in mind?"

"Have you anything with an Eiffel Tower?" Milo inquired.

I was impressed that he had remembered the description of Mrs. Barrington's most easily recognizable piece of jewelry. He really was frightfully efficient when he chose to be.

"An Eiffel Tower?"

"Yes, you know: a jeweled replica of some sort. We sometimes" — Milo offered another suggestive smile — "holiday in Paris, you see."

"When we can get away from your wife," I chimed in.

The corner of Milo's mouth tipped up.

"I'm afraid I haven't anything like that," the proprietor said. "But I've got a lovely sapphire necklace that would suit the lady perfectly."

"No, I'm afraid it's an Eiffel Tower she wants," Milo said. "Isn't it, darling?"

"Yes," I confirmed. "You've promised me again and again. I intend to get it."

Milo looked at the man and shrugged his shoulders, as if at a loss in the face of a woman's demands.

I thought of Mrs. Barrington's other pieces. "But," I said slowly, "I would like a sapphire bracelet. But there's a certain one I want. I saw it on a rich lady once, and I've wanted one ever since. There was a diamond bracelet she had too, now that I think of it. They were both lovely." I proceeded to describe the missing pieces in great detail.

"I haven't got either one of those," the proprietor said a bit wearily when I had finished.

"Well, then I suppose we must keep looking." I took Milo's arm and pressed myself against him in what I could only hope was a fair impression of coquettish behavior. "You've promised me, lovey," I purred.

"That I have. And you know I can't resist you, darling." Without warning, his arm came around me, and he pulled me against him, giving me a lingering kiss on the mouth before releasing me.

317

My eyes shot daggers at him, but he only smiled and turned to the proprietor. "You'll have to excuse me. I am sometimes overcome by Mary's charms."

The man, it seemed, was completely unfazed by our behavior. "You certain nothing else will do?" he asked.

"I don't think so," I said. "I want one of those things specifically."

The man seemed disappointed, but he nodded and gave Milo a look that seemed to say he understood the trials of high-spirited women.

"If you come across any of those things, you'll let me know?" Milo asked.

"Certainly, sir. Certainly."

Milo took a card from his pocket and scribbled something on it, handing it to the man.

"Pleasure to assist you, Mr. Ames. Gibbs is my name, sir. If you think of anything else you need, you've only to ask."

"Thank you, Mr. Gibbs. I shall."

Milo turned to me. "Come, Mary. I'll buy you a sable coat."

I smiled. "I suppose that will do until the jewelry comes along."

I came back to where he stood and smiled at the shopkeeper. "Thank you for your trouble, Mr. Gibbs."

"It was my pleasure." He leaned a bit closer over the counter. "And I wouldn't worry myself none about his wife, miss," he said warmly. "I'm sure she's nothing compared to you."

23

"Brava, darling," Milo said when we were safely outside. "You were magnificent."

He took my hands in his, turning me to face him. His eyes were alight with amusement, and I could tell that he had enjoyed our little charade immensely. Against my will, I felt caught up in his enthusiasm.

"We were rather convincing, I think," I said.

"You were perfection. You should be on the stage."

"But if you ever refer to me as 'skittish' again . . ."

"That was your admirer, Mr. Gibbs, not me."

"You needn't have kissed me," I told him, attempting to be cross.

"I never like to miss an opportunity to kiss you, darling," he said with a smile.

"I'm not certain why it was necessary for Mary to be your mistress," I said, disengaging my hands from his. "Wouldn't it have been just as effective for me to be your wife?"

"It was merely for effect, and you must admit that it seemed to be a point in our favor."

It was true. The story seemed to have shifted Mr. Gibbs's sympathies almost at once.

"How did you know that would work?" I asked.

"When one wants to associate with un-scrupulous people, it is best to behave un-scrupulously."

"Something you know all about, I'm sure," I said, only half in jest.

"Come now, darling. You see that he was inclined to be much friendlier when he thought we were on an illicit errand."

"That is not to his credit," I replied, "though he was pleasant enough once he had relaxed his guard. If only someone will try to sell him Mrs. Barrington's pin or bracelet."

"If I spread it about that I'm looking for that particular piece, I think it will reach the right person eventually. I'm a trifle optimistic perhaps, but, then again, you know I'm inclined to be lucky." That was an understatement. Milo lived a charmed life.

Everything he touched seemed to bend to his will and yield excellent results. Except, perhaps, our marriage.

"You gave him your real name," I said, recalling that Mr. Gibbs had addressed him as Mr. Ames.

"Certainly. Do you expect I carry cards about with a false name on them?"

"I wouldn't be surprised."

He was unruffled by my cynicism.

"It's not a bad idea, actually. Alas, I hadn't the foresight to have them made up. I will have to suffer aspersions cast upon the humble name of Ames." He gave me a challenging look. "It's not as though I'm not accustomed to it."

If he was expecting sympathy from me, he was sadly mistaken. He had made his bed, and he could lie in it. Although I didn't particularly care for the metaphor in this instance.

"Shall we try a few more shops?" Milo asked, drawing my thoughts back to the task at hand.

I wavered for only a moment. I didn't quite know how we had gone from talk of divorce to an amiable partnership in the space of one morning, but I supposed it wouldn't hurt to continue our search for the brooch.

"Very well." I relented. "Only if you'll stop talking incessantly about your wife."

We had no better luck with any of the other shops we visited, but Milo left his card at several establishments. It was fortunate that Mrs. Barrington's Eiffel Tower pin was so distinctive a piece, for I suspected it would be much easier to identify than either her missing necklace or bracelet. With any luck, one of the pieces would eventually come into the possession of one of the shopkeepers we had visited. Milo had made it very plain that anyone who came across them would be richly rewarded. I hoped this would induce someone to contact us.

"I think we've visited enough shops for now," I said at last. I had had enough of playing Mary. As much fun as she was, I was ready to go back to being myself. It was much less exhausting.

It seemed that he had read my thoughts, for he said, "As charming as Mary is, you are infinitely preferable."

He was being suspiciously sweet-tempered, and I had the distinct feeling that he was up to something.

"Will you have lunch with me?" he asked as we approached the car.

I considered. We had been behaving very

prettily toward one another all morning, and I saw no reason why we shouldn't have lunch together. In fact, I was, against my better judgment, rather inclined to be hopeful about his sudden appearance. That he had not absconded to France seemed to bode well for his willingness to work toward some sort of resolution.

"Let's go back to the flat," I said. "I don't want to be seen in public looking like this. Besides, Winnelda was dreadfully worried that I should be abducted or slashed to bits by Jack the Ripper."

"If I thought she had the remotest chance of being able to deter you from your ridiculous schemes, I should be quite put out with Winnelda for allowing you to run about unaccompanied. As it is, I must acknowledge that it's impossible to stop you from doing just as you please." It seemed to me that, despite the levity of his words, there was some deeper meaning in them.

"It's not always impossible," I said softly.

His eyes met mine, but he said no more about it.

Back at the flat, Winnelda was overjoyed to find that I had not been seized by fiendish persons in the course of my pursuits. I think that she refrained from hugging me by only the slimmest of margins.

"I'm ever so relieved that Mr. Ames was there to look after you, madam."

She must have seen my eyebrows rise, for she added quickly, "Not that you're not very well able to take care of yourself. I'll just see to lunch now, shall I?"

I changed into a dress with a pink and lavender floral print, wiping the remainder of the heavy makeup from my face. Then Milo and I enjoyed a companionable luncheon, our discussion always returning to various aspects of the case.

There was, I sensed, something just below the surface, but neither of us seemed in a hurry to bring that particular conversation to light. I knew, of course, that we couldn't just go on sweeping things under the rug. There were so many things there already that the rug barely touched the floor anymore.

"We didn't really learn anything today," I said, pushing my plate away. "I will confess that I had hoped we would be able to find the jewelry. I suppose it was ridiculous for me to expect to solve the crime in one morning's work."

"Patience, darling. It may turn up yet. Besides, you enjoyed it, didn't you?"

"It was rather exciting," I admitted.

"And Mary is so very fetching." His eyes

moved over me. "I suspect you would look rather alluring in a maid's uniform."

I frowned at him as Winnelda cleared away our plates, and we rose from the table and went into the sitting room. Milo sat down on the sofa and lit a cigarette.

"What now, my lovely?" he asked. "Shall we infiltrate a smuggling ring or some such thing this afternoon?"

"Oh, I'm afraid I must be getting ready to go soon." I had suddenly remembered that I was engaged to dine with Lord Dunmore, and I was surprised to find that I very much wished I wasn't. What would have pleased me most, just then, would have been to remain at home with Milo, sharing a quiet dinner and discussing the case. I knew, however, that I could not, for a number of reasons.

"I take it, then, that you're not going to invite me to stay for dinner?" he said lightly, though it seemed that his gaze had grown more intent. I wondered if I was looking suspicious. I was normally very good at hiding my feelings, but Milo had a way of seeing beneath my façades.

I hesitated. "I have a dinner engagement."

His look was definitely intent now, even as he sat back in his chair, his relaxed posture indicating he hadn't a care in the world.

"With whom?" he asked.

I had thought, initially, that I would be pleased to inform him that I had dinner plans with Lord Dunmore. However, after the camaraderie we had shared today, I found myself suddenly reluctant to tell him. Milo had never been jealous, but something told me he would not approve, and I was hesitant to upset the delicate balance.

"Oh, just a friend," I said lightly.

The corner of his mouth tipped up. "Amory darling, there's something you're not telling me." It wasn't a question. I found myself irritated by the way he could see past my pretenses so easily when it was always impossible for me to read him.

I sighed. "It's no great secret. If you must know, I'm dining with Lord Dunmore."

I was surprised at the annoyance that he allowed to cross his face. He was normally so very closed that I hadn't expected him to reveal his true feelings on the subject.

"I'd rather you didn't," he said calmly, and I was again surprised. Milo seldom took any interest in my affairs. In fact, I could not remember an instance where he had told me he'd "rather I didn't" about anything.

"I don't see any harm in it," I replied, throwing back at him the words he had used about his drink with Helene Renault.

His eyes came up to mine, and I felt suddenly that we had been standing on the edge of a precipice all day, and we were now leaning precariously close to the edge. This was not going to end well. I could sense it.

"Amory, whatever is going on between us, Dunmore is not the sort of person you should toy with."

I sighed. "For pity's sake, Milo. I'm not a child."

"No, you're certainly not. You're a beautiful woman, and Dunmore's taken notice of it. I know he puts up a good front, but he is not what he appears to be, Amory."

I might have thought his concern touching under other circumstances. As it was, I found it ludicrous that he should lecture me on the company I was keeping.

"You don't think I know that?" I answered lightly. "His charm is much more transparent than yours, Milo. I can tell when he is in earnest and when he's not. In any event, I don't think you're in much position to quibble about my choice of dinner companions, do you?" There was no malice in the words, only simple fact, but I knew as soon as I said them that they might not have been the right thing to say.

I saw his jaw clench, and then he mastered

himself, the familiar look of indifference falling over his handsome features. "You're certainly entitled to do as you please, darling. By all means, dine with Lord Dunmore. I hope you enjoy yourself."

He went out of the room before I could reply, and a moment later I heard the front door close behind him.

I dropped into a chair and rubbed a hand across my face. I felt that somehow I had lost the bit of ground we might have made up this morning. It seemed that no matter what I did, things only got worse.

Lord Dunmore arrived punctually to collect me for dinner. I wore a gown of aubergine satin, and he was all smiles and profuse compliments, looking as dashing as ever in his evening clothes.

"I must confess, I was a bit afraid you'd cancel our engagement this evening," he said, as he helped me into my coat.

"Why should I do that?"

"I've heard that you've been keeping company with your husband. I thought he might have dissuaded you."

"Milo doesn't dictate my social schedule," I said lightly.

I turned to tell Winnelda that I should not be home too late. She was nowhere to be seen, however. She had made a very concentrated effort to stay out of the way, and I found myself wondering what she was thinking. I had no doubt that she disapproved. She was my staunchest supporter, but I rather suspected she was also very much a devotee of my husband. In general, Milo's good looks made it difficult for women to hold things against him for long. Unfortunately, I knew this from personal experience.

"Shall we?" Lord Dunmore asked, offering me his arm.

We went down the lift and out to his long, shining car.

"Where are we dining?" I asked.

"It's a little place called French's," he said. "Not very well known, but it's a favorite of mine."

"It sounds delightful."

"It is. Add to that the charming company, and I think we're going to have a wonderful evening."

I tried to fight my misgivings. Despite the fact I was dining with Lord Dunmore as a means to an end, I felt, somehow, that it was poor behavior on my part to do so. After all, Milo had obviously been making an attempt to patch things up between us, and I couldn't help but feel that this dinner would only make things worse.

Then again, it was not as though there was anything wrong in it. I had made my feelings very clear to Lord Dunmore. It would be rude of me to cry off, and if I had done so, it was very likely he would not agree to using the Dunmore Diamond as bait.

Besides, I thought Milo had worried for naught. I could sense nothing in Lord Dunmore's behavior that was inappropriate. I had intimated to him that I wanted only to be friends, and he seemed to have accepted it. The distance between us on the seat was proper, and the conversation never strayed into uncomfortable territory.

I had never heard of French's. It was located on a quiet street in Covent Garden, and I was somehow glad that there would be less chance of us being spotted together by people that I knew. Despite my assertions to Milo that I should be free to do as I chose, I didn't want to cause any more waves than I already had.

The restaurant was, despite its name, done in the rustic Italian style with dark wood, beamed ceilings, and brick arches creating little alcoves for more intimate dining. It was to one of these alcoves that we were ushered by the enthusiastic maître d' upon our arrival. "Ah, Lord Dunmore," he said, "I am so pleased to see you again."

"It's good to see you again, Antoine."

"We have been waiting for you to visit us again. And you have brought a friend with you this time," he said, turning to me with a bright smile. *"Enchanté, mademoiselle."*

"Good evening," I said. So Lord Dunmore has brought a woman "this time." It was all very smoothly done. Lord Dunmore must have taken many women here for Antoine to be so very well versed in the script.

"Well," I said, when we had placed our orders from an extensive menu, "have you thought any more about using the Dunmore Diamond to catch the thief?"

"Straight to business, aren't you, Amory?" he said with a smile. "I admire forthrightness in a woman."

"It would mean so much to Mrs. Barrington. Even if she's wrong in her suspicions, at least we will have tried."

"You don't think this is a matter best left to the police?"

I hesitated, unwilling to let him know how closely associated with the police I was. "I'm sure they are doing what they can," I answered. "But the thief won't be as wary of us."

He leaned forward a bit, his arms resting

on the table. "Would it mean a lot to you?"

"Yes," I said. "It would."

"Then we'll do it."

I smiled, surprised at how quickly he had capitulated. "Now we've only to determine how we shall work it."

"Let's not talk about that now," he said with a wave of his hand. "There'll be plenty of time for business later. For now, I'm interested in pleasure."

"Very well," I replied, a bit warily. "What shall we talk about?"

He shrugged. "Whatever you like."

In that case, I might as well steer the conversation along the lines of the mystery.

"May I ask you something?"

He smiled. "Of course."

"Who do you think might've had reason to murder Mr. Harker?"

I had hoped to see some sign of guilt or secret knowledge, but what I saw was something very like boredom. "I haven't the faintest idea."

I was a bit surprised at the apparent carelessness in his answer. After all, the man had been killed in Lord Dunmore's house. I would have thought the problem would present a bit more interest to him. Besides, Mrs. Garmond had told me that he seemed very upset about the matter. Why should he feign complete indifference with me?

"Surely you must have some idea," I said.

He regarded me from across the table, trying to determine, I suppose, why I should suddenly appear so interested.

"I had forgotten that business you were involved in at the seashore," he said suddenly, comprehension dawning. "So you fancy yourself a detective, do you?"

I wasn't certain I cared for the condescension in his tone, but I was determined not to let him see my annoyance. Instead, I affected a bit of embarrassment. "I'm afraid you've found me out, my lord. I do love a good mystery, and I thought, perhaps with a bit of pondering, I might be able to figure out why someone would have wished to kill him."

My ploy seemed to have worked, for he smiled indulgently. "I must say you're very charming when you've set your mind to something."

"I'm just curious." I returned his smile, not wanting to give him the impression of how involved I truly was.

He sat back in his seat and appeared to consider it. "I really couldn't say why anyone would want to kill James Harker. He was a bore, perhaps, but a harmless enough fellow. If I had to choose who might have done it, however, I suppose I would pick one of the Echols girls."

He said this in a casual way as he picked up his wineglass, and my brows shot up in surprise. "Really? What makes you say so?"

"Who knows? Jealousy, perhaps. I believe they were all mad about each other and didn't quite know how to work it out."

This was an interesting perspective indeed. "I saw Mr. Foster with Marjorie Echols when I dined with the Douglas-Hugheses last night. I thought perhaps they were a couple."

"I wouldn't think so. Foster prefers a different type of woman. Marjorie Echols is a . . . well, I shouldn't say such things . . ." He smiled, as though to disarm the harshness of his words. I wondered briefly if there was more to his comment than he let on.

"I confess I don't know the Echols sisters very well," I told him.

Again, a smile I could not quite interpret. "Felicity is a lovely girl," he said. "Very unlike her sister. There's something vague and slightly eerie about her, though, isn't there? She seems the type that would kill over unrequited love or some such rot."

"It has been very exciting meeting Mr. Foster. One doesn't often encounter such celebrity." It seemed that, just for an instant, something like irritation flashed across his eyes, but it was gone so swiftly that I could not be entirely sure it had even been there at all.

"Were you at Wimbledon the year he lost?" he asked.

"Yes," I answered, thinking it was somewhat petty of him to mention one crushing loss among a sea of victories. "That was unfortunate."

He smiled. "Misfortune for some is fortune for others."

"Yes, I suppose so," I replied.

The waiter arrived then with our food, and I had a moment to contemplate what Lord Dunmore had told me. Was it possible that he was right? Had one — or even both — of the Echols sisters been involved in the murder? I hadn't placed them high on my list of suspects, but they couldn't be ruled out. I would need to find a way to talk to them again as soon as possible.

24

The food at French's was excellent, and as we ate, the conversation shifted to less morbid things. I found Lord Dunmore to be intelligent, witty, and very well-informed. Yet, for all that, some part of me was on guard. I didn't know if it was the murder, Milo's warning, or some instinct of my own. I only knew that I seemed to sense something superficial about his friendliness, and for some reason I did not feel completely at ease.

"It's too early for me to take you home," he said, when we had finished and he called for Antoine to settle our bill.

"It's not so very early," I pointed out. Nonetheless, we had not yet discussed the particulars of how we would use the Dunmore Diamond to lure the thief, and I supposed a late night would be the cost of his agreeing to such schemes.

"Come, Mrs. Ames. The evening is young.

There is a great deal of fun left to be had." The way in which he said this made me slightly wary, but an idea had come to me suddenly. Perhaps a way to accomplish two things at once.

"There is a nightclub I've heard a bit about," I told him. "It's called the Sparrow."

It seemed that surprise flickered across his face. "The Sparrow?" he repeated. "I shouldn't have pictured you in a place like that, Mrs. Ames."

The words sounded ominous, and I wondered if perhaps the Sparrow was not the sort of establishment I had imagined. "Is it a sordid place?" I asked. "I don't know much about it. I only heard that it was popular with some of my friends."

"Not sordid," he said. "Only perhaps a bit more . . . lively than the places you are accustomed to. I've not been there often, but I understand many of our mutual acquaintances have been known to frequent it, including the Echols girls, Mr. Harker, and even Mr. Foster."

"Well, perhaps we'll see them there tonight," I said with a smile. "I'd very much like to see it. I'm not afraid of a little excitement."

This seemed to amuse him. "No? Well, neither am I. In fact, I think that sounds like a rather enjoyable way to spend an evening. It's not far from here, in fact. Shall we go?"

We walked into the Sparrow not half an hour later, and I could see at once that Lord Dunmore's assessment had been correct. The nightclub was not the sort of place I was accustomed to frequenting. Once inside, we were engulfed in the thick, smoky atmosphere. The lights were dim, and the music being played by a large band at the front of the room was cacophonous. A great many couples moved about the dance floor, and most of the dances were, to say the least, unfamiliar to me.

The nightclubs Milo and I frequented tended to be much more reserved. And, though Milo was, to put it politely, much more adventurous than I, I suspected this place would have been beneath his notice as well. It lacked the elegant recklessness of some of the more popular nightspots and seemed somehow shabby instead.

I was most definitely out of my milieu.

Lord Dunmore, it seemed, felt no such qualms. In fact, he seemed very much at home. He took my arm, and we threaded through the crowded tables, raucous laughter breaking out around us, almost indistinguishable in the din. The air smelled very strongly of alcohol and stale perfume. I wished now that I hadn't been so hasty in suggesting that we come here.

"I've seen someone I must say hello to," he told me. "I'll find you in a moment." Lord Dunmore's grip on my arm loosened, and then he had disappeared into the crowd.

I took a moment to get my bearings. Perhaps I was too old for such frivolity, but I noticed that several of the women around me looked a good deal older than me, though they were certainly making valiant attempts to hide it.

I tried to see where Lord Dunmore had gone, but the crowds and inadequate lighting, not to mention the haze of cigarette smoke, made it difficult to see much of anything. I began making my way through the crowds in hopes of finding some inconspicuous spot where I could await his return. I didn't expect that there would be much to be learned here, after all, and I was rather anxious that he should take me home.

I wondered what Milo would think of all of this when I told him. Then I remembered that he was cross with me and would likely be very disinterested in anything that I should have to say about this evening.

I refused an offer to dance and two much less polite offers by the time I neared the perimeter of the room.

Then I turned around and, as luck would have it, bumped directly into one of the suspects I had been hoping to encounter.

"Hello, Miss Echols," I said, as brightly as I could manage. It was Felicity, the younger sister. She was wearing a wrinkled gown of gold lamé, and her face, already pale, seemed to grow paler as she realized who I was.

"Oh . . ." She looked at me with her wide, vague eyes. "Mrs. Ames, isn't it?"

The glass in her hand was nearly empty, and it occurred to me to wonder how much she had had to drink, for she seemed to sway slightly on her feet. I fought the urge to reach out and steady her.

"How have you been?" I asked, keeping up the pretense of polite conversation, which was difficult considering I fairly had to shout to be heard.

"Dreadful." She drained the remainder of the liquid from her glass, and then looked at me again. "That is to say . . . I've been all right. How are you, Mrs. Ames?"

"The murder upset me quite a lot," I told her.

It appeared my comment had struck

341

home, for her eyes filled at once with tears. I should have known better than to speak so bluntly, but I had been hoping to trigger some sort of response. This was not what I had hoped for.

"Oh, it's all so very dreadful," she said, covering her face with her free hand, her shoulders shaking.

"I'm sorry, dear," I said. I took a handkerchief from my handbag and handed it to her, while taking one arm and ushering her to an unoccupied seat in the corner. She sat heavily in a chair, and I took her glass and then sat at the table beside her.

"I didn't mean to upset you," I told her sincerely. I hadn't foreseen this reaction, and I felt bad now for having spoken so callously of the death of the man to whom she had been rumored to be attached. I glanced around for some sign of Marjorie. She would know better than I how to comfort her sister.

"It's just that I feel so sorry about poor James." Felicity sobbed. "He was so very sweet, and it was so cruel what happened to him."

"Yes, we're all very sad about that," I agreed.

"He was always a gentleman," she said. "No matter what anyone says about him, he was always a gentleman."

To my knowledge, no one had ever accused him of being otherwise.

"Were you . . . on good terms with him?" I asked.

"Did I love him, do you mean?" she asked with disarming frankness. "No, I didn't. Not really, anyway. Not in the romantic sense . . . but he was very kind to Marjorie and me."

"It must be hard to lose such a good friend," I said.

She reached for her glass, and I handed it to her, despite the fact that it was empty. She lifted it to her lips and then set it down sadly. "It's all gone," she told me.

"Yes, dear. Perhaps some water . . ."

She shook her head, her blond curls bouncing. "I never thought that it would come to that, that he would be killed."

"I'm sure no one did."

"He didn't mean it," she said. "I'm sure he didn't."

"Who didn't mean what?" I asked.

It seemed for just a moment that her gaze cleared ever so slightly and she seemed aware of what she had just said.

"What are you doing here?" she asked suddenly. "This isn't your type of place, Mrs. Ames."

"Lord Dunmore told me that several of

our mutual acquaintances enjoyed coming here, including Mr. Harker and Mr. Foster. We decided to drop by and see if there was anyone here we knew."

She looked at me, her eyes wide. "Is he here?"

"Yes, we've just come from having dinner."

Her eyes darted behind me, searching the crowd. "You shouldn't . . . He isn't . . . Don't trust him, Mrs. Ames. He's dangerous."

I was surprised by the alarm in her expression. "I'll certainly keep that in mind."

"I'd better go before he comes," she said, and there was something very much like fear in her voice.

"I'm sure there's no need to be alarmed," I said soothingly. She had obviously had too much to drink if the presence of Lord Dunmore put her in such a state.

I turned to see if I could spot him anywhere in the room. When I turned back, I was startled to see Felicity Echols was gone. She had disappeared into the crowd.

A moment later, Lord Dunmore found me. "Enjoying yourself?"

"Not especially," I admitted. I was suddenly tired, and I didn't want to be in this place any longer.

"It is a bit . . . exuberant, I suppose." As if to confirm this, a row of scantily clad chorus girls made their way out onto the floor, warbling a song at the top of their lungs.

I turned to look at him. "Would you take me home now?"

"Are you certain you don't want a drink?" he asked.

"Thank you, no."

"We haven't even had a chance to dance yet."

"I wouldn't think you'd enjoy dancing in a place like this," I said frankly. I was hard-pressed to picture the elegant Viscount Dunmore moving about the dance floor to the somewhat-frantic jazz tune the band had begun to play.

His eyes caught mine and held, a small smile forming on his lips. "Perhaps not, but I would enjoy having you in my arms."

"I'm afraid my ankle is not quite healed, in any event," I replied, though, in truth, it had nearly ceased to trouble me at all.

"Of course. Well, if you're ready, I'm quite willing."

He put his hand on my elbow, and we walked toward the door. I couldn't seem to get my mind off what Felicity Echols had said. How strange it was that Lord Dunmore should have implicated the Echols sisters and Felicity Echols should have warned me against him.

There couldn't be anything serious in it. Dangerous could have more than one definition. I couldn't believe that Lord Dunmore was involved in James Harker's death. Then again, I was well aware of the loosening effect alcohol had on the tongue. Perhaps she had been willing to tell me something that she might not have under other circumstances.

The thought was certainly not a pleasant one as I once again slid into the cool backseat of Lord Dunmore's automobile.

"Are you sure you want to go home?" Lord Dunmore asked as the car pulled onto the busy streets. Although the hour was growing late, the London nightlife was just beginning to come alive. I couldn't help but wonder where Milo might be. This time of night was when he was most in his element, and that was not an especially comforting thought.

"There are any number of other nightclubs we could visit, you know. Or we could go to a jazz club, if you like music."

He was sitting very close on the seat, so close that I could feel the warmth coming off him. I was not, as a general rule, uneasy

346

when I found myself alone with a gentleman, but there was something about his
nearness that was making me slightly uncomfortable. It was as though my body was
picking up some subtle signal that my mind
had not yet interpreted. I wondered how
much of it had to do with what Felicity
Echols had told me.

"Yes, I'm afraid I'm rather tired."

"Might I ask you an impertinent question,
Amory?" he said suddenly.

I was a bit afraid of what it might be, but
I nodded. "If you like."

"Where exactly do things stand with you
and your husband?"

I hesitated. I wasn't certain where this
conversation was leading, but I didn't wish
to appear rude by refusing to answer him.

"Things are a bit complicated at the moment," I said at last.

"Perhaps you're not sure what you want.
Perhaps I can help you figure it out." His
fingers were caressing my arm in a slow,
hypnotic movement. I felt a shift in the
atmosphere.

"I . . . don't think . . ." I was trying to
determine how best to play this, but he
moved rather quickly, and it was difficult to
find the countermoves.

"Why don't you come back to my house

for a drink," he said in a low voice.

"Thank you, but no."

"I heard that you were out to dinner with your husband last night," he said, his fingers still on my arm. "Trying to keep up pretenses?"

"Milo and I are not on unfriendly terms." I felt somehow that I didn't want to share any more than I had to. There was something slightly intrusive in his questions and his behavior.

"I've always taken Ames for an intelligent man. If so, I assume he's trying to make up for his . . . indiscretions."

"There are just a few matters that need to be settled between us," I said carefully.

Lord Dunmore smiled. "In the meantime, perhaps you'd like to take advantage of your freedom."

He was leaning closer, and it seemed that in a moment he would try to kiss me.

He was handsome, attentive, and very sure of himself, but I wasn't even slightly tempted. Despite what Milo may or may not have done, I had absolutely no desire to engage in an affair of my own . . . with Lord Dunmore or anyone else.

"You promised to discuss the use of the Dunmore Diamond with me, my lord," I said, hoping my very obvious change of subject would halt his advances.

A knowing smile flickered across his face, and, by some subtle shift of posture, he contrived to ease the intensity that had been so apparent only a moment before. "I think you should wear it to the ball," he said.

This I hadn't expected. "Oh, I don't know if that is a good idea."

"It would look lovely on you, and you can arrange to set it somewhere as a trap at some point in the evening."

I found it surprising how he spoke of a priceless heirloom as some trinket to be tossed about at will. Nevertheless, the idea was not entirely without merit.

"Yes, I suppose that might work," I said. "I shall think it over."

"Certainly." He smiled. "Call on me before the party, if you like. I'll give it to you to wear."

I was relieved to see we had arrived back at my building. "You needn't see me to my door," I said, hoping he would take the hint.

To his credit, he did not insist. "Very well. I'll leave you here then. You'll be in touch about our other arrangements, I suppose."

"Yes. Thank you. And thank you for a lovely evening, Lord Dunmore."

"Alexander," he corrected, taking my hand in his.

"Alexander," I repeated with a smile. "Good night."

"Good night, Amory." He squeezed my hand. Then he turned and got back into his car. I watched it pull away before turning toward the door, feeling very much relieved. The evening had not gone exactly as I had expected, but I still felt that I had learned a few things.

I stopped in the lobby before going to the lift. Although I was tired, I somehow dreaded going back to the dark, quiet flat. Winnelda had gone to bed long ago, and I wished there was someone to talk to.

I was trying to fool myself, of course. I knew perfectly well that I was making excuses to go and see Milo. It was intensely irritating to me that I should want to talk to him at all, given everything that had happened between us as of late. Nevertheless, I was perfectly aware that I would break down, so I might as well just go see him.

I went back outside and hailed a cab.

25

The Ritz lobby was busy, despite the hour, with people in evening dress coming and going along the brightly lit hall, their footsteps muted by the dark rugs. I could hear faint strains of music drifting from the direction of the dining room, where guests were no doubt enjoying a carefree evening of after-dinner dancing. For some reason, it recalled the early days of my marriage. We had been very young and carefree then, and I had loved nothing more than floating about the room in Milo's arms.

Brushing away my growing nostalgia, I walked toward the lift. It occurred to me suddenly, however, that I probably should have telephoned to warn him of my arrival. In fact, I began to wonder if I had been foolish in coming here. After all, Milo might not want to talk to me at all. Just because we had enjoyed engaging in subterfuge together this afternoon didn't mean that everything was all right between us.

There was also the possibility he might not be there. There were any number of ways he might have chosen to spend his evening while I spent mine with Lord Dunmore. An even worse possibility than a night on the town occurred to me: he might very well be in his room and . . . entertaining. I felt vaguely sick at the idea that Helene Renault — or some other woman — might be there now.

I hesitated for a just a moment, and then I turned and approached the front desk.

"May I help you, madam?" asked the man who stood behind it.

"Can you tell me if Mr. Ames is in? He's in the Trafalgar Suite."

He didn't hesitate. "Mr. Ames is still in the dining room, madam," he said, indicating the direction I should take.

I thought of asking if Milo was alone but decided against it. I could find that out for myself.

I made my way to the dining room, admiring, as I always did, the elegant opulence of it. It was a beautiful room, glowing golden in the night. The elaborate frescoes, heavy draped curtains, and soft lighting in the gilded chandeliers that hung from high ceilings gave the large room a feeling of warmth and intimacy. Laughter and the soft murmur of conversation mingled with the clinking of glasses, and I couldn't help but contrast the quiet elegance of this place with the cacophony of the Sparrow.

I spotted Milo at a table near the dance floor and was immensely relieved to see that he was alone.

His brows rose when he saw me, and he stood as I approached the table. He was dressed in spotless evening attire, and I felt a little pang. In some cruel twist of fate, he always seemed most handsome when things were the worst between us.

"Hello, Milo," I said.

"Good evening," he replied politely.

We stood there for a moment, looking at one another.

"May I join you?" I asked at last.

He pulled out a chair and motioned with exaggerated courtesy for me sit.

"To what do I owe this unexpected pleasure?" he asked, taking the chair across from me. He didn't sound as though my answer would be of any particular interest to him. His dinner plates had been cleared away, but he was drinking a glass of wine, and his fingers toyed with the stem.

"I wanted you to see that I had arrived home in one piece," I said.

"I am gratified to learn that you escaped your evening unscathed."

"Lord Dunmore was . . ." I began to say "a perfect gentleman," but that was not exactly the case. Milo noticed my hesitation. "Very pleasant."

"Did he kiss you?" He asked this casually, as though he was not questioning his wife about her behavior with another man.

"No, of course not," I replied irritably.

"Did he try to?"

I paused. I wanted very much to lie to my husband, but I couldn't bring myself to do it.

"Not exactly," I said.

His eyes met mine. "I knew perfectly well that he wouldn't be able to resist you, darling."

"But I didn't allow him to kiss me," I said. My meaning was implied. I had resisted Lord Dunmore's advances, while Milo had been caught kissing Helene Renault.

"But if a photographer had been present in that moment when he tried, it might, in fact, have been interpreted as more than it was."

I sighed. He had a point. However, I was very hesitant to admit it. No matter how well he presented his arguments, I still didn't know if I believed him. That was the maddening part. No matter how much I wanted to trust him, there was always some part of me that found it impossible to do so.

He was watching me as these ideas flashed through my head, and I couldn't help but feel as though he was reading my thoughts.

"Do you want something to drink?" he asked. "Coffee, perhaps?"

I was prepared to decline, but, in truth, a cup of coffee sounded wonderful. "That would be lovely. Thank you."

I think he had thought I would turn him down, for, though it may have been wishful thinking, he almost looked pleased. He motioned to the waiter and placed the order before turning back to me. He appeared perfectly at ease, but there was something watchful about him.

"I learned a few interesting things this evening," I said, more to fill the silence than anything else. "I . . . I went to the Sparrow."

"Did you?"

"You don't sound surprised."

"Do you expect me to be? It's perfectly obvious you revel in doing things I warn you against." I couldn't tell whether or not he was jesting with me, so I ignored him.

"I ran into Felicity Echols, and she was quite drunk. She said some rather interesting things."

He waited.

"For one thing, she warned me against Lord Dunmore. She said he is dangerous."

Milo's brow rose ever so slightly, and I could detect the faintest hint of derision on his features.

"She seems genuinely afraid of him. I wonder if she believes he might have killed James Harker. She also said, 'He didn't mean it. I'm sure he didn't,' but she wouldn't say of whom she was speaking. I thought she might mean Mr. Harker, but it doesn't really make sense. And, if not him, does that mean she knows who the killer is?"

"It's all very interesting," Milo said blandly.

"And Lord Dunmore thinks one of the Echols sisters might have done it. He seems to believe that there was some sort of love triangle transpiring and one of them might have killed Mr. Harker out of jealousy. It seems a bit ridiculous to me, but I suppose it's always a possibility."

"Indeed."

"It's not much," I admitted. I sighed, leaning back in my chair. "It doesn't feel as though we're getting anywhere. I can only hope that something will happen with the

Dunmore Diamond."

"The Dunmore Diamond?" Milo repeated.

The waiter arrived at that moment with my coffee, and I had a moment to decide how to answer. I had not yet revealed this part of the plan to Milo, and I was not at all certain he would be receptive to it. There was no going back now, however. "Yes," I said when the waiter had gone. "Lord Dunmore has agreed to use the Dunmore Diamond as bait at the ball on Sunday. It may prove the perfect opportunity to catch the killer."

Milo seemed extremely unimpressed. "I think you'd be better off letting the police do the dirty work, don't you? After all, Inspector Jones gets paid to do that sort of thing."

I ignored this bit of skepticism and took a sip of my coffee. "I think it's an excellent plan."

"Yes, I'm sure you do." There was something vaguely like sarcasm in Milo's tone, but I decided to overlook it.

"We'll make a show of the diamond," I said, purposefully neglecting to mention that Lord Dunmore intended for me to wear it. "Then I will relate to each of the suspects that we've set it down somewhere.

If the thief was desperate enough to commit murder, there is every chance he or she will be willing to risk being caught for a piece of such magnitude."

Milo seemed to consider this. "It might work," he said, "in theory. But I don't see how you'll convince the killer to believe that Lord Dunmore would be so careless with the diamond."

"It's worth a try, isn't it?"

"If you say so, darling."

"I just wish I could be certain that the thief is the killer," I said. "I keep coming back to the idea that Mr. Harker surprised the thief in some way and was killed to ensure his silence, but his confronting the thief seems to go against what we've learned of his personality."

"I would not have taken him for a confident man," Milo said.

"No." I frowned, as his words sank in. "You're right. Then what was he doing with the paste jewels from the bracelet . . . and the gun? And furthermore, where is the rest of the bracelet?"

"All very good questions."

"There is, of course, the possibility that Lord Dunmore is either the thief or the killer and it was a mistake to take him into my confidence. I thought it a risk worth taking, however, for even if he is guilty, he will be less on his guard thinking he is taking part in the trap."

"You don't mean you allow that your Lord Dunmore might possibly not be the gallant gentleman that he seems?"

"For pity's sake, Milo." I sighed. "You're not going to develop a jealous streak now?"

"Certainly not." His eyes met mine. "After all, I may not have the right to that particular honor for much longer. Although, I must admit, I thought I'd merit a better replacement than Dunmore."

He was trying to make me angry, and he'd succeeded.

"Certainly," I retorted. "After all, if I wanted flattery and lies, I could get them from you."

"Do you still believe that I am having an affair with Helene Renault?"

His eyes met mine and held. I wanted so very much to tell him no, but I just wasn't sure. I never knew what was true and what wasn't. "I don't know."

"Have you made up your mind about divorcing me?"

"Milo . . . do we have to talk about this now?"

"Yes," he said.

I sighed. "I don't know what to tell you. I

don't want to divorce you. But I meant what I said. I won't . . . I can't go on with things as they are."

"I'm not going to try to stop you, if it's what you want."

"Is it what you want?" I asked softly.

"Certainly not. I'm very happy being married to you, Amory."

It was almost laughable, how very polite we were being to one another, but I didn't feel like laughing. In fact, the knot in my throat made it impossible to speak.

"Dance with me," he said suddenly. He stood and held out his hand.

I wavered. "Milo, I don't think . . ."

"There's no harm in it," he said, that familiar enchanter's smile flickering at the corners of his mouth. "It's only a dance, darling."

It was more than that. We both knew it. I recognized too well that look in his eyes, the glint of intensity that appeared when he had made up his mind to accomplish something. My instincts warned me that it would be better not to give him the opportunity to put his arms around me, for I was infuriatingly susceptible to him at close distances. My head and my heart were at war, and I found my head was much too tired for the fight.

I took his hand and allowed him to lead me to the dance floor. He turned to me, his eyes meeting mine, before his arms went around me, pulling me against him. And, just like that, it seemed the room and the other couples around us faded away until it was only us and the music.

As we moved across the floor, lost in the gentle sway of the music, I was very aware of the weight of his hand on my back, of the warm pressure of his body against me. My face close to his, I could smell the subtle, spicy scent of his aftershave mingling with the starch of his collar.

"Do you remember that night in Paris?" he asked.

"Yes," I whispered.

I knew just the night he meant. It had been the last night of our honeymoon and the sort of thing that fairy tales were made of. We had danced until after midnight to the slow, heady strains of the orchestra, and then we had taken a moonlight stroll along the banks of the Seine. I clung to his arm as we walked, and I had thought, in the naïveté of youthful bliss, that the glow of lights in the rippling water seemed like a reflection of my happiness.

We had stopped on a bridge, and I leaned against the balustrade, looking up. "I'm so very happy," I told him.

He had looked at me intently, his eyes moving over my face as though he had never quite seen me before. "You're so beautiful," he said, and there was something in his voice that was different from his normal murmured endearments. "I adore you, Amory."

He had leaned to kiss me then, and the love that surged through me had been almost dizzying. Looking back, I didn't know if I had ever been happier than I was in that moment.

Even now, our marriage crumbling beneath us, I felt the ghostly flutter of that euphoric moment in my stomach. Milo, as always, had known just what to say, what I would feel at the mention of that night. I think that was what I both loved and hated most about him, how easily he could make me forget all the things I needed to remember and remember what I wanted to forget.

"You're just as lovely tonight as you were then," he said. "Lovelier." If possible, he pulled me more tightly against him. "It's impossible for me to hold you like this without remembering."

My heart had begun to beat madly, and I forced myself to take slow, deep breaths. I didn't trust myself to answer. I knew I was dangerously close to losing myself in his hypnotic seduction.

"Come upstairs," he said in a low voice in my ear. "Spend the night with me, Amory."

I closed my eyes. In that moment I wanted nothing more than to relent, to forget everything except how much I loved him. But some part of me knew that if I did, nothing would change.

And I couldn't do it. I could not let things go on as they had always done.

I stepped back suddenly, cool air rushing in to take the place of his warmth against me. "I can't, Milo," I said, and my voice sounded strained.

"Why not?" He still held my hand in his, his thumb caressing my palm.

"Do you want the truth?"

"Of course."

I looked down at my hand in his, and then I gently pulled it away. "For things to work between us, I need you to behave as my husband, to show that you care, not only when it's convenient or you're in danger of losing me. I love you desperately, Milo," I whispered, tears welling in my eyes, threatening to spill over. "But I'm not sure I can trust you. And sometimes love just isn't enough."

26

I awoke with a heavy feeling in my chest, the sort of thing that befitted the broken-hearted heroines of the radio dramas my life was rapidly beginning to resemble, but there was nothing to be done about that at the moment. I had made myself very clear to Milo. It was up to him to make up his mind.

After a breakfast of toast and coffee, I felt a renewed sense of purpose. Lord Dunmore's ball was tomorrow, and I needed to start putting things in order. My romantic difficulties could wait until afterward.

I had just finished dressing in a light wool suit of pale blue over an ivory crêpe de chine blouse with a flounced collar when I heard the telephone ring. I refused to hope that it was Milo calling. Since I was not expecting it, I was not disappointed when Winnelda came to say that Inspector Jones was on the line. I was rather glad to hear it, in fact. Now that I had come up with a plan for catching the killer, I had only to convince the inspector that it was a worthwhile endeavor.

"Good morning, Mrs. Ames," he said, as I picked up the telephone. "I hope I'm not disturbing you."

"Not at all, Inspector. I was hoping to hear from you, in fact. I've something I'd like to talk to you about."

"How fortunate. I was wondering if you would like to have tea with me this afternoon. Do you know Lyon's Corner House in Piccadilly?"

"Certainly," I said readily, very glad he hadn't suggested tea at the Ritz.

"Very good. I'll see you at four." He rang off without further ado. He certainly hadn't been talkative, but that was not particularly unusual.

I wondered why he had decided not to come by the flat this time, but I certainly was not going to quibble over the meeting place.

I set the telephone back on the receiver and tried to think of how best to spend my morning. I wasn't entirely sure that Inspector Jones would be receptive to my plan, but I intended to convince him.

■ ■ ■ ■

The second telephone call of the day came shortly after lunch. Once again, it was not Milo.

"Mrs. Ames, you'll never believe it," said Mrs. Barrington without preamble as soon as I had picked up the telephone. "I've found my Eiffel Tower pin! It was in the trinket box on the mantelpiece!"

This was a very unexpected development. "I don't understand, Mrs. Barrington," I said, when I had recovered from my surprise. "It just appeared there?"

"Yes. I've been through the house again and again, and the servants have searched behind me. It wasn't there when last I looked. I'm certain of it."

"When did you discover it?"

"Just now. I was looking for matches and happened to open the box, and there it was, as blatant as you please. I'm not imagining things, Mrs. Ames. It wasn't here before."

I believed her. Mrs. Barrington was not a silly woman. I was certain she had made a thorough and comprehensive search. That could mean only one thing. Someone must have placed it back in the box.

"When did you last make a search?" I

asked, hoping that, if she could pinpoint the time, it would help us determine who might have had access to the box.

"I've tried to remember that. I think it was the night before the dinner party. I wanted to make one final search before I came to you with my problem."

So she had not looked in the box since that evening at her house. That meant that anyone at the dinner party that night might have slipped it inside when no one was looking. I tried to recall seeing anyone near the fireplace, but I hadn't been paying much attention.

"But why should someone have put it back?" I asked.

"I don't know," she answered with a sigh. "I've been trying to figure out who might have done it, but it just doesn't make any sense."

The door buzzer rang, and Winnelda went to answer it.

"I'm sorry, Mrs. Barrington," I said. "There's someone here. Shall I call you back?"

"No, no, that's all right," she said. "I just thought you should know. If I think of anything else, I'll ring you again."

I set the phone down, frowning. Why would someone have stolen something only to put it back? Surely they didn't think the crime would have gone undetected.

"A package has come for you, madam," said Winnelda, coming away from the door with a brown parcel in her hand.

I took the package and opened the attached card. It read:

I suspected you wouldn't come to collect it, so I've sent it along. I look forward to seeing you wear it.

— A

It couldn't be.

I removed a flat, midnight-blue case from the package and opened it. Winnelda and I both stared.

Nestled on a bed of black velvet was an enormous oval diamond in a platinum setting, suspended from a chain of diamonds that glittered wildly as if they had been waiting to be exposed to light.

The Dunmore Diamond.

It had already been quite an eventful day by the time I left the flat to meet Inspector Jones for our tea appointment. I had put the Dunmore Diamond in the safe, though I still felt a bit uneasy leaving it unattended. I wished that Lord Dunmore hadn't sent it to me in that casual way. The thing was priceless, and he had sent it over wrapped in brown parchment paper.

Markham drove me to Piccadilly, and I went inside Lyon's Corner House. It was busy this time of day, the large crowds at the white-clothed tables being served by nippies in their black dresses with starched white collars, caps, and aprons.

The room was large, and most of the tables were full, but I spotted Inspector Jones sitting at one of the tables near the long steel food counter, reading a newspaper. I made my way over to him, weaving among the tables.

"Hello, Inspector Jones," I said. He had risen to his feet, but I waved him back into his chair. "I'm sorry I've kept you waiting."

"No need to apologize, Mrs. Ames. I appreciate your taking the time to meet me."

Though he was a difficult man to read at times, I had come to be able to detect a certain something in his posture that indicated when he was about to reveal something. There was something he was going tell me, or, more likely, he was up to something.

It seemed my latter supposition was the correct one, for a moment later I heard a familiar voice. "Well, isn't this a charming

369

reunion."

I turned to see Milo making his way to our table. I looked back at Inspector Jones, who met my gaze with a pleasant expression. I suddenly understood why he had chosen this neutral meeting place. No doubt he had been keeping tabs on my unraveling marriage and knew I would be unlikely to meet with him if I knew Milo would be in attendance. I felt I should be a bit angry with him for not telling me my husband would be at tea. Until I heard what he had to say, however, I would grudgingly overlook his underhanded tactics.

I glanced at Milo, but he was not looking at me.

"Inspector Jones. How nice to see you again," he said, by way of greeting. It was polite of him to say so, considering Inspector Jones had suspected that Milo might be guilty of murder when last they had met.

"Thank you for coming, Mr. Ames. How have you been?"

Milo took the seat beside me, his attention still focused on the inspector. "I'm excellent, thank you. I trust the London air is agreeing with you?"

"It's been an adjustment from the seaside," Inspector Jones responded. "I have been enjoying it immensely, however. We've adapted quite readily to life here."

"We? Are you married?" I asked. It had suddenly occurred to me that I knew very little about Inspector Jones. It was silly of me to think so, of course, but it seemed strange somehow that he should have a life outside of his role as a policeman.

"I am. Mrs. Jones is delighted with London."

"And have you any children?"

"Yes, two daughters."

He answered the questions willingly enough, but did not elaborate. I supposed that it was against his nature to give more information than he received.

The nippy came to our table, and we placed our orders.

"I hear Lord Dunmore is going ahead with his ball tomorrow night," Inspector Jones said, when she had gone.

"Yes," I replied warily. Now that I had my own plans for the ball, I hoped Inspector Jones didn't mean to tell me that the police planned to prohibit another event at Dunmore House. It would spoil everything. "Is there any reason that he shouldn't?"

"Aside from the sake of propriety?" he replied dryly.

"Well, yes," I admitted. "I think it's rather in poor taste, but you'll admit that societal approval has never been chief among Lord Dunmore's concerns." I didn't dare look at Milo as I said it.

"No. Indeed it hasn't," Inspector Jones agreed.

"If he wants to have another ball, I don't really see what harm it could do." I could hear myself protesting too strenuously, but I couldn't seem to make myself be quiet.

It seemed that Inspector Jones's rather searching gaze settled on my face for a moment longer than made me comfortable. With the inspector, I always had the feeling that his mild eyes were boring into my brain and reading all the thoughts I most wanted to keep from him. While this was, no doubt, an excellent skill for a policeman to have, it always put me a bit out when I was the one from whom unspoken confessions were being pried.

"Are you planning to attend?"

"It's going to be one of the biggest events of the season," I said, dodging the question he was really asking.

"And you, Mr. Ames?" he asked, turning to Milo.

Milo was, as ever, unimpressed with Inspector Jones's interrogations. "I expect Amory will drag me along with her," he answered blandly. "I have no patience for balls, but one must do as one's wife requests."

"I have often found that to be the case," Inspector Jones agreed pleasantly before turning his gaze back to me. "And I expect you have some sort of plan to catch the killer?"

My eyes flickered to Milo, and I saw the barest hint of sardonic amusement cross his features. I looked back to the inspector and affected my best innocent expression. "Why, Inspector Jones, I don't know what you mean."

He was not fooled. Apparently, despite my moderate success with Mr. Gibbs, I was not cut out for the stage. "Why don't you tell me what it is that you're planning? You'll agree that things will go better if we work together."

I had intended to tell him anyway, knowing it would be beneficial in many ways to operate under the canopy of police sanction. Nevertheless, I felt a bit annoyed that he should have predicted my intentions so correctly. No doubt he had suspected I was plotting something, and that was the reason he had asked me here.

"Very well," I conceded. "It will make things easier if we have a policeman at hand."

"I'm so glad you think so." There was definite sarcasm in his tone, but I chose to ignore it.

"I've been thinking that the best way to catch the killer is to lure them with another piece of jewelry," I said.

"Do you think that it will be as easy as that?" There was no derision in his tone, for which I was grateful.

"I don't know," I confessed. "But it seems worth a try. And Lord Dunmore has agreed to provide a piece worth stealing: the Dunmore Diamond."

Inspector Jones's brows rose. "I am unfamiliar with that particular piece, but it sounds most impressive."

"It's been in the Dunmore family for generations, I believe."

The nippy came then with our tea things: a pot of steaming black tea, and a tiered platter of little sandwiches, crumpets, tea cakes, and shortbread biscuits. Though I had very little appetite, I took a biscuit and nibbled at it half heartedly.

"And how, exactly, is the thief to gain access to it?" Inspector Jones asked, once our tea was poured. I was gratified that he was taking my plan under consideration, rather than dismissing it out of hand.

"I . . . I'm going to wear it." I found I

couldn't look at Milo as I said it and focused instead on the cup and saucer on the table before me.

"Indeed?" Inspector Jones said.

"At some point in the evening, I will leave it unattended in a room upstairs. Perhaps the card room. It is familiar to all of the suspects, as nearly all of them had been to that room at some point on the night of the murder. Then we've only to wait in the room across for the thief to reveal himself."

"That's a very pretty plan, Mrs. Ames, but you overlook the danger of wearing the diamond. If the thief was willing to kill once, what will stop him from trying again?"

I hadn't, until that moment, really considered that I might be in any particular danger. I had thought to leave the necklace in the card room and then give the thief time to try to collect it. It hadn't occurred to me that the thief might try to take it from around my neck. It was rather stupid of me to have overlooked the possibility. Nevertheless, I intended to go ahead with the plan.

"It's worth the risk," I said resolutely.

Inspector Jones looked at Milo. "And you agree with her, Mr. Ames?"

Milo lit a cigarette, waving out the match. "You know as well as I do, Inspector, that there is no stopping her once she gets an idea in her head."

A small smile appeared on the inspector's face. "Yes, I am beginning to realize that."

"There's only one thing that might cause a problem," I said.

"Only one?" Inspector Jones asked wryly.

"What if all of the suspects don't come to the ball? A death might have been enough to keep the innocent ones away, and the guilty party might just as well decide that it's too dangerous to attend."

"You leave that to me, Mrs. Ames. I believe I can be trusted to carry out that small part of the plan. And I'll put an officer across from the card room to keep an eye on things." He rose then, placing several bills on the table. "Thank you for meeting with me. I shall leave the two of you to enjoy your tea."

"One more thing, Inspector," I said.

"Yes?"

"Who inherits Mr. Harker's money?"

He looked as though he wondered why I asked, but didn't question me. "There is a brother in America."

Then his death would not have benefitted the Barringtons. "I just wondered. Thank you for the tea, Inspector Jones. We shall see you tomorrow."

He hesitated, his gaze shifting to Milo. "I

meant to ask you, Mr. Ames, if you learned anything of interest the night of the murder. Inspector Harris mentioned that he saw you speaking to several of the people on the first floor after the incident."

This was news to me. I had assumed Milo had gone to Helene Renault after the shooting. Why hadn't he told me that he had been asking questions of the suspects? He had professed to be uninterested in the circumstances surrounding Mr. Harker's death, but it seemed that was not quite the case.

If Milo was caught off guard by the inspector's sudden question, he gave no indication of it. "I was vaguely curious," he allowed, "but no one seemed to know anything."

"I see," Inspector Jones said. "Well, I suppose that will be all for now. I'll see you at the ball."

I watched him go. He had never explained precisely why he had invited both of us to tea, but I wondered if he had simply been trying to push us together. If it didn't seem counter to his character, I might have suspected him of having a romantic streak. We both knew, however, that it would take more than a few scones and biscuits to mend things between Milo and me.

I turned to my husband. "Why didn't you

tell me you were asking questions that night?"

"There was nothing to tell."

I accepted this answer, knowing it would do no good to push him. I couldn't help but wonder, however, if he had been gathering information on my behalf. Perhaps he had even suspected it was murder and had been trying to steer me clear of it. It was a comforting thought, somehow, that he had cared, but I wasn't sure it mattered now.

"What do you make of Inspector Jones?" I asked, attempting to ascertain my own thoughts. "I can't quite decide what he's about."

Milo observed the burning end of his cigarette disinterestedly. "I'm a bit surprised he would allow you to proceed in so harebrained a scheme."

"It's a very good scheme," I protested. "Perhaps he realizes that it will be the easiest way to flush the killer out of hiding and feels that I am capable of assisting."

"Do you really think it will be accomplished so neatly? Lord Dunmore throws another ball, you wear his necklace and produce a killer, tied with a bow?"

"We can always hope." I hesitated. "Are you going to take me to the ball?"

His brows rose. "Oh, are we friends again

now? You change your mind so quickly, darling. I can barely keep up."

"Milo," I said calmly. "I don't like to quarrel with you."

"I don't particularly care for it myself."

"Then let us work together. For now, let us put aside everything else and try to solve this murder. If we learned anything at the Brightwell, it's that it would have been much better if we had cooperated." It might have saved me getting shot at, in fact.

"If you say so, darling." He ground out his cigarette and rose. "I'll be there, but I'm not certain what time. You'd better go on without me. In the words of the good inspector, I'll see you at the ball."

27

The morning of the ball arrived, and I greeted it with a mixture of anticipation and apprehension. On the one hand, I was looking forward to some sort of resolution. On the other, I was a little concerned about what that resolution might be. Perhaps it was my past experience with such things, but I could not help but feel there would be a great deal of unpleasantness before the evening was out. After all, there was a very good chance that I would encounter a murderer tonight, and my last such experience had not been an agreeable one.

There was one consolation: at least it was not another masked ball. I didn't know if I could bear another evening of concealed faces. In fact, if I never attended a masked ball again, it would be fine with me. It is difficult enough to read people in real life, to sort through the masks we wear, all of us pretending to be something or someone that we are not. Indeed, nothing in this case was what it seemed. Even the jewels had been masked in deception.

In a way, all of this had started with masks. I wondered again about the connection between James Harker's tiger mask and the one that Mr. Foster had worn. Inspector Jones had seemed convinced that Mr. Harker's death was not a matter of mistaken identity, but I still felt that there was some connection with the mask.

I wondered suddenly if Inspector Jones had thought to contact the mask maker. He hadn't mentioned it, and it seemed to me that it might prove a useful thing to do. I remembered at the dinner party Lord Dunmore had told me the name of the fancy dress shop where he and many of the others got their masks. Frederick's, was it? No, Friedrich's.

I went to the telephone and asked the operator to locate and ring up the shop. She was a very efficient young woman, and a few moments later I was on the telephone with Mr. Bertelli, Lord Dunmore's costumier.

"Hello," I said. "My name is Mrs. Ames. I was admiring the mask you made for Lord Dunmore's masquerade, and I was thinking of having something made up. Your work is magnificent."

He was obviously flattered. "Thank you, madam. We do have an excellent selection of masks ready-made. Or we can make something specific for you, if you'd rather."

"I think I'd like an original," I said quickly. "Something along the lines of . . ." I searched my mind for something suitable, "a Columbina mask. Perhaps in black velvet with gold leaf?"

"Oh, yes, madam," he said. "I can do something of that sort, certainly."

"Thank you. I understand you made the mask for Mr. Nigel Foster," I said casually. "The tiger one he wore to his recent masquerade?"

"Yes, I designed Mr. Foster's mask personally. He specifically requested a tiger mask. I thought it a bit outré myself, but, of course, I was determined to give satisfaction. I was not going to quibble with him, but . . ." He paused significantly and tsked into the phone. "It was not what we had originally agreed upon."

"Did he say why it was that he wanted a tiger?" I asked.

"Oh, yes," Mr. Bertelli answered. "He said he knew someone else who was wearing a tiger mask, and he wanted one as well. It was some joke." Again, a disapproving sound from the other end of the line. "When the one I created would have looked so much better."

This was very interesting indeed. Why should Mr. Foster have wanted a mask to match Mr. Harker's? If anything, I should have thought he wanted his own unique mask. He had told Mr. Bertelli that it was meant to be a joke, but he had led me to believe that he and Mr. Harker were not well acquainted. If that was true, what joke could have been between them?

"Now about your mask, Mrs. Ames," Mr. Bertelli said. "Did you want it to include feathers or jewels of any sort?"

I paused. "Jewels?" I repeated.

"Yes, madam. We've a wide array of gemstones we can put on the mask. They're paste, of course, but very high quality.

"I . . . might I think a bit about it and call you back?"

"Certainly, certainly."

I rang off and stood for a moment, lost in thought. The conversation had given me much to consider.

Almost before I knew it, it was time to begin dressing for the ball. I had chosen for the evening a gown of silver silk charmeuse that flowed like molten lead as I walked. It had a fitted bodice, very thin straps, and a low-cut back. It hugged my shape to the hip and gave way to a gently flowing skirt with a slight train. It was not nearly as elaborate as the gown I had worn to the first ball, but I had no wish to go tripping about the house when I was on the heels of a murderer. Besides, I couldn't help but feel that this less-extravagant ensemble suited me better, especially when I would be wearing so ostentatious a piece of jewelry.

I hadn't heard from Milo since our visit with Inspector Jones, and I hoped that something wouldn't come up to detain him from attending the ball. One never knew where Milo might dash off to next. Some part of me felt that I could rely on him, but I knew better than to have my heart set on it. Hopefully, when push came to shove, I would not be left alone to grapple with a murderer.

I was nearly dressed when I heard the ringing of the telephone. I wondered if it might be Inspector Jones calling in regard to the ball, but Winnelda didn't come to fetch me, so I went on with my makeup.

A moment later, she came into the room, one of my furs draped over her arm. "The white fur for tonight, Mrs. Ames?" she asked.

"Yes, I think so. Who was on the telephone, Winnelda?"

She wrinkled her nose. "An unsavory gentleman, to be sure."

"Oh? With whom did he wish to speak?"

"He was calling for Mr. Ames."

This was intriguing. "Did he leave his name or a message?"

"Yes, madam," she said, draping the fur over the back of a chair and running her hand along it. "He said his name was Mr. Gibbs."

"Mr. Gibbs?" I exclaimed. "What did he want?"

She looked up, surprised at my interest. "He wanted me to tell Mr. Ames that he thinks he's found just the piece Mr. Ames is looking for."

Mercifully, Markham was not in the habit of asking questions, and he drove me back to the pawnbroker's shop in Whitechapel without comment. I thought I had just enough time to stop before the ball, and it could be that this was the piece of the puzzle we had been waiting for.

I'm sure I must have looked a sight, rushing up to the shop in an evening gown and mink stole. I had left the Dunmore Diamond in its case in the car. I didn't intend to take any chances with it.

I rapped on the door, dust collecting on the knuckles of my white gloves. Mr. Gibbs had not answered the telephone when I had phoned him back, and I was a bit worried that he might not be at his shop at all. Luckily, after a few moments of energetic rapping, I heard shuffling steps inside, and the key turned in the lock. The door gave a protesting creak as it opened ever so slightly, and I saw one eye regard me suspiciously from within.

"Good evening, Mr. Gibbs. May I come in for a moment?" I asked, pushing my way past him into the shop.

He was, I think, not entirely pleased to see me. On the one hand, he was fairly certain that Milo was prepared to reward him handsomely if the piece he had proved to be satisfactory. On the other, Milo was not with me, and I think he was not entirely convinced I would be able to pay him. The possibility of reward won the day, however, and he smiled at me.

"I'm happy to be of service to you, Miss . . . Mary, was it? Is your gentleman friend with you?"

"No, he's otherwise engaged this evening."

Mr. Gibbs nodded knowingly, as though he commiserated with me that Mr. Ames should be required to spend the evening with his bothersome wife.

"I understand that you found a piece similar to the one I was searching for?"

"Yes. I asked around after the gentleman told me what he wanted, and I think I may have found it. But perhaps you'd better come back later with Mr. Ames, just to be sure it's the right thing."

He was worried that I, as the rich man's little mistress, would be unable to compensate him appropriately.

I wondered which piece it might be. I had listed all of the missing jewelry, but I suspected, for some reason, that the piece he had found was Mrs. Barrington's missing sapphire bracelet. After all, it was the piece most recently stolen.

"Would you show me the piece?" I asked. "Please?"

He hesitated before making his way behind the counter. He pulled out a small bundle. It looked to be something wrapped in a dirty handkerchief. Pulling back the corners to reveal the piece inside, he pushed it toward me on the counter.

My eyes widened in surprise. It appeared to be Mrs. Barrington's Eiffel Tower brooch.

I picked it up and studied it closely. Flipping it over, I saw what I was looking for:

the date of the Barringtons' anniversary engraved beneath the clasp.

If this was in fact her brooch, however, what was the piece she had found in her trinket box only yesterday? One of them was a replica. But which? "Are these real diamonds?" I asked.

He drew himself up. "Of course they are. I don't sell worthless trinkets."

"No, no. Of course not. I only wanted to be sure."

"You can bring that to any jeweler in town, miss. He'll tell you."

"That won't be necessary. This is exactly what I'm looking for," I told him.

"I aim to please," he replied with an expectant smile.

I hesitated. I felt suddenly that there was no way to get the information I wanted without revealing my true motives to Mr. Gibbs. Unfortunately, I was relatively certain that he would not be appreciative of my ploy. Well, there was nothing to be done about that now.

"May I be honest with you, Mr. Gibbs?"

He looked suddenly very wary, as though honesty was a commodity he did not often trade in. "If you like, Miss Mary."

I plunged ahead before I could think better of it. "I'm afraid my name isn't Mary, and I'm not Mr. Ames's mistress. I'm his wife."

He frowned.

I rushed ahead. "I am looking for this brooch because it was stolen from one of my friends."

His face hardened suddenly, and as he crossed his arms over his chest, I knew I was on the verge of losing him. "I don't know anything about that."

"No, I'm certain you don't. You see, it's all very complicated, but I need to know who it was that stole it. I assure you, none of it will come back on you or your associates. And Mr. Ames and I are still willing to compensate you handsomely for your trouble."

This seemed to appease him a bit, for his scowl softened ever so slightly.

"It's something of a private matter, and I would be very grateful if you could help me."

I hoped he would interpret "grateful" to mean generous.

"I didn't get any of the particulars about who sold it," he told me at last. "Perhaps I could find out . . ." The rest of the sentence was heavily implied: for a price.

I thought about this for a moment and came to a decision. "Can you telephone your friend and find out? I need a description of the person who sold it. As detailed as possible."

He appeared to consider.

"There will be a reward in it for both you and your associate," I assured him.

"I suppose I could find out," he said grudgingly. "A description is all you're wanting?"

"Well, dates would be quite helpful as well. But the most important thing is to find out who it was that sold it. And I need to know tonight, if at all possible."

"It may take me a while to locate my associate."

I suspected a rundown of nearby pubs would be in order. I glanced at the clock. The ball was getting ready to begin, and I didn't want to be late. I reached into my handbag and took out several bills. "This is a down payment on the information, Mr. Gibbs," I said, pressing it into his hand. "The sooner you can find out, the more there will be in it for you. When you have the information, call the number on the card Mr. Ames gave you, the number you used today. Leave a message with my maid, Winnelda, and I'll call her later to find out what you've learned."

"Very good, Mrs. Ames. I'll find out as

quickly as I can and let you know."

He seemed much more amiable now that I had greased his palms, if that was indeed the correct expression.

"Thank you so much, Mr. Gibbs. You've been ever so helpful." I felt suddenly elated by the promise of success. With any luck, we would have a description of the killer before the night was out.

"His wife, you say?" he said, giving me a thorough going over with his eyes. "I guess he's a smarter gent than I took him for."

I arrived at Dunmore House shortly after nine o'clock, and the street was already packed with automobiles. The crowds were even denser than they had been at the last party; I reflected grimly that it seemed the murder had only whetted society's appetite for scandal. There were people of every description flowing into Lord Dunmore's house in a sea of evening jackets, top hats, glimmering gowns, furs, and jewels. The mingled scents of a hundred expensive perfumes hung in the air like a pleasant cloud.

Lord Dunmore was standing in the foyer greeting guests when I entered the house. It seemed almost as though he was holding court — and enjoying it immensely —

despite the macabre outcome of his last such event. He saw me come in and excused himself from the group he was with, working his way through the crowd to reach me.

"Amory, I'm so glad you've arrived," he said, taking my hands in his and squeezing them. He stepped back as if to survey me. "You look ravishing."

"Thank you."

His eyes strayed to my neckline. "It suits you."

My hand reached up to touch the Dunmore Diamond. I had put it on in the car after leaving Mr. Gibbs's shop, and I had been aware of the cold weight of it against my chest ever since. "I hope it works," I said.

"People are beginning to notice, I think." It was true. I had seen several curious glances in my direction since I had discarded my furs.

"I've thought it over," I told him in a low voice to avoid being overheard. "At some point in the evening, I'll take it off and leave it upstairs. Then I'll tell each of the suspects that the latch is loose and I've set it aside. We shall hope that it proves too great a prize to resist."

"Just be careful," he said, his hand on my arm. "I should hate for you to put yourself in danger."

"I'll be careful," I assured him. I certainly didn't intend to take any unnecessary risks.

"Alexander." A slim blond woman had appeared at his side, clutching his arm. "You've promised to introduce me to your friends."

He smiled at me with a shrug. "Duty calls, Mrs. Ames. Save a dance for me?"

"Certainly."

He allowed the blonde to lead him away, and I followed the crowds into the ballroom. The decorations were a bit different from what they had been at the last ball, but no less elaborate. If Lord Dunmore was indeed the culprit, it was not money he was after. He had far too much of that at his disposal already.

I was still taking it all in when Mrs. Barrington met my gaze from across the room and waved me toward her. She was wearing a gown of dark purple satin, but the gown was hardly noticeable against the veritable glare of her jewels. She wore a necklace of diamonds set in bright gold, and it gleamed in the light, rivaling the chandeliers.

"Good evening, Mrs. Barrington," I said when I had reached her. "You look lovely this evening. Your necklace is beautiful."

"These are paste, my dear. Lloyd had

them made up for me. I didn't dare arrive in real diamonds, and I've let everyone know as much."

"Yes, that seems the safest thing to do." I thought of the Eiffel Tower brooch in Mr. Gibbs's shop but decided against mentioning it at present. I wanted a bit more time to sort things out in my mind.

"So that's the Dunmore Diamond, is it?" she said, her eyes on the gem at my neck. "It certainly is a lovely stone."

"Yes. I feel a bit conspicuous wearing it." It seemed the weight of responsibility made it heavier around my neck. I had a good deal of very expensive jewelry, much of it given to me by Milo, but it was another thing entirely to wear someone else's priceless family heirloom. Especially when one considered that I was, in essence, advertising it like wares at a market to a jewel thief and killer.

"Conspicuous is just what we want, isn't it?" she pointed out. "Now you've only to be seen by the suspects so that they know the diamond is in play."

"I suppose I shall make my way around so that they can," I told her.

She nodded. "Good luck, Mrs. Ames." She looked strained, anxious, and I could only assume that the tension of the evening was beginning to weigh on her. I felt a bit nervy myself.

I reached out and patted her arm. "I think it will all work out."

She tried to smile but didn't quite succeed. "Mrs. Ames, there's something else that concerns me. What Mrs. Douglas-Hughes told you, about James's comment that night that my necklace looked like it belonged to someone's mistress. Do you think . . . I've begun to wonder if perhaps Lloyd has a mistress. He's been acting so strangely as of late, going out at strange hours."

I was surprised. "He seems very fond of you, Mrs. Barrington," I said, and I meant it. I had seen nothing but devotion in Mr. Barrington's behavior. "Perhaps he's only been upset about Mr. Harker."

"Yes," she said. "Yes, I suppose you're right. If you'll excuse me, I will see where he's gone off to."

I took a glass of punch and began to make my way around the perimeter of the ballroom, looking for any of the suspects that might be induced to admire, and presumably covet, the Dunmore Diamond. There was a good deal of lovely jewelry in play tonight, but I thought none of it would be as tempting as the piece at my throat.

"Yoo-hoo, Mrs. Ames!" I stilled as I heard the voice behind me, cutting through the music of the orchestra with ease. It was Mrs. Roland.

I turned to see her approaching me in a brilliant scarlet silk kimono that might have been better suited to a boudoir than a ballroom. It seemed she had made good her threat to arrive uninvited at Lord Dunmore's ball.

"How are you, Mrs. Roland?" I asked resignedly as she reached me.

"Wonderful, wonderful! What a lovely party this is. I'm so glad you suggested I come."

There was nothing I could say to this, but, luckily, no response was required.

"You look lovely, as always, my dear," she went on, without stopping for breath. "Silver is so becoming with those gray eyes of yours, and . . ." Her eyebrows rose so high they nearly disappeared into the row of ringlets arranged low across her forehead. "That's the Dunmore Diamond, isn't it?"

"Yes," I said, trying to think of some good excuse for wearing it. "I was speaking about it with Lord Dunmore, and he felt it was time it made an appearance. He asked me to wear it."

"Indeed?" she asked, and I could hear the

speculation in her voice. "And is your husband here, dear?"

That was a very good question. I had yet to see any sign of Milo.

"He should be here somewhere," I said, inching away from her. "If you'll excuse me, Mrs. Roland, I have someone I must speak to."

"Of course, dear. Of course. The diamond looks magnificent on you. Much better than it did on Lord Dunmore's mother!"

I did my best to disappear into the crowd and breathed a sigh of relief when I was sure I had been able to escape her. Her questions had become too pointed too quickly, and I hoped I would be able to avoid her for the rest of the night.

The evening was certainly off to an interesting start. I glanced at the clock. It was nearly ten o'clock. Things were spiraling toward a conclusion. If all went as planned, we would catch a killer by midnight.

28

An hour later, I decided I had mingled sufficiently and that it was time to put the plan into action. I had flaunted the necklace before all of the suspects, except Mr. and Mrs. Douglas-Hughes, whom I had not yet seen. I wondered if they had decided not to attend the ball. Inspector Jones had intended to encourage attendance, but Mr. Douglas-Hughes had friends in government, and I thought he would not be induced to come if he felt disinclined to do so.

There was still no sign of Milo either, but I would not wait forever. I would have to catch a killer without him.

I slipped into the foyer and made my way up the wide red stairs, treading carefully to avoid another mishap. There was no one sitting on the steps tonight, and the stairway seemed more sinister somehow. The inspector's warning was fresh in my mind, and, though I tried to act casual, I was very alert to be certain I was not being followed. All other considerations aside, it would be quite embarrassing to be murdered.

Speaking of Detective Inspector Jones, I had seen no sign of him as of yet. Nevertheless, I had no doubt that he was skulking about the premises somewhere, and I was confident that he had stationed a policeman in the bedroom across from the card room as we had discussed.

The upstairs hallway was quiet, and I reached the card room without encountering anyone. I carefully removed the necklace and set it on the card table. I stepped back to be certain it would offer sufficient enticement and was satisfied by the way it glittered even in the dimly lit room. It was rather an obvious ruse, I thought, but I hoped the thief would be too caught up by such a prize to notice.

With one final glance over my shoulder, I left the room, closing the door behind me, and went back downstairs.

In the foyer I spotted Mr. and Mrs. Douglas-Hughes, who had just come in. I wished I had waited a few more moments, so they might have seen the diamond. Perhaps I could find a way to bring it into the conversation.

"Good evening," I said, approaching them. "I was just wondering if you were here somewhere."

"Good evening, Mrs. Ames," Mr. Douglas-Hughes replied pleasantly. "I'm afraid I was detained."

"Nothing unpleasant has happened yet tonight, has it?" Mamie asked. The "yet" did not escape me. She expected something to happen, too. I wondered if everyone could feel the vague sense of anticipation in the air.

"No, not at all," I said. The unpleasantness was still to come.

"I was a little uneasy about coming here tonight," Mamie admitted with a rueful smile.

"There's nothing to worry about, darling," her husband said, but I noticed that his eyes moved around the room in a restless, watchful way. I wondered what he was looking for.

"I think none of us are very easy," I said.

"But we've all come, haven't we?" Mamie replied. "The police wanted us here for some reason, and I think that is what frightens me a bit. That Inspector Jones asked in the politest way if we could attend, and we really didn't want to say no. Of course, judging from the crowds, it seems half of London is interested in seeing if anything is going to happen this evening."

"Yes," I answered. "It will certainly be interesting." I wanted to say more, but I held my tongue, despite my instinct that they could be trusted. They had both lied to me about the missing earring, but I still felt somehow that they were not involved in the theft or murder. Mamie seemed much too kind to be guilty, and, while I thought Mr. Douglas-Hughes the type of gentleman who would not hesitate to kill in the service of his country, I did not think that he would have carried out a killing in such a public place and in so untidy a manner.

Nevertheless, despite my belief in their innocence, I could afford to trust no one at this point. We were too close. I could feel it.

As luck would have it, the Echols sisters approached us just then. I had crossed paths with them earlier in the ballroom. Marjorie had been cool and Felicity uneasy, and I knew it was not my company they were seeking now. Mamie had obviously won them over as well.

"You both look lovely," Mamie told them after exchanging pleasantries. I had to admit that it was true. Marjorie looked stunning in a gown of bright red, and Felicity looked ethereal in violet. I thought again how very different the two of them were. It was not especially surprising that Mr. Harker should have been torn in his affections, if that was indeed the case. Felicity's gentleness would have been well matched with his quiet nature, but Marjorie's vibrant boldness would have been appealing to a shy, un-confident gentleman.

"You've taken off the diamond, I see," Marjorie said suddenly, acknowledging me for the first time since she had joined us. Really, it couldn't have been more perfect an opening.

"Oh, yes," I said. "It seemed the clasp was loose. I left it in the card room until Lord Dunmore can put it back in his safe."

"Diamond?" Mamie asked.

"Yes, Lord Dunmore lent me the Dun-more Diamond for the evening. It's only too bad the clasp was broken. I didn't dare risk losing so valuable a piece."

The more I said this, the more often I felt like this was all much too obvious. Would the thief really think that I would be so care-less as to leave it unattended in the card room? Were the situations reversed, I would find the entire thing extremely suspect. I supposed only time would tell, however. I just needed to be sure that all the suspects were properly informed.

"If you'll all excuse me, I must see if I can find my husband." It was a flimsy excuse, considering I was fairly certain Milo was not even here, but it would work as well as any.

I made my way back into the ballroom. The din had grown louder, and people were talking and laughing with what seemed to be an almost frantic merriment. There was a sense of expectation in the air, as though they were anticipating further calamity. I only hoped this evening's events would not end up obliging them to too great a degree.

I had only just entered the room and begun sipping a glass of punch given to me by a passing waiter when Mr. Foster approached.

"Mrs. Ames, I've been waiting all evening for the chance to dance with you," he said with a charming smile. "Would you do me the honor?"

"Certainly," I told him, setting aside my glass. In addition to the possibility of conversing with a suspect, my nervous energy was building, and I thought the exercise would do me good.

He was an excellent dancer, and there was something very appealing about him, a boyish charm that combined with his athletic physique. I saw many of the women looking

403

his way, and I knew it wasn't just his storied sporting career that interested them.

"You're looking very lovely this evening," he told me. "That color suits you."

"Thank you." I supposed I might as well set up the trap while an opportunity presented itself. "My neck is feeling a bit bare."

"Yes, I noticed you had taken the necklace off."

He was a rather observant gentleman. "The clasp was loose, and I was forced to leave it in the card room until Lord Dunmore has time to put it in the safe."

"Indeed? Well, I think your neck couldn't possibly have looked any lovelier with the necklace than it does now."

I laughed. "It's a stunning piece of jewelry."

"Yes, I suppose it is."

He seemed disinclined to discuss jewelry, and we talked of other things. As we moved about the dance floor, something caught my eye. Lord Dunmore and Vivian Garmond stood at the edge of room, talking to one another. It was the first time I had seen them together, but there was no romance in what was happening now. I could tell that at once from their body language and the expression on Mrs. Garmond's face as she looked up at him. I couldn't help but feel I had not helped matters between them by wearing the Dunmore Diamond tonight. Perhaps I would have the opportunity later to explain the situation to Mrs. Garmond.

The dance ended, and Mr. Foster escorted me from the dance floor, his hand resting lightly on my waist.

"Can I get you another drink?" he asked.

"Not just now, thank you."

"Here you are, Amory." I hadn't seen Lord Dunmore approaching until he appeared at my side. I glanced to where he had been standing with Mrs. Garmond, but she was gone. "I've been looking for you. You don't mind if I steal her away, do you, Foster?"

Mr. Foster stepped back, a smile flashing across his face. "Not at all. I'll take another turn with her later."

It seemed that Lord Dunmore looked a bit annoyed, but the expression was gone so quickly that I couldn't be sure. I wondered if he was still preoccupied by his encounter with Mrs. Garmond.

Mr. Foster walked away, and Lord Dunmore turned to me. I thought he might ask me to dance, but it seemed that was not his intention. "I want to talk to you for a moment."

I glanced around. It was so loud in the

ballroom that I was certain that no one would overhear us. "What is it?"

"It's too hot in here," he said. "Let's go somewhere where we can get a bit of air."

"Outside?" I suggested, indicating the doors that led from the ballroom out onto the terrace.

"No. It's too windy. It would muss your hair, and we wouldn't want that, would we?"

"No, I suppose not," I replied.

He smiled and took my hand in his. "I know. Come with me."

I let him lead me out into the foyer and across to the small sitting room on the other side, where I had sat the day I had come to visit him. We entered, and he closed the door behind us, the heavy oak muting some of the noise of the ball. The room was cooler than the ballroom had been, but there was something slightly intimate about the setting, and I wondered what it was that he wanted to talk to me about.

He didn't release my hand as he turned to face me. "There? That's better, isn't it?"

"I suppose it is," I answered. "What is it you wanted to talk to me about, Alexander? Is it the diamond? I've left it in the card room as we discussed."

"No, it isn't that. Wanting to be alone with

you isn't reason enough for me to spirit you away?"

I felt a subtle shift in the atmosphere, as though Lord Dunmore had flipped some sort of switch. Really, it was almost impressive.

"It is cooler in here," I conceded, unsure of where this might be leading. The various warnings I had heard about Lord Dunmore nagged at the back of my mind.

"I'm still feeling a bit warm." His voice had taken on a silky quality that put me on guard.

"I believe dancing has that effect," I replied as blandly as possible. So did arguing with one's mistress in a crowded ballroom.

"It isn't only dancing," he answered. "I've found many much more effective means of warming the blood." There was something practiced yet oddly natural in his approach, like an actor who had played a role so long that he forgot he was someone other than the character he embodied.

"I'm sure you have."

His eyes locked on mine. "If you'd let me, Amory, I can have a fire lit in no time."

It was only with great effort that I kept my brows from flying upward in surprise. He really was shameless. What I found remarkable, however, was that the blatant suggestion that would have been completely offensive from another man somehow managed to be almost flattering coming from Lord Dunmore. Almost.

He stepped closer, and I put up a hand to halt his progress. "I shouldn't think that necessary, Lord Dunmore," I said firmly.

"A moment ago I was Alexander."

"It seems that using your Christian name has given you unwarranted encouragement. That was my mistake."

He smiled suddenly, and some little change in his posture completely dispersed the intimacy of the moment. "Am I annoying you, Mrs. Ames?"

"I think you're very charming," I answered carefully, "but you should know that I am quite immune to it."

"In other words, I am wasting my time."

"You are wasting your time, my lord."

His eyes searched my face for a moment, and, apparently seeing that I meant it, he sighed and gave an elegant shrug. "Fair enough. You can't blame a man for trying."

You could, in fact. But I decided that was an opinion best kept to myself.

"I hope we shall be friends," I told him. "But only friends."

"If you insist," he said with faux ill humor.

"I do. We don't need people talking. In fact," I said, "it would probably be better if we aren't seen coming out of this room together. Why don't you go back to your guests, and I'll follow in a moment."

He lifted my hand to his lips and kissed it before turning to go. At the door, he stopped. "We could have had a lot of fun together, you and I," he said wistfully.

" 'Fun' is quite overrated," I told him. "Love and devotion have a much more lasting appeal."

He looked at me, and I knew he understood my meaning. His quarrel with Mrs. Garmond had no doubt spurred on his unseemly advances, but I hoped he could see the error in such logic.

"You're quite a woman, Amory," he said. Then he left the room and closed the door behind him.

I didn't quite know how to feel about what had just happened. On the one hand, it had been inappropriate in the extreme. On the other, perhaps Lord Dunmore had been too much used to getting his way. I hoped this was a lesson he could profit by. And that perhaps he could find a way to work things out with Mrs. Garmond.

I dropped into a chair and rubbed a hand across my forehead. This night was already turning out to be much too eventful, and we had yet to encounter the killer.

My eyes fell on the telephone, and I remembered that I needed to ring Winnelda and see if Mr. Gibbs had had any luck in identifying the thief. I went to the telephone and gave the operator the number to the flat. She connected me, and a moment later Winnelda picked up. "Ames residence," she said crisply.

"Winnelda, it's Mrs. Ames."

"Oh, hello, Mrs. Ames!" she said cheerfully. "How are you?"

"I'm fine, thank you. I asked Mr. Gibbs — the gentleman who called for Mr. Ames earlier this evening — to telephone me and leave a message with you. Has he phoned yet?"

"Oh, yes, madam! He phoned about twenty minutes ago."

I felt a rush of excitement. "What did he say?"

"He said to tell you . . . wait just a moment . . ." I could hear the crinkling of a piece of paper, and then Winnelda read carefully. "The gent was of medium height with dark hair."

I waited, but she did not continue. "That's all?" I asked at last, disappointed.

"That's all he said, madam."

"Thank you, Winnelda."

"Is the ball going well? Did the ladies like your dress? And the necklace?"

"Yes, everything's going quite well. I'll be sure to tell you all about it tomorrow."

"I shall look forward to it, madam!"

I rang off, lost in thought. Medium height with dark hair. I realized suddenly that that description could conceivably be applied to any of the male suspects. And if it was one of the women, they might have had a gentleman acquaintance sell the pieces for them. Really, this clue had turned out to be of very little help.

I heard the door open behind me, and I wondered if Lord Dunmore had come back.

I turned. "Oh, hello, Mr. Foster."

He closed the door behind him and glanced around the room before his eyes came back to me. "I see Dunmore's abandoned you, and I hate to see so lovely a lady all alone."

I didn't know why, but I suddenly felt a bit uneasy. Mr. Foster had never been anything but polite, but there was some slight change in him now that I couldn't quite name. He seemed different somehow. But perhaps it was only that my nerves were all on edge this evening.

"I was just getting ready to rejoin the

festivities," I told him.

"Don't hurry out on my account," he said. My eyes flickered past him to the door. He was standing before it, and I would have to go around him to leave.

"Oh, it's not that," I said lightly. "I think perhaps I'd better go and see if my husband has arrived. If you'll excuse me." I walked purposefully toward the door.

"Wait a moment." He held out a hand, and I stopped myself just before I walked into it.

He looked down at me, his expression not quite as pleasant as it had been a moment ago. The faint warning bell that had been going off in my head seemed to get louder.

"There's no need for you to rush away."

I looked at him warily. There was something in his tone that I didn't quite like, a hint of something dangerous beneath the light words.

"I'm afraid I must be getting back."

"Or you could stay, and we could take advantage of our time alone."

"I beg your pardon?" I had heard him correctly, but I thought I would give him a chance to retract it.

"I believe I've made myself clear enough," he said. "Surely you haven't misinterpreted it."

I felt a surge of irritation at his insinuation and at the direction in which this conversation was headed. I was not certain how he had come to believe that I would be in any way receptive to advances.

"It appears you are under some misapprehension about me, Mr. Foster," I said coolly, hoping to put the conversation to rest.

It didn't seem to have worked, for he smiled, and it was not a very nice smile. "Come now, Mrs. Ames. You needn't play the prude. After all, you've been toying with Dunmore. Well, I won't let that worry me. You wouldn't be the first woman we've shared."

I was not easily given to embarrassment, but I flushed at his crudeness.

"There is nothing untoward occurring between Lord Dunmore and myself," I said, fighting to keep my voice steady in the face of my growing anger and repugnance. I pushed past him and reached the door, but he pressed his hand against it and prevented me from opening it.

"You can protest all you like, but we both know the truth."

"Please let me past, Mr. Foster." My voice was calm, though, in truth, I was both furious and alarmed. His posture made it very clear that he did not intend to let me out of the room.

He smiled again. "I don't think you really want to go. I've known many women like you. You're tired of your husband's philandering and want to get even. Perhaps you're just bored and looking for excitement. In either case, I can offer you a remedy."

"I don't want . . ."

"I think you do." He stepped closer, pressing his body against mine as his hands dropped to my waist. I tried to step back and create a space between us, but he propelled me backward, pressed me between himself and the wall near the door.

"Let me go at once," I said. I considered screaming, but I doubted very much I would be heard above the noise of the ball.

I put my hands against his chest to push him back, but it only seemed to encourage him. "Don't play hard to get, Mrs. Ames."

He tried to kiss me then, and I turned my face away, pushing against him as hard as I could. He was strong, lean, and muscled from his years on the tennis court, and I didn't move him in the slightest. I felt the first surge of real fear as I realized he did not intend to release me.

"I like a woman with fight in her," he said with a laugh. His mouth dropped to my neck, and I tensed at the sensation of his lips on my skin.

"Mr. Foster, let me go," I demanded, struggling against him as hard as I could.

He grasped my arms, his fingers boring into my skin, as he pressed me more tightly against the wall. His eyes came up to mine, and there was something unpleasant in them. "I'm tired of playing games with you." He tried to kiss me again, and when I turned my face away he whispered something very coarse in my ear.

I'm afraid he gave me no choice. I brought my knee up quickly and very hard.

He released me and staggered back, doubled over and swearing vigorously. I stepped quickly past him, pulling open the door. "I do not play games, Mr. Foster."

I left the room without a backward glance.

29

Under any other circumstances, I would
have left the house at once. As it was, I
could not leave before our plot had been
carried out. I just had to be sure to steer
clear of Mr. Foster for the rest of the
evening. I wondered if I should tell Inspector Jones what had happened, but I doubted
anything much could be done about it. It
was my word against Mr. Foster's, after all.

I could scarcely believe it myself. Mr.
Foster had never appeared anything but
pleasant and polite, the very picture of a
gentleman. Then again, I knew perfectly
well how deceiving appearances could be. It
only took the right circumstances for the
mask to drop away.

One thing I now knew. Mr. Foster was a
very likely suspect. If he was capable of
treating women in such a fashion, I didn't
doubt for a moment that he might be
capable of worse.

I was so lost in thought, still shaking with anger and the residue of fear, that I didn't hear the voice until it had called me three times.

"Mrs. Ames."

I looked up and saw Vivian Garmond standing near the stairs.

"Hello, Mrs. Garmond," I said, trying to compose myself.

"Might I speak to you for a moment?"

I looked back at the door to the sitting room. Mr. Foster had yet to emerge, but I didn't particularly want to be there when he did.

"Certainly," I told her. I was not at all in the mood for another confrontation at present, but I supposed now was as good a time as any to talk to her.

"There's a little room just this way," she told me. She led me without hesitation down the wood-paneled corridor just beyond the sitting room, obviously familiar with the house. She stopped before a door and opened it, switching on the lights, and we stepped inside. It was a small study, the impersonal décor indicating it was not much used.

She closed the door behind us and turned to me. "I saw you go into the sitting room, and I knew that he was with you, so I waited outside," she said. "Much longer, and I would have come in."

"Mrs. Garmond, please believe me when I say there is nothing between me and the viscount."

She shook her head. "No, Mrs. Ames. I was talking about Nigel Foster."

I frowned, confused.

She hesitated, as though trying to decide something. Then she went on in a quiet, steady voice, her sad, dark eyes meeting mine. "I know what people say about me, Mrs. Ames. I see the way they look at me with contempt, how they avoid talking to me whenever they can."

I wasn't sure what to make of what she was telling me, so I waited.

"People believe that my son is Alexander's. Well, he isn't."

I was surprised. Frankly, I wasn't sure she was telling the truth, but the paternity of her son was none of my affair, and I certainly didn't intend to judge her for it.

She must have read the sympathy in my expression, for she went on. "I think I can trust you to keep this to yourself, Mrs. Ames," she said. "I . . . I was married to Mr. Garmond very briefly before his death. Alexander came along later. But when I came home afterward and people started

418

talking, I let them. Alexander doesn't care what people think. He never has. And it was better people thinking my son is his than knowing the truth. You see, Mr. Garmond was not my son's father either. Nigel Foster is."

I stared at her. This I had not been expecting.

She continued in a calm voice, as though it was someone else's story she was telling from memory. "We were in Greece at the same time, and I got caught up in the romance of an affair with a handsome, charming tennis star. I fell quickly for him, but our romance was short-lived. By the time I discovered I was expecting a child, he had left the country. Mr. Garmond came along then, and shortly after we met he asked me to marry him. I accepted, but he died unexpectedly of an illness, and I found myself quite alone and pregnant in a strange country. It was then I met Alexander. He was very kind to me. I gave birth to my son in Greece, and Alexander accompanied us home."

"Did you ever tell Mr. Foster he had a child?" It was none of my business, but I couldn't stop myself from asking.

She shook her head. "I didn't want him to know. You see, he's not a good man. I realized that almost at once. There were always other women, a great many of them. And he . . . he has a bit of a violent streak. He expects people to give him what he wants, and he is willing to take it if they don't."

This I had seen firsthand.

"He was engaged once to a young woman, but I had heard they broke it off. Did you hear that?"

"Yes," I said, remembering what Mrs. Roland had told me.

"They said she had been in an accident of some sort, but the truth of it was that he beat her and she fell down the stairs."

I stared at her, horrified. "Why wasn't he arrested?"

"I can only assume she was too afraid to tell what had happened. I counted myself fortunate to have parted ways with him, and I had never thought to see him again. But then we were both invited to the Barringtons' dinner parties. I tried to act normally, as though we didn't have history, but it soon became apparent that he wanted to . . . renew our acquaintance. That night at the ball, he had followed me upstairs and tried to push me into one of the bedrooms. We struggled, and it was only when someone came along that I managed to slip away. I think he intended to move on to someone else after that. I was, well, hiding in one of the bedrooms when the shot sounded."

I thought of the bruises I had seen on her chest at the hat shop. That explained them, her uneasiness when I had mentioned Nigel Foster, and why she had lied about being in the ballroom when the murder had happened.

"I don't think he would have cared about me in the slightest, if it hadn't been for Alexander. But once he knew I cared for someone else, he decided he would stop at nothing. It isn't as though he loves me. He only wanted to prove that he could have me."

An athlete's competitiveness, I thought. Combined with the violent streak of a ruthless man, it might prove deadly.

"Nigel's attentions made Alexander jealous at first, though he'd never admit it. But things have often been uneasy between us. We've quarreled frequently, almost since the beginning. He is kind but often thoughtless. He always does just as he pleases with no consideration for anyone else. Nigel's return to London was just the final straw. Alexander and I had a terrific row and said some terrible things to one another. Until that night at the Barringtons' home, we hadn't seen each other in weeks. Mrs. Barrington didn't know, of course, and I think it was all rather awkward for her."

It made sense that Lord Dunmore had begun dangling after me that night. Perhaps it had been his own attempt at inducing jealousy in the woman he loved. I never ceased to be amazed at the games we play with the people we love. I had been guilty of it myself, to some degree.

"I've been planning to go away," she said, "saving money to go to my sister in Australia. Then I went to see him a few nights ago, and . . . Well, I thought it might be possible to make amends. But now I just don't know. We quarreled again tonight . . ."

"Was it about the diamond?" I asked, hoping to make amends for that at least. "There's an explanation."

She shook her head. "It wasn't that. It's just so many things," she said sadly. "I think Alexander cares for me, in his way, but I can't go on the way I have been. I just can't."

"I'm sorry," I told her. I could think of nothing else to say. I knew only too well that one-sided devotion just wasn't enough.

"I just thought you should know," she said, turning toward the door. "I didn't like to leave the country without someone knowing the truth."

I stood in the room for a moment when she had gone, digesting what she had told me. I didn't know what to make of this unexpected confidence. While I did not wish sympathy to bring down my guard, her story had had the ring of truth to it, and I didn't believe she was the killer.

I felt sorry for her, and I hoped that, if she could not find happiness here, she would find it in Australia, starting a new life with her son.

The clock on the wall chimed eleven, drawing me back to the matter at hand. I had informed all the suspects of the location of the Dunmore Diamond. I supposed I needed to go upstairs and see if the trap would have any effect.

I went out into the hall and was walking back toward the foyer but stopped before turning the corner when I heard voices.

I recognized one of the speakers as Milo. His arrival did not so much catch my attention as did the fact that there was a woman with him.

They were speaking in French.

I hadn't seen Helene Renault at the ball tonight, but I could think of no one else with whom my husband would be conversing in that particular language.

"Come into this room with me," she was saying. "I must speak to you."

I hazarded a glance around the corner and saw them enter the sitting room in which my earlier dramatic scene had been enacted. Luckily, they did not close the door completely behind them.

Naturally, I did what any self-respecting wife would do and moved to listen. I leaned against the wall, hoping that anyone who happened to see me would think I was only resting after a particularly strenuous waltz.

"I had to come and see you tonight," she told him. She had a low, sultry voice that was only enhanced by the fluidity of her native tongue. It was exactly the kind of voice I would have expected a French seductress to have, and I found it intensely irritating. "I think, perhaps, that you're angry with me, and I couldn't bear that."

"Not at all," Milo answered in an amiable tone. "Why should I be?"

"Because we were caught in that photograph. I knew that it would displease you."

"It wasn't so much the photograph that surprised me."

"You mean the kiss?" She laughed, a throaty laugh that sounded well-rehearsed. "You didn't like it?"

"It was, shall we say, ill-timed."

I felt a sinking feeling, as though all my worst suspicions had been confirmed. Milo was chiding her for her indiscretion and nothing more. I wanted to walk away, but I found that I couldn't. Not just yet. I had to know how things really stood between them, the extent to which she had captured my husband's affections.

She laughed again. "The photographers follow me around. They like to see interesting things. And you, Milo," she purred his name, "are very interesting indeed."

She was laying it on rather thickly. If Milo was entranced by such obvious charms, I had greatly underestimated him.

"What did your wife say?" she asked with a giggle that made me grit my teeth.

"She was not pleased." Milo had always had a knack for understatement.

"Did she curse and hit you and throw things at you?"

I felt a surge of indignation. What did she think I was? A sailor?

"Hardly," Milo replied, and I could hear the humor in his tone. "But she was displeased, nonetheless."

She sniffed. "You English are inclined to take things much too seriously. Did you tell her it was only a bit of fun?"

"I told her that we were photographed at

an inopportune moment and that it went no further."

"So sad," she lamented. "But there are no photographers now." The invitation in her tone was very clear, but she said the words anyway. "Kiss me."

I tensed, waiting for a telling silence as he acquiesced. I was rather surprised when I heard his answer.

"No, Helene," he replied, in the same calm tone. "As I told you before, I'm not interested."

"I think you are teasing me," she taunted him. "Perhaps you think to drive me mad with desire. Is that it?"

I clenched my teeth. For pity's sake. She spoke exactly as if she was playing a role in some absurd melodrama. I had never seen one of her films, but if this performance was any indication of her talent, I was not missing anything.

I recognized the growing impatience in Milo's tone. "I'm not teasing you, Helene. And I'm not going to kiss you."

She gave a little sniff of displeasure.

"I hope you don't think I don't appreciate the offer," he continued. "You're a very beautiful woman, and I am flattered, but I'm afraid the answer is still no. You see, it may be dreadfully English of me, but I'm

426

very fond of my wife."

I stood very still, relief coursing through me. I felt oddly as though I might cry. Naturally, a husband should care for his wife, but it was different to hear it from Milo's lips when he didn't know that I was listening.

He was going to come out of the room soon, so I passed quickly by and moved toward the stairway.

I must have looked quite the fool rushing up the stairs, a ridiculous smile on my face.

Once upstairs, I tapped at the door of the bedroom across from the card room. It was opened instantly by a portly sergeant who must have been hovering just inside, waiting for the culprit to make an appearance.

"Good evening," I said, brushing past him and into the room. "No sign of a thief yet?"

He was, I think, caught a bit off guard by my arrival, but he recovered quickly. "Not a peep out of anyone yet, ma'am," he said.

I felt a nagging bit of worry. Perhaps the trap had been too ridiculous to work. Or perhaps one of the Barringtons or even Lord Dunmore was the killer and was privy to the entire thing. In retrospect, it all seemed quite hopeless.

I took a seat in a brown velvet chair. I

might as well wait a bit longer. It was still possible that something would happen.

The sergeant seemed ill at ease with my presence. I thought it possible he wasn't entirely sure who I was and what I was doing bursting in upon his clandestine assignment. Nevertheless, he was too polite to say so, and we chatted for a few moments about the weather.

The door opened a moment later, interrupting the sergeant just as he was beginning to regale me with his own highly developed theory regarding the best climates in which to catch criminals. It was Inspector Jones, and Milo was behind him. "Good evening, Mrs. Ames," said the inspector as they entered and he closed the door behind him, leaving it open the barest of cracks. "I thought we might find you here."

I looked at Milo and found his eyes were already on me. I smiled. "Hello," I said.

He gave me a little smile in return, and I felt a rush of love for him. There was so much I wanted to say to him, but I knew perfectly well that now was not the time.

"Nothing yet, eh?" Inspector Jones said, calling my attention back to the matter at hand.

"No, no one has taken the bait yet," I said glumly.

"Well, with any luck it won't be much longer."

The sergeant stationed himself near the door, where he could see through the crack out into the hallway. Milo and Inspector Jones both took a seat, and we waited in expectant, yet not exactly optimistic, silence. I thought how dull the evening would prove to be if we had only sitting around looking at one another to keep us entertained. Someone should have thought to bring a deck of cards. We might have played bridge.

As it turned out, however, we did not have long to wait. As usual, the inspector's instincts were correct. It was only a short while later that the sergeant signaled to us. Then I detected the faint sound of footsteps outside the door. The inspector held up his hand for silence.

We waited a moment, and then Inspector Jones moved silently to the door and eased it open a bit wider. I couldn't see from my vantage point, but a moment later he pulled the door open fully, and I could see out into the hallway.

Marjorie Echols stood there, the Dunmore Diamond dangling from her hand.

I stood, my eyes wide. I couldn't believe that it had worked. It seemed almost absurd that it had. Yet there she stood, as guilty as

429

you please.

"Good evening, Miss Echols," Inspector Jones said in a tone that somehow managed to be both polite and accusatory at the same time. "Would you mind telling me what you're doing with that necklace?"

I saw something flash across her face, and I thought that she was going to be stubborn about it, make up some preposterous excuse. Then it seemed almost as though she wilted a bit. "I suppose you've found me out, haven't you? I knew it was too good to be true." She shot an angry glance at me. "I should have known it was some sort of trap."

"Perhaps you'd better step into this room," Inspector Jones said. He took the diamond from her hand and deposited it in his pocket.

"Oh, wait!" cried another voice. "She hasn't done anything." It was Felicity Echols who had come down the hall. She was pale and wringing her hands. "Please don't arrest her. She didn't mean it."

"Be quiet, Felicity," Marjorie said, though her tone was kind.

"If there is an explanation to be had," Inspector Jones said calmly, "it would be best if you gave it to me now."

They filed after him, and he closed the door. We all sat down, and Inspector Jones looked at Marjorie Echols. "Now, why don't you tell me what's been going on."

She let out a sigh and shrugged. "If you must know, Jim had been giving me pieces of his aunt's jewelry to sell."

This surprised me. James Harker had been stealing his aunt's jewelry? This I hadn't expected. In fact, it didn't make sense.

"Why would he do that?" Inspector Jones asked pleasantly.

She smiled, a flash of confidence returning. "Because I asked him to."

"I see. He was in love with you, then?"

She shrugged again. "I don't think Jim ever really thought of it in those terms. We were just great friends. He wanted to help me when he could. And he wanted to help Felicity. Truth be told, I think he was perhaps a little in love with her. Felicity cared for him, too, in her own way. She was very fond of him."

Inspector Jones glanced at Felicity, who was quite pale, and then back to Marjorie. "He wanted to help your sister how?"

Marjorie looked at her sister, and I saw Felicity give an almost imperceptible nod.

"She was being harassed by Mr. Foster."

"Harassed?" Inspector Jones repeated skeptically. I marveled again at the way in which the man could convey so much while saying so little.

"Yes, he is quite mad to get Felicity to . . . succumb to his charms. She doesn't like him and never has, but he doesn't let that worry him. He's been rather relentless about it."

Her words had the ring of truth to them. I had, unfortunately, had a glimpse of the lengths to which Mr. Foster would go. And Mrs. Garmond confirmed that he would stop at nothing to get what he felt was being denied to him.

I had been able to escape him, but I wondered if Felicity had been less fortunate in the past. I hoped not. I remembered what she had told me that night at the Sparrow. She had been drunk and confused about who had brought me there. It had not been Lord Dunmore she had been warning me against, but Mr. Foster.

"We were going to wait a while to sell the things, and then we were going to leave London and go abroad," Marjorie went on. "Jim gave us a few pieces, but then he thought his aunt was growing suspicious that the things were disappearing in her house. So he said he would meet us at the ball and give us one last piece. However, when he met up with us that night, he said that his aunt had decided to wear a paste bracelet and we would have to wait."

So Mr. Harker hadn't taken his aunt's bracelet. Then who had? I felt as though we were turning around in circles.

"The night of the murder, did he have a gun with him?" I asked suddenly. Inspector Jones looked as though he didn't quite appreciate my butting in.

"Yes." She let out a laugh. "Poor fool. He said he would protect us from Mr. Foster, if need be. It was his own gun that he was killed with, wasn't it? I was afraid something like that would happen."

"Did you kill him, Miss Echols?" Inspector Jones asked.

"Oh, no!" cried Felicity.

Marjorie looked genuinely surprised. "Certainly not! I was truly fond of Jim."

"Despite the fact that you were forcing him to steal from his aunt and give you the jewels," Inspector Jones said.

She shrugged. "I needed the money. Mrs. Barrington has a lot of jewels. I didn't think it would matter that much in the end."

"We shouldn't have done it," Felicity whispered. "We shouldn't have taken those things. Jim didn't mean to be a thief. He thought of us as a charity, people who needed his help. He was so very sweet. He only wanted to . . ." She broke off suddenly, weeping into her hands. The sergeant handed her his handkerchief.

"It wasn't all that nice to take advantage of Jim, perhaps," Marjorie admitted. "But he said that he wanted to help us, and I wasn't going to say no. Besides, he didn't help us much in the end."

"What do you mean?" I asked.

"Things escalated quickly. Mr. Foster began turning up everywhere we went, trying to get Felicity alone. Even that night at the ball, he arrived in the same mask as Jim. I think he meant to try to trick Felicity into going off alone with him."

So that accounted for the duplicate mask, why he had called Mr. Bertelli about a "joke" he wished to play. Mr. Foster had meant to use it as a trap of his own. I found the man utterly detestable.

She looked at me. "That night we had dinner with you and the Douglas-Hugheses, Felicity stayed home because we expected Mr. Foster would be there. I thought maybe if I tried to talk to him, he would leave her alone, but it was no use. He's a cad through and through. So I decided to sell one of the pieces sooner than we had planned. And that's when I found out."

"Found out what?" Inspector Jones asked.

"That all the things Jim had given us were paste."

30

I stared at her. For just a moment, the room was silent and I could hear the loud ticking of the clock on the wall. I think we were all a bit stunned at this newest revelation.

"What do you mean?" Inspector Jones asked at last.

Marjorie sighed, as though we were quite dense and explaining all of this was becoming a great inconvenience. "I took them to sell them, and the proprietor told me that they weren't real. Just costume pieces, he said."

I frowned. James Harker had been giving them paste jewels all along? Then where were the real things? None of this seemed to make any sense.

"Are you certain?" I asked.

She looked at me impatiently. "The jeweler ought to know, I think."

Then the piece she had attempted to sell hadn't been the piece Mr. Gibbs had found for me in Whitechapel. He had insisted the pin tonight was genuine, and I was inclined to believe him.

"Either James was very stupid and took the wrong things," Marjorie said, "or he did it on purpose."

"Oh, no," Felicity insisted softly. "He wouldn't have done that."

Inspector Jones glanced at me and then rose to his feet. "You ladies had better come with me, nonetheless," he said to the Echols sisters. "There are a few more questions we'll need to ask you."

Inspector Jones and the sergeant led the Echols sisters, Marjorie sauntering and Felicity sniffling, out of the room. I sat back in my chair with a sigh.

Milo lit a cigarette, his eyes on my face. "I can see the wheels spinning. That's rarely a good thing."

I sat forward. "Something isn't right. There is something that we're missing. It's all so very unsatisfactory."

"Alas, such is life. Perhaps that's all there is to it. Perhaps they'll confess to the murder after a thorough interrogation."

I shook my head. "I don't think so. I believe Miss Echols's story."

"It's very bizarre," he said skeptically.

"That's just why I think it's true. Why

should she make up something like that?"

"I imagine Foster would have a rather different account of events if questioned."

"I wouldn't put him past theft and murder," I said darkly. "The way he behaved this evening . . ." I stopped. I had not really intended to share that with Milo.

As usual, however, he missed nothing. His gaze, I thought, was suddenly very sharp. "Exactly how did he behave this evening?"

"Oh, it was nothing I couldn't handle," I said. "But let us say Lord Dunmore is a mere child in comparison."

"Indeed?" There was a hard glint in his eyes. "I think I shall have a word with Mr. Foster."

"Oh, Milo. You needn't make a fuss," I said, secretly pleased that he should care. "But we have more important things to consider. It doesn't make sense that Mr. Harker might have been selling the jewels for himself and giving paste replicas to the Echols sisters. Surely he would have known they would discover it eventually if he did."

Milo shrugged. "Perhaps he would have gotten what he wanted from one — or both — of them by then."

This wasn't satisfactory either. I didn't see Mr. Harker as the type of man to string women along to see what he could get from them. Then again, I certainly wouldn't have styled him a jewel thief.

"Someone was certainly selling the pieces in Whitechapel." I had not yet had time to tell Milo of the most recent development with Mr. Gibbs, how I had gone to look at the Eiffel Tower brooch. I related the events of the evening to him.

"Did Mr. Gibbs say who had sold it?" he asked.

"He told Winnelda, and I quote: 'The gent was of medium height with dark hair.' "

"How very enlightening."

"The description could fit Mr. Harker, I suppose. Then again, it could fit most anyone. One thing we know for certain: someone was having copies made. But why? If they thought to confuse Mrs. Barrington by covering up the theft, it doesn't make sense to have only replaced a select piece. And what happened to the paste bracelet that was stolen at the ball? It was never discovered, and they searched all of the people who were on this floor at the time of the murder." A thought occurred to me suddenly. "Do you think it might still be here somewhere?"

"Unlikely," Milo said, squelching my enthusiasm. "The killer would have had ample opportunity to retrieve it by now."

"Not necessarily," I said stubbornly. "What excuse would they have had to come here since the ball?"

I thought suddenly of Mr. Douglas-Hughes's visit to this house on the day I had come to see Lord Dunmore, of the false story he had told me of a missing earring. Was it possible he had come to retrieve the stolen bracelet from its hiding place? If so, then we were too late.

Somehow, I didn't believe that to be the case. Was it possible the bracelet might still be in the library? Perhaps the thief had taken it while Mrs. Barrington slept and had decided to hide it until it could be safely retrieved.

"Let's go to the library," I said. "Perhaps we'll find something."

I rose to my feet and Milo stood, grinding out his cigarette in a nearby ashtray.

"I think, my darling, that, in spite of what all the slanderers say about me, you are the reckless one in our marriage."

I ignored him, going out into the hallway and walking toward the library. He followed me.

We went into the room, and I walked to the chair where Mrs. Barrington had been sitting. I glanced around the floor and saw nothing. I slid my hands around the cushions of the chair and even knelt to look under the chair, but there was nothing to be seen. I stood and looked around the room, trying to think of any other place it might be.

One thing didn't make sense. If the gems had been removed from the bracelet, why hadn't we found the empty setting? It seemed almost as if the bracelet might still be intact. If that was the case, how had the gems been found on Mr. Harker's body?

I felt the vague stirring of a memory. There was something I had heard, some bit of information that would help make sense of all of this. And then it came to me.

Paste gemstones. They had been present in more than just the jewelry.

What if the stones found with Mr. Harker's body weren't from the bracelet at all? What if they had been from a masquerade mask? I knew of only one of the suspects who had been wearing a blue mask that night.

The description of the thief that Mr. Gibbs had given might have matched James Harker.

It would also match his uncle.

"Milo," I said suddenly. "I think I . . ." My words cut off as I heard the sound of footsteps in the hallway outside. It was pos-

sible that it was just Inspector Jones returning, but something made me pause.

I walked silently to the door. We had left it
open a crack, and I could see out into the
hallway. There, near the grandfather clock
against the wall, stood Mr. Barrington. He
glanced back down the hall, but I was
confident I could not be seen. Then he
opened the clock case and pulled something
out.

I pushed open the library door and
stepped into the hall.

He was surprised to see us and concealed
it badly. "Oh. Er . . . Good evening. I was
just . . . If you'll excuse me."

"Just a moment, Mr. Barrington," I said.
"What is that in your hand?"

I could now see quite clearly what it was:
a blue masquerade mask and a sapphire
bracelet.

I was aware of Milo behind me, and I was
sure that I could feel his displeasure. No
doubt he thought that I should have let Mr.
Barrington retreat. Perhaps he was right,
but I couldn't do that, not when we were at
the resolution of the case.

"It's . . . well, I'm afraid it's rather a long
story." Mr. Barrington tried to look casually
chagrined, but sweat had begun to bead on
his forehead, and his eyes were darting past

me, as though he intended to run.

"Why don't you come into the library and talk to us for a moment," I said gently.

Milo let out a disapproving breath through his nose, but I ignored him. If I could convince Mr. Barrington to come and talk for a moment, we could summon Inspector Jones and do things in an orderly way.

Mr. Barrington wavered, attempting to decide between flight and the possibility of formulating a plausible explanation, and then he walked past us and into the library.

"Why don't you go get Inspector Jones," I whispered to Milo.

"And leave you alone with a murderer?" he asked. "I think not."

Then we would just have to hope that he returned to us after speaking with the Echols sisters, for I had no intention of leaving either.

We followed Mr. Barrington into the room. He hadn't taken a seat, but stood facing us. His face was red, his dark hair damp with perspiration.

"So you killed Mr. Harker." I hadn't meant the words to sound quite as accusatory as they had come out, but there was no taking them back now.

"Amory . . ." The warning note in Milo's

voice held just the faintest tinge of exaspera-
tion.

Mr. Barrington's face flushed, but his
expression remained steady. "Nonsense,
Mrs. Ames," he said, something of an
uneasy smile on his face. "I didn't have
anything to do with my nephew's murder. I
just forgot I had placed these things there
for safekeeping."

"It's your mask from the masquerade,
isn't it?" I asked, nodding toward the
disguise in his hand. "Might I see it?"

"No," he said.

"That's because there are stones missing,
aren't there? They were the paste stones
found on James Harker's body."

"This is nonsense," he said stubbornly.

"That isn't true," I said. "At some point,
Mr. Harker must have turned his back to
you, and you took advantage of it to kill
him with his own gun."

I thought I heard what might have been
another disapproving sigh come from Milo,
but it was so faint I couldn't be sure.

Mr. Barrington said nothing, but I didn't
need him to at present. Things were beginning to make sense, and I was warming to
the tale. "It was you who was stealing your
wife's jewelry, wasn't it? He knew that you
were selling Mrs. Barrington's jewels and

replacing them with paste copies, and he had to be silenced."

Mr. Barrington looked stunned. "How did you know about the jewels?" He stopped, as though he realized he had said too much.

Though now was not the time for gloating, I couldn't help but feel a bit smug.

"We have our sources," I told him grandly. I remembered his love of sport. "What was it? Gambling debts?"

He hesitated. He had wanted to deny it all, but it was really impossible now. He had already said too much. He looked suddenly very weary, as though confession would be something of a relief.

"I've had a streak of rotten luck the past few months," he said. "It's been one loss after another. I only intended to sell one or two of Serena's things in order to cover the most pressing of my losses, but then I realized how easy it was. I had an efficient system going. I would take one of her pieces at a time to be copied and then put the replicas back in her jewel case. She only noticed once, when I took a ruby earring to have a paste pair made, but I put it back in her bureau and she was convinced she had only misplaced it. The replicas were excellent. Serena never knew the difference."

"But Mr. Harker did," I said.

He snorted. "James didn't know about the jewelry. I only recently discovered the night of the ball that he was stealing from Serena as well. Only he didn't know that the pieces were paste. Almost everything in her jewel box is a replica now. Apparently, he has been taking things during dinner parties to divert suspicion from himself. The idiot. Served him right that they weren't worth a thing."

I was suddenly confused. If James Harker hadn't known about the jewels, then why had he been killed?

"But why steal the paste bracelet from your wife that night?" I asked.

"You don't know as much as you think, do you, Mrs. Ames?" he asked. "This bracelet is made of real sapphires. I told her they were paste so she wouldn't be much alarmed when I stole them later, but they were actually genuine. One of the few genuine pieces left. I went into the library when she was asleep and took it. She had told me about her trap, of course, but she sleeps like the dead, and it was easy."

"Did James see you?"

"No, he knew nothing about it."

I was still puzzled. "If it wasn't the jewels, then why?"

He sighed. "It got to be where I was in

desperate need of money again. I put off selling that brooch, knowing how she loved it. But it was the most valuable thing left. When that was gone, there was only the bracelet and one or two smaller things remaining. I knew I needed to do something else. There wasn't enough left of value to sell, only one or two pieces. I had heard rumors, of course, about Foster."

"What sort of rumors?" I asked.

"Rumors that, though he is almost impossible to beat, it is not impossible for him to lose."

"What do you mean?"

"He did it once before, you see."

"That match at Wimbledon," I said, as things clicked into place. I remembered Lord Dunmore's reference to Mr. Foster's loss, the vague aspersion he had cast upon it.

"Yes. Foster and I had agreed to meet and discuss the possibility of a . . . joint venture. He is heavily favored at the match in Switzerland, and if we bet on his opponent, we could stand to make a good deal of money if he loses."

It was beginning to become clear now, but that didn't make it any less horrible. And there was one thing I still didn't understand.

"What did any of it have to do with the ball?"

"I thought it would be less suspicious if I stole the bracelet at the ball rather than at home. Serena had begun to notice things missing. I thought at first that she was looking for things in the intervals when I had taken them to be copied, though I had tried to be careful, but then I realized there was another thief. You can't imagine my surprise that night when I arrived home to discover that someone had stolen the replica of the Eiffel Tower brooch. I had to have a second replica made, and it was only recently completed. At that point, I didn't know who might have done it, but I couldn't take any more chances. She was expecting a thief at the ball, and that suited my plans quite well.

"I arranged to meet with Foster that night. When the time was right, I went into that empty room and let him in through the balcony door so we wouldn't be seen together. We were talking about the possibility of his throwing the match and our splitting the profits if we bet on his opponent. I tried to give him the bracelet as my portion of the bet, but he said I'd have to sell it myself, so I kept it in my pocket. After we'd talked, I let Foster back out through the balcony. No one would know we had met. I thought that was the end of it."

"But it wasn't," I said.

"I realized that Serena might raise the alarm once she discovered the bracelet missing, and there was the possibility we might be searched. It was then I realized that a stone was missing from the bracelet."

I remembered suddenly how Mrs. Barrington had snagged the bracelet on her gown. Perhaps a stone had come loose. That must have been the gemstone near the stairway that had become lodged in my shoe.

"That was what gave me the idea," he said. "The stones were nearly the same size as the gemstones on my mask. I could replace them, wear the gems away, and no one would be the wiser. I had pried a few loose when James came into the room."

"And he saw you with the bracelet," I prodded.

"It was more than that. He must have been listening to my conversation with Foster. He always was a snoop. He said, 'That wretched Mr. Foster' didn't deserve the money, and nor did I. He said he intended to take the sapphires to give them to someone who had more need of them. He removed a gun from his pocket and set it on the table. Then he scooped up the gemstones from the mask to put them in his pocket. A few slid from the table and fell onto the floor, and he bent to pick them up. I suddenly knew that there was nothing else to be done."

There was a moment of silence as his words hung in the air.

"I had to do it," he said. I thought, in addition to the glint of sorrow, there was something a bit desperate in his gaze that made me uneasy. It was desperation that had led him to kill his own nephew. I somehow thought that he would have no qualms about doing away with Milo and me.

"I didn't want to do it. I had to," he said again. "Don't you see? There wasn't any other choice."

"He was your nephew," I said. "He would have known to keep quiet."

He let out a strangled laugh. "James couldn't keep his mouth shut about anything. It was as if information just poured out of him at the most inconvenient times."

I remembered what Milo had told me. James Harker had blurted out his uncle's financial difficulties at an inopportune moment, and it had cost Mr. Barrington a business deal. I hadn't thought revenge was likely, but I had never considered that there might have been a greater secret that Mr.

Barrington thought was worth killing for.

"I knew that if this came out, it would cause an immense scandal . . . for me and for Foster."

I thought of Nigel Foster's part in this for the first time. Surely he must have suspected that Mr. Barrington might have killed James. But the secret was his as well, and he had been unwilling to risk his own reputation.

"I didn't have time to collect the paste gems from his pocket after the shot sounded. I hurried from the room, hiding the mask and bracelet in the first place I saw, that clock. I shoved them inside, intending to come back for them later. Then I walked back toward the room as though I was investigating the shot." He rubbed a hand across his face. "I have relived that wretched night in my mind a thousand times."

"Mr. Barrington," I said soothingly, "perhaps the best thing would be for you to turn yourself over to the police."

"No!" he said. He fumbled in his pocket and pulled out a pistol.

Now was not the time to reflect on the irony of facing down the barrel of a gun held by a killer for the second time in as many months.

"This is getting to be a very bad habit of yours, Amory," Milo remarked, as though he had followed my train of thought.

I ignored him, my eyes still on Mr. Barrington. Great beads of sweat quivered on his forehead and began to roll down his face, and I could see that his hand was trembling. I hoped he was not gripping the trigger too tightly. Perspiration and unsteady hands seemed a very poor combination.

"Dunmore was so very smug about tonight. I was sure he knew something. I brought this gun along in case I needed to deal with him, too."

"There's no need to do anything desperate, Mr. Barrington," I said calmly. "The police are in the house, and you'll be caught. The best thing to do is just to give yourself up."

He seemed suddenly sad, defeated. The gun wavered in his hand, almost as though he had deflated. I was aware of Milo moving slowly to stand beside me, and I wondered what he intended to do.

"Let me have the mask and bracelet, Mr. Barrington," I said gently.

I took a step forward, and he pulled the gun upward. "No," he said, jerking his hand back. At the same moment, Milo pushed me behind him even as the gun went off with a deafening boom.

Mr. Barrington stared at us for a moment, as though he was more surprised than anyone that he had done it. Then he turned and fled from the room.

I turned back to Milo, and something about his face stopped me cold.

"What is it?" I asked, a strange sense of dread creeping over me.

"I don't want to alarm you, darling," Milo said, pulling back his dinner jacket to reveal a growing red stain on the white shirt beneath, "but I'm afraid I've been shot."

31

"Milo," I gasped. I rushed to his side, fear coursing through me with such force that I felt almost dizzy. I realized instantly what had happened. Milo had pushed me aside, but, in doing so, he had put himself in the path of the bullet.

"It's all right," he said calmly. "I'm fairly certain it's only a scratch, but perhaps I'd better sit down nonetheless."

As he moved to a chair, there was a shout from the hallway and the sound of a scuffle. A moment later, Inspector Jones came into the room, followed by Mr. Douglas-Hughes. The inspector's eyes fell on Milo, and he came quickly to his side.

"Inspector Jones, please call for a doctor. Milo's been shot," I said, as though he couldn't see for himself. My voice sounded calm to my own ears, but it seemed as though it had come from very far away, as though I wasn't the one talking at all.

Inspector Jones turned back to Mr. Douglas-Hughes. "Will you telephone, sir?"

"Certainly," he replied promptly, going from the room.

"Did you catch him?" Milo asked conversationally.

"Yes. We apprehended him in the hallway. Sergeant Lawrence has taken him in charge," Inspector Jones replied, his calm gaze taking in the location of the blood on Milo's shirt.

"Excellent work," Milo said in congratulation. "I didn't have much time to think about apprehending him after the gun went off."

"We'd better take off your jacket, sir."

He helped Milo gently out of it. Milo appeared as unperturbed as ever, but his face had gone pale. I had never seen him any shade but bronzed, and it frightened me badly to see the color leeched from his face. He was in pain, and I feared that he was losing too much blood.

My eyes fell to the steadily growing red stain against his white shirt, and I felt my legs go a bit weak as the corners of my vision began to swim.

"It's all right, Amory," Milo said soothingly as he reached out and took my hand. It was not until his warm fingers enclosed my icy ones that I realized he was trying to comfort me and not the other way around. "Sit down, darling," he said. "You've gone all white."

I pulled over a chair and sat at his side. I was glad for the support; my legs felt like straw.

"Oh, Milo, does it hurt very much?" I was fighting tears. I didn't want him to know how afraid I was, for that would only make him more uncomfortable than he already was. I had never felt so helpless.

"Not at all," he said, lying. My eyes searched his face, and he smiled, squeezing my hand reassuringly.

"It appears it's only a flesh wound," Inspector Jones said.

"Oh, thank God," I whispered.

"He didn't really mean to shoot me," Milo commented. "Amory made him uneasy, and the gun went off."

"It seems Mrs. Ames is always confronting armed killers just before the police can arrive," Inspector Jones said dryly.

"At least this time I was able to intercept things, so to speak."

"Perhaps you shouldn't be talking, Milo," I said.

"I'm not dying, darling. I'm perfectly capable of carrying on a conversation."

Inspector Jones pulled a crisp white handkerchief from his pocket and pressed it against the wound. Milo's jaw tightened almost imperceptibly.

"Are you certain he's going to be all right?" I whispered to the inspector. "Is he losing too much blood?"

"I haven't been shot in the ear, Amory," Milo said. "You needn't talk about me as though I can't hear you."

I frowned at him affectionately. "Do be serious for once, Milo. You've got a bullet in you."

"I don't think the bullet is in him," Inspector Jones reassured me. "I think it merely grazed him. Quite a lucky thing."

"You see?" Milo told me. "A scratch."

He was being brave to reassure me, and I adored him for it. I still felt like I was one step away from falling into sudden hysteria. My husband had been shot protecting me from a desperate murderer. It sounded too melodramatic to be true.

"The doctor will be here shortly," said Mr. Douglas-Hughes, coming back into the room. "Is everything all right?"

"I think so," Inspector Jones said. "I think Mr. and Mrs. Ames may be more careful about confronting killers in the future." He smiled to soften the reprimand. "I must commend you both, however. You've managed to see yet another murderer brought to justice. Well done."

Coming from Inspector Jones, this was high praise indeed.

"That wretched man killed his nephew for fear of being found out in a gambling plot," I said, feeling extremely uncharitable toward Mr. Barrington. "Mr. Harker had overheard his uncle plotting with Mr. Foster to throw a match in Switzerland next month. He'd done it before, you see, at Wimbledon. There were rumors circulating at the time that there was something wrong about his loss, and he left the country while things died down."

"And yet he planned to do it again," Inspector Jones said.

"It's nothing along the scale of Wimbledon, of course. They probably could have managed it without much suspicion. But even a hint of scandal could have ruined both of them. Mr. Barrington felt Mr. Harker must be silenced."

"Did he say if Foster has anything to do with the murder?" questioned the inspector.

"I don't know," I admitted. "I wouldn't put it past him, though it's more likely that he suspected that Mr. Barrington had something to do with it but chose to keep silent."

"We'll find out what his involvement in all of this is," Inspector Jones said.

"I'm afraid that won't be possible," Mr. Douglas-Hughes said calmly, breaking into the conversation for the first time. I looked up at him, surprised.

He went on in his cool, steady voice. "Mr. Foster is involved in some, shall we say, highly sensitive work with the Foreign Office. I'm afraid we can't jeopardize that."

"Not even if he's an accomplice to murder?" I asked.

He looked at me gravely. "There are more lives at stake than you know, Mrs. Ames."

I thought it somewhat unjust that Mr. Foster, a liar, a cheat, and a violent man, was outside the reach of the law.

Mr. Douglas-Hughes seemed to have read my thoughts, for he continued. "I know he is an unsavory character, Mrs. Ames. And believe me when I say that measures will be taken to ensure he puts no one else in jeopardy."

That would have to be sufficient, I supposed. However, it still left my question unanswered.

"You came here that day claiming to be looking for your wife's missing earring, and she confirmed your story later. But Mrs. Douglas-Hughes wore no earrings to the ball."

Mr. Douglas-Hughes smiled. "You're very perceptive, Mrs. Ames. We could use more people like you in the Foreign Office."

"Don't give her any ideas," Milo said.

"I thought," Mr. Douglas-Hughes said slowly, carefully weighing his words, "that it might be possible that Mr. Foster was somehow involved with Mr. Harker's death. He had been much interested in Miss Felicity Echols, with whom Mr. Harker was on friendly terms, and I thought Mr. Foster might have wanted his competition out of the way. My wife and I were in the card room at the time the shot sounded, and Mr. Foster came in from the balcony. I came back to check the door to the murder room, just to ascertain whether it might have been possible for him to lock the door behind himself and then retreat to the balcony. I found the bolt could only be activated from inside, and I was satisfied that he was not the killer."

Not the killer, perhaps, but despicable nonetheless.

I thought suddenly of Mrs. Barrington and felt very sorry for her. I knew it would come as a dreadful blow after the death of her nephew to find out that her husband was responsible. I felt sorry, too, for poor James Harker, who had trusted his uncle and had been sorely deceived.

It seemed proper, somehow, that this had started at a masked ball, for nothing had been as it seemed. Even death had worn a disguise.

The doctor arrived and confirmed Inspector Jones's assessment of Milo's injury. He cleaned and bandaged the wound, which thankfully hadn't even required stitches, and instructed Milo to consult with our doctor in a day or two.

After he had gone, Milo and I were left alone for the moment, Inspector Jones and Mr. Douglas-Hughes having gone to tend to the unpleasant aftermath of the investigation. I could only imagine what sort of chaos was happening downstairs as the guests began to realize what had occurred.

"The worst part in all of this," Milo said, examining the bullet hole in his dinner jacket, "is how furious my tailor is going to be."

"He can't fault you for being shot at."

"Trust me, darling. He can fault me for anything." He stood and gave a slight wince. "I will admit that being shot is not as

461

glamorous as it has been made out to be."

"You're going to relish this story for years to come."

"Naturally. One doesn't get shot every day."

Despite the levity of his words, I knew that he had likely saved my life. Had he not pushed me aside, the bullet would have hit me squarely. I stood and went to him, taking his hand in mine.

"Thank you, Milo," I said, sincerely.

This seemed to surprise him. He hadn't been expecting me to grow suddenly sincere. "I'd do it again in a heartbeat," he replied.

"Yes, well. Next time we face a killer, I hope he or she will use something other than a gun."

"Good heavens, Amory. Next time?"

I laughed. "Never say never."

"Speaking of never, you do realize," he said suddenly, a mischievous glint in his eyes, "that it will hereafter be impossible for you to divorce me."

"A pity," I said, in keeping with his lack of gravity. "I might have been a viscountess."

"Only a viscountess?" he chided. "If you're going to do something, do it right. I expect you could get an earl, or perhaps even a marquess if you set your mind to it."

"Why stop there? What about a duke? Or even a prince?"

"Not as a divorced woman. Unless perhaps you went to the Continent."

I laughed. "I don't want a prince."

"Well, that's a relief. Life would be much too dull without you, darling."

"It would be less constraining," I said. "You could do as you pleased without having me to answer to."

"Nonsense. Who would there be to drag me about solving murders and getting shot?"

"You're rather an idiot, Milo," I said with a smile.

"But you love me anyway," he said.

"Yes," I answered softly. "I love you anyway."

"Then let's go home. I'm quite sick of the Ritz."

"Milo," I said suddenly, stopping him at the doorway. "I happened to overhear a bit of your conversation with Helene Renault downstairs."

"Happened to overhear?" he repeated. There was the slightest loosening of the corner of his mouth, as though he was almost tempted to smile. I had no doubt that he was perfectly aware of what I meant by that.

"I heard you . . . ~~fight her off,~~" I said, my own lips trembling at the corners. "She's quite tenacious, isn't she?"

He smiled then, one of those smiles that made my stomach flutter. "I may not be a model husband, my darling, but I hope I am a better one than I am often given credit for being."

And there it was, a précis of our marriage. I couldn't change who he was, not really. He would never be a sentimental, dutiful husband at my beck and call, dedicating himself to my whims. But that was not why I had married him. What I had wanted most, I now had: the reassurance that I could rely on him when it mattered most. He had, after all, just taken a bullet for me.

He opened the door for me, and we went back out into the hall just as Lord Dunmore and Mrs. Garmond came up the stairs. I noticed a significant change at once. Mrs. Garmond's face was radiant, her dark eyes glistening with happiness. Something must have occurred since last we spoke.

"That police inspector has informed me of what's happened," Lord Dunmore said when they reached us. "Are you all right, Ames?"

"Quite all right," Milo answered.

"I can't believe it was Barrington," Lord

Dunmore said. "I never would have suspected him."

"Is Foster still here?" Milo asked suddenly. "I'd like a word with him."

"Milo . . ." I began to protest, but Lord Dunmore interrupted smoothly.

"Mr. Foster has had an unfortunate accident and broke his nose."

The gentlemen met eyes, and Milo smiled. "Perhaps another time, then."

Mrs. Garmond turned to me. "There's one more piece of news. You'll never guess. Alexander has asked me to marry him."

"Has he?" I asked, considerably surprised. "Well, allow me to offer my congratulations."

"He says I have you to thank," she said.

My brows rose. "Oh?"

"I've realized the benefits of a loving and devoted wife," he said, with a smile and a wink. "You're a lucky man, Ames."

"That I am, Dunmore," Milo agreed.

"I hope you will be very happy," I told them, and I meant it.

"I'm certain we shall be." Mrs. Garmond smiled up at him, her face aglow. She would have her work cut out for her with Lord Dunmore as a husband, but I suspected she was more than willing to try her hand at it. Furthermore, I thought she would enjoy it immensely.

Milo and I left them and were making our way down the stairs carefully, to keep from jarring Milo's wound, when a voice rang out. "Oh, Mrs. Ames! Mr. Ames!" Mrs. Roland came up the last few steps to meet us. "How dreadful, how absolutely dreadful! Are you all right, Mr. Ames?" she asked, surveying the blood on his clothes with something very like ill-concealed glee.

"Quite all right. Thank you," he replied with a smile.

"But you've been injured."

"Yes, but I've learned my lesson," he said. "And Amory has promised she will be less violent in the future."

She stopped, speechless, and I fought the urge to laugh. I doubted that Mrs. Roland's being at a loss for words had ever happened before and was unlikely to ever happen again, so I could not bring myself to be angry with Milo for so outrageous a remark.

We took advantage of her disconcertment, crossing the foyer and going out into the night. Bright lights flashed as we stepped outside, and I realized that reporters had gathered as they began to shout questions at us. News had spread with remarkable speed. I somehow suspected that Mrs. Roland was to thank for that.

466

"Mrs. Ames! How did you manage to catch another killer?"

"Mr. Ames! Are you gravely wounded?"

This was the last thing we needed. I was sure we made quite a pair, me in my evening gown and Milo in his bloodstained shirt. "Let's hurry to the car, Milo." I made a move to descend the front steps, ready to push my way through the crowd, but Milo stopped me with a hand on my arm.

"Just a moment, darling."

"What is it?"

"Let's give them something to put in the gossip columns first, shall we?" And he pulled me to him and kissed me thoroughly in the blinding glare of the flashbulbs.

ABOUT THE AUTHOR

Ashley Weaver is the Technical Services Coordinator at the Allen Parish Libraries in Oberlin, Louisiana. Weaver has worked in libraries since she was 14; she was a page and then a clerk before obtaining her MLIS from Louisiana State University. Weaver lives in Oakdale, Louisiana.

The employees of Thorndike Press hope you have enjoyed this Large Print book. All our Thorndike, Wheeler, and Kennebec Large Print titles are designed for easy reading, and all our books are made to last. Other Thorndike Press Large Print books are available at your library, through selected bookstores, or directly from us.

For information about titles, please call:
  (800) 223-1244

or visit our Web site at:
  http://gale.cengage.com/thorndike

To share your comments, please write:
Publisher
Thorndike Press
10 Water St., Suite 310
Waterville, ME 04901

471